Our Lady OF THE INFERNO

PRESTON FASSEL

FANGORIA.COM
@FANGORIA
DALLAS, TX

"Dripping in 1980s nostalgia... a great character study... very entertaining."
—**Leigh Monson, Birth.Movies.Death**

"...reminiscent of a 70s grindhouse style, using transgressive violence to elevate and illuminate... fantastic and and will leave your gut churning."
—**Rebekah McKendry, Ph. D.,**
Shock Waves Podcast

"...the final showdown is a fitting knockdown, dragout battle between two of the toughest broads in the Big Apple. If you've ever felt the '80s needed more chicks that kicked ass, Inferno has them in spades."
—**Monica S. Kuebler,** *Rue Morgue Magazine*

"Fassel's writing, quite simply, is spectacular... like a fiery lighthouse beam pinning me to the page."
—**Herman Raucher, Author of** *Summer of '42*

Our Lady of the Inferno
Copyright © 2018 by Preston Fassel

ISBN 9781946487087 *(paperback)*
ISBN 9781946487056 *(e-book)*

Library of Congress Control Number: 2018932065

Published by Fangoria
www.fangoria.com
Dallas, Texas

COVER BY **ASHLEY DETMERING**

DESIGN & LAYOUT **ASHLEY DETMERING**
COPYEDITORS **KAYLEIGH OVERMAN-FASSEL & FRANCIE CRAWFORD**
DISTRIBUTOR **CONSORTIUM BOOK SALES & DISTRIBUTION**
ASSOCIATE PUBLISHER **JESSICA SAFAVIMEHR**
PRODUCER & PUBLISHER **DALLAS SONNIER**
AUTHOR **PRESTON FASSEL**

First Edition September 2018

Printed in the United States of America

Table of Contents

To my wife and soul-mate, Kayleigh; and my brother,
Brian, my earliest and most faithful reader.
You make me feel feelings.

And to the memory of the great lost rental chains that
introduced me to 42nd Street and were my second home:
Schnucks, Hollywood, Hastings. You will be missed.

"And on the border of the broken chasm
The infamy of Crete was stretched along,
Who was conceived in the fictitious cow;
My Sage towards him shouted-'Peradventure
Thou think'st that here may be the Duke of Athens,
Who in the world above brought death to thee?
Get thee gone, beast... he comes
In order to behold your punishments.'"
-Dante Dante Alighieri
Canto XII, The Inferno
Translation by Longfellow

"You say that you are my judge; I do not know if you are;
but take good heed not to judge me ill, because you would
put yourself in great peril."
-Joan of Arc

Prologue

I T'S THE STENCH THAT AWAKENS TINA. NOT THE INTER-
minable cry of the gulls echoing across the hills and
gulfs of refuse that surround her, not the intensity of
the heat leeching sweat from her every pore, but the stench.
It is the summation of every odor she has ever inhaled:
rotted eggs and rotting animal flesh, cabbage gone bad and
meat gone bad and stale urine and fetid baby shit wrapped
in decaying cotton. As she is jerked to consciousness, the
smell is her totality, the entirety of her being, thought and
sensation lost completely to the smell, so that the smell is
her universe, her soul, her god.

Coherence comes slowly, a pinprick of a thought,
"Where am I?" growing, sparking, becoming more: *who am
I, what happened?* The thoughts ease her back to existence,
separating her mind from the stench. The van; the john;
the wad of bills, tempting her further along, more than
she'd ever seen in her life and the offer so simple...

She rises, legs heavy, gropes around in the dark to
steady herself, hands brushing against rusted iron, the wet
sop of ancient fast food. Her fingers briefly find an anchor
in the side of a garbage bag before the plastic rips and spills

out a torrent of decay that finally pushes her over, sends her back to her knees. The half-digested remnants of her last meal cascade out of her, running down her chin, her breasts, a black waterfall of filth in the dull fluorescence of the new moon. The one pitiful mercy bestowed upon her: She can't smell it.

She begins screaming, wordless, terrified, the adrenaline surge enough to lift her to her legs, still weighted down with listlessness and malnutrition but cartwheeling for her now, providing enough balance to propel her through the trash heaps. She exits from between the mounds where she awoke, hopes to find some thoroughfare beyond, some pathway to escape, discovers more paths snaking around her, dozens of them laid out before her, around her, like the myriad tentacles of a vicious squid.

Running, she starts running, chooses a path arbitrarily, any path better than standing still, instinct kicking in: the instinct to flee, to survive, the instinct that's saved her in the past but not last night. One instance, she'll chalk it up to one failed instance but not now. Now her gut will save her again like it has before, she messed up last night but she won't mess up now, running, feet slipping and skidding over garbage, garbage and more garbage but not faltering, managing to keep on her feet.

She reaches the end of a trail, a mountain before her, two paths to take from here and instinct says fork left so she forks left and keeps on cartwheeling, occasional sobs escaping her unwillingly, conscious thought still only coming in fits and bursts. Will figure things out when she gets back to the Misanthrope, why she ended up here. Has dealt with some sick, weird fucks in her time but this by far the sickest, the weirdest. Robbed, most assuredly raped, was she supposed to be dead, was that it, was her body supposed to be rotting here instead of running, a botched murder, beaten, raped, robbed, murdered, dumped? *Well fuck you, Johnny, I'm heading back to civilization and Ginny's going to rip your lungs out once she finds your narrow ass.*

Another break in the path, another turn, nothing distinct to direct her, nothing unique about her surroundings to indicate that this is the correct path, an incorrect path, if she is going in circles, just the motion of her legs, just the echo of her grunts as her lungs chafe. Rounds another corner when she hears the growl, fierce in its reverberations, turns behind her to see the dog, a mutt, feral, raw intensity in its hunter's gaze. Its shoulder muscles are bunched and its body is arched downward, hair mangy and filthy, one eye milked over white and seemingly cracked, like a broken, warped marble shoved into the socket. She screams and it lunges into a bolt towards her and she is running even faster now, even more directionless, tears and snot streaming down her face and her arms pinioning in front of her to prevent a fall, to keep some semblance of balance, and as she turns her head behind her to track the progress of her predator, she finds not one dog in pursuit now but three, four, more dogs pouring from behind piles, over piles, spilling out in droves to join the pack.

Exhaustion sets in, muscles tightening, body burning, the throbbing in her head drowning out the sound of the dogs and her own breathing, a whining buzz flooding her ears as she swings herself around a corner. With a defeated whimper her calves give out and she finds herself on her knees, turning around as the dogs close in, mouths opened wide to bare bloody, broken fangs and blackened tongues dripping yellowed, frothy ooze. Her own hands grip helplessly at the pile beside her, to pull herself up, if the remnants of energy in her are enough to purchase six more feet of life then she wants them with bitter desperation, and the dogs are nearly upon her when the whistle breaks through the whine in her ears, high pitched, reedy and broken, like someone playing a cracked recorder. The dogs retreat, some of the mutts bungling up on one another, lost to their own momentum, knocking one another over. The whistle sounds again and the dogs are retreating, falling back, whimpering, tails tucked between legs, and again the whistle, *a dog whistle, must be a dog whistle, someone near, sending them away, saving her*—and out from behind a pillar of flattened car chassis a figure emerges, the whistle emanating from it. Tina is stretching her arms towards it when her sight returns fully, focuses, adjusts, and she can see the helmet the figure wears, the dull bronze glowing in the moonlight, the red streaked horns, the massive, bloody axe, and her instinct tells her that her trouble has only really now begun.

1

Tuesday, June 14th, 1983

"T INA NOT COME HOME LAST NIGHT." COLONEL
Baniszewski says this to Ginny near the end of
dinner, his sixth glass of wine as nearly depleted as the candles burning on the table between them, reducing the light in the Misanthrope dining room to a sick,
green-copper haze. Ginny, raising her own glass to her lips,
getting a steady buzz on in preparation for the night's events,
thinks she hears the Polish accent slip. She wonders, as she
often does, about the true extent of his linguistic limitations,
if she is in fact hearing his best efforts at the English language or if his butchered speech is another dissimulation, an
affectation to go along with his polo shirts and deck shoes
and pleated jeans to present an image to the world of someone weak and vulnerable and who most certainly would
not carry a 9mm pistol at the small of his back.

"Are you surprised, sweetheart?" Ginny says, tries to
spear something with her fork, can't quite make out the
food on her plate any longer in the dimming light. Tonight's meal: two dollar steak, boxed mashed potatoes, frozen corn, whipped up with something a few degrees north
of apathy by the Misanthrope chef, presently sitting on the

opposite side of the dining room beneath a sheaf of peeling silk wallpaper, waiting for the pair to leave so he can clean up and turn in. "Do you have any idea how many times she threatened not to come back? I mean, we better put out an APB."

"Girls not come home, girls not bring money," the Colonel says, shifting around on his side of the table. "Girls not bring home money, I not get money. I not like it when I not get money. I especially not like it I have seven girls working. *Eight* is good number."

"*Numero Uno,* Tina's no big loss. The girl was too vanilla for her own good. Was never gonna last. At best she was, like, a rent-a-car. Get your money's worth, back to the lot."

"That your problem. *You* break in girls."

Ginny winces. "...*Die zwei:* The hours are shit, the pay basically sucks, and, like, we don't even have any health benefits."

"Girls live here, not on street. Someone fuck with them, you fuck them back. Someone fuck with you, I fuck them back. I fuck you back, you never fuck anyone again. That girl's health benefits."

Ginny looks askance, nods conciliatorily. "Okay, I'll give on that one. But, three, hell-o, we aren't exactly the Plaza, right? I mean, honestly? You're surprised people don't come back here at night? Shannon found, like, rats in her toilet two days ago."

"Rat," the Colonel repeats.

"Rats, like, in the non-singular. Synchronized swimming. They were playing like, the Blue Danube."

The Colonel sighs and shifts some more. "Maybe I think about hire exterminator." What discomfort Ginny can make out on his face seems to come from self-interest—repugnance at the thought of rats making nests out of his silk sheets, reducing his suite to the same Spartan conditions as the rest of the hotel. "But exterminator cost money. And there no money if girls not come home! There's no money if only seven girls!"

Ginny sighs. Tinny music fills the silence between them, piped in on the Mistanthrope's ancient sound system, Debbie Harry wafting through the halls, a synth-pop lullaby for the lost boys and girls that fill its rooms. The Colonel fidgets more; the wine working through him, guiding him down the road that Ginny has well mapped, taking him from agitated sobriety to the dulled paranoia of a buzz, to the not unpleasant joviality of tipsiness, to the manageable doldrums of sense-dulled drunkenness. Based on his consumption, she judges him to be on the cusp of the buzz and tipsiness. She can relax now, knows which part to play. "Sweetheart, *darling,* don't you worry your little head one sorry second! You know that this time tomorrow Ginny'll have brought you home three brand new girls. Just for you. You know, like she always does?"

"Like you always do." The Colonel grins.

"Beautiful girls. Fresh off the bus. Kentucky? Ohio? Texas? One with an accent?"

"Accents not matter. Long as you bring some girl back."

"But beautiful. Young."

"Yes. Very good. You very good, Ginny. Bring home lot of girls, make sure they bring home lot of money. The Colonel not forget that." He gestures at her loosely with his fork, drops it onto his plate. The fork splashes up the juice from his steak and it splatters his face, his polo shirt, and The Colonel stares at it dumbfounded for several moments before Ginny reaches across the table and places the utensil back into his hand, lifts his napkin to dab his face.

"Just, like, helping out, you know. Just doing my job."

"You do very good job. Good bottom lady. You help a lot." The Colonel reaches back across the table, his hand leathery, little bigger than Ginny's, mottled with uneven and randomly distributed patches of hair so that it looks like a small, balding tarantula when it closes over her own. "Help the Colonel do lots of things."

The sun has long since given herself up to the horizon by the time Ginny makes it back to her suite, the corridor blindingly lit, overtaxed sconces blazing against the lemon yellow wallpaper to create a hangover's worst nightmare. The Colonel's insurance policy: Keep the halls well-lit as a deterrent—against burglars, against kids fucking in the hall, against kids shooting up in the hall, against kids graffiting the halls. The Colonel's folly: the hallways ceaselessly full of kids fucking, kids shooting up, here, beside Ginny's own door, in iridescent pink made brighter by an adjoining sconce, the words "WERE THE KIDS IN AMERIKA," above a poorly rendered anarchy symbol.

Breath in, breath out, key in the lock and turn, flip the switch, take off the hat. Another role; another woman.

"Hey, Trish. I'm home." Closes the door behind her, locks it, seals in the cool air wafting through their rooms, courtesy of the window unit bequeathed by the Colonel, a privilege not bestowed unto the other miscreants that fill the rooms of the Motel Misanthrope. In contrast to the hall, the quarters are dimly lit though clean, the fruit of Tricia's enforced solitude.

"Oh, motherfucking shit, Batman, like, where the fuck were you?" Tricia Kurva, grinning wickedly, pushes her wheelchair to the door, stretches out two gloved hands. The sisters embrace; pangs of guilt rise up on Ginny's palette, irrational in origin and intensity, not for how she's spent her night, or for the girl's condition, but that her little sister looks too old for seventeen, her face drawn, an occasional gray hair amongst the blonde. Guilt that, in having behaved differently in the past, she might have prevented this. "I was, like, crying, like, I totally thought you were dead and that I'd, like, never see you again. Also, I was hungry."

"Steak. Catch." Ginny digs in her bag, comes out with the remnants of the Colonel's steak, kept warm in tin foil, tosses it to Trish. Trish catches it, turns her wheelchair around towards the living room, managing to both propel herself forward and unwrap the meat without spinning herself in a circle.

"Oh, fuck yes, it's, like, all bloody and stuff. Was this still mooing when you ripped its heart out and showed it to her?"

"One hundred percent grade-A fresh." Ginny follows her, into their tiny den, towards the sounds of Carson a little too loud on the television. Trish situates herself in front of the tube, sets to unwrapping the meat. "I did the wash," she says, tearing into the steak. "Your stockings are over the shower rod. They were, like, all grody with blood and perv juice."

Ginny detours to the kitchen, takes a glass and a fistful of ice, continues on to the bathroom, surprised to find her stockings hanging over the rod exactly as her sister said, not sure how she manages to get them up there, doesn't want to ask and spoil the trick. She retrieves the bottle of vodka she keeps beside the shower, pours a glass.

Trish, in front of the set, beer in one hand, a sliver of steak in the other, eyes transfixed on Carson, calls out: "You know this is probably cat, right?"

"Oh, at least fifteen percent. Ten percent possum. Five percent possum droppings." Ginny turns on the shower, strips, enters, cranks up the temperature. "Hey, look in my purse. I got you something." She brings the remnants of the vodka into the tub with her, holds it aloft with one hand, soaps with the other. Tricia wipes her hands on her jeans, wheels herself towards Ginny's purse, rummages, and finds her prize.

"Oh, fuck me sideways underwater, you are the mother-loving queen shit big sister."

"I take it I got the right issues?"

"Well, I don't read *Wonder Woman*, but, it's the right *X-Men*."

"I thought you might be interested in trying something new. If you don't like it, I can trade it to Roger."

Ginny places her now empty glass on the rim of the tub, lets her arms rest at her sides. Intermittently, a single bead of water will form on the lower lip of the shower head, distend, dangle, and then drop to the floor of the tub, vanishing into the swirl of water. Layer by layer, Ginny begins to strip away the noise. She starts with the television, the music in the hall; then, the turning pages of Tricia's comic book, her sister's noisy and eager chewing, the murmur of neighbors through the wall. Layer by layer the sounds vanish, peeled away and discarded like onion skin, until there is just the rush of the water, its low, droning melody; and at last, here, in the quiet, her sister safe beyond the door, her body dripping wet and internally scorched, the warmth just receding between her thighs, there is sterility. Cleanliness. Something particularly demoralizing about the times the Colonel forces her to be on top, required to buck about as though she were the instigator of their coupling. Prefers the supine position: the passivity, the loss of agency, the opportunity to drift away as she does in her nightly showers, the view looking up, the lovely mahogany of the bedposts and the supple ripple of the red satin canopy, hypnotic, almost peaceful when she can tune out the noise and see it not as fabric but as the billowing dusts and gasses of a nebula, eternal beauty churning silently in the blackest corner of the universe, beyond the reaches of humanity.

When she's out and dry and in her robe, Ginny hunkers onto the couch beside her sister, second vodka of the night in hand. Tricia's eyes vacillate between the television and her comic; Ginny's eyes remain glued to the set, slowly glazing, her speech retaining its effervescence even as her mind at last begins to slow down.

"Oh, I am so glad that I did not miss the end of Carson. I... love those curtains, man. I mean, there is absolute-o-mento no better thing on this Earth to get blazed to than Johnny's curtains. When I die, I totally want you to steal those curtains and burn my body in them. No, wait. When I'm dying, steal them and wrap me in them so they're the last thing I see."

"Oh, bullshit. You like to catch it because you've got, like, a total old-man crush."

"Oh, fuck you."

Tricia gleefully slaps the pages of her book shut. "Omigawsh, you so totally do! You want him to swing his golf club on your putting green." She holds the comic against her forehead, closes her eyes. "Johnny Carson's dick." Trishia lowers her comic, opens it. "What does Ginny Kurva want to ride to work tomorrow instead of the subway?"

Ginny snatches the book away from her sister. "All right, you little shit." She grabs the arm of her sister's chair, spins her around so that they're facing each other. "It's late. You've got an assignment due."

"Oh, man, now you're harshing my buzz."

"C'mon. What'd you learn today? History." Ginny snaps her fingers at her sister's ear. Tricia sighs, settles back, playing with the empty aluminum foil in her lap.

"Okay, so, like, the Tudor family took over England in the War of the Roses, which is, like, a totally radcore name for a war, though, like nobody can agree on when it really started or ended; but mostly they say it ended when Richard III, who, like, might or might not have been Quasimodo, so righteously got his ass handed to him in the Battle of Bosworth by Henry Tudor, who became Henry VII. The last guy to get killed by Richard was Henry's standard bearer..."

"Which is?"

"The dude who, like, carries the flag, like, in Revolutionary War shows, he's like the guy next to the guy with the pipe and drums. And so, like, the standard bearer was the last guy to buy it, and his son, Charles Brandon, became Henry VIII—Bosworth Henry's son—best dude for life. Cause, like, Henry VII doesn't get a lot of attention except for killing a hunchback, cause his son was like a total fucking Bond villain."

Ginny sinks back into the couch, finishes her drink. The beginnings of a smile twitch at the corners of her mouth as she listens to her sister go on. From Tudor England they move to anatomy, the bones of the head, before a stab at mathematics, Ginny too inebriated to assess the algebra work she herself wrote this morning, and then it's on to the final challenge of the evening.

"Good. *Nun, Deutsch.*"

"Oh, fuck you. I'm tired."

"*Nein, nein. In Deutsch, fraulein.*"

"*Fick dich.*"

Ginny sighs. In German: "*Of course you would start with the dirty words.*"

"*Come on, it's late.*"

"*Okay. I'll give you a break tonight. But I expect you to be at a fourth grade equivalency by the end of summer. And you will sing me '99 Luftballoons' in its entirety. No errors."*

"I, like, only understood half of that."

The sisters return to the television, moving now to music videos, Ginny rewarding her efforts in sisterly education with another glass. Pastel and neon explode across the screen, Trish occasionally dialing down the volume so that the images seem to sync up to the music drifting from the hallway. Both of them snicker in delight when the song on the Misanthrope sound system matches up with the video onscreen. After a while, Ginny closes her eyes, lets the color blasting from the set sink into the front of her eyelids, filling her up with flashing reds and blues and yellows, the vibrations gently rattling her body, an aural massage, relaxing her muscles and lulling her off into blissfully dreamless sleep.

Mindful of her sister's descent into unconsciousness, Tricia is careful to pluck the glass from her hand before it falls. Spends the next hour in pursuit of something dirty on the airwaves, disappointed that, even with the cable package they've been granted, the geezers are right, there really *is nothing* on television these days. When Ginny awakens hours later, the lights off in the apartment, the music in the hall turned down a notch, she's unsurprised to find herself wrapped in a blanket. She staggers to the bedroom. In the aureolin glow of the light slipping in from around their blinds, Ginny can see her sister curled in bed, her chair folded neatly beside her, her rosary wrapped around the narrow fingers of a limp hand. She wants very much to sit beside her, to place a hand on her back, to offer her in her slumber some reassurance that her sober mind cannot articulate; knows that this would very much be a bad idea. Doesn't care to conjure any bad memories; the fear that unfamiliar weight at the foot of the bed brings. She opts instead to crouch on the floor, propped on her haunches.

She reaches to her nightstand, collects her cassette player, puts on her headphones. Activates the tape. The narrator's prim, pleasant voice begins where Ginny last left off: "*Bien dans sa peau. Bien dans sa peau.*"

"*Bien dans sa peau,*" Ginny whispers, wraps the blanket tight around herself.

"*J'en peux plus,*" the narrator intones.

"*J'en peux… j'en…*" Ginny mutters. She watches her sister sleep for a good long while before she closes her eyes and once more gives herself over to darkness.

2

Wednesday, June 15th, 1983

CLOUDS ARE BUILDING ACROSS THE HORIZON WHEN Ginny Kurva awakes, the glow of the lights creeping in from the window replaced now by a gray haze that, coupled with the efforts of the window unit, make her think of winter in St. Louis. She half closes her eyes; for the groggy duration of the struggle up the peak from waking to awake, she thinks of snow; carries the thought with her as she heads to the television room, switches it on for company, volume turned down so as not to wake Tricia. She assumes the *musubi-dachi*, bows to an imaginary sensei before she begins her exercises. Her morning routine has allowed her to not only maintain her training but her figure; has seen too many girls on their diets of snack foods and hot dogs begin to grow fat with time, start bringing home less at night, and in doing so incurred the wrath of the Colonel.

When her practice is complete, she dresses, returns to the couch with her notebook, Tricia's textbooks, chosen on the basis of availability and cost from the city's bookstores. Decides to give her a break today on history; has been forcing the girl through the middle ages for long enough, really just needs to only open the blinds to see them repeating themselves. Today: A continued emphasis on algebra and the anatomy of the head; further German work; and, for a cross-curriculum activity, a thousand-word essay on Uranus. Stops a moment, reconsiders, scratches out Uranus and replaces it with Neptune.

If nighttime in the hallways of the Misanthrope recalls the aftermath of a rock concert, then morning in the dining room summons images of a haunted house movie, cavernously empty, the chairs upended on the tables, faulty wiring in the florescent lighting keeping them at only half-power, bathing the room in a dull, gray flicker. The atmosphere does not disturb Ginny; absent the Colonel and his candles, the dining room—next to her room— is perhaps her favorite place in the Misanthrope. The disused libraries of her youth taught her to find solace in isolation, peace in places of abandonment. Half-hidden in the shadows that envelop every few feet of the room, she pauses, looks to the back corner table laid out with donuts, coffee, a platter of hastily-cooked scrambled eggs. Gathered around it, partaking of the Colonel's daily bread, preparing themselves physically and emotionally for what lies ahead, sit her girls. Six now, gathered here not just for sustenance but for *her*; waiting for her word, her command, their trust placed in her wisdom to guide them through another shift. Watching from her pillar of shadow, Ginny does not utter any prayers; she has not done that for over three years. Yet, in this moment, as it occurs every morning, she acknowledges to herself that if she were still the praying kind, then she *would* be praying now, for their safety, for their return to the Misanthrope tonight, for her to be able to lie down beside Tricia this evening in their bed and know that no harm has come to them.

"Good morning, ladies," Ginny calls as she moves towards the table. Some of the girls, the younger ones, those more in thrall to her command, half rise from the table. She nods agreeably to each of them—Mary, Constance, Candice, Michelle, Shannon, Sandra—making sure to make eye contact with every girl, ensure they are all acknowledged and aware that they have been acknowledged, let none of them feel neglected or less special. There are no addicts among them—not to Ginny's knowledge—but some of the girls who have been with her the longest are beginning to show signs of the early wear that accompany the hard life: the eye-shadows of sleepless nights, the lines around the mouth from a tightly-held jaw, the pallor of the chronic drinker that Ginny wishes away every morning when looking into her own mirror.

"Late morning for you," Candice says jovially, deepest voiced of the group, a booming volcano of a larynx buried in her throat. "Must mean a late night."

Ginny bows. "Just taking the bullet so that none of you have to, dear ladies."

"Twenty-two caliber bullet," Constance titters. The girls laugh.

"Dear hearts, *please*. I *am* thoroughly exhausted today, from worrying my tiny little head over each and every one of you. Now, as I'm sure you're all well aware, our table is absent by one this morning."

"Absent by *half* of one," someone says.

"Most totally," Ginny concurs. "So in acknowledgment of this, let us like, have half a moment of silence." She thrusts out her lower lip in an exaggerated frown and bows her head. It takes only a few seconds before someone begins giggling.

"And let us never speak her name again," Ginny says.

"Bout time that bitch got her ass off on the dusty trail," Candice says. "Six of us doing seven hos' work."

"I admit, I made a failing in my assessment, and for that,

I am totally sorry," Ginny says, hands clasped over her heart. "If anything, though, I think each and every one of you can agree that I am most righteously guilty of a large heart, and you *know* I couldn't force a poor girl onto the streets, don't you? Be that as it may, I take full responsibility for feeling too much for a sad little lady that I found lolling around the gutter and brought here in a *very* misguided attempt to rectify her bad situation. We must move on now, though, ladies. There *are* hard times ahead…"

"There's *hard* times ahead *every day*!"

"Open mic is tonight, sweetheart, but, ladies, we all appreciate the preview, don't we? Now, let's be serious for a second. I am totally going to do my best to bring home someone new tonight, okay?" Ginny gestures to her own body; left her fuck-me shoes at home this morning in favor of sensible pumps, a bow neck blouse, smart suit. A different kind of business ahead of her today.

"But until then, all of you have got to keep picking up that slack. I promise, things will even out. Until then, though, prices go up an extra two dollars, and you all make extra sure that you're making yourselves worth it, hmmm? Each and every one of you is an extraordinary young woman, and you all need to make sure that each and every one of your dates knows that by the time you're through. *Verstehst du?*"

"*Ja, Frau Kurva,*" the girls reply in unison.

"*Gut,*" Ginny says. She takes her seat at the table; dutifully, little Mary, sixteen, smallest, youngest of the group, gathers up donuts, eggs, brings them to her on a plate. Shannon pumps coffee from the pot, prepares it with just the right ratio of cream to sugar. Ginny checks the time on her watch, red LEDs glowing back at her in the half-dark. Running late, but not *too* late.

"All right then," Ginny says. "So we've still got fifteen

WEDNESDAY, JUNE 15TH, 1983

minutes. Last week was Chapter 3. What are our first impressions? Like, what did you think? Mary, we'll start with you, and remember, there are no wrong answers."

Mary dabs sheepishly at donut glaze stuck to her bottom lip. "I'm... really enjoying it. And I'm glad that Gatsby finally showed up. I want to know what's going on with him. And... I really like Nick. I think he's really... nice."

"Anything else you have to say right now?"

"No, that's all."

"That's all right. Sandra?"

"I wanna go to a party like *that*. That's some classy shit, right there. Suits and dresses, fuck. You try and throw a party like that around *here,* someone's gonna burn this mother down."

Ginny smiles, relaxes, and drinks deeply from her cup. In fifteen minutes, book club will be over, and it will be time to take to the streets. The girls around her will be filling their bodies not with the artistry of long dead scribes but with all of the filth and needy longing that the city has to vomit up to them. Fifteen minutes; tomorrow, she hopes, the full thirty. Half hours, quarter hours, moments. One day, in the future- soon in the future, she hopes- when each of them have left vacant rooms at the Misanthrope, it is her warmest wish that they remember not the weight of bodies on theirs or the smell of blood and jizz, but these moments; and that, in these moments, they are, as Ginny feels she is, most wholly and completely themselves.

———

"Containment." The word, muttered in Nicolette's strained warble, hangs above the room like the sword of Damocles, ready to plunge into the skulls of every man sitting around the meeting table. Staring out at them, she supposes she is expected to demonstrate a reaction to her own words, as though they are a surprise to her, like she didn't just say them after formulating them in her own mind. Though she has made leaps in her socialization skills, she cannot conceptualize what the expected reaction is, so she reverts instead to the default face she uses when attempting to fill gaps in conversation: mouth slightly open and twitching at the corner, super magnified eyes stretched wide and blinking behind the lenses of her tortoiseshell glasses.

"Shit," someone mutters. Though Nicolette can see his face, she is not entirely sure who he is; she finds it incredibly difficult to differentiate the faces of men of a single race. In this regard, her body has been of great benefit: She has found that most men of authority do not care if a woman only refers to them as "sir." Indeed, it can be quite beneficial. She has advanced nicely through her career without knowing the names of many of her superiors.

"It may be our only option at this point, sir," Nicolette continues. "We've been dealing with wild dogs in the landfill for years. They're just another component of the job, along with the birds and the rats."

"We brought in the birds to kill the rats," someone says.

Nicolette stares for a moment, unsure if she was meant to stop or keep going. When no one says anything, she keeps going: "The attacks we're here to discuss have been more severe." She turns back to the wall, the map of the landfill behind her, gestures to the relevant sector. "Pinpointing them, they all appear to be isolated to this region, near the West Mound. That would indicate that they're all coming from a new, unique pack."

"Pack?" someone says. Nicolette believes that the emotion they are conveying is 'incredulity.' "You're talking, like, a pack of wolves?"

"Any grouping of canines is called a pack," Nicolette says. "Yes. Like a pack of wolves."

"All right, this is bullshit, right?" another someone says. He looks around to the rest of the men. "I mean, I'm not alone, right? This is 1983, not the damn stone age. We've got dozers, we've got guns. We go out there and we *kill them*."

"That would be very difficult," Nicolette says. "It's common for feral dogs to burrow."

"So the poison didn't work," someone else says. Nicolette feels confused. She has already reviewed this. It frustrates her that people can be so careless in their acquisition of information.

"It killed three dogs. Even if no more have joined the pack, it's hardly a significant number."

"Okay, answer me this: How quickly do these things breed? Do we know that?"

Nicolette looks to the ceiling, consults the notes she memorized, her own knowledge of canine behavior. The ceiling is made up of rows of fiberglass tiles stained brown with ages of rain. There are exactly twenty-four tiles in the room. "One female tends to be responsible for most of the breeding," Nicolette says. "Even in packs where there are multiple bitches…"

Several someones snicker. Oblivious, Nicolette goes on: "…only one tends to give birth, even over extended periods of time."

"Good," the someone who had been talking says. "Okay, so, they don't breed quick. Lord knows where these things came from, but, if more aren't getting in—hell, even if they are—if we can keep knocking a few out here and there, it gives us a chance. Up the dosage, do another round, see what turns up. If we can knock some more out, who knows? Sound good to you?"

Uncomfortable silence permeates the room. It occurs to Nicolette that she is being addressed. "Yes. I can personally supervise the administration of the next round. I still think you need to consider containment, though."

More mutters from around the table.

"If the attacks are isolated to one pack operating in one region, containment might be the best option. Quarantine the area and the attacks stop. We lose a small area, but..."

Someone at the head of the table stands up. "So jack up the poison. Another round, two more rounds, dammit, we gotta slaughter the fatted calf and dump it out there with a stomach fulla strychnine for these bastards to choke on. Bring on the axe. I ain't gonna be the guy who loses turf to a bunch of fucking animals."

The someone leaves; murmurs fill the room as the rest of the men begin to drift out as well. Nicolette watches them go. A while later, after they're all gone, she supposes it's time for her to leave, too.

———

It's begun raining by the time Ginny makes it to the Port Authority, and while the day demands a great deal of her, she spends a long while across the street, smoking, listening to the tuneless music of raindrops smacking the hoods of taxis, breathing in the mist that rises up from the hot pavement. Drops a butt to the ground; about to reach for another, her pack half depleted, checks her watch; forty minutes wasted. Foregoes another smoke, takes the next red light across the street, into the building. For the first time since last evening, her thoughts drift to Tina, and what a stupid bitch Tina is, how Tina can go fuck herself for putting her in this position and how what Tina needs is to get fucked in the face with a shard of glass and just plain fucking die.

The key to surviving at the terminal, Ginny has learned, learned the night she and Tricia unloaded here three years ago, is to not look at anyone while looking at everyone, to glimpse surreptitiously yet thoroughly, to analyze every passing and stationary individual for their capacity for violence, and so scouting the terminal for suitable trade is an even finer talent, one at which Ginny has become exceedingly proficient. The art is in the scan, in taking a quick glimpse and creating a mental polaroid, looking away and analyzing it, looking for signs of desirability. She has learned to scope out the desperate look of the runaway, the dropout, the debutant, the petty crook, girls of once great means suddenly deprived of daddy's credit card and mommy's car. Girls from broken homes. Stupid, arty girls from permissive families thinking that adventure is a bus trip away.

Girls lined up at the stock gate begging for a mallet to come careening down into their skulls.

The rain outside grows harder, something closer to real music, and now that she's indoors it's not such a bad thing, the rain an elimination system of its own, girls who'll run into a storm like this in an unfamiliar city too brave for the Colonel's purposes, too self-reliant. Ginny directs gray eyes towards the girls watching television, the ones feeding quarter after quarter into slots to watch static-ravaged network news, biting their nails, waiting out the rain, taking the opportunity to try and determine if this is really the best idea, being here, from upstate or the burbs, Maine, Boulder, Wichita, high schoolers playing hooky on daytrips losing their cool at the last moment, businesswomen putting in time for companies too cheap to front air fare. There, a nervous looking girl, scrunched forehead, concerned look, blonde, curly, her face not yet showing the ravages of the tobacco abuse indicated by her lightly yellowed nails, her skin bearing that tan particular to girls of a rural extraction, not the relaxed brown of a pool hopper or beach bunny but a working girl, her time in the sun spent in labor, her jeans not purchased for fashion but for practicality. As Ginny takes stolen glimpses of her and analyzes them, she recognizes in the girl's demeanor a complete vulnerability, and so Ginny ceases her game of look-look away, and sets her sights fully on the girl, watching her for a long minute until she worries that one of the bums will chase her off begging, that one of the flashers will hobble by and send her screaming into the storm. With practiced, purposeful indifference, Ginny strolls over and takes a seat beside the girl in one of the cramped plastic bowls of the terminal chairs.

Ginny sits there for several moments, eyes completely off the girl except for occasional glances in her periphery to ensure that she's still there. She checks her nails, sighs audibly but unexaggeratedly, shifts in her chair occasionally to convey frustration, boredom. After the appropriate amount of time has passed, she turns, says politely, without any artifice, "I just love your hair."

"Oh, uh, what?" The girl turns, startled, face indicating a combination of shock and delight, probably the first kind words she's heard all day, perhaps in a long while. "Oh, well, thank you." Twinge of an accent. Appalachia, maybe?

"I'm so jealous." Ginny touches her own head, exaggeratedly tangles her fingers in the jet-black strands of her well-cared for hair. "A bob's, like, the only thing I can manage. If I let it get any longer it's hello, major bed head. All day long, I look like I just got out of a hurricane." She reaches into her purse, comes out with her cigarettes, lighter. The girl eyes them hungrily.

"Smoke?"

"S-sure." Trying and failing not to seem desperate. Probably ran out of her own somewhere on the way up here, trying to budget whatever she's got left in her own purse between food and her craving.

The two sit and smoke a moment, camaraderie established, joined now in their shared habit. "This rain is just, like, murder, isn't it? I mean, it's like, just take me out back and shoot me rain."

"It's pretty bad," the girl says. "I haven't wanted to leave since I got here."

"Just off the bus?"

"Yeah."

"Where you in from?"

"West Virginia."

"Oh, wow, really? First time in the city?"

The girl nods. "How about you?"

"Me? Oh, well, I live here and all. I was just out shopping when the rain hit, so I ducked in. I'm just killing time."

"What were you looking for?"

"Hmmm?"

"You said you were out shopping."

"Oh, you know, some new dresses, maybe jewelry. Yesterday was payday, and, like, you really have to keep up with the latest fashion if you want to make it here."

"What do you do?"

"Public relations," Ginny says. "I manage a group of entertainers. Strictly local, but very successful."

"Oh, wow. That must be really exciting." Genuinely impressed; little Loretta in from Butcher Hollow, getting her first taste of a cosmopolitan city girl.

"Ginny Kurva," Ginny says, extends her hand. The girl takes it, smiles.

"Tammy Struthers. Nice to meet you."

"Well, Tammy Struthers, what do you say a couple of girls with nothing else to do on a rainy afternoon grab some coffee? The rain's not going anywhere, and I could totally use the company."

Tammy mutters something.

"Sorry, sweetie?"

"I... don't have any money."

"Oh, darling, don't tell me you got mugged? Left your purse on the bus?" She feigns giving the girl an opportunity to speak, cuts her off: "Look, my treat, okay? I provide the coffee, you give me the conversation."

"Really?"

"I'm going to go in the bathroom and drown myself in the john if I have to sit here for another hour watching daytime TV. Gag me with a spoon."

The girl smiles. "All right."

"Got any stuff you need to take?"

"Just my bag."

"All right. Let's go."

Ginny guides her, careful not to lose her quarry, mindful of the hundreds of eyes moving across their bodies as they wade through the sea of tourists, families, businessmen, homeless kids, hustlers, pushers and pimps that crowd the terminal; mindful too of Tammy Struthers, watching that washed-out, wrist cutter look on her face begin to shift into something resembling cautious optimism.

Ginny lets the girl enjoy her coffee and another cigarette. The two sit for a while listening to the clamor of travelers and transients, Ginny pointing out different archetypes as they pass: the adulterous suburbanite visiting his mistress, the spendthrift businessman risking his wallet to save a dime, the drifters and vagrants and dropouts whose parents don't know they've dropped out. Tammy watching in delight as the color of the city ceases being something threatening and predatory, and becomes something more akin to a film to be experienced and wondered at. At last,

Ginny turns to Tammy, and with the same impassive gaze she's fixed upon the passerby, asks, "And what about you, urban adventurer? What brings young Tammy Struthers into the heart of the big city?"

The game has been so distracting, the coffee so relaxing, that almost without thought Tammy responds, "Oh, I ran away from home." The gravity of the revelation hits her immediately; her face flushes; a hand covers her mouth.

Ginny smiles incredulously. "No way. You're not here for college?"

Tammy shakes her head, eyes downcast.

"Oh, come on. NYU? Columbia? You're trying to majorly embarrass me."

"No, I... I really did run away."

Ginny puts her hand over Tammy's, her grin widening. She squeals with delight. "Omigawsh, so did I!"

Tammy shakes her head, confused. "I'm sorry, what?"

"This is so amazing," Ginny says. "I mean, what are the odds?"

"No...really?"

Ginny points to the nearest arrival gate. "Three years ago. I was eighteen and my sister was fourteen, and we got off the bus right over there. Right there! My dad was in the Corps. He was, like, a major joy kill. Everything was *do this, don't do that, go to this school, don't hang out with those boys,* and I was all, 'forget you, Mister Man, this is the 80s. You can't tell us what to do.' So we climbed out the window one night, pawned our stereo, and three years later, here I am." Ginny gestures to herself with all of the splendor and confidence of a woman with the world not only figured out, but under her complete dominion.

Tammy's face twists and contorts, the optimism approaching hope now, something inside of her twisting, ready to break.

"What about you, sweetie? Did you just decide to say 'forget it,' too?"

"Well…My family… We own a farm. It was my grandad's and then my dad's… hell, you don't wanna hear this. This ain't nothing like your story."

"Sweetheart, right now we're just two girls, sharing coffee and stories. I'm all ears."

Tammy runs the back of a hand over her face, trying to keep herself composed. "It was great when I was little. Money was just coming in left and right, and dad put it all into the farm. More land, more land. Said it was the best investment 'cause God wasn't making any more of it. Then, a few years ago, things went bad. First it was President Carter and us not being able to sell grain to the Commies. Then dad said that the harvest had been so good for everyone that the prices went down… I'd never seen him worry so much… He and mom would tell me things were fine, but at night, I'd sneak out of my room… Dad would be in the kitchen drinking…"

"That's awful," Ginny interjects.

"I could help around the place, but I was just another mouth to feed. No, that's a lie. I didn't want to watch it happen. I knew what was comin' next and I didn't want to be around for it. I know that makes me awful but I couldn't do it. I ain't got that in me. I know this is where everyone who wants to run away goes if they don't want to be found, so this is where I came." She wipes her face again, mutters, "Just didn't know what I planned on next."

Ginny puts an arm on Tammy's shoulder, doe eyes at their most compassionate, her smile at its most wickedly delightful. "You don't know it, but you made the best decision you're ever going to make."

"I… what?"

"That's what's so amazing about New York. You can

come here dirt-broke and ready to get kicked in the teeth, and the next thing you know, you're living in a hotel and making a hundred dollars a day."

"A hundred dollars?"

"And do you know who happens to be hiring?"

Tammy wipes her nose. "Now you're messing with me."

"Messing nothing. This total bimbette, Tina, totally quit on me. Left us high and dry. Our boss is like, super rad, but he's got this thing that he has to have eight girls working for him. You know, old timers and superstitions?"

Tammy nods. "Sure. My grandfather has this thing about never walking under ladders."

"Exactly. So, anyway, I was set to start interviews tomorrow, but I think I might have found what I need."

"But I... This is really quick here. I mean, I... I don't got no experience and..."

"Oh, no, no, no, sweetheart! Are you turning down money? I'm offering to train you, doll! Think of it as an apprenticeship. You don't need any experience if you're just willing to listen, learn, and do your best. I mean, just look at you—you've got that look."

Tammy looks down—the dirty t-shirt, faded jeans, peeling boots—and comes back puzzled. "I do?"

"Glammed up, big-haired, city chicks are a dime a dozen here. It's like, hello, if you want to see a show, do you really want to pay money to see what you can look at for free?"

Tammy considers this. "Well, no, I guess you don't."

"Exact-a-mundo! People here want to see a good country girl. They want Miss All American Heartland. The girl next door. And you have that in spades, sweetheart. And you're going to get a place to live too, you know."

"What're you getting at with all this? I ain't dumb, you know, if you're thinking of trying something funny with me..."

"Tammy, if I'm lying to you, then, I'm, like, totally screwed, right now and forever. I am just a *very* desperate woman. My boss is going to absolutely *kill* me if I don't get us back on schedule, and you, well, I don't mean to be mean, sweetie, but you are totally not in a position to turn down available work." Ginny stands, abruptly. "I think the rain's stopped." She sighs deeply, and stubs out her cigarette. "Look, sweetheart, the coffee and conversation were totally awesome, but, I really have to get back to the rest of my day..."

"I'll take it," Tammy says. "If it'll get me money... I can send it back home. I can make up for running off. And if you can make it... Well, maybe I can, too."

Ginny smiles with all of the warmth and generosity she gives to her sister, takes both of Tammy's hands in her own. "You are, like, a total lifesaver. Omigawsh, this is so totally out of the fifth dimension incredible! Come on, girl. Let's not wait another minute."

"All right! Where are we headed?"

"I've got to show you your new home."

———

Though the Misanthrope is within walking distance of the terminal, Ginny hails a cab. It's a grander introduction to city life, the luxury of paying for a twenty-minute ride instead of taking a ten-minute walk, and it affords Ginny the rare opportunity to re-experience seeing Manhattan for the first time through unmolested eyes. The awe that comes over Tammy as they enter into Times Square, at the billboards and the colossal scope of the architecture, creates a quiet bitterness in Ginny, that she and Tricia were never given that split second of wonder, not allowed something so innocent as looking towards a building and recognizing it from a movie they'd seen on television.

The façade of the Misanthrope—Ginny laughs inside at the appropriateness of the term— is immaculate, the bricks free from graffiti and even the sidewalk kept relatively clean for occasional spots on the nightly news, intermittent features in the *Times,* The Hotel St. Jude, where the wayward youth of Manhattan can find their place in the world for dollars a day and keep off the streets after dark. It is a clever tactic to not only keep the city off of The Colonel's back but also to lull the new recruits, give them a first impression of someplace gentle, a portal into a time of family dinners and songs around campfires and crisp Christmas mornings that never really existed.

"Here we are," Ginny says, puts a welcoming hand on Tammy's shoulder. "My home for three years, and hopefully yours for many years to come. The Motel Misanthrope."

"But that sign there says 'Hotel St. Jude.'"

"It's a sort of unofficial name. I came up with it." Ginny is struck by the question of whether she really ought to be proud of this.

"What's it mean?"

"Oh, it's just the name of this book I like. You read a lot?"

"I like Erich Segal."

"…Anyway, let's go on ahead inside. You are going to *flip.* If you want the authentic New York experience, then this is so totally where it's happening."

As they enter the building, Ginny directs her towards the stairs, passing her quickly through the lobby, past the front desk, trying not to give her an opportunity to absorb too much of *this.* "Interior art's a big thing here now," Ginny says, gesturing broadly to the graffiti, genuine stabs at art intermixed with lewd phrases, gang insignias, and renderings of male genitals in varying degrees of accuracy and arousal. "Most places you're going to go into will look something like this. It's the way that people all living together in one space can, like, come together and make it both totally their own but also something that belongs to everyone."

"That's really beautiful," Tammy says.

"You'll be up here on the second floor," Ginny says, leads her down the corridor, thankful that the revelry hasn't kicked up into full swing yet; no bodies strewn about the hall, few syringes. She guides her towards Tina's old room, opens the door, ushers her inside. She forgets sometimes how meager the girls' accommodations are in contrast to her and Tricia's. Nonetheless: cozy, clean, the ceiling fan left on to keep the place cool. Ginny shuts the door and the two women stand there in the stillness of the room, the fan's pull chain rattling quietly on a crooked axis.

"Well," Ginny says, "here we are!"

She flops herself down onto the room's small sofa, pats the cushion beside her. "Have a seat, sweetheart. We need to discuss your interview."

Tammy, exploring the small space, says, "I thought you said I had the job," finds her way back to the sofa and sits.

"*I've* hired you. I'm sort of the, like, HR director. But we're a small organization, so, there's a lot of oversight. So you've got to have an interview with *my* boss."

"What's he like?"

"The Colonel's super awesome. Real legit. You know, he's the one who runs, like, this whole place? When he came to New York, there was no place safe for girls like us to go when we first got here. So he opened the Misanthrope. Everyone in the building's, like, pretty much our age. Nobody over thirty allowed. You *are* under thirty, aren't you?"

"I'm seventeen."

"Perfect. Now, listen, Tammy, I know that your work experience is primarily in farming. But do you have any experience in *entertaining?*"

"Oh… Well, I mean, I was in a few talent shows. I guess I can sing okay."

"Wonderful, sweetheart, wonderful. I bet your boyfriend loved it when you sang for him."

"Oh, well, I never really sang for anybody… I mean, maybe in the car to the stereo, sure, but, I never *sang* sang."

Ginny shakes her head. "Well, he sure missed out."

"It wasn't that serious."

Ginny puts her hands together, tents her fingers beneath her nose. "And that is what we need to talk about. Sweetie, when people in New York pay to be entertained, they expect a lot more than they would in other parts of the country. Like, if you go to the dollar double feature at the drive in, you're going to expect a different type of show than the opera, right?"

"I guess so."

"So, New York is the ultimate entertainment experience. Like, if you're going to see a show, the performers interact with you."

Tammy considers this, fascinated and confused.

"So you're going to be interacting with the men you're entertaining."

"The men I'll be entertaining?"

"It is super stressful to be a guy in New York. You have no idea. Just as bad as things were going for your family, they're going super well here. There are guys who work eighteen hours a day and sleep in their offices just to keep their businesses running. If they slacked off at all, entire companies could go bankrupt overnight. Thousands of people would be out of jobs. So these are very important guys."

"Sounds like it."

"So, once in a while, they get an afternoon off. Like, just a few hours. And they need something to take their minds off of all that stress; something to distract them from everything they have to deal with." Ginny pauses for effect: the make it or break it moment. "Sweetie, you're going to be that something."

A beat. Tammy stands up, ready to walk out when she realizes she doesn't have a place to walk *to,* no idea how to get back to the Port Authority, not sure she'd even want to return there anyway, a few dollars short of penniless and completely friendless and...

"Sweetie, sweetie? Please, sit down. It's all right."

"What are you talking about?"

"Sweetie, please, calm down. Tammy. Tammy." Ginny stands, places her hands on Tammy's shoulders, sits her back down with equal parts gentility and force. "Shhh, shhh. Sweetie, I know you're scared. It's scary, at first. I was scared, too. Three years ago I was sitting right where you are, right now, thinking the same thing." A twinge of guilt at that particular lie, but Ginny figures better to tell it that way; the concept of being ushered into the profession in a New York hotel *is* so much more glamorous than a proposition at a truck stop in Akron. "And I was, like, totally honest about what I told you in the terminal. A hundred dollars a day, sweetie. My sister has her own television—color!—and a VCR... do you know what a VCR is, sweetie?"

Tammy shakes her head, still trying to catch her breath.

"You'd be working with some very rich, powerful men, sweetheart. Generous men. This is classy. Free shows. Rides in expensive cars. Tammy... Tammy, I want you to listen to me for a moment. This is me speaking to you as another woman. We have very few options in the world, you know? I mean, we can't all be Sally Ride, right?"

"Who's Sally Ride?"

Ginny bristles. "The point is, we're limited. Now you can go to college and get a degree, or be born into something big, but, that one-in-a-million-chance aside, you and I sweetie? The world doesn't want good things for us. Anything good that's ever going to come to us, we have to take. I think you get that, don't you? I know you do. That's why I came up to you at the terminal. I could just tell that you were the perfect girl. That you would take an opportunity like this by the balls and *twist.*"

"I don't think I'm ready for something like this," Tammy says, trying to choke back the tears.

"You can do this, Tammy. I know you can. If you can't do it for yourself, then I know you can do it for your folks." She wants to add: *You can do anything for someone you love;* doesn't want to push it. "A hundred dollars a day. So you get yourself a few nice outfits, some things for yourself, and then you can start sending money back home. Sweetie, play your cards right, and you can, like, save the farm."

"Do you really believe that?"

"I *do,* Tammy." Ginny has Tammy's hands in hers now, kneading them encouragingly. "And I am going to be there for you every step of the way, watching your back. And you are going to do just fine, darling. You are going to do such awesome, wonderful things."

"Okay," Tammy nods. "You're right. I'm so grateful I met you. I'm… I'm glad it wasn't someone else found me there. You got a good heart. I can tell that." Tammy wipes her eyes with the side of her hand. Ginny can't tell if it's the girl's honest assessment or if she's really just trying to convince herself. "So what happens now? How do… How do I start?"

"We go back downstairs so you can meet the Colonel. And have your audition."

————

Though he does not employ a regular secretary, the Colonel has had his office partitioned in two, the outer portion dedicated to a perpetually empty desk decorated with a blotter, pens, a telephone that Ginny herself has never heard ring and a typewriter she has never seen used, a cramped, green vinyl sofa that has been utilized far too much. Tucked away in a back corner of the ground floor of the Misanthrope, it is perhaps the only undisturbed part of the building, its walls clean, the carpet free from debris, the lighting moderate and well maintained. Tammy's eyes drift around the room cautiously as Ginny leads her in, her head turned down towards the floor, hands folded in front of her.

"You're going to love the Colonel," Ginny says, guiding Tammy towards the sofa, gesturing for her to sit down. "He's a very classy guy, real sophisticated. Just let me tell him you're here and he'll be, like, right out."

Ginny moves to the second door, knocks, waits, can see the shadow of the Colonel's feet move across the base of the door, the glimmer of light from the peephole darken. Deadbolts turn. The door opens a crack, the Colonel never fully opening the door, opting instead to unlock it, step back, wait for his audience to enter, the better to prepare himself in the event of an ambush.

The Colonel's inner office is more Spartan than the exterior, undecorated but for a single photograph of some nameless Polish city, an ancient desk in the center of the room occupied by a pair of ledgers, one containing the finances he presents at tax time, the other holding the actual figures of the Colonel's business empire, the money generated not only by rent coming into the Misanthrope but also the profits from his side ventures, what Ginny collects from the girls at the end of every shift, the cut taken from the dealers who do business in the Misanthrope's rooms.

The Colonel observes Ginny as she enters the office, nods to her, closes the door and locks it, one hand kept securely on his pistol until he's certain they're alone in the room.

"It good to see you." Ginny has long learned to suppress visibly flinching when the Colonel kisses her. "New suit?"

"Thank you for noticing."

"That not a compliment. Too manly. Not show enough." The Colonel stops a moment, waves a hand dismissively with a look of disgust, the expression of someone who's just realized they've made a faux pas and wishes to continue the conversation without acknowledging it. "I need second opinion on something. Have dream last night. You smart girl, need advice on what it means."

"That's like, totally cool that you want to come to me with that, but, sweetheart, I have got a surprise for you sitting out front, and, well, I don't want the blushing bride to get cold feet."

"Hmmm?" The Colonel moves to the door, looks through the peephole again.

"For me?"

"Your number eight."

The Colonel stares out the peephole a long while. "Beautiful. Like something out of dream."

"The one you had last night?"

"No, no. Dream last night, I back home, in Poland. Bodies in ditches on either side of road. Faceless men dig more ditches for more bodies. Smell of death everywhere. In the distance, some camp. Auschwitz, Treblinka? Who knows. Smoke fill sky. More smell of death. I behind wheel of big truck, only it hovering in air, not driving on wheels. On either side of truck, there two chains, and on the end of chains, Rottweiler dogs. The dogs on fire but they not burn."

"That's, like, totally fascinating."

"She young?"

"Seventeen."

"Have much experience?"

"Zilch."

"Hmmm." The Colonel steps away from the door, rubs his chin as though stroking an invisible beard. "I teach her."

"It's why I brought her to you."

"You very understanding." The Colonel returns to his desk, retrieves a cigarette, lights up. "Most women get jealous, their man get involved with other women. Not you. You know one woman not enough for me. You also know that you always Number One. Best bottom girl."

"Well, like, totally."

"You special. I never marry you, you know." He moves to the door, looks out again at Tammy, fidgeting on the sofa. "I marry girl like that. Blonde, tall, real American girl, kind of girl that make other men jealous, turn heads. Girl that men at war think about when bullets rain down. You beautiful girl, but not American enough."

"Excuse me?"

"You too… *Slavic.*"

"*Excuse me?*" Ginny can't be sure, but the Colonel's accent seems to briefly disappear on the word.

"You make good mistress; woman Colonel really cares about."

"You wouldn't care about your wife?" Ginny finds this curiously amusing.

"Wife gives children, raises them. Provides good home… Wife a *practical* decision. Mistress… Mistress listens, understands problems. Maybe I marry this girl. Young enough to have many children. Beautiful." The Colonel steps back from the door. "What does dream mean?"

"You're feeling powerful, which is why you're driving the big truck, and you're feeling that no one can stop you, which is why it's hovering above the ground. The dogs are, like, your worries, that are chained to you, and which you're trying to forget. That's why they're on fire. But you can't let go of them, which is why they won't burn out."

The Colonel listens intently, nodding slowly. "Very good. But you wrong."

"Am I?" Ginny knows she is; patently sure the dream has something to do with necrophilia.

"I have no worries." He nods politely. "I get ready now. Be out in a moment." The Colonel turns, pulls the picture off of the wall, reveals the safe hidden therein. Turns the combination, opens it, sets about packing away the ledgers amongst the stacks of cash he keeps there en route to whatever financial institution holds the bulk of his fortune.

Ginny returns to the anteroom, hairs on the back of her neck and between her legs standing on end. "Well, sweetheart, this is it."

Tammy nods, eyes fixed on the ground.

"He'll be out in just a second."

"Ginny?"

"Yes, sweetheart?"

"Is it gonna hurt?"

"What, sweetheart?"

"When he…" Tammy trails off.

Ginny stands still before the girl; ponders the relativity of time, how slowly it can pass for one observer, how quickly for another, how anticipation can turn observable seconds into experienced hours. She breathes in. Something hitches in her throat.

"Tammy?"

"Yes?"

Tammy is still looking at the ground when Ginny's rigid composure fluctuates for one fleeting second before she rights her posture and smiles warmly.

"You're going to do fine. The Colonel's a very experienced man. It'll be just like a hard pinch, and then it's going to be *fantastic.*"

"I never thought about it happening like this. All the different ways I thought about, it wasn't ever like this."

"Darling, it never is."

The door behind her opens. Tammy raises her head and Ginny turns to see the Colonel enter, tugging at the hem of his shirt. In the time since Ginny left him he's poured some sort of oil into his hair, slicked it flat against his scalp.

"Tammy, this is..."

"Colonel Zarek Baniszewski," the Colonel says, thrusts an arm out towards Tammy. The girl stands on trembling legs, extends a hand. The Colonel takes it, gives it a single, powerful thrust, drops it.

"You very beautiful girl," the Colonel says. Seeing the two beside one another, Ginny is struck by how tall Tammy is, five eight, five nine maybe, a good six inches taller than herself, an inch taller than the Colonel.

"Thank you," Tammy whispers. "Ginny's said a lot of nice things about you. She says you're a war hero."

"I serve my country honorably."

"My daddy always said that war heroes don't get enough respect," Tammy says.

"Your father sound like wise man. You should listen to him." His tarantula hand dances up Tammy's arm, his fingertips raising goosebumps on her flesh. "Ginny leave us now. You impress me, I give you back to her. Then, she do great things with you."

Ginny leaves the room; no further words for Tammy nor the Colonel. Someone locks the door behind her as soon as she closes it.

There's a shredded leather sofa across the hall from the Colonel's office, mended and re-mended with duct tape over the course of its long and brutal life; beside it, a coffee table with a lamp, a section of today's *Times*. Ginny positions herself on one of the corner cushions, lights up a smoke, takes up the paper. Keeps her eyes mindful of the time on her watch; a good half hour passes before the door to the office unlocks. Tammy emerges, looking no worse for the wear, no visible scratches or bruises, her clothes intact.

"Sweetheart," Ginny says, rising to her feet. Tammy walks past, head down, long, quick strides as she disappears down the main corridor of the Misanthrope.

Ginny looks back to the office, The Colonel, leaning in the doorway, cigarette in one hand, looking flushed, bemused.

"She make good number eight," he says, takes a drag. "Not wife material, though."

———

"Ms. Aster?"

Nicolette looks up from the puzzle book on her desk. It's lunch time. She has already finished her sandwich and banana and is working on her coffee. The meal provides the appropriate balance of nutrients and eliminates guesswork as to what she will eat each day. The coffee, brewed weak, provides just enough of a caffeine boost to see her through the day without an unpleasant crash after work. The food is a necessity but the coffee is a reward.

"May I have a moment?" Someone says. He has brown hair that is thinning at the crown but not the temples. Nicolette believes that this is the most fortunate way to go bald.

"Yes, sir." Nicolette pushes her book aside. It is a first edition copy of Greg Bright's *Maze Book: Puzzles for Everyone*. She has solved every puzzle in the book at least once. It pleases her to study them again, seeking alternative routes. Lately, she has begun to contemplate reconceptualizing the puzzles in three dimensions rather than two. She wonders, if this is the case, if they have infinite exits accessible by moving vertically rather than horizontally through the contours of the maze.

"I hate to spring this on you, Ms. Aster, but we got a tour coming through tomorrow," the someone says. He sits in the chair opposite Nicolette, uninvited. It displeases Nicolette when individuals presume temporary ownership over an area of her space simply because she invites them to address her. Granting permission to speak to her is not the same as granting permission to physically interact. "Girl's school, nothing major, bunch of eight, nine year olds, learning about civics, city processes, stuff like that. Bright girls, good girls, private school. They'd, uh, they'd been supposed to have a tour of a, uh, I think a police department, but that fell through, and you know how kids are, getting a field trip cancelled…"

"Yes sir," Nicolette says. She never particularly cared for field trips as a child. They were simply an opportunity for her to feel uncomfortable around others in a strange environment.

"Anyway, the principal gets through to us—real nice lady—all in a tizzy, wants the kids to be able to go someplace, see something that has to do with the stuff that keeps life movin' that you don't necessarily see, thought bringing them out here might be, uh, educational."

"Okay."

"What I'm getting towards is this, I'd like for you to give the tour. I know it's sudden, but, uh, you always done real good with orientation—I don't know if I ever said that before, but, I'm real pleased with how you handle orientation…"

"Okay."

"And I just think it might all be better coming from you. Girl to girl, you know?"

"Yes, sir."

"Knew I could count on you, Ms. Aster. You always know how to keep crap out of my hair. What's left of it." Someone laughs. Nicolette has learned that when someone says something and then begins to laugh that it is considered appropriate to laugh along. It is a sign of camaraderie. Nicolette lets her mouth open and pull up at either corner. She approximates the sound of laughter, a series of ululating "huh" sounds that, to those familiar with her general disposition, sound like a genuine demonstration of amusement.

"Hey, look, there'll be a little extra something in your next envelope." Nicolette supposes this is an indication of a bonus on her next paycheck. "Sound good?"

"Yes, sir," Nicolette says. One of her hands moves towards her puzzle book. She does this as a means of indicating to Someone that she is ready to be left alone. It pleases her that she has been able to learn this skill.

"You're a lifesaver." Someone stands up. "I'll let you finish lunch." Someone looks like he's ready to leave when he stops and turns back around. Nicolette briefly feels uncomfortable but recomposes herself. She has become accustomed to people not physically behaving in a manner that their speech indicates.

"Take care," Someone says.

"Yes, sir," Nicolette says. She opens her mouth and lets one corner rise up. Someone leaves. When she's sure he's not coming back, she returns to her puzzle book. The puzzle she has been working on today is one of her favorites. The pages of the book are filled with the shining gray graphite of myriad pencil marks from her numerous trips through the maze. It is in the shape of a wheel. Its interiors are composed of meanders, designated in recent artistic theory as the Greek key. Károly Kerényi, one of Nicolette's favorite authors, said that the meander is the figure of the Labyrinth in linear form. This observation pleases Nicolette. It means that a maze made up of meanders, like this one, is a maze made up of a maze. A labyrinth within a labyrinth.

Nicolette moves her pencil towards the center of the maze. At the center, rendered in red ink, is a small grid. There are fourteen squares in the grid. Two have been filled in. Twelve are empty.

———

It's late afternoon and the sun has begun its descent by the time Ginny changes into her work clothes and hits 42nd; there are few hours left and much to be accomplished.

Getting dates has never been an issue for Ginny. While she would tend to be assessed as average in appearance outside of 42nd, she falls to the more attractive end of the spectrum of Times Square trade, the bulk of which tends towards either the malnourished or the morbidly obese. Ginny has also cultivated her wardrobe to specifically appeal to the clientele walking the street from dawn until dusk. For the college boys looking for a reprieve from their studies, she is a New Wave goddess, a siren risen up from the depths of their most aching fantasies. For the businessmen slumming on their lunch breaks, the suburban dads taking a vacation from domesticity, the outfit coolly recalls the wrong type of girl at their children's schools. This is the fantasy she sells, and the sale is effortless; she only need stand on a corner, in a doorway, show the right amount of smooth, muscular thigh, bend just enough to grant a hint of cleavage, and within moments the date has been made, the price agreed upon. What exhausts Ginny is the loss of time. She has mastered the craft so well that she has found herself on more than one occasion standing before the entrance to the Misanthrope in the early evening, the smell of sweat and semen clinging to her, a rancid taste in her mouth and a pain between her buttocks, with no memory of the time spent since leaving her room that morning. Though she is not oblivious to the virtue in forgetting how she spends the majority of her day, there is a frustration in that the lost time is *her* time, hours of *her* life which she will never recall, and that when she lay on her deathbed she will be no better than a woman who's spent a good portion of her life in a coma, sleeping away time that might have been spent at work or play, writing or drawing or creating or inventing or sleeping or boozing or fucking or TV watching but *spent* nonetheless, fully realized and remembered. Then, the day will come when the sun beats hot on the street and the sweat pours from her armpits, when she can barely breathe in the stagnant air of the Misanthrope guest rooms, some fumbling boy on top of her, staring up at the ceiling trying not to feel either the pain of clumsiness or the cruel, coaxed encroachment of climax, and the idea of lost time becomes appealing to her after all.

Ginny manages to turn four tricks in an hour and a half, a tidy sum tucked away in her B-cup, when she decides to run a spot check on her girls. For safety's sake, they work in pairs, one keeping watch over the other while she operates, so that one can act as a runner to retrieve Ginny in the event of a beating, an attempted rape, a john trying to shirk them, the pairs gravitating around the sex-laden region of 42nd street between 7th and 8th unaffectionately known as The Deuce.

She checks in on Constance and Candice, catcalling potential dates as they shuffle in and out of Eddie's Adult Books; Sandra and Mary, playing the sheepish Lolitas outside Playland Arcade; saves, for last, Shannon and Michelle, operating near the box office of the Colossus Theater, Michelle idling time chit-chatting with the ticket girl while Shannon runs her fingers up and down the hem of a leather skirt, black-lined eyes calling to the theater patrons.

"*Darling,*" Ginny says to Shannon, air-kisses either cheek, careful not to impale herself on the spikes of the girl's dog collar. "I bring you greetings from the far away land of three blocks that-away. How *does* this awfully gorgeous, gorgeously awful day find you?"

Shannon shrugs. "Fuckin' same old. Hoping to pull in a little extra this week. Lana's birthday is coming up. First one since she moved in with me. I wanna get her something special, you know, some kind of like, real meaningful shit. Like, a cubic zirconium tongue stud, something like that."

"You're a thoughtful girl."

"You still ain't met Lana. I wish you'd come by some night."

"An employer doesn't socialize with her employees outside of work, sweetheart. That goes double for a teacher and her students. I've got to maintain standards. No one else is."

Shannon smiles. "One of these days, man."

Ginny's ears prick up, the hair on the back of her neck rising with the sensation of eyes on her body. Her head turns and Shannon follows her gaze so that they look in unison on the pair of boys eyeing them, twenty-two, twenty-three, burly in an athletic sort of way.

"Now, now, boys, didn't your mothers tell you that it isn't polite to stare?" Ginny says, moving towards them, swagger in her hips, the most gently menacing of smiles on her lips. "Don't be naughty, now. Or I might have to punish you. Unless you want to be punished?" Shannon moves up behind her, bad cop to her slutty cop, eyeing the boys with an intensity that indicates she might as soon fuck them as slit their throats.

The boys snicker to each other—defense against unease. Ginny can tell from the lack of forthrightness neither of them has ever procured professional services before.

"Don't be bashful, sweethearts. Fortune favors the bold, don't you know that? If you see something you want, *say so.*"

"Oh, shit," one of the boys says, the larger of the two, blonde, moon faced, high-forehead. Ginny unsure if the bulk of his chest is just the weight or a woefully undiagnosed case of gynecomastia. "Are you, like, a hooker?"

"Oh, darling, no, no, *no.* Where did you learn such filthy words? I am a girl looking for a good time, and someone to have a good time *with.* Now my question to you is: are you and your friend *generous* enough to treat my friend and I here to a show? It is, like, so hot, and we would both be, like, so *grateful* to get out of this heat. Wouldn't we, Shan?"

"Ecstatic," Shannon says to the boy's friend, a growl followed by a flick of the tongue.

"How generous do we have to be?"

"Well, sweetheart, how grateful do you want us to be?"

———

In another era, the Colossus, like all the theaters on 42nd Street, was a palace. In the victorious days and years that followed the Second World War, stoic veterans in their Sunday best led women in pearls and Summer dresses into the cavernous chambers of the auditoriums, where they luxuriated in the silver glow of the movie screen. Yet, if video did indeed kill the radio star, it killed the theater first. For all their brief splendor, the palaces could not do battle with the cozy threat of television, and eager men with a little money and few morals were more than happy to buy the palaces out from the desperate owners. The Colossus has gone through half a dozen owners since then, each with their own visions for the theater; it's showcased pornography and Spanish erotica, Scandinavian art films and kung-fu beat-em-ups. The previous owners, a small chain based out of Southern California, took a stab at middle-American legitimacy, running only box-office blockbusters and employing security guards in bow ties and red velvet jackets in an attempt to keep particular elements out of the auditorium. Few on The Deuce find it a coincidence that, shortly after the initiation of this program, the Colossus was set ablaze. The company sold the charred remnants to a local pornographer who, in need of legitimate cash flow on a limited budget, refurbished the single auditorium into four smaller, separate rooms, and purchased a set of video projectors to broadcast VHS tapes. Such was it that the Colossus became The Deuce's resident video art gallery, brutal slashers appearing beside Academy award winners, Redford and Gere sharing space with blood sucking demons.

Against Ginny's expectations, the air conditioning is working today in the Number Three auditorium, well enough that the patrons are wrapping their arms around their torsos to warm themselves against the AC's merciless onslaught. Though, under different circumstances, she would not be averse to the cold, she finds it numbing her joints this afternoon, frustrating her efforts to manipulate the boy's not unimpressive cock in her gloved hands. Though she'd been exposed to her fair share of labials majoris in the locker rooms and showers she drifted through before shuttling off to Manhattan, her intimate knowledge of the male anatomy was restricted to textbooks and hygiene class films; and while the medium of her education has been less than ideal, the diversity she has encountered has been intensely fascinating, if not completely from a place of sexual intrigue, then most certainly from an academic standpoint. It is not without some consternation that she will find herself, as she does now, studying an erect member with more than a professional eye, admiring the formation and the heft as she imagines she would with a lover; and though the initial sense of repulsion led her to justification, excitement as coping mechanism, phallic Stockholm Syndrome, she long ago jettisoned any attempts to rationalize her feelings towards the bodies of her clients.

Against the growing numbness in her wrist, Ginny completes her task. Her date slumps back into his seat, a serene look spreading across his cherubic face. A few seats away, his compatriot stares blank-faced at the movie screen, turning Shannon's dog dollar round and round in his hands, her face buried in the darkness of his crotch. With a contented sigh, Ginny collects her payment, rises, and sets to finding a better spot in the auditorium.

Towards the front of the theater, something catches Ginny's eye, a peculiar yet not unfamiliar gleam of light emanating from a small cloud of smoke in the front row. She pauses, waits for the appropriate level of light to reappear onscreen, sees it again, smiles, begins to move towards it: the telltale reflection of the movie screen off of the slick-shaved head of Roger Neiderman.

"Omigawsh, I didn't realize they let people like *you* in

here."

"Shhhhh." Roger raises a finger to the part of his tangled beard that she supposes hides his lips. In the darkness of the auditorium, his black clad torso is invisible, making it seem that his hands and head are separate, detached entities. "It's coming up." Blank-faced, he raises his hand, takes a hit off of his joint, encircling himself once more in thick smoke.

Ginny sits, removes her hip flask, drinks. Onscreen, the woman in the car insists she and her boyfriend leave the make out spot. The boyfriend reluctantly puts the key in the ignition. The girlfriend screams. Silhouetted in the beams stands the killer, shotgun at the ready. Ginny grins, grabs Roger's free hand; the killer performs an awkward running leap onto the hood of the car, drops the shotgun into position, pulls the trigger. The windshield explodes. So too, does the boyfriend's head, a psychedelic burst of grainy, red matter arcing out across the screen. Ginny squeezes Roger's hand, tugs at it.

"Say it, say it!"

"When life gets tough, get stronger. Excedrin."

Ginny squeals with delight, claps her hands. "I never get tired of seeing that."

"Nothing beats an exploding head," Roger says.

"*Galaxy of Terror,*" Ginny says.

"See you that, raise you *The Fury.*"

"*Dawn of the Dead.*"

"*Scanners.*"

"Ecstasy!" Ginny swoons in her chair. Roger makes the ticking little "heh" sound that passes for his laugh.

"You know, every Halloween, we'd get pumpkins for our front porch," Roger says. "And, ah, when I was in high school, every All Saints Day, I'd take them out back, and I'd, ah, I'd try to recreate the best exploding heads with my dad's shotgun. Trajectory, angles. Fun times. Of course, if I tried that here, I'd get arrested."

"You own a gun?"

"I'm a Jew from Oklahoma. Of course I own a gun... You mean you don't? *Here?*"

"I don't need any more trouble with the law, sweetheart." Doesn't want to tell Roger the real reason she prefers a switchblade to a firearm: afraid that if she had a gun in her room the day might come when she'd decide to use it on herself.

"Hey, you're not going to bogart the stash, are you?"

"What? Oh, ah, no. Sorry; where're my manners?"

"Omigawsh, Roger, I was, like kidding."

"Oh." He passes her the joint. From behind the lenses of his gold-rimmed glasses, giant eyes look pleadingly to her flask. Ginny takes a drag from the joint, glares back coyly.

"See something you like?"

"The, uh, booze."

"You damn romantic, you." She hands him the flask, Roger eagerly moving to drink it, stops and considers something.

"You didn't, ah, rinse and spit with this, did you? No, ah, backwash?"

"Sweetheart, I wouldn't be offering it if I had."

"Heh." Roger drinks. Onscreen, the plump killer, re-splendent in goldenrod pajamas, blubbers helplessly as he cradles a blood-drenched mannequin.

"Off-off Broadway brings you a startlingly lavish pro-duction of *Cat on a Hot Tin Roof,* starring Ron Jeremy as Maggie the Cat."

"Ohmigawsh, Roger. Why do we like this stuff?"

"Are you asking me academically or practically?"

"Give me both?"

"As members of a counterculture, we, ah, eschew the

false narratives of Hollywood in favor of, ah, more nihilistic fare that we, ah, see as being more authentic, more honest, and, therefore, less spiritually corrupt."

"Practically?"

"We're fucked up people who like fucked up shit."

"Speaking of fucked up people, Trish loved the comics, by the way."

"Heh."

"Well, not *Wonder Woman*. I'm trying to get her to read more stuff with female protagonists. Until this year it's been all *Batman, Spider-Man, Wolfman*."

"Wolverine. There are plenty of women in *X-Men*."

"Mmmm, still, I'd like for her to have, like, a singular role model, you know?"

"I got a guy maybe I'm gonna be buying some *Sheenas* from, blew all his rent dough on ice."

"How much you want for them?"

"I'll make sure some end up in your hands. No charge."

Ginny is about to protest when Roger says abruptly, "Other than that, how is our little daughter of darkness?"

Ginny rubs her temple. "I'm worried about her German. If she's going to get in anywhere decent, she's got to get the second language down. All she wants to learn are the swears."

"Oh. But the swears are the fun ones."

Ginny shakes her head. "Look, a fat man is wearing cat eye glasses and doing a dead woman's hair. I think that calls for a silence on our part, doesn't it?"

"Hmmmm, yeah, yeah."

The pair sit without speaking, Roger's eyes never leaving the movie, one or the other occasionally shouting obscenities or advertising slogans at the screen. There is a peace that comes over Ginny in moments such as these, when she finds herself sitting beside Roger in a theater on a hot afternoon, the work day behind her, time left on the clock but not enough to practically do anything with; moments when the best use of the time at hand is to idle in the laziness of a late Spring day with somebody who makes no demands.

The movie ends sooner than Ginny would have cared for; the credits roll. Roger stretches, joints cracking, and rises out of his chair.

"Aren't you going to stick around for the second feature?"

Roger checks his watch. "I've got ten minutes to get to the Oracle for *The Burning.*"

"Parting is such sweet sorrow. Think of me, please, would you? Remember, when you lose feeling in your ass, and the cold air sweeps over your bald head, and you really need to take a whiz but you don't want to miss something totally grody... that's me."

"I'll make a fried wiener joke just for you."

Roger is halfway down the aisle when he pauses, half-turns. He looks like he wants to say something, not sure whether to speak or keep going.

"You forget something?"

He walks back, sits beside Ginny.

"Look, ah, I know it isn't any of my business, ah, about *your* business...I mean, your, ah, *professional* business..."

Ginny bristles. "No, it isn't, but, go ahead..."

"I don't know if it's true or not, but, is it true that Tina didn't come back last night?"

She tenses up. "What if it is?"

Roger drums his fingers on his head. "Look, it probably isn't anything, but, ah, coming out of the Roxy last night, I saw her talking to some guy in a green van."

Ginny takes Roger's free hand between her own, pats it. "Roger, sweetheart, I hate to break it to you, but... that's what we do."

"Ah, no, no, I, ah, get that and all, but… Look, it probably isn't anything, but, I just got a weird feeling. Something wasn't right about the guy."

Ginny smiles and sighs. "Roger… There isn't anything right about any guy on 42nd."

"Uh, yeah, sure, but, ah… Look, you gotta know what this is like, you see a guy, something just tells you he's bad news, right?"

"Was he yelling at her, threatening her?"

"No, no, they were just talking."

"You didn't see a knife, a gun?"

"No."

Ginny puts a hand on Roger's face, realizes which hand it is, places her other hand on his face. "Roger, darling, you are an absolute *doll,* you know that? But don't worry your sweet little head about anything. Tina was, like, a totally lousy worker, and she just bailed, okay? It's happened before, it'll happen again."

Roger nods, still looks concerned.

"Sweetie, don't give me that look. Please. You're worried about something happening to *me*? Darling, *please."*

"It's just…" Roger looks around the theater. "Who's, ah, who's gonna laugh at my jokes, then?"

Ginny stands. "Sweetheart, the peanut gallery will always be here."

She rubs his scalp, turns, and exits the theater. The sun is halfway below the horizon when she steps out onto the pavement, invisible beyond the skyline of the city but still high enough that the heavens are gold and soft. Ginny has to stop and consider, for just a second, turning around, heading to the box office of the Oracle. The color of the sky is just right, the vibe of the encroaching night just perfect, like when she would get into Dad's Impala, drive against the dying light out to the park, and there, beneath the sunset, "Rhiannon" cranked on the stereo, practice her *pas de chats* until her knees gave out and she'd flop onto the grass and let the dew soak into her jeans, dark by then, but everything square at home and Tricia safe and so it was okay to lie back and pick out the constellations as she watched the stars blink to life—

She checks her watch; enough time to make it back to the Misanthrope, collect today's kick-up from the girls, dine with the Colonel. She doesn't look back towards the Oracle on the walk to the Misanthrope. Traffic crawls past her, green vans chugging by at irregular intervals. She only looks at them askance.

———

Though she could leave much sooner in the day, Nicolette waits until sunset before heading home. She needs to see the sky changing color above the mounds of the landfill before it feels safe to leave. Tonight, the sky turns a deep shade of salmon. This is a good color, and makes Nicolette feel particularly calm on the ride back to her house. She puts Zamfir on the stereo. Combined with the richly churning reds of the sunset, it helps her feel especially at peace.

Once she is home, Nicolette strips and bathes. Smell is her weakest sense and she fails to register when odors from work cling to her body. To avoid conflict or confrontation with her coworkers, she has learned to adhere to a regimen of thorough, nightly bathing with a loofah and perfumed soap and shampoo. She turns the water up to maximum heat to ensure thorough sanitation. To distract herself from the pain, she fixates on the water dripping from the base of the shower head and tries to count the drops.

Once she is bathed, Nicolette goes to the living room. The room is sparsely decorated with a couch, a lamp, a table, and a record player. The window faces west and affords her a view of the last moments of the sunset. Because she felt so soothed on the ride home, she puts a Zamfir record on the turntable. The deep salmon of the sunset has sunk into a series of luminescent bands of color. Crimson. Purple. Deep navy. Nicolette fixes her eyes on the purple strip and meditates upon it. Sufficient meditation on the proper color of the sunset helps Nicolette determine whether the next day will be good or bad. She is beginning to feel worried about the tour. New responsibilities tend to be difficult for her to initially conceptualize, and this makes her nervous. She closes her eyes and captures the purple behind her lids. The purple fills the darkness inside of her. She swims in it. Tomorrow will be a good day. She opens her eyes. It's almost dark outside. She does not feel worried anymore.

Nicolette sits perfectly still with her hands resting on her knees and her mouth slightly open. In her mind, she is sitting on top of a warm, smooth rock. A light breeze blows. Below her are endless fields of rose bushes, rustling in the wind. Bulls graze amongst the bushes, oblivious to the thorns around them. Figures in white tend to the bulls, bathing their bodies from clay pitchers. Beyond the bushes, rising up towards the heavens, is The Altar. Above, the sky is a pale azure and the sun a muddy ochre. The Meadow does not represent any physical place but is entirely of Nicolette's own mental construction.

Nicolette rises. She moves through the passage that winds down the rock face towards the Meadow. Her horns scrape the sides of the passage. The issue of the dogs is becoming a hindrance at work. In the beginning, when the Altar was small, there had been little concern for its discovery. As it grew in scope, though, and the tributes began to rise in number, it had been necessary for Nicolette to protect it. The presence of an occasional stray dog or two in the landfill had given her the idea for the pack. She had assumed that the sudden appearance of multiple dogs would lead to a quarantine of the area. That had failed. Now, it's having unforeseen consequences. One of the benefits of her job is that as long as things are going well, there is a minimal amount of human contact. Most of her days are spent filling out paper work. There are occasional spot checks of equipment. If no one has been injured and everything is up to code, she can largely count on being left alone. Months-long stretches have gone by during which Nicolette has only had to exchange the most superficial of pleasantries with her coworkers. Since the dogs became a problem, she has had to attend several meetings. Men come to her office with increasing regularity. The situation is unique enough that she does not fear for her job. She knows that anyone else in similar circumstances would be under the same amount of pressure. She also knows that the safety record during her tenure has been one of the best in the landfill's history. She will need to act soon to restore the status quo, though. She is certain she can convince her superiors that containment is the best option.

In the Meadow, Nicolette begins to move through the bushes. The Meadow is one of her earliest memories. As a girl, she would spend long hours here lying among the roses and watching the sky change colors with the day. It was not until she was ten, and under the care of her first psychiatrist, that she came to realize the Meadow existed in her mind. The psychiatrist explained that when she went to the Meadow, it looked to the rest of the world like she had gone into a trance, and this frightened people. The psychiatrist told Nicolette that this was not normative behavior. He encouraged her to stop going to the Meadow and to try and focus on the real, external world around her. Nicolette did not yet have the appropriate vocabulary to explain that the Meadow *was* the real world.

Nicolette comes across a grazing bull. It's the color of coal. She runs her hands along its body and feels the powerful muscles beneath. The bulls were not always a part of the Meadow. Along with the attendants, the Altar, and the rock face, they are more recent additions. Nicolette lays her head against the bull. She listens to the sound of its breathing. It matches the sound of her own breath. The moment is peace. The moment is truth. Nicolette closes her eyes. When she opens them, she is on the couch and the sun is shining bright, white light through the windows, and it's time to dressed and go to work.

In the kitchen, the egg beaters kick up, scream incessantly for the better part of a minute, then die down. A moment later, Tricia wheels into the bedroom, the beaters balanced in a plate on her lap.

"Hey, you wanna lick these?"

"What I want is a blackout," Ginny says, staring out the window. "I want for something on the electric grid to just, like, blow up. For, like, some slovenly guy with his stomach sticking out under his shirt to spill his coffee on something and just wipe out the whole city. I want to look up and see just… blackness. Stars… and blackness."

"Omigawsh, you are so fucking morbid!" Tricia sets to licking one of the beaters herself. "Fuck you, Vampira, fuck you and your smelly fat guy's stomach."

"I never said he smelled."

"If his stomach is sticking out under his shirt, he *has* to smell. It's, like, the fucking *law*."

"You gonna get up and watch the launch with me Saturday morning? Go up to the roof afterwards?

"I'm going to sleep Saturday morning. But, I'll totally dream of something not boring for you, okay?"

"This is big, Trish. This should interest you. The Russians were sending women up before we were born. You need role models. Sally Ride…"

"…is going to go up in space and the Pope and the Ayatollah are going to declare world peace and they'll cure herpes and you're going to completely fucking cream yourself over your girl crush." Tricia spins around, heads back towards the kitchen. "Omigawsh, seriously, you could've just said you didn't want to lick the beaters."

"Hey, Trish?"

"If this is about fat guys with coffee…"

"So, I like, ran into Roger tonight."

Tricia turns around. "Did you? How is he? Did he ask about me? Tell me he asked about me. What was he wearing?" After the first time Ginny had seen Roger, stocking the shelves at Hobbs' End Comic Emporium one day early last Summer, she had made the terminal mistake of calling him "cute" in conversation with her sister. Ever since, it has since become Tricia's mission in life to make her sister as uncomfortable as humanly possible whenever the topic of Roger Neiderman arises.

"Shit, Trish, he's, like, twenty-seven."

"Hell-o, I'm like, legal here?"

"We are so not going there. But, he did say something really weird."

"Sexy weird, or creepy weird?"

"…He said he saw Tina talking to some spooky guy in a van the other night. He said he had a bad feeling about it." Ginny follows Tricia into the kitchen. Sugar, flour, chocolate chips, and vodka litter the kitchen, dusted and spilled and splashed in myriad configurations around the giant plastic mixing bowl from which Tricia has set to scooping balls of cookie dough onto an aluminum pan.

"I mean, girls bail all the time, right? And if anyone was going to bail, I'd have picked Tina. But, Roger's pretty on the ball, right? I mean, he's never said anything weird like that to me before. It's kind of creepy, right?"

"Well, he does always know when it's going to rain."

Ginny sits at the table, takes a drink from the flour-dusted vodka bottle. "He also lives in movie theaters."

"I thought he lived downstairs?"

"His mind is probably completely shot from watching that shit all day." Ginny takes another drink, pleased with this observation. "I mean, this afternoon, we watched *Maniac* for, like, the fifth time."

"The fifth time? You're sleeping on the couch tonight. If you bring home mannequins tomorrow, I am, like, totally moving out."

"Roger." Ginny shakes her head. "Shit. He's going to fry his brain out there."

"Well, if he does, I call dibs on his body."

Ginny presses her hand down into a pile of flour, flicks it in her sister's face. Tricia shrieks.

"Oh, cock-a-doodle fuck! I am, like, so totally going to poison you!" She sticks her hand into the remaining cookie dough, rips off a chunk, flings it in Ginny's hair.

"Bitch!" Ginny flings two handfuls of flour. The kitchen air turns white.

"Geek!" Another wad of dough hits Tricia in the face. "Nerd! Star fucker!"

"Oh, that is personal, you little shit!"

The Kurva kitchen descends into a torrent of dough and flour and sugar and chocolate chips and laughter, and while Ginny can't stop thinking for a moment about the stars or Sally Ride or green vans crawling through the glowing night, it's fun, for a little while, to pretend that she can.

———

Though the Kurva sisters usually share their bed at the Misanthrope amicably, the arrangement is not without its drawbacks. Ginny's habit of assuming the spread-eagle position in her sleep has led on more than one occasion to Tricia physically throwing her out of bed in the middle of the night. Arguments arise, too, come morning, over the presence of drool on pillows, what percentage belongs to whom, and who is the more disgusting for it. Winter does, of course, lead to requisite cover-fights, subsequent name calling, death threats, exhaustion or love or both leading to the pair wrapped around one another in the center of the bed. Still, Ginny is glad to endure it; love for her sister and an acceptance of their circumstances notwithstanding, it gives her comfort, if she happens to awake in the night, to be able to turn her head and see another body and know she is not yet completely alone in the world.

For all of this, though, there is one drawback to sharing their bed that turns Ginny's blood to ice, and which, in its worst iterations, causes her to fantasize all through the next day about relocating to the couch.

It always begins the same, Tricia twitching about the waist, her unconscious mind attempting to activate her legs, unaware or unwilling to admit that they ceased to function long ago. The sweat comes next, followed by the thrashing of her head side to side, eyes lolling beneath their lids as memories and nightmares mingle in the most scarred recesses of her mind, before she sits upright in bed, eyes open but still asleep, screaming with enough terror to wake their neighbors. Ginny has observed no pattern to the occurrence of these night terrors, though she has learned from experience that sitting at the foot of the bed or attempting to enter it after Tricia has fallen too deeply asleep tends to activate them. Though the correlation puzzled her at first, she was quick to make the connection in her own memories: Dad staggering drunkenly away from her bedroom door, Mom at the foot of her bed, shushing her sweetly, and so she has taken to sleeping on the floor or couch those nights that she stays up later or passes out first. On the nights that Ginny happens to be awake beside her sister when the thrashing starts, she is usually able to stop the attack from becoming full blown; stroking Tricia's hair tends to work, though, if it proves ineffective, Ginny has found that the most surefire—though embarrassing—method is singing to her sister; since moving into the Misanthrope, she has had to learn and recite more Hall and Oates lyrics than she truly cares to remember.

If Ginny is asleep when an attack comes on, though, the results are less manageable.

As they are tonight.

The sisters have been in bed for less than an hour, freshly cleaned from their culinary battle, when Tricia's screams wake Ginny. Ginny's initial response is slow, a series of her own shouts of surprise accompanying groping for the switchblade she keeps behind the alarm clock. Then the realization of what is happening sets in, along with stone cold sobriety.

"Trish! Trish!"

The screams continue, high pitched, staccato. Her eyes, bulging from their sockets, stare lifelessly into some horrible, starless night.

"Tricia! Sweetie, sweetie, wake up." Ginny grabs her by

the shoulders. "Tricia, darling?" She begins singing "Private Eyes;" no luck.

"Wake up!"

The screams become louder, more strained, more animal panic slipping in, intermingling with the music in the hall, and a confused, drunk voice slurring outside their door, "Hey, can I come in?" Ginny feels each scream like a dagger in her hungover brain, rage building within her with such undirected fury that, at last, when she swings her own palm and strikes her sister in the side of the face, she isn't even aware that she has moved until the sound of the blow registers, the screams stop, and Tricia collapses sobbing into her lap.

"You fucking bitch! What the fuck? Why did you do that? Why did you do that?"

"Oh, Trish, I'm... Trish, I didn't mean it, you were... you were having one of your fits." Hesitantly, Ginny lowers a hand to her sister's hair, begins stroking it. "I'm sorry, sweetheart, I'm so sorry."

"I was having a nightmare," Tricia sobs against her sister's thigh.

"I'm so sorry, sweetie. Sweetie, please, I'm sorry."

"I was all alone, downstairs, on the street, and, and something was coming for me, and I could... And I could... And I could feel my legs but I was in my chair... And I couldn't get... get out and... My arms couldn't push the wheels fast enough and... *Ginny.*" Her voice cracks in a last, anguished squeal before she rights herself and wraps her arms around her sister, the pain of the blow lost to the need for comfort.

Ginny kisses her sister's face, strokes her hair. The strength of her sister's arms around her is startling.

"It was... awful... And then it got me and... And it..."

Ginny pulls her sister's face away from her so she can

look directly at her. The expression on her sister's face is almost as terrifying to Tricia as the content of her nightmare.

"Tricia… No one is ever going to get you. All right? If anyone ever tries to hurt you, ever again… I'll kill them."

"I know."

"You don't have anything to be afraid of." Ginny lays back, easing her sister down with her. They lay face-to-face on their own pillows, Ginny running her fingers through her sister's hair.

"Now that's *my* nightmare. Why the fuck can you grow it out without it turning to shit?"

"I'm special."

"Damn straight you are."

"Best of the best."

"Princess Patty."

"Oh, shit. I'd forgotten that."

"Who remembers shit about when they were seven?"

"Omigawsh, that dress was, like, so fucking girly, I think I actually might have gone lesbian and then straight again."

"Bullshit. You loved every fucking second of it. You wouldn't take it off for, like, days. Your teachers were so pissed… And when they took you to the office, you told the principal, 'I don't have to take it off, I'm Princess Patty and this is my royal *degree*'."

"Oh, gag me with a spoon. When you invent time travel—because like, I know you're going to invent time — travel—please go back in time and kick my ass, okay?"

"Right after I kill Hitler. Now go to sleep. There are no monsters here. The Princess is safe."

"Ginny?"

"Yeah?"

"I'd like to go for a walk, Ginny."

Ginny sits up. Upon first arriving in New York, it had occurred to her that, for the duration of their stay, Tricia would require a sort of de facto imprisonment, not only for the purpose of honing her sister's mind to her studies but also for keeping her in a position that would ensure the highest level of safety. It has been to Tricia's advantage that she requires little in the way of entertainment beyond what their room can house and what Ginny can provide. Even as children, while Ginny would spend her summer vacations in the backyard, at the lens of her telescope or digging for bugs, Tricia could be counted on to be parked in front of the television, attention divided between the screen and the pages of a comic book, checking the egg timer to make sure she didn't overcook the brownies in her Easy Bake. True to her prediction, Tricia has adapted well to spending the majority of her time in isolation. As such, Ginny takes seriously any unscheduled requests to go outside.

"Yeah. Sure. Let's go."

———

Ginny tends not to mind that the Colonel is too cheap to have the Misanthrope's elevators repaired. She has always considered her legs one of her best features, and the regular ascensions and descents from she and Tricia's room have done wonders for them. Only when she must transport Tricia downstairs, her sister's arms hooked around her shoulders, her legs propped onto Ginny's elbows, does it become a concern.

"Omigawsh, Trish, like, are you putting on weight?"

"Not even."

"You feel heavier than two weeks ago."

"And you sound bitchier."

At the bottom of the first flight of stairs, Ginny sets Tricia down, jaunts back up to retrieve her wheelchair. Those residents of the Misanthrope who have stuck around longer than the customary week invariably learn the basic details of the sisters living on the fifth floor and of the grievous bodily harm that will come to them should they transgress against either. More transient guests do not have the benefit of learning such details. On one of the earliest occasions Ginny took her sister out, she attempted to leave her wheelchair outside of their room, carry her sister to the lobby, and go back to retrieve it, only to find another guest in the process of wheeling it into his room. The resultant argument lasted something short of five seconds and ended with the unfortunate boy's nose flattened against his face, a hairline fracture from the multiple blows to the head with the edge of the door. Ever since, Ginny has employed the process of first depositing her sister on a landing and then immediately returning to the top of the stairs to retrieve her chair; whether the efficacy of the process or the scope of her reputation, there have been no further incidents.

"You know, you've got, like, influence with the Colonel," Tricia says once Ginny is carrying her down the next flight of stairs. "You should make him fix the elevator."

"Omigawsh, if someone doesn't give him the money first, he's not going to give away anything." She neglects to mention that, even when the Colonel is in the gift giving mood, there are always conditions. She tries not to remember how they got their toaster oven.

"Okay, so, like, he can convert the stairs into an escalator."

"That makes no sense."

"Okay, so, then, like, he can put in those things in the walls, like, in old movies, with like, you know the pulleys and shit."

"Dumbwaiters?"

"Yes! And he can have them operated by dwarfs."

"Tiny, polite dwarfs."

"Wearing tweed suits."

Bodies are drifting in and out of the lobby of the Misanthrope when Ginny at last reaches the bottom with Tricia's wheelchair. Her sister waits on the bottom step with her head against the wall, her eyes following a pair of attractive boys conversing outside the dining room, Tricia ineffectually attempting to make eyes at them, batting her lashes, tossing her hair back again and again. Ginny sighs as she unfolds the chair, Tricia making a final effort at being noticed by making a show of getting herself into the chair, thrusting herself up on her triceps and crab walking off of the step over to her sister. She flings herself into the seat with such exaggerated finesse that she nearly topples herself over, the feat still not earning her any attention. Ginny takes the handles at the back of the chair as Tricia casually raises her middle finger at the boys as they pass, the two oblivious as to what they've done to raise her ire.

The Deuce is as heavily populated by night as it is by day, but while sunlight attracts outsiders, the artificial lights of the night bring out the denizens of 42nd Street; the pushers and pimps, shirtless hustlers in jean shorts, gaggles of drag queens strutting through crosswalks with indifferent pride, pipe heads and ice heads riding out fixes in the gutter or in phone booths; needy men gnawing their cuticles outside of bathhouses; the occasional tourist looking on in awe or gruesome curiosity at the grotesque carnival that forms the core of the Big Apple; *the girls,* propped in doorways, submitting themselves to the night as Ginny does to the day. For Ginny, there is no fear for her here, nor for her sister; at least not beyond what she experiences every waking moment of her life, the fear which accompanies the very fact of her womanhood and all of the predation which that entails, the vigilance required of her in even the most pedestrian of settings, a fear compounded even further by her particular occupation in this particular city.

Following Tricia along the sidewalk, her chair cutting a swath for them amongst the writhing crowd, Ginny slowly imagines that only the two of them exist. While her unconscious mind remains vigilant, scans the faces around her for any sign of potential harassment, she permits herself to imagine the bodies around her fading away one by one into the haunted, emerald and magenta glow of the neon signs, till there is only her and Tricia, drifting along endless sidewalk. She can hear, swelling in her memory, the melody of Skateaway, played on an eternal loop on the long drive home for Christmas break, three years ago now, her first semester at Avila behind her and the song seeming to speak to her of what wonder and romance lay ahead, the true struggles of her life, she thought, finally behind her, and only bright mornings and Paul Saunders in her future. The real struggles, she was to learn, when she got home, yet to face her. Yet, the music, playing on now in her memory, soothes her; even if it no longer speaks to her of fantastic tomorrows, it still fills her with a sense of peaceful solitude, of the fantastic now. For many years, she has seen herself as someone capable of digging a pearl of sanguinity from even the most atrocious of circumstances, of taking ill conditions and manipulating them to her benefit.

If she has found one positive to her current situation, it is this: She has learned to stop looking to the future and love the present.

Such an endeavor is easy when one sees nothing to look towards.

"Hey, Trish?"

"Yeah?"

"You ever think about what you want to do? I mean,

like, when you get to school?"

"Omigawsh, did you hear that?"

"What?"

"The sound of my joy dying. It went ker–woooop and then it crashed and it died. It was very sad. Why do you hate joy? Does it make you feel powerful?"

"I mean, I'm getting you ready for anything you can possibly want to do. I don't know if you realize this, but you're really smart. And you're going to have a lot of options. You're good at math. You can do a lot with that. Have you ever thought of being an engineer?"

"I've thought of *killing* an engineer."

"You could figure out a way to trick your chair out with like, I don't know, a little gasoline engine, or, you know, barbed wire and spikes or whatever you'd want to put on it."

"Or I could, oh, I don't know, do something that doesn't end with my last words being, 'My life was a waste.'"

Ginny sighs. "I'm tired. Let's go home."

Tricia grips the wheels of her chair, prevents Ginny from pushing it forward. She leans back, looks up at her sister. Though she is putting forth her best effort not to look troubled, Ginny knows too well the subtleties of her face, the little inward tremor between her eyebrows. "Hey, Ginny? Not yet, okay? I don't want to go back to sleep yet. Okay?"

"Sure. Fine. You let me know."

Ginny and Tricia walk for the next half hour. Tricia soars past storefronts, occasionally slamming the breaks of her chair, threatening to fling herself out, laughing at her own recklessness as she presses her face to windows to stare at sheaves of cardboard propped behind glass to block out the view of what's inside.

"I am so making you take me into one of these places

someday."

"Omigawsh, like, you really have no shame, do you?"

"Shame is for the weak. How about my birthday? You don't even have to buy me anything. But, like, you know, if you were wondering, if they make, blowup dolls of the *Godfather* cast…"

"Oh, shut your mouth."

"It is, like, the sexiest movie ever made. Everyone except Brando. I'll take *Streetcar* Brando. But he's, like, number four."

"Who're one through three?"

"Al Pacino, then John Cazale, then James Caan. And I mean Part One John Cazale, without the mustache."

Ginny almost drops the chair. "Have I ever told you that I think you might be seriously fucked in the head?"

"Oh, like, fuck you on a band saw, bitch. You get it up for that, like, electricity guy…"

Ginny stops the chair. "Nikola Tesla was a brilliant, gorgeous, brilliant man."

"Virgin," Tricia coughs.

"Excuse me, what?"

"It was in *your* book."

"Since when do you read my books?"

"Back home, when I'd get bored pooping. I hated to be bored when I pooped. And, like, hello, I don't know if you blocked it out, but *virgin!*" Tricia shouts the word so loud that a nearby man turns, looks at her quizzically. Tricia giggles as she clasps her hands over her mouth.

"Well, fine," Ginny says. "He was passionate about his work. He had better things to do." She neglects to mention that this is part of the fantasy—that her intellect, linguistic prowess, fantastic legs and quick wit are able to crack the mad genius' stalwart celibacy, inspiring him to thrust the contents of his desk onto the floor, tear open her cardigan and take her right there beneath the magnifying transmitter.

"Omigawsh. You are, like, so totally more fucked in the head than me."

Ginny begins to push the chair again. "Bullshit. *You're* the fucked one. Cazale was way more doable with the mustache."

"Omigawsh, I get it!"

"What?"

"You're, like, a total hair slut."

"Shut up. And, so? I like the way that hair feels."

"*Sooo* you like men who look like porn stars."

"And *you're* going to turn into a walking VD bath the second I let go of you. I am so totally not raising your two dozen illegitimate children."

Tricia grips the wheels of her chair, stopping herself so abruptly that Ginny nearly topples over. "…I can still have kids?"

"What?"

"I didn't think I could have kids."

"Well, I mean, sure you can. I mean, they'd need to do a C-section, but, like, your reproductive system is intact. So, you know… Sure, yeah. Sure you can have kids. Do you… want kids?"

Tricia shrugs. "I don't know. It's just something I didn't think I could do." She begins pushing herself in her chair again. Something profound strikes Ginny deep in her stomach; she can't quite articulate what.

"Hey, Ginny? Push me for a while? My arms are getting tired."

"Sure."

"I want to look at the lights."

Tricia folds her hands in her lap, tilting her head back to watch the signs as they go passing by. Slowly, her eyes begin to grow heavy, twitching gently, neon glow reflected in progressively disappearing pupils until her eyes shut and she begins to snore quietly.

Ginny watches her sister sleep, a sad yet comfortable familiarity in the experience. This is how it is now, has been, forever shall be, world without end; Tricia dead to the world, the valiant efforts of another day rewarded with the undisturbed sleep of the innocent; and Ginny, the eternal sentry, standing on guard, the last one awake in the theater for the midnight show, watching as the movie goes on, and on, and on, and on. Ginny sighs, checks her watch. Pathetic little time until her day begins. She lights a cigarette, brings it to her lips with one trembling, exhausted hand, staring up, the electric drowned navy of the sky beginning to wane into a sickly slate blue. Her eyes ache; the cigarette slowly burns to ash as she contemplates the many hours that lay ahead of her until she can drink herself into oblivion. She drops it on the ground, doesn't bother to stub it out, heads back home.

She's going to have a hell of a time getting her sister upstairs.

3

Thursday, June 16th, 1983

I T TAKES MORE THAN THE USUAL AMOUNT OF EFFORT
for Ginny to prepare herself for work this morning.
Though she has long become accustomed to dealing with hangovers, she does not function well on a sleep
deficit. As alcohol has become so much a part of her life
at the Misanthrope, she has come to expect, and even find
comfort in, waking with a throbbing headache, her vision matted and chalky, the first minutes of the day spent
hunched over the bathroom sink, desperately chugging
water from the tap. Ginny considers the hangover to be
a signifier of progress. A hangover means she managed to
achieve a good, hard drunk the night before, and a good,
hard drunk means that she slept a dreamless sleep. Drunk
Ginny is asleep at one in the morning, oblivious to the
world, stirred to consciousness only by the presence of a
threat. Sober Ginny would appear, to an outside observer,
to be in the final stages of a nervous breakdown: the muttering, the swearing, the erratic pacing culminating in the
inevitable crying jag. As spirit-breakingly awful as the dry
nights are the following mornings: The welcome symp-
toms of a hangover replaced by frightening, alien sensa-

tions and an eerie, still disorientation, the world around her moving in hyper-slow motion, a raw, creeping feeling moving over her throughout the day.

Such is how Ginny feels today.

Ginny completes her morning exercises, her form sloppier than usual, her timing sludgy. Moving to the kitchen on wooden knees, she prepares to sit down for her lesson planning, stops. She stands for a long while hovering over the table, her mind drifting. At last, on one of the sheets of loose-leaf paper she uses to leave Tricia her day's work, Ginny scrawls in great, looping letters, "SICK DAY." Satisfied with this, she puts on her sunglasses—American Optical aviators, *the same brand favored by Sally Ride,* she thinks with a smile— and staggers out the door.

Ginny's feet are even clumsier on the steps this morning than with Tricia's weight on her back. Five steps away from the second floor landing, she gives up and lets her legs slide out from under her, a semi-controlled slide ending in a near collision with the floor. Righting herself, the appropriate response seems to be to strike the wall as hard as she can. Although she succeeds in creating a sizable crack and releasing some of her bottled adrenaline, the agony from her knuckles to her elbow hardly seems worth the endeavor.

Once the pain has subsided, Ginny makes her way to Tammy's door. She looks at the numbers for a few seconds, breathing deeply, attempting, as best she can in her present state, to meditate, rid herself as much as possible of any negative thoughts. It wasn't terribly long ago she stood in this very spot and prepared to walk Tina through her first day. Tina, the unremarkable. For the first time since her hasty departure, Ginny dedicates actual, concentrated thought on the girl. Gorgeous, to be sure. While Ginny has always been proud of her own Slavic good looks, there was something enviable in Tina's California-blonde aesthetic, a sort of least-common-denominator, thoroughly American beauty that would have let her take over 42nd, if the girl had only been willing to put forth an iota of effort. It *was* her looks, really, Ginny realizes now, that made her suited for the trade, and not any *talent* on the girl's part. Though she takes no particular pride in it, Ginny is quite assured of her own abilities in giving physical gratification. She is certain she could be violently disfigured and still keep herself in business through a reputation as one of the best lays to be had in Times Square. Tina's talents were all God given, uncultivated, unearned. She didn't have to spend eternal, debasing hours in the backs of cars or the balconies of movie theaters or the rooms of the Misanthrope learning how to satisfy clients. All that was ever needed was a wink, a toss of the hair, and the men were forking over their money before they had the opportunity to realize there was no depth to the performance. Demands for refunds were not uncommon with Tina; Ginny cringes to think of the number of johns she had to deal with on Tina's behalf, the blackened eyes and broken wrists she had to deal out in the name of preventing the sniveling dipshit from getting raped or beaten because she took payment for something she refused to deliver. Tina, the ultimate crapshoot . When she was in good form, the money flowed like manna in the wilderness. When—more often than not—she was feeling bashful or unconfident, when a date critiqued some aspect of her appearance and she set herself to moping for days, when she went off the pill and hit the rag and refused to do anything but the rub and tug, her income dwindling, when she threatened to just not come home some night and hitchhike her way back to Sacramento, there were days when, in her darkest moments of intoxication, Ginny considered wasting the bitch herself.

Green van or not, good riddance.

Ginny knocks on the door. It takes several seconds for it to crack open, chain lock in place, Tammy's frightened face peeking out. It's clear the girl has had as little sleep as Ginny.

"Rise and shine, sweetheart. Is the new girl ready for her first day?"

Tammy stares back, motionless.

"Sweetie, will you let me in? Just do that. Just let down the chain and let me in?"

Without taking her eyes off of Ginny, Tammy removes the chain and steps back. Ginny moves into the room.

"It looks like you and I both had real bummers of a night."

Tammy nods. Ginny takes her hands in hers, holding them in front of her. "Look, sweetie, you don't realize it, but today is one of the most exciting days of your life."

"You sure look different when you aren't dressed all nice," Tammy says. "Yesterday I thought you looked all like one of them women on *Dynasty*. Now you just look slutty." Tammy puts her hands in front of her face and stifles a sob.

"Darling, sweetie, shhhh, shhhh. You're fine, I'm fine, everyone is fine. You are not a victim anymore, don't you get that? Starting today, you are in total control. Look, when I started doing this, I was just as terrified. And then, I realized something. You know what I realized, sweetie?"

"No."

"I realized that this was one of the most empowering things that ever could have happened to me. Do you know what empowerment means, Tammy?"

"You mean like all that women's lib stuff?"

"…Yes, just like that. Men are going to be paying for you, Tammy. Not for you to clean their cars or farm their corn or serve them hash browns, but for *you*. *You* are worth something now, Tammy. Not what you can *do* for some-one. *You.* Do you know how many people are out there right now, starving for validation? Just wanting to know that someone cares about them, that they matter? Your en-tire job is getting to know that you matter. And people just won't *tell* you that you matter, sweetie. Any asshole can tell you that. They're going to *pay* you. Doesn't that sound, like, totally awesome?"

"When you're saying it like that... But the stuff you're gonna want me to do ..." She prepares to break down again.

"You never, ever do anything you don't want, sweetie. Different girls all have things they're comfortable with, and if you decide you don't want to do something, you just say, 'No sir!' And, boom, you just move on."

"There're gonna be other girls?"

"Of course, sweetie. And they are, like, the nicest, sweet-est, most supportive girlfriends you are *ever* going to have, because not a single one of them is going to judge you. We're all alike here, sweetie. Anything you ever need, any-thing at all, and all you have to do is ask one of them. This is a turnaround for you, Tammy. This is where you stop worrying about what's around the corner and you start *deciding* what's around the corner. But first, you've got to come downstairs with me, and you've got to start your day. I know it's scary, but do you know what fear is, sweetheart? Fear is just your body's natural response to something it's not familiar with. And do you know how scientists define intelligence? Intelligence is the ability to adapt to a new situation. So the choice is yours, sweetheart. You can either be afraid or you can be intelligent. Which is it going to be, darling?"

"I... I don't want to be afraid."

"And you don't have to be. I'm going to be with you

the whole way, and so are the other girls. No one's going to let you fall. But you've got to make the first step. Are you ready for that, sweetie?"

Tammy nods.

"Good. Now, come with me."

Ginny leads Tammy out into the hallway, locks her door for her with one of the many keys on her ring. "I'll get you a copy of a key later," she says. "The last girl ran off with hers. Now, I don't want you to rest on your laurels. I expect a lot from my girls. There's no use in having a rocking bod if it isn't carrying around an awesome brain. Don't expect to hit the streets in the morning and then come back here at night and live it up until dawn. If all you do is work and party, the next thing you know you have no teeth and you're screaming at people for nickels in front of the Pussycat Club. So! You're going to be doing some reading in your down time. Now, the girls and I are already three chapters into *The Great Gatsby*. Have you read it?"

"I seen the movie."

This impresses Ginny. "Okay, that's cool, but I really want you to appreciate the prose. It's a short book so it won't be too hard to catch up, but I'm going to pair you up with Mary—she is, like, the most darling girl you are ever going to meet. She'll also be your German partner."

"My what?"

"Now don't be intimidated, I don't expect you to be a natural off the bat. Mary will help you to get started. You'll be surprised how quick you can learn. Michelle, the newest girl after you? Already speaking at a second grade level."

Ginny and Tammy enter the lobby, move into the dining room. Tammy stops a few feet beyond the entrance, looking at the girls gathered around the table, the darkened room. Ginny takes her hand, squeezes it.

"Remember what I said about fear, sweetie. Come on.

Let's go on ahead and have some breakfast, and you can meet your new friends." Ginny leads Tammy by the hand as she approaches the table.

"*Guten tag, damen.*"

"*Guten tag,* Frau Kurva."

"I know I'm late, again, and for this, I utterly and wholly apologize. Please don't think that I feel my time is any more valuable than yours. But, I have some exciting news this morning! Ladies, please meet Miss Tammy Struthers, the newest addition to our club!" Ginny claps, encouraging the rest of the girls on. Most of them clap; Candice, more boldly, rises and puts a bear hug on Tammy.

"Damn, girl, get over here! This table's getting lonely with an empty chair."

"Thank you, Candice. Tammy, why don't you tell us all about yourself?"

"Sorry, what?"

"What's your story, girl?" Candice shouts.

"You had your opportunity to introduce yourself, Candice, this is Tammy's time now." Ginny turns to Tammy. "Who are you? Where did you come from? What do you like?"

"Well I....Well, I came here from West Virginia... I was born there."

"Mary, can you tell us the capitol of West Virginia?"

"Char...Charleston."

"Very good. Tammy, please, continue."

"I grew up on a farm there. I like... chicken legs, and... Glen Campbell and... Willie Nelson and... I like... red."

Ginny smiles. "And what a coincidence! Red is my favorite color! Tammy, why don't you tell the girls why you're here?"

"Because.... Because you found me at the..."

"No, no, sweetie, what brings you to New York, what

you hope to *accomplish*."

"My… my momma and daddy… Their farm's in real trouble, and I… I was hoping that, maybe, I might be able to help them out."

"And have you ever heard anything less selfish in your lives, *damen?* Tammy is a model for us all. There is not a selfish bone in your body, is there? And, sweetie, I want to say this—and, ladies, please forgive me if I'm not speaking for any of you— but I truly, honestly feel that you are going to so totally succeed. Ladies, let's all give Tammy a great, big Misanthrope *yes!*"

"*Yes!*"

"*Yes!*" Ginny raises her arms above her head, begins pumping them in unison. "Yes! Yes! Yes!"

"Yes! Yes! Yes! Yes! Yes!"

Ginny looks to Mary, gestures with her eyes towards Tammy. Mary takes the cue, rises, moves to Tammy, wraps her arms around her. Sandra follows, then Candice, the rest of the girls, the chorus dying down as each one rises to embrace Tammy, their warmth sincere. Tammy, overwhelmed , begins to cry, sinks her head into Michelle's shoulder. Michelle strokes her hair; Sandra reaches back to retrieve a napkin for use as a tissue. Ginny has vouched for this girl; Ginny, whose guidance has profited them, whose protection has kept them safe. They require no greater endorsement.

Now, she is one of them.

———

"The first rule is, you never trick alone." Ginny says this to Tammy as they stroll along 42nd Street, Mary struggling to keep up, her legs a good deal shorter than either woman's. Tammy's eyes try to remain in front of her, but they can't quite seem to focus, drifting all around, 42nd Street more awesomely terrifying and monolithic than the Port Authority, the great mass of people all moving as though in unison, the traffic congested street, the men with sandwich boards standing before theaters advertising nude live girls, the men with sandwich boards standing before liquor stores advertising the end of the world, newsstands and kiosks and movie marquees advertising everything from *Young and Wet* to *Return of the Jedi*.

"If you trick alone," Ginny continues ,"I cannot be held responsible for what happens. If a date gets violent, tries to make you do something you don't want, if he won't pay, underpays, if, like, anything non-kosher goes down, your sister will find me. I'll never be far away. And then I'll take care of things."

Car horns honk; catcalls drift out from a Cadillac. Ginny keeps walking, Tammy close beside her. "Rule number two—no glove, no love. You've heard of AIDS, sweetheart?"

"Sort of. But don't just the gays and junkies get it?"

"If you screw or shoot you can get it, sweetie, and if everything goes well, there's going to be a lot of the former and zero of the latter. Here." Ginny reaches into the pocket of her shorts, brings out a new package of condoms. "The first one's on me. After this, it's your investment. No glove, no love. Last fall, this entire stable of girls over on 8th? Wiped out, boom, done. One night this girl noticed, like, these big welts popping up all over her face. It turned out she'd shared an infected sailor with one of the girls she worked with, *and* was fooling around with another girl. Now, of course I wasn't around to see it, but I do *hear* from some of my little birdies that the lucky ones were the pair who gassed themselves before the end."

"I used to have lunch with one of them sometimes," Mary says. Her voice is tiny, like a little girl in a vaudeville routine. "Rebecca… I went to her funeral. She got so thin."

Tammy stares at the package, looking simultaneously repulsed and terrified.

"Just be careful and you'll be fine, sweetheart. Every occupation has its hazards. You've just got to be careful. And make sure you get yourself a flask and fill it with something hard, for rinse and spits."

"What?"

"Now, you're going to need an image," Ginny says, stopping, looking Tammy over. "The jeans are really working for you. You've got, like, fantastic hips. I'm thinking something a little more in-your-face country, though, you know? *Urban Cowboy* is still *very* big here. Some plaid, maybe a halter top, get your hair all nice and big."

"We all have an image," Mary pipes up. "Like you saw this morning. Shannon and Michelle and Ginny are our punk and New Wave girls, Constance and Candice get the R&B crowd."

"What about you?"

Mary pouts, grabs one pigtail and pulls it to her mouth. She chews on in while casting her eyes up at Tammy. "Have I been a bad girl, daddy? Are you going to punish me?"

Tammy flushes. Ginny scratches the back of her neck. Though she can't deny the profitability of Mary's incest routine, it's never quite sat right with her.

"It's a role you'll play, is all," Ginny says. "Acting. Like a part in a play. You just need to find what works for you, what comes natural. Once you get that figured out, everything will just fall right into place. I'll have you shadowing me today, and then we'll decide who you'll partner up with, where you'll flourish the best, whose iron will sharpen yours."

Tammy stops in her tracks. "Whose iron sharpens mine?"

"Yes, it's a…"

"You read the Bible?"

Ginny suddenly feels immensely irritated, Tammy looking to her now like a nice combination between a wall at the Misanthrope and Tina's stupid, bitch face. "Yes, I am familiar with it. Would you like to interrogate me any further, or can we discuss something that's relevant?"

Tammy says nothing. Cars on the street go by, their passengers oblivious to the strange retinue holding court on the sidewalk. Mary, in a voice even softer than usual, squeaks out, "I was raised Methodist."

"So was I," Tammy says. To Ginny, it looks like the first genuine smile she's seen on the girl's face since the Port Authority. On another day, Ginny might be able to turn it into a learning moment. Today, with the sensation of teeth gnawing into either one of her temples, feeling like her skin is receding backwards into itself and collapsing into her bones, she's just plain pissed off.

"This is all very fascinating," Ginny says, glaring at Mary through her sunglasses. Mary puts her head down, looks away. Satisfied that order has been restored, Ginny turns back to Tammy. "Now, you'll arrive to breakfast every morning in the dining room. That's taken out of your rent, so don't concern yourself with paying for any of it. Lunch and dinner are your problem. We go to work right afterwards, on the dot. Your routine is yours to come up with, but I don't advise more than a half hour for lunch. You rest too much, you get lazy, you don't want to get back into the swing of things, and then the second half of your day is totally wasted. We work until eight, then it's back to the Misanthrope. I cannot stress this, sweetie, but do *not* try to play hero and go looking for dates after dark. There will be no one to look out for you, and the Colonel has, like, a very tenuous agreement with the other... element... on 42nd."

"Element?"

"The Colonel's not the only show in town, sweetie, and when he set up shop, there were some other…enterprising gentlemen who weren't very fond of it. It took, like, a big sit down and a lot of negotiation for everyone to find an agreement they were happy with. We own the day, they own the night, and no one has to get her face tic-tac-toed with a razor anymore."

Tammy stumbles in her tracks, doubles over, grabbing her knees.

"Sweetie, sweetie… That's what's *not* going to happen, all right? Now, like I said, dinner is your problem, but we meet in the dining room for kick-up. The Colonel gets seventy-five percent of your day's wages…"

"Seventy-five percent?"

"Understand, he's providing you with a service as much as you are him."

"Exactly what kind of service?"

"Me, sweetheart."

Ginny stops, puts her arm up to still her companions, lowers her sunglasses. Her ears have pricked up, the little tingling sensation at the sides of her head that she's always felt when men are watching her, a soft burn that pinkens her lobes and which haunted her through middle school, high school. Her body's warning bell that she was being talked about again, snickered at, notes passed around her, the cold fish, the frigid bitch, the spiteful remarks of loathsome and lustful boys, angry, hungry eyes moving over her body, repugnant fantasies swirling in their brains, indignation that this pretty, slender cooze would have less interest in them than in the written word, the splendor of the cosmos, never grasping that while she might have interest in boys she had no interest in *them*. The thing that embarrassed and humiliated her is now her tool, her weapon: In less time and with more accuracy than the hollered propositions that most Deuce trade relies upon, Ginny can identify and pick up a date simply by that feeling, by knowing who is gazing at her with enough longing, the same boys grown into sad young men, still chasing the dream that eluded them in another, happier life; a dream she no longer has the privilege of denying them.

Ginny scans The Deuce for the source, eyes roving every man and boy, zeroes in on a suit across the street, still in the liquor store doorway, brown wrapped bottle under his arm, absently fiddling with the knot of his tie as he gazes out at the trio of sirens waiting for him across the asphalt ocean.

"All right, Tammy. This is it. I want you to watch me very carefully, all right? This, like, will so totally be on the test."

"There's gonna be a test?"

———

"Es tut mir leid, Frau Kurva." Mary's voice sounds ready to break as she says this, she and Ginny sharing smokes, each with a leg propped against the wall of the Misanthrope, the suit's belabored grunts coming from the room beside them. Ginny takes a long drag off her cigarette, nearly hotboxes it, stops. Wants to give herself something to look forward to in the next moment.

"What?"

"I didn't mean to speak out of turn, before. With Tammy."

"Don't even think about it." Ginny checks her watch, glances at the door. Taking more time than she expected or would have liked; had planned on taking Tammy along on a few more tricks after this, but, at the present rate, she won't make anything herself today. Being the bottom girl only affords her the privilege of giving up just sixty-five percent of her income; she earns no commission on the girls' earnings. She checks her watch again, retrieves her hip flask. Normally she hates to drink before lunch, but figures she can make small exceptions for herself now and again.

"Miss Ginny... You know, if there's anything I can ever do to help you, you can, you know, you can let me know," Mary says, fiddling with her pigtails. "You know, just like, stuff around the Misanthrope, or, like, I don't know, anything really, right? I mean, even if you need me to... help out with the Colonel, sometimes?" Her voice trails off, her head beginning to move towards Ginny, then jerking away at the last moment.

"Mary, sweetie, what are you talking about?"

"I just... I don't know if I really let you know how grateful I am," Mary says. "For everything you've done for me. I don't just mean taking care of me and stuff, but... Trying to, like, help me out, teaching me things, trying to make me smart. I mean, when I go out, and I'm working, or I'm studying, it's like I'm not just doing it for me, but I'm doing it for you, too, you know? Because I want to make you proud. I've only ever wanted you to be proud of me." Mary's voice, straining for the duration of her speech, at last cracks.

"Mary, sweetie, sweetie, you don't owe me anything, sweetheart."

Mary sobs more violently, grabbing at Ginny's tank top, bunching it up in her fist. "I been bad, Miss Ginny. I messed up. I messed up so bad, Ginny."

"Mary, sweetheart, shhh, shhh. You didn't do anything wrong. I shouldn't have gotten mad at you. Please, sweetie. It's all right."

"It's not that. It's not that at all."

"What, sweetie? What is it? Tell me so I can help you, darling. You know that's why I'm here, don't you? " Ginny puts her flask to Mary's lips, Mary reluctantly drinking from it.

"I... I haven't been on my pills. They were making me *fat,* Ginny, and Sandra's so thin and tan and... I was afraid I wouldn't be able to work anymore. And I, you know, I always used a rubber, right? But then, I found out those don't always work a hundred percent?"

Ginny can feel her face run the light speed gamut from confusion to realization to ice dread. She pulls her sunglasses off, pulls Mary's head back to look her in the eyes. Mary jerks away, startled.

"Mary...?"

"I'm pregnant, Ginny. I... I took, like, a few tests, and, like, they all said the same thing, and..." Her voice trails off. Ginny holds her face back to her chest, rocking her slowly, gloved fingers combing her hair.

"Is everything okay?"

Both women jump as Tammy emerges from the room, hair tousled, face wet with sweat and tears, her body trembling with such subtlety that Ginny doesn't realize the girl is shaking until she hears the soft rustle of bills rubbing against one another in her palm.

"It's that time," Ginny says to Tammy. "You know how it is."

Tammy nods sympathetically to Mary, puts a hand on her shoulder. Mary smiles back weakly. Tammy turns to Ginny, offers her the money.

"I... I ain't ever held this much money in my hand before," Tammy says.

"So hold it a little longer," Ginny says. "Your bra's a safe bet." She steps away from Mary. She wants to hold her longer, settles for patting the side of her face. "Don't try your panties. If you're going around the world, it'll end up spilling out and some wiseass will, like, totally try and snatch a few if he thinks you're not looking."

"Okay."

"And that's it. You remember Shannon from this morning?"

"The girl who looked like a vampire?"

Mary has to giggle at this, Ginny joining in against her will. "Yeah, but, like, totally don't tell her that. She'll be back up the block, near the Colossus theater, with Michelle. Go tell them I sent you. You're going to shadow them the rest of the day. They can give you some ideas."

Tammy nods, stuffs the wadded bills into her bra. As she leaves the hallway, she stops to put a hand on Mary's shoulder, smiles. Just as she's about to vanish around the corner, Ginny runs to her, grabs her by the wrist.

"Hey, Tammy? You did great, sweetheart. You did great, and you're going to do just fine."

———

Nicolette knows that she will be expected to be presentable when conducting the tour, so she is sure to wear her best outfit and her father's watch. Her best outfit is a red double-breasted jacket with matching capri trousers, stockings, and a white blouse lightly starched and buttoned at the neck. The watch is made of gold with a single diamond at the 12.

Dressing appropriately has been one of Nicolette's greatest challenges. For much of her life, her own external appearance was a cipher to her. She dressed for the tactile experience of clothing. The right texture. The right degree of tightness against her flesh. Among her first experiments in observation and mimicry came following her initial job interview. Her college grades were impressive enough to secure her the position but the outfit she'd chosen of jeans, a starched flannel shirt, and duck boots was off-putting to the interviewer. She'd said, "If we're going to keep you around, sweetheart, you need to look like you belong in the office, not rolling around the mounds with the boys." That evening, in her apartment, visiting the Meadow, she'd had a revelation. In the week before her first day of work, she began going to a nearby bar frequented by business-men and women from local offices. The crowd was over-whelming. It was lit a dim but wise shade of aurelion that made the crowd bearable. She watched the women and made several notes on cocktail napkins. She observed the frequency of dresses and the frequency of suits. She kept a running tally of what colors of dresses and suits women wore. She tracked the styles of shoes and in what colors they wore them. At the end of the week she developed an appropriate formula for determining the best wardrobe with which to begin her career. A skilled tailor aided her in maintaining the proper tactile stimulation. Though she remains oblivious to it, the endeavor made her the best dressed woman at the landfill. Two years ago, it came to Nicolette's attention that women had begun to emulate the appearance of Diana, Princess of Wales. It was with no small degree of pleasure that Nicolette began to emulate her, too. This only improved Nicolette's sartorial standing at the office.

As the descendent of a queen, Nicolette feels it appro-priate that the world look towards royalty for influence.

Nicolette checks her watch. The time is precise and set to the United States Naval Observatory. She saves it for special occasions, when she likes to feel particularly pow-erful. Important business meetings. Review days. Receiving tribute. Each tick is like the beat of her own heart. She can feel the reverberations through her wrist. They remind her of the strength that courses through her own veins. The strength of her true self, that no man can see.

There is still purple trapped behind Nicolette's eyes this morning, and so she is feeling confident as she boards the bus. Rows of noisy children greet her. Their tiny, invisible mouths form senseless words that assault her ears and fill her mind with aural garbage. She stares at them with bulging eyes. She wonders if they can feel her hate the way that she can feel theirs.

"Miss Aster?" Someone says. The someone is a woman. She wears a black and white nun's habit that hides her hair. Nicolette wonders if the woman is bald beneath the habit. She keeps her own strawberry-blonde hair trimmed into a neat, Princess Di pageboy cut.

"Hello," Nicolette says. "I'm Nicolette Aster. Pleased to meet you." She does not extend her hand.

"Thank you so much for doing this," the Someone says. "The children were so disappointed when they found out their original trip had been cancelled. I'm going to warn you, they aren't very excited about being... here... but I've told them to keep an open mind. They're all very bright girls. I think you'll find them very well behaved."

"Okay," Nicolette says.

"Girls?" The Someone calls out. "I want you all to say hello to Miss Aster. Miss Aster has been kind enough to agree to give us a tour of this very important, very special place. Can you girls say, 'Hello, Miss Aster?'"

"Hello, Miss Aster," the reply comes. The tiny, spiteful voices are like daggers in Nicolette's mind. She smiles to show them that they cannot hurt her. She digs deep within herself, reaches into the Meadow to retrieve some hidden power.

"Hello, children," Nicolette says. She raises her voice an octave as she speaks; she understands that this conveys excitement. "How are we all doing today?"

"Good," the reply comes.

"I'm very happy you're all here to see me today," Nicolette says. "I was so lonely. Now who's ready to take a nice long tour of… oh no. What happened? It looks like… it looks like someone dumped a bunch of garbage outside!"

"We're at a dump!" A girl yells from the back of the bus.

"Well, what do you know, it looks like we are," Nicolette says. "But you know what? I wouldn't want to be anyplace else right now. Because this is one of the most important places in the whole city. Did you all know that?" The words coming out of her mouth are painful, false, but she can feel the hatred coming towards her diminishing, weakening. If she could see any of the children's faces from behind their veils of smoke, she thinks they might even be smiling. "Someone tell me… what do you see?"

"A bunch of junk!"

"Trash!"

"Garbage!"

"Oh, no," Nicolette says. "That's not what I see. You know what I see? I see clean kitchens. I see empty trash cans in your neighborhoods. I see bathrooms that don't stink and refrigerators that don't have any rotten, smelly old food in them. You know why? Because all the bad stuff that makes your kitchens dirty and your refrigerator stink comes right here. And I make sure it gets taken care of. Now who's ready to take a little ride?"

A few quiet cheers come up from throughout the bus. Good. The little sluts are placated. Nicolette signals to the driver to start the bus. She keeps her balance by gripping the seat before her. In it, a little girl stares up at her. The girl has a thin blue raincoat laid over her lap. The blue sings to

Nicolette. It gingerly touches her arm and invites her to follow it down a winding path through a twilight cavern. There are tigers on either side of the path, crouched. They are not crouched to attack. The tigers crouch out of reverence. Nicolette smiles down at the girl.

"The building you're at now is Plant 1," Nicolette says, parroting from memory the speech she was given on her first day. She is unsure the children will understand all of it. She does not care. "All administrative functions for the landfill occur here. We also unload from barges. Plant 2 is on the North side of the Landfill. It's exclusively a marine unload operation. Barges arrive there from Manhattan and Brooklyn to be unloaded. The third operations site is the Brookfield Avenue Plant. Brookfield is exclusively a truck unload operation."

The children are quiet. They seem to be listening. They are well behaved, or they know how to appear well behaved. The girls with whom Nicolette attended school were well versed in such arts. They smiled sweetly to the teachers. They waited until backs were turned to deliver their taunts to Nicolette. Nicolette, who was too quiet; Nicolette, who always stared; Nicolette, pasty-skinned and square-jawed and hook-nosed amongst a throng of beautiful girls born to beautiful parents, beautiful parents who whispered secret things that their children heard from their hiding places, children who brought word back to Nicolette in playground taunts and locker room gossip.

The girl with the blue raincoat raises her hand. The Someone in the habit says, "Yes, Alicia?"

"How big is this place?" Alicia asks.

"Twenty-two hundred acres," Nicolette says. "The highest point in the landfill is eighty-two feet taller than the Statue of Liberty." To her surprise, Nicolette adds, for no particular reason, "It's visible from outer space."

"Wow," Alicia says.

"We receive garbage from eight until midnight," Nicolette says as the bus continues on. "Crews run maintenance back at Plant 1 from midnight to eight but the landfill itself is shut down."

Alicia's hand goes up again. Nicolette's body tenses. Why can't the little shit just shut up?

"Why did you want to work here?"

"How many of you like to play with your friends?" Nicolette asks. Most of the hands on the bus raise. "How many of you like to play alone?" Slightly fewer hands raise: the smaller girls, the heavier girls, the infirm and sniveling little bitches who waddle at the rear of the pack. It is almost as though they, like Nicolette, can see into their own futures: the rolls of dough that will sprout from their baby fat and the already birdly faces that will hollow out with acne and pock mocks and the endless nights the hungry little sluts will spend drooling over the phone, aching for the filth they'll never get, and their raised hands beckon to Nicolette: *end it now, end it now.*

"Well, I always liked to play alone," Nicolette says. "And working here, as long as I do my job right, I mostly get to play alone."

"That's sad," Alicia says.

"No, it isn't," Nicolette says.

"Yes it is. It's always more fun to play with someone else."

Nicolette stares and smiles. Her blood boils. Two years ago, after the Great Revelation, it had seemed to Nicolette that The City was offering her these little ones as its tribute. They were, after all, simple to obtain; promises of candy were all it required to entreat them into the back of her van. Even still, after the first five or six, it had begun to occur that perhaps she was misreading The City's intentions. Whatever aura of intense vitality they might project on the street, it was gone once the hunt began. They cowered. They cried. They begged for their parents. Only one or two permitted any satisfactory pursuit. Even still, the resultant meals were unnourishing. Bland. The furor that rose up across the island only solidified Nicolette's growing belief that she had misread The City's intentions. Parents held vigils in schoolyards. Searches were conducted. A detective even came to Nicolette's door, showing her pictures, asking if she had seen any of the girls. Nicolette had said "no." She had known that her sex would shield her from suspicions. Still, she should have known that The City would not offer those who would be missed. After the First Cycle, it had become expedient to spend long hours in the Meadow, focusing, understanding whom The City intended as its tributes.

"Miss Aster?" The Someone asks.

"Yes?"

"Are you all right?"

"Yes. Why?"

"You stopped speaking," the Someone says. Nicolette checks her watch. The Someone is correct. Five minutes have elapsed. Alicia stares up at her.

"Oh," Nicolette says. She smiles, addresses the bus. "All right now, children. I'm going to talk to you about something called the leachate process."

When the tour is over, the bus parks back at Plant 1. The Someone asks the children to thank Nicolette; asks if they would like to take a photo as a souvenir. The overwhelming response is to the affirmative. The children disembark the bus, some attempting to hug Nicolette as they file out. Nicolette recoils, guards herself behind one of the bus seats. Alicia is the last to leave.

"Thank you for the tour, Ms. Aster," Alicia says.

"You're welcome," Nicolette says. She stares at the

raincoat; her hands shake. Different circumstances would permit her to throw the coat around the little cunt's neck, fashion it into a garrote, twist the sleeves until her eyes swelled red with blood and popped from their sockets.

"When I grow up, I want to have an important job like you," Alicia says.

Nicolette reaches towards the raincoat. It's blue, blue, blue. Perhaps the girl shouldn't grow up. "You're smart," Nicolette says.

"Thank you."

"Why did you say thank you?"

Alicia doesn't say anything.

"Do you have friends?"

"Not a lot."

"Smart people often don't. Smart girls have even fewer." Nicolette makes a low keening sound.

"Are you okay, Miss Aster?"

"Do the other girls tease you?"

"...Sometimes."

"Do they make you eat lunch by yourself?"

Alicia doesn't respond.

"It's better to eat by yourself, anyway. It's more fun. Do the other girls ever ask you about boys? Do you like boys?"

"Boys are gross."

"Do they ever ask if you've kissed a boy?" Nicolette's voice has dropped to a whisper. "Have you ever?"

Alicia attempts to move around Nicolette. Nicolette grasps the raincoat. She nearly reels at the electricity that surges through her veins. She whimpers. Her massive eyes loom large above the girl's face. "Stop pretending. I know what you are, you filthy little slut."

"Alicia?" The Someone is coming back onto the bus. Alicia darts around Nicolette, past the Someone, out to join her classmates. Nicolette is left holding the raincoat.

The residual vitality left behind is overwhelming. She forces herself to remain in place as it assaults her body. It is almost too powerful. She travels to the Meadow. In the Meadow, as her true self, she can harness any power. She finds the girl's essence waiting there for her. It's a ball of fire hovering above the ground. The attendants swarm around it, staring at it with their hollow faces. Nicolette grasps it in her hands. She opens her maw. She takes it into herself.

Nicolette opens her eyes. Her face is wet. She is sweating. She checks her watch. She needs to have lunch. Her nutrients are low. Then, she thinks she would like to visit The Girl.

———

"How much money do you have?" Ginny asks Mary when they have situated themselves in the diner booth and gotten coffees.

"Maybe a few hundred? I think, maybe? I don't know."

"Sweetie. You've got to keep track of your finances."

"I try! I'm sorry. I try, but… You told me we couldn't use any of the banks. It's a lot to keep track of."

"Can you guess? Can you give me an estimate?"

"I don't know. I think, like, two hundred? Maybe, like, I don't know, maybe two fifty?"

Ginny rubs her eyes. "Two hundred, okay, okay. So we're looking at two hundred dollars." She looks up to the ceiling, hands folded before her as she once folded them in prayer. "That's what you've got to look at first, sweetie, and then you've got to ask yourself, how much more of that can you make in three, four months? Because, sweetie, in another few months, you aren't going to be out on that street anymore. There's a lot of shit people on this street will tolerate. There're are a lot of things the cops turn their backs on. But a pregnant working girl is not one of them. "

Mary, staring at her coffee, begins to cry quietly, her body jerking with small, silent sobs.

"The first thing that's going to happen is that your dates are going to dry up. The guys you'd normally pick up, like, no problemo, are going to start looking at you like you're a needle in their dicks. Then, different men are going to come. And they aren't the kind of men you want to trick with, sweetie. They aren't the kind of men *Shannon* would trick with. Think of the sickest, most fucked up son of a bitch you ever pulled a date with, and sweetie, he is, like Mr. Rogers next to who's going to come knocking at your door. And if one of them doesn't take you on a one-way-ride, some totally self-righteous boy in blue is going to pick you up anyway. And even if the Colonel bails you out the first time, you'll go back again. And maybe I can talk him into getting you out the second time. But, sweetie, you need to realize, he's not a generous man. He'll realize that you're a drain on his wallet. And that is, like, the cardinal sin in the Book of Baniszewski."

Mary's cries have become audible at this point. In the time-honored Deuce tradition of nobody giving a damn about anyone but themselves, not a single head in the place turns to look at her.

"Sweetie. Shhhh. Shhhh. It's all right."

Ginny moves around the table to sit beside Mary, letting the girl's head rest against her shoulder. The sight of two women holding one another *does* draw some attention.

"You're scaring me," Mary sobs. "Why are you trying to scare me?"

"I'm not, sweetie. I'm telling you the truth. I'm telling you what I've seen happen."

Mary continues to cry, nuzzling her face against the shoulder of Ginny's tank top. "I'm so scared, Ginny. What do you want me to do?" She looks up at her, pleading. "You always know what to do. Tell me what to do."

"I'm not telling you to do anything, sweetie. I'm so sorry, darling, but I can't tell you to do anything. All I can do is tell you that no matter what you decide to do, I'll be there with you."

"How much do I have to make? How much will I need?"

"A baby's expensive, sweetheart. It's tough for me to take care of my sister on what I'm making, and she's almost a grown woman. She doesn't need doctor's visits and shots, and we don't mind eating like shit." At this, Mary has to let out a wry giggle. "We manage, but it's tight, sweetheart, it's very tight. You will need to work your ass off for the next few months and save, like, everything. And in the meantime you're going to have to find a job doing *something.*" Ginny finagles a cigarette out of her pack, lights it awkwardly so as not to set Mary's hair on fire.

"This is all… this is all… this is all I've ever done," Mary sobs.

"I'll see what I can turn up. You know I know people. We can't let them know about your situation, though. No one wants the new girl going on maternity leave right after she starts."

"I'm going to end up as some waitress. I'm going to have to work for some old asshole whose cock I have to suck and not even really get paid for it."

"That doesn't have to happen, sweetie."

"What else am I going to do, Ginny?"

"I told you, sweetie, I can't tell you what to do. But you can do anything you want, you know? And I told you, whatever you decide to do, I'll be there for you. And I can help you."

Ginny and Mary stare at one another after Ginny has said this. There is no expression on Ginny's face; the sly grin and beatific eyes that normally define her are gone, replaced with a placid, neutral pallor that is chilling in the mellow light of the diner. Mary gags, begins to heave.

"I don't... I can't do that."

"Do what, sweetheart? I'm not telling you to do anything."

"You're telling me to... you're telling me to get rid of it. To get rid of him, or her."

"Mary... Sweetheart, please, get this into your adorable little head... I'm not telling you to do anything at all. This is all completely up to you. If you want to get rid of it, that is completely up to you. That is completely between you and the Colonel."

Mary's face contorts. "He can... he knows how to do that?"

"Oh, natch. It was, like, apparently really valuable during the war."

"Has he... have you...?"

"*Fuck you!*" Mary recoils at the ferocity of the response. Ginny clears her throat and recomposes herself. "I'm sorry... No. But plenty of other girls have. You're not the first one I've had to have this talk with."

"Who else?"

"That's not for me to say, sweetie. But they're all still here, aren't they?"

Mary nods, sadly.

"You've just been telling me what to do for so long. Ever since you found me, you've told me when to get up and when to go to bed, and what I'm going to read and where I'm going to work. And, I've, you know, I've been okay with that because I know I'd be dead if you hadn't have gotten to me first. So that's been cool, that's all been really cool because, you know, like you said, I know I'm a lot better than I was when you found me. And, I'm so glad for you, Ginny, you know that?" Mary grabs a napkin from the table, wipes her nose. "I know you don't believe in it, but, when I pray at night, I thank God for you because I know you're right. I know I'm gonna get out of here one day, and I'm gonna be able to do stuff a lot of other girls won't, because so many other girls don't have someone like you. But, I'm not ready for that yet. I'm not ready for the big decisions. Just tell me what to do."

Ginny kisses Mary on the forehead. "You're so much brighter than you give yourself credit for, you know that? You're growing by leaps and bounds, sweetie. That's why you don't need me to make the decision for you. And that's why I know you're going to make the right decision."

Mary looks up at Ginny; the expression she finds there is implacable, inscrutable. She searches her face for any hint, any twitch of the lip or glimmer of the eye that could be interpreted as instruction, any tell-tale sign that might guide her down the correct path. She finds none; and in that absence, it seems, there lies her answer.

"Take me to the Colonel," Mary says, and wiping her face, reaches across the table, grabs her cup, and finishes her coffee.

———

A good hour has passed by the time Ginny finally sits Mary down on the Colonel's couch, wiping her eyes with the knuckles of her gloves, stroking her hair, counting down in her own mind the number of tricks she's lost by now, the number of dates she'll have to pull to make up for the lost time.

"Now, just wait here, sweetheart, and don't even think about any of this."

"How can I not think about this?"

"Think about something else. Think about what you'll do the next time you've got some free time. Are there any movies you want to see?"

"I hear *Flashdance* is good."

"It's fabulous, sweetheart."

"You seen it?"

"Oh, at least... twice."

"Is it as good as the videos on MTV make it look?"

"Even better. So you just clear your sweet little head of all of this bullshit and you think how nice it's going to be to settle down over at the Colossus and have a nice, relaxing night at the movies. And don't forget, sweetheart, the space launch is this Saturday. You've got that to look forward to."

Mary nods. "I wrote it on my calendar so I don't forget to set my clock. Like you told us to."

"And you've never believed that you're my best student? Shame, shame, shame on you!"

Mary smirks, plays with her pigtails. Ginny rises from the couch, prepares to go face the Colonel.

"Ginny?"

"Yes, sweetie?"

"I've been reading ahead in our book."

"Fabulous, darling. Where are you at now?"

"Everyone's gone to the hotel in the city. I keep wondering if maybe, like, if it might've even been this hotel, back before it turned into a shithole."

Ginny considers this. "I doubt it, but I wouldn't rule out the possibility."

"Ginny? I hate sad endings. I don't want you to spoil it for me, but, does Gatsby get a happy ending? I mean, he's, like, kind of a dumbass, but I kind of like him, too."

"He turns out all right in the end."

Mary nods. "That's cool. I like it when people get happy endings. It makes me think I can get one too, right? And maybe you can, too."

Ginny pats her cheek, then heads to the Colonel's door. It cracks somewhat more than usual, the Colonel uncharacteristically exposing more of the office, giving Ginny a wider berth than he normally affords. She wonders if he's coming to trust her even more than he already does, or if the daytime booze is finally making him careless. Even with his gun drawn, at this close of a range she could easily kick it out of his hand, a chop to the neck while he was still stunned, his reflexes slowed while hers are scarcely affected, and then he'd be on his knees …

"It's about Mary," Ginny says, closing the Colonel's office door behind her. The Colonel secures his gun back in the belt of his pants, settles down behind his desk. He sits rigidly in his chair, hands splayed out on the blotter, as though he already knows what's about to be said, already prepared to make arrangements, bring an end to the whole fuck awful conversation before she even has to have it. It takes her a good while before she realizes that he's so completely blitzed that she could stand there for the rest of the night and not get a peep out of him unless she speaks first.

"She's gotten herself pregnant. We need to get rid of it," Ginny says at last. "We need *you* to get rid of it."

"Which one Mary?"

"The little one. With the pigtails? Cute, terribly sweet. And, darling, we cannot let that precious little girl…"

"What it matter to me, girl get pregnant? That her problem. I buy you all pills. Girl too stupid to take one pill, that her problem."

"Darling, don't be so short-sighted. Do you know how much of the kick comes from her? She's our little Lolita. We have got a tremendous corner on a very lucrative market with her."

"Get a new one. Plenty of high schools around here. Junior high. Plenty of girls to choose from. In Poland, I see girl eleven, twelve years old work, make money for family. Girls that young even easier to control."

"…Sweetheart," Ginny says, leaning across the desk, stroking the Colonel's hair, "We're talking about *not* being short-sighted. You know there are certain things we can get away with here, and that is, like, so totally not one of them."

The Colonel snorts. "Stupid. American men fuck girl dressed like little girl, look like little girl. Fuck girl sixteen years old, this okay, fuck girl fifteen years old, this man gets arrested, go to prison, men fuck him. Fuck girl five minutes before she turns sixteen, that a problem, five minutes later, that fine. What difference five minutes make?"

"Darling, I totally see what you're saying, but it's hardly relevant to what we're discussing. Mary. Remember, Mary? We need her. *You* need her for what she brings in. I need her for what she gives the group. She's, like, our little mascot."

"We have mascot in Poland," the Colonel says. "Men I travel with once, have dog they carry with them. Small dog. They put little vest on it. Feed it scraps of food. One day, food run out. We eat dog."

"Cannibalism is, like, *really* not cool over here, sweetie."

The Colonel snorts again.

"I don't see what the big deal is, darling. You've done it before. Jennifer, Shannon, what's her face…"

"Big deal is just that. I do it for other girls, what do I get? Girls cry a lot, sit around for days, not make money. Not even say 'thank you.' This not charity, Ginny, this business. Mary want me to throw her garbage out, Mary pay me to throw it out."

Ginny flinches. "Sweetheart, I could take her someplace else, the idea was that this would be part of the services you provide…"

"I not charge so much as other place, how about that? Cost how much normal? Two hundred? I do it one hundred. You pay. Cash now; more later. You show me you grateful, maybe you not have to pay so much." He reaches over the desk, running his hand up the side of her butt cheek.

"You are a saint among men, sweetheart."

————

Mary has taken to crying again by the time Ginny exits the Colonel's office. Ginny stands in the office doorway, watching her, waiting for Mary to look up, takes a bit to realize that the girl's slipped off into the fifth dimension. She moves to her, kneels before the couch, gingerly puts her hands on Mary's knees.

"Sweetie," Ginny whispers. "I've taken care of everything. The Colonel's just going to… compose himself, and then he's going to take you upstairs."

Mary tilts her head quizzically, sticks the ends of her pigtails in her mouth. "What's upstairs?"

"The Colonel's suite, darling. He has his equipment there."

Mary's body jerks, stiffens. She bites down on the end of her hair. "Upstairs? Right… now?"

"It's just down the hall from my room, sweetie. Just think of me. Right next door, enjoying a big cup of tea and watching Carson, just like you will tonight. Safe and sound."

Mary tries to stand; Ginny squeezes her knees, forces her back down.

"The last thing you want to do is sit around meditating

on this, sweetheart. The sooner you get it done with, the sooner you can stop thinking about it. Don't you know that waiting for something to happen is the worst part?"

"I thought you said you never did this before."

"I haven't. But I did have to make a huge decision once, just as big as what you're doing now. And even though I made it quick, the time before I did it was, like, some of the most awful fucking time I've ever had in my life. And... as incredibly fucking terrible as it was... I have never, ever, sweetie, *ever* looked back on it and wished I'd done it different. I am so sorry that this is happening, but sometimes we have got to do really, really awful things. And..."

And then it comes on her, suddenly, awfully, as it does on cursed afternoons such as this, when the sun's heat penetrates even the air-conditioned walls of the Misanthrope, when she is sleep-starved and weakened, when she is, regrettably above all things, not at all drunk. Without warning, Ginny is hearing her own voice, seeing her own body. She is watching herself, this approximation of herself, the girl who'd worn a pink bow neck blouse and matching skirt for her senior picture now looking like some reject from CBGB, squatting like an animal in a squalid room...

"We do this now. Make it quick."

The Colonel marches from his office, his stray hairs combed into place, the wrinkles of his khakis smoothed out, even his voice strangely unaccented. Nothing about his demeanor indicates a man with enough alcohol coursing through his blood to kill an eager college freshman. If Ginny did not know better, she'd think the man was stone sober.

Ginny remembers, from the much beloved book of quotes her father gave her for her fifteenth birthday, that Einstein called time a stubbornly persistent illusion; that those who believe in physics see no distinction between the things most people call the past, the present, the future. Kneeling here, before Mary, Ginny feels the truth of this acutely. Time ceases to move forward. The wings of the hummingbird and the bee become static. Even the particles of the air around her still their rotations, hovering immobile in space.

"Come on."

Mary's knees slip out from beneath Ginny's palms as she takes the Colonel's hand. Mary is slowly turning her head to look over her shoulder and Ginny is watching herself watch them go, Mary so small even beside the Colonel, so dumbly trusting, believing in spite of all prior knowledge and evidence that the path she is walking on leads to some place bright, and for a second Mary hovers in the doorway, pretty as a picture, frozen eternally in this infernal moment, time reaccelerating, the heart beating again, the air swirling…

And then she's gone.

———

Nicolette finds Someone and informs him that she is unwell. She dabs at her damp forehead and places a hand over her abdomen and bemoans female difficulties. She says she believes it would be best if she went home. Someone is sympathetic. He thanks her for her effort on the tour and wishes her a quick recovery. To Nicolette's ears, his tone seems to be something that might be genuine concern, and she thinks that she might not ever have directly spoken with this Someone before.

Nicolette collects her lunch from her desk and leaves the landfill. She eats on her way out to The Deuce. On Friday nights, Nicolette enjoys taking the forty-minute trek from Staten Island out to Manhattan, to drive up and down Times Square. The flashing lights and the distant hum of neons and fluorescents soothe her nerves and speak to her of a pleasant weekend to come. It is her reward to herself for making it through another work week. Last year, in the weeks leading up to the beginning of the Second Cycle, Nicolette had been caught in traffic near one of the numerous adult theaters on the street when she had seen a woman in fishnets and barely existent shorts lead a man inside. Nearby lights cast a sallow pink cone onto the sidewalk that beckoned to Nicolette. Nicolette had listened and obeyed. She watched the theater. Traffic had been slow enough that it allowed Nicolette to see the pair exit later and the man hand the woman a sum of money. She had squeezed her steering wheel with enough force that she had driven her nails into her own flesh and drawn blood. The message conveyed to her by The City had been received clearly. When the Second Cycle had begun, Nicolette began returning to 42nd Street to collect her tributes. The *pornai* came to her willingly. They entered her van. They were desperate and careless and often physically weak. They succumbed easily to the chemical rag. They tended to perform more admirably than their diminutive predecessors. They ran. They fled. An occasional few attempted a fight. On the whole, the vitality they offered her was sufficiently pleasing.

There were no search parties. There were no vigils.

Nicolette drives up and down The Deuce for a half hour before she spots her. The Girl is exiting the hotel, adjusting the strap of her tank top. She is small and slender and has short, carefully maintained black hair. Her skin is the color of fresh copy paper. She is dressed like one of the girls from the album covers in the "Punk" and "New Wave" sections of the record store Nicolette frequents for her albums. Nicolette first became aware of The Girl late last year, after the Second Cycle had been completed. She'd had a day off and decided to spend it browsing some of the book and music stores on 42nd. She had been passing by the hotel when she had witnessed a curious sight: A group of pornai, seven of them, crowded together on a fire escape, all holding small objects. On the pavement below, an eighth pornai, The Girl, looking up. The Girl had waved her arms and one of the pornai had thrown her object off the fire escape. It had hung there in the air a moment, and then drifted down to the ground. The Girl had said something and the other pornai had applauded. Then The Girl had waved her arm again and the next pornai had dropped her object. This object descended more rapidly and appeared to break. The process continued until all of the pornai had thrown their objects. Then they had disappeared back into the hotel. Moments later, they and The Girl had reappeared at the entrance of the hotel and drifted off in different directions. Nicolette had parked her van and returned to the hotel as quickly as she could. She had gone and inspected the objects. They were shoeboxes and paper boats and wicker baskets. They had crude parachutes attached to them made from bandanas and bits of fabric and magazine pages. In each object was an egg. Some were broken, some were not. Then she had seen the paper on the ground. It was wadded up and discarded near where The Girl had stood. Nicolette had opened it. Though she could not decipher the entirety of the paper's contents, she remembered enough from high school science to recognize it as physics equations.

Nicolette had interacted with enough of the pornai by then to know their nature. They were stupid and venal. They begged to be violated for spare change. They let their bodies decay like corpses. This Girl was different. This Girl possessed intelligence. The Girl was attempting to transfer this intelligence to the pornai. She commanded them. She controlled them.

For the weeks that followed, Nicolette had observed the routine of The Girl and her pornai on 42nd Street. She had seen The Girl walk down 42nd like a general, inspecting her troops. She had seen The Girl put a man's face through a car windshield.

The Girl begins walking down The Deuce, looking around. Nicolette feels the peculiar sensation in her bowels that The Girl induces. Her stomach clenches. The fury is so great she trembles. The Girl approaches two of her pornai. One is the Beta, the one dressed all in leather, who knowingly wears the collar of a dog. The other is new; she is dressed like a farmhand. The Girl moves quickly.

Nicolette opens her mouth and lets one corner twitch. The Girl thinks she is smart. The Girl sees herself as an instructor, a teacher. The Girl has no idea that her little Omega has been given over for tribute.

The Girl continues on her way. Nicolette watches. Her hands tingle.

When she seeks tribute from The City, Nicolette feels its vibrations in her bones and hears the soundless voices whispering up to her through the gutter; it delivers unto her tribute in waxing and waning patterns, weak and strong, weak and strong. The weak sustain her but permit her rest between collecting the strong tributes. The final tribute is the strongest of all. It must keep her an entire year. It is the last great offering from The City before the contract has been fulfilled and the Fourteen have been given unto her. This year, The Girl will be her final offering. It will be unlike any other she has ever received.

Nicolette has never taken an Alpha bitch before.

———

Since leaving Mary with the Colonel, the afternoon has become a haze, a chain of interconnected, unrelated events; Ginny staggering up and down The Deuce in her best effort to appear in control; dozing off beneath a date, waking up ten minutes later to find him still on top of her, bills totaling twice the normal cost stuffed into her bra; checking in on the girls, Candice expressing surprise for the sweep when she'd just conducted one fifteen minutes before. With precious little time left in the day and pathetic amount of cash to show for the effort expended, it seemed that, rather than further embarrass herself on the street, the best course of action was to hunker down someplace safe and wait out the remainder of the afternoon.

Onscreen, Jennifer Beals drips sweat in her sun-drenched studio. Ginny closes her eyes, letting the oranges and ochres and sepias sink into her eyelids, entering the space between sleep and consciousness. Ginny does not need to see what is happening onscreen in order to enjoy the film; the movie's images are firmly recorded in her mind, every step of choreography memorized with such detail that, should she wish, Ginny could recreate it herself. Though watching the film has become one of her favorite past times, her first viewing was strictly out of curiosity. Music videos for the film's songs play in heavy rotation on MTV, and, after seeing each of them numerous times over during their nightly music video binges, Tricia expressed interest in going to see the movie. The next afternoon, Ginny slipped into a showing to pre-screen it—against her sister's protestations, and in spite of her age, she will not permit her to see any R-rated films that she has not already viewed. As the end credits began, Ginny feigned vomiting into her popcorn to hide the tears rolling down her face, holding her head inside the bucket all the way to the bathroom. That night, she excused Tricia from her homework and eagerly wheeled her back to the Colossus to wait in the ten-minute line for tickets. Later, both sisters sat rapt in anticipation in the crowded, freezing, stinking theater, surrounded by a sea of men and women who remained oblivious to the women's shared response to the film's end, when Ginny, turning to her sister, asked through her bucket of popcorn, "Did it make you feel feelings, too?" and Tricia, her bucket placed over her head, nodded in the affirmative.

As of this screening, Ginny has seen *Flashdance* approximately sixteen times. If she continues at this rate, she will easily surpass last summer's record of twenty-one showings of *The Wrath of Khan*.

In the vermillion-tinted world of her mind, Ginny senses a presence beside her, a body hovering above the next seat over and then settling into it, a low grunt and a sigh. No danger registers, no need to open her eyes and assess the potential threat, knows based upon this non-response that it could only be one of two people, one of them presently confined to their room at the Misanthrope.

"Good afternoon, sweetheart. I'm sorry you had to find me like this. I would so much rather be watching *Friday the 13th,* but it's been one of those days, you know?"

Roger grunts. "It looks like shit without the 3D. Number two is better anyway. The smart girl has your name. And she lives."

"But the guy in the wheelchair dies."

Roger grunts sadly. "Ah, yeah. But, in Number Three, the killer gets an axe in the face. So it's like payback."

Ginny sighs deeply, wishes the boy in the wheelchair hadn't gotten that axe to his face so she could have liked the thing; wants so much to have a slasher of her own, where the smart girl lives to outsmart the killer at his own game, success of intellect and measured ass-kicking above dumb luck, hates it when the moronic bimbo lives just because she's fortune enough to aimlessly throw enough junk in the killer's way, and the smart friend gets wasted halfway through the picture without even the pretense of a fight.

In high school, Ginny *was* the smart friend.

Ginny stirs in her seat, opens her eyes painfully to look at Roger. He is, perhaps, the one welcome sight she has seen all day, sitting there motionless, expressionless, fiddling with his beard, the film reflected in the lenses of his glasses, a strangely unsexy girl in sports gear conducting an exotic dance that comes across to Ginny as more threatening than titillating. When slow points of films arise, she likes, sometimes, to watch the screen on Roger's lenses, two little mirrored images dancing in front of his eyes, the way she used to turn around in the theater as a little girl and watch the image reflected on the window of the projector booth, a miniature show all her own while the rest of the world looked forward, sharing the wonder only with the dust motes swirling around in the projector's beam. It takes Roger a few seconds to realize he's being watched, turns his head slowly towards Ginny, smiles obliviously, turns back to the screen.

"I didn't see that van last night."

"You were watching?"

"I missed *Basket Case* at the Roxy. I didn't have anything else to do."

"What about sleep?"

"I try to avoid it when possible. I, ah, saw you and your sister out. Everything okay? I'm not used to seeing the two of you out together when it isn't the weekend. I, ah, thought maybe something was wrong so I didn't want to bother the two of you."

"Oh, wouldn't you know it, the little dickens got herself strung out on caffeine yesterday afternoon while I was gone and I had to tire the rascal out. You should have come said 'hello.' Trish likes you." Ginny yawns. "It's good for her to have attention from someone who isn't a total creep."

Onscreen, the girl in baseball gear collapses exhausted, her dance routine having reached its Sapphic apex, the audience cheering in spite of the apparent possibility of her onstage demise.

"She gave her life for stripping," Roger says. "May her sacrifice never be forgotten."

The laughter which strikes Ginny is so sudden and forceful that she jerks forward, stifling an involuntary snort against Roger's shoulder. She feels Roger's arm tense beneath her, pulls away from him, composes herself.

"Anyway, thank you, sweetheart, for your lovely little vigil, but I do believe the streets of 42nd are no more unsafe than you feared. But I thank you, and I can assure you that each and every one of my ladies would thank you as well."

"That, ah, doesn't necessarily mean anything."

"What're you talking about?"

"If, ah, if someone whacked Tina, and, ah, they haven't found her, then there's a good chance that it's someone who's done something like this before. And if it is, then guys like that don't just run around killing people left and right. That there's your, ah, spree killer."

Ginny cocks her head, one eye shut, the other open. "Oh, shit, Roger. Really? We've gone from some perv in a van to, like, a serial killer?"

"They've got these, ah, they're called cooling off periods, in between when they kill people. They're totally normal then... or, as normal as they usually are." Roger pauses. "I, ah, read this in a book, just so you know."

"Sweetheart, darling...." Ginny yawns. "I'm really glad you're here, do you know that? Because you really, *really* need to watch something other than a horror movie once in a while. Cleanse your palette."

"Is that what you're doing?"

"A girl's got to get a little protein in her diet once in a while, sweetheart. She can't just live on the fat and sweets. But I'll be back to binging on goodies with you soon enough. And, pray tell, what exactly are you doing here? In between movies? Did you really buy a ticket just to talk to me? You could've caught me in the lobby of the Misanthrope. You live, like, three floors down."

Roger grunts. "I wanted to see this."

"Omigawsh, Roger, you little sleaze! You are totally perving out on this, aren't you?"

Roger shifts in his seat. "I, ah, I saw the music videos on MTV, and... it's got great music."

"Oh, I know, right? But, like, good luck getting the soundtrack. Trish has been trying to make her own mixtape. She's been recording the music videos from television, and then she's going to try, like, putting her cassette recorder next to the TV and recording all the songs. It's probably going to sound like shit, but, you know, it gives her a hobby."

"Her, ah, her German doing any better?"

"Like, not even."

"Have you thought about maybe getting her some movies? I could get you some tapes with subtitles. What does she like?"

"Love stories and movies where lots of guys get shot."

"She takes after big sis, huh?"

"Sweetheart, the only love stories I like are the ones where someone dies at the end."

"No one dies at the end of this."

"I thought you'd never seen this?"

"I, ah, I've never seen it with you."

Ginny feels herself begin to sweat. Roger opens his mouth to speak, Ginny tensing as she prepares for him to say something, feels relieved when he doesn't, completely caught off guard when he finally speaks:

"I mean, you know, we don't have to just hang out here all the time. We could.... we could go someplace, ah, sometime, for, ah, coffee, or drinks, and, ah, you know, just talk there, or... you could, I don't know, ah... just come to my room. I mean, not for... ah... but, ah... just, you know, to hang out."

Ginny pipes up, her voice higher than she intends it. "Sweetheart, you are an absolute *doll,* but I have had the most exhausting twenty-four hours, and I have really just got to get some rest. So I'm just going to treat myself to a nice little zone out here before I've got to head back. I'll, like, so totally love catching up with you next time, but, until then, au revoir, *mon petit boule.*"

"You're going to sleep here?"

"No, sweetheart. I'm not suicidal. I'm just going to rest my eyes."

Ginny shuts both eyes now, her elbow going slack against the armrest, fighting to stay awake, to listen to the music, to see the movie in her mind's eye, Jennifer Beals and Michael Nouri walking through delightful cityscapes of pipe and steel, the skyline of Pittsburgh running over with persimmon, a warm beach on a late, sunny, Summer afternoon, the sky just beginning to turn over into a soothing shade of crimson and the light reflecting amber off of the rolling waves that she and Tricia run through, ash-fine sand sticking to the bottoms of their feet as they ascend the dunes—

The hand on her shoulder brings her back to life with a start, her own hand gripping the wrist, preparing to break it, her other hand reaching for the switchblade strapped to her hip, stops herself when her eyes clear themselves. She looks around, startled; the movie is over, the auditorium lights turned up, and Roger stands over her, regarding her quizzically.

"The movie's over. It's time to go home."

————

Shannon is running up to the entrance of the Colossus just as Ginny is leaving, her eyeliner smeared, Mohawk askew, desperation seeping through the cracks of her stony face in enough volume that Ginny knows before she's heard a word that she's needed immediately.

"What happened? " Ginny says, and she and Shannon are off and running together down The Deuce.

"You know the Colonel was working on Mary this afternoon?"

The warmth of the evening fades as Ginny's body turns to ice. "Sweetheart, that's a question, not an answer."

"I'm just asking. The point is he fucked her up good."

"...what?"

"Mary lost her shit, said she changed her mind, tried to leave. The Colonel went bat shit. He beat the fucking shit out of her. Then he went ahead and finished the job. *Badly.*"

Ginny stumbles in her tracks, grabs her knees to steady herself. She grabs Shannon and pulls her down so she can look her in the eye, teeth gritted, all of her lofty ideals faded now with the sun, the electric darkness of the 42nd Street night surrounding and filling her, the desire for violence pumping through her veins with such force that she can feel them throbbing in the sides of her head, her wrists, her abdomen.

"Is she dead, Shannon?"

"It isn't good, Ginny..."

"Give me a straight answer, you fucking bitch, or you die first."

"Shit, Ginny. Yeah, she's alive. She's alive, but she's fucked up real good."

Ginny stands back up, puts her hands over her face.

"I'm so sorry, Shannon." She puts her arms out; Shannon walks into them obediently, the two women embracing.

"Hey, it's cool, man."

"Tell me. Everything."

"I got a pretty sweet date with a couple of guys out of Boston. I'm coming out of a room at the Misanthrope and some kid's running bloody towels down the hallway screaming fucking murder, and, like, people are freaking the fuck out and shit, right? And I follow him, I'm thinking maybe something's gone down with one of the other girls, right? And he dumps them on one of the maid carts, and the kid just grabs up another load of towels and I follow him back to the Colonel's suite, and the Colonel's in the door in his fucking tighty whities and he's totally fucking drenched in blood, just, like fucking standing there in the doorway, totally red, smoking a cigarette, and the kid's crying when he hands the Colonel the fresh towels and he jams the cigarette into the kid's face and takes the towels and slams the door."

"Son of a bitch." Ginny steps away from Shannon. Her thoughts are sludgy, coming to her slower than she needs.

"I grabbed the kid and asked him what was going on. I slipped him a bill not to talk to anyone, and then I came to find you."

"So no one else knows about this?"

"I came straight to get you."

"Listen to me very carefully, okay, sweetie? I'm placing, like, a tremendous amount of responsibility on you right

117

now."

"You know you can trust me. After what you did to those guys who... You know I'd do anything for you, Ginny."

"I know that, sweetheart. Now I want you to go to the dining room and collect tonight's kick up. Mary has very severe food poisoning. The new girl knows she and I went off somewhere this afternoon. They know she wasn't tricking so a story about a rough john isn't going to fly. Let them know I'm not feeling well either but that Mary got the worst of it. She is, like, totally hurling everywhere, *explosive* diarrhea. It really isn't a good idea for anyone to see her. *Explosive.*"

Shannon nods, taking this all in, a small crease in her forehead the only indicator of distress.

"Listen, sweetie, we cannot have a panic. Once our darling little Mary is back on her feet, then we can all sit down and have a very serious discussion about what's happened, but in the meantime, I don't want anyone scared. How well do you think some of the other girls would handle this? Sandra? Tammy? They will just pack their little bags and disappear into the night, and what happens to them then? The same ones who'd run are the exact same ones who will absolutely not make it in another stable."

"All right. Okay. So I get the kick. Then?"

"Then you bring it to me. And I'll bring it to the Colonel. And he and I will have ourselves a very civilized discussion."

———

And here she is again, Ginny Kurva, in front of a shut door leading to a dark room, the fear gripping her not borne of the abstract terror of the unknown but of the full knowledge of what awaits her on the other side. A lurking dread down in her bowels that, no matter her intentions, no matter her plans, it always leads back here, to the hallway, to the crying girl in bed, to the living death of knowing that she put her there, and that nothing within her power can ever take it back. A dread that the theories of the oscillating model of the universe are correct, that time will continue to move forward until the universe collapses in on itself and the Big Bang repeats and all that has ever happened will happen again, that she is not only standing here now but that she will always be here, *has* always been here, that there are infinite Ginnys, each in her own stage of agony, and that in the grand cosmology of the universe they will remain that way forever, each frozen in her own personal moment of hell for eternity.

The room is more well-lit than Ginny had anticipated. Someone left the curtains open, light spilling in from the neon signs of the buildings around the Misanthrope, the pale electric blue of the dying horizon casting a glow over the bed that fills Ginny with a sense of anxiety that, for a few paralytic moments, keeps her rooted to her place. Then she finds her own trembling legs moving forward, towards the bed, towards the frail shape lying there, a girl so ashen that she looks like an inhabitant of a medieval plague ward, welts and bruises beginning to flourish in congregation around a massively blackened eye. Ginny looms at the foot of the bed, her body swaying, one hand outstretched before her, hovering above the sheet. Hesitantly, gingerly, she lifts it up, looks beneath at the extent of the damage. A cursory glance is all that is required. She drops the sheet, turns around, grips the windowsill. There is a brief moment when the nausea is so intense that the prospect of vomiting up her own bowels seems quite plausible. It passes.

Once Ginny has regained control of her body, she moves to the windows, draws the curtains. The darkness that washes over the room soothes her, lets her breathe again.

"Mary, sweetheart?" Ginny sits at the foot of the bed, nearly springs back to her feet, anticipating a scream, remembers where she is and settles down. Mary does not move; Ginny strains against the music in the hall to hear her breathing, cannot, places a hand on her back, keeps it there even after she feels it rising and falling with the staccato rhythms of belabored breathing. "Mary?"

"Mmmm?"

"Mary, sweetheart? It's Ginny."

"...Ginny?"

"Yes, sweetheart. I'm here."

She waits for a response. For seconds, it's quiet, then, a series of low, groaning wails rise up out of the darkness, Mary's body twisting under her hand.

"What did he do to me, Ginny? What did he do?"

"I'm so sorry, sweetheart."

"Ginny," she moans, "Ginny, Ginny, Ginny. What did he do to me? What did he do?"

Ginny lies down beside Mary, finds her head, puts her hands around it. "Something that never should have happened, sweetheart. I am so sorry. Please, sweetheart, believe me, this was never supposed to happen. This has never happened before."

"I feel dizzy. I feel funny."

"I'm sure the Colonel's given you, like, some kind of dope. Just... try and enjoy the ride, sweetie."

"Ginny..."

"Yes?"

"I can't... I can't feel anything. Down there."

Ginny flinches. "Your legs?"

"No. Just... down there."

Ginny wipes her face. "You're just sore. You've got to, like... Just let it heal up."

"It's bad, isn't it?"

"You're going to be okay, sweetie."

Mary sniffs. "Have you ever lied to me, Ginny?"

"What, sweetheart?"

"You've never lied to me before, have you? I mean, maybe you've lied to me about little things, like if one of the girls was doing better than me, or if I'd done something to make you kind of upset but you didn't want to hurt my feelings, like, I mean, I know you've probably lied to me about stuff like that, right? But, you've never lied to me about anything big, have you?"

"Never, sweetheart."

"Please don't lie to me now."

"I won't."

"I'm messed up pretty bad, right?"

"I think so, sweetheart. I... didn't take a very close look."

"But you're smart. You know a lot of science stuff. I know you do, you talk about it all the time."

"I like... astronomy and chemistry, sweetheart. I... I, like... I wasn't that good at biology."

"You said you weren't going to lie."

"A-Plus, with honors."

"I'm never going to have any babies, am I? Any of my own."

"I don't... No, you're probably not." A chill runs up Ginny's spine when there's no response. "I'm not a doctor so I can't tell you that for sure, but... No, sweetheart, I'm sorry."

"I wasn't planning on it for a while, you know? I mean, I wanted to get away from here, first, you know? Like you and me always talked about. Use my money to go to school, do something else. I thought, school's where it's going to start over for me. I mean, like, I'd have the money I'd made here, but, other than that, I always sort of figured I'd never have to think about any of this again… And, you know, it's stupid, but I figured, I'd meet some guy, and he'd be really cool, and he wouldn't be anything like my dad or my brothers." Mary stops abruptly; only the sensation of her hot breath against Ginny's face prevents her from thinking that the girl's simply up and died on her right there.

"That's not happening now, is it?"

"You can still do all of that, sweetheart. You have no idea how many girls have gone through what you're going through right now. Lots of them. There are, like, tons of women out there right now with kids they've adopted because they were in a situation just like yours, and, sweetheart, those little boys and girls don't love their mothers any less. Sweetheart, believe me, just because something is yours doesn't make it special. Do you have any idea how many miserable, awful mothers there are?"

"My mother never did anything to me."

"*That's not what I meant,*" Ginny snaps. "I'm sorry, I'm sorry. I'm not mad at you, sweetheart, not at all. I'm… I'm mad at this, this, what's happened to you."

"I'm never going to be a whole woman again."

"You will, and you are."

"Not the way it matters. Not the way it matters for this job."

"You don't worry about the job one little bit right now, sweetheart, do you understand? You do not worry your darling, precious little head one absolute iota. Your job right now is to rest. Rest, and get better. And once you're all better, I will figure out exactly what we are going to do with you, all right? You are going to be just fine."

"Will you stay with me?"

"It's just past sunset. I can't."

"Just for a while, then?"

"A little bit."

"You got any stories to tell me, Ginny?"

"Sweetie, my mind is, like, absolutely fucking shot right now. I couldn't tell you who was on Carson last night."

"Just hold me then?"

"Of course."

And Ginny holds her, and Mary, having struggled this long against the lull of the sedatives coursing through her veins, lets herself sink down into the peaceful recesses of opiate sleep. She dreams, Ginny supposes, of the un-formed thing eviscerated from her this afternoon in the heat-soaked daze of a lunatic's parlor abattoir, the life it might have led and the babies it might have called brother and sister, the children she will never bear, the futures they will never lead; and Ginny, silent tears streaking her cheeks, strokes the girl's hair in slow, even movements, a story to tell her after all, a story that she can do anything to help her now; that she has any future at the Motel Misanthrope.

––––––

Finding the dining room bereft of her usual dinner companion, Ginny lets herself into the Colonel's suite, one hand on the black satchel with which she presents him the nightly kick-up, the other on her switchblade. Since coming to work for the Colonel, the prospect of him com-pletely losing his mind has loomed large over her. Her me-teoric rise from simple street walker to bottom girl came not just because of her intelligence, her cunning, her will-ingness and ability to inflict physical punishment, but be-cause she learned quickly that the Colonel's brain, whether from war or drink or an accident of birth, looks and functions more properly like a piece of Swiss cheese than the average person's. From here, it was a simple matter of playing to his vanity, to the twisted version of the world which he inhabits. While her dearly departed predecessor— a rather intellectually disadvantaged piece of work named Maggie, currently screaming at people for nickels in front of the Pussycat Club— sniveled before him, absorbing his abuse, showing up to greet the girls at the start of the day bearing on her face the marks of her impotence and her insolence, Ginny whispered into his ear of greater things. While Maggie cowered and begged, Ginny filled his polluted brain with tales of glory: of a stable kept together not out of fear but of love; of a shared bond of sisterhood that would fortify them into a happily functioning, profitable unit; of the power that she could manufacture for him if only given the opportunity; of the things—both financially and physically—she could provide him with. For all of her confidence in her own abilities, though, for as artfully as she has played the Colonel like her own personal violin (an irony, Ginny now thinks, considering her ineptitude for any musical instrument), she has never let one reality slip far from her mind: Colonel Zarek Baniszewski is now, and always has been, one step away from a complete mental break.

"Colonel, sweetheart? Where are you, darling? I'm, like, totally starving over here. I waited around for you downstairs but you never came, and it didn't feel right to eat any of Georgie's food without you there. You have no idea how hungry I am. I could eat *anything* right now. *Anything.*"

Like a genie from a lamp, the Colonel steps out of the bathroom, naked, wet, idly twisting a wadded up washcloth round and round one ear. He stares not at Ginny but through her, a damp cigarette bobbing up and down between his lips. He walks across the room to an object wrapped in tin foil sitting beside the television set. Ginny watches as he unwraps it, revealing a miniature baked potato, microwaved corn, a processed hamburger patty with no bun. "I order room service. Not as hungry as I thought. You eat."

Ginny places the bag on the floor, cautiously moves to the food, taking the plate and sitting down at the foot of the bed. The Colonel moves around the room aimlessly, muttering quietly.

"You, aren't really yourself tonight, sweetheart."

"I like neat things. Not loose ends. I think there collaborator in Armia Krajowa, I say kill all suspects. Never know who enemy is. Women could be enemy, old men could be enemy. Children. Children do anything for candy, presents. Take information, hide guns. There town I think have collaborators, I say, bring suspects together, take them into room, give children toys. Children no idea what happening. Brrt! Brrt!" The Colonel imitates the sound of a machine gun firing, holds his arms out like a rifle and swings them back and forth in front of Ginny. "Kill everyone. No survivors means no risk."

"Oh, totally," Ginny says, cutting into the hamburger patty. "You've got to cover all your bases."

"Yes. This is the neat way to do things. Today not neat. Today messy. I not like mess."

"Sweetheart, it's all right," Ginny says, putting her food aside. She gestures for the Colonel to sit beside her. He stays motionless before her. "Darling, it's nothing to get bent out of shape over. Things happen. People make mistakes. We just have to figure out what to *do* about that mistake."

"I not make mistake. I act out of kindness."

"Sweetie?"

"*She* make mistake," the Colonel says, rubbing his head

with his free hand. "I do this dozen times before. Hundred times. Mary not trust me. Things go wrong. Girl never bleed this way. Mary never meant to have baby. Never meant to get rid of baby. She should have died." Ginny watches him pleasantly even as she reaches for her knife, does not pull it out.

"I should have let her die. But I know you like her. I fix her as favor to Ginny."

"You are, like the sweetest man on the face of the Earth."

The Colonel puts a hand on her shoulder, shoves her back onto the bed. "You flatter. But I not stupid. I know you not pleased with what I do for you."

"That's simply not true, darling. I am so totally grateful."

"You say I make mistake. You say I have to fix mistake."

"*Do about* mistake, darling, not fix, *do about*."

"I give girl life. What you want me to do next? Make water into wine?" He moves to the mini-fridge, opens it and retrieves a half-empty bottle of merlot. He pops the cork, begins to drink.

"It's my fault," Ginny says, setting her plate aside, rising, moving to the Colonel, "that, I'm, like, not effectively communicating how righteously grateful I am." She takes the bottle from him with one hand, begins to drink from it, then slips the other between his legs and gets to work. "I am, like, so relieved that Mary is still alive, I am, darling, you *know* that I am. But, like, since she's still alive, I've got to worry about her future, you know?"

"Future?"

"What she's going to do with herself now, sweetie. We're looking at her being down for, like, at least a week."

"Not my problem."

"But, sweetheart, it is, don't you see? Let's say she's ready and able to come back, like, one week from today. That's one week of Mary's income you are, like, totally out. And

Mary is an absolute little *peach* of a moneymaker for you. *Die zwei,* the other girls are going to find out she's sick, even if they don't know why; if you kick her sweet little behind to the curb, they're going to get scared, and I have never made those darlings work out of fear."

The Colonel swats Ginny's hand away, takes the bottle back. He moves to the bed, plucks the remnants of the hamburger from the plate, begins to stuff the patty into his mouth. "Mary want charity, she can go to Salvation Army."

Ginny sighs breathily, runs one hand down the back of her own head, saunters towards the Colonel, bends over, crawls up onto the bed on her hands and knees, letting her tank top sag, exposing cleavage. "Zarek, darling, you're not looking at the bigger picture, here. Happy girls are productive girls. You have a totally righteous opportunity in front of you. Show them that you're, like, as powerful as you are kind. Take care of her. Just a week. Let her stay, let her eat. It will, like, totally blow everyone's mind. They won't just appreciate you, then, they'll *love* you."

The Colonel watches Ginny, his eyes travelling from hers to her breasts, down the length of her body, his jaw moving in a slow, determined circle, like a cow chewing cud. He nods slowly.

"Let me see."

Familiar by now with the Colonel's awkward euphemism, Ginny obediently removes her tank top, her bra. When initially seducing the Colonel, she put an artistic effort into removing her clothes, calling on her dance training to strip with a fluid grace she is certain would have reduced other men to undulating jelly before her. With scant experience she learned that he had no appreciation for the slow burn, for the smoldering reveal, only for the quickest exposition of the flesh possible under any given circumstances.

"Good. So you still know how to listen. Good. So you listen. I not need to do anything. I already do everything. You nothing without me. There men more dangerous than me on Deuce. I keep them in line. I better man. Other men cut girls, kill girls. I make sure you and girls not hurt by those men. I keep the peace. Yes?"

"Yes."

"You bottom girl. I top. Only thing you top of is gutter. You runs girls. I run you. I say Mary through. Mary broken now, only freak want ripped up cunt, I not cater to freaks. Mary still alive; that best thing she can get, I already give it to her. You understand?"

"Yes, sweetheart. And I am so totally…"

"Not say grateful. You shut up and listen. You need me. I not need you. Without you, I everything. Without me, you nothing."

"Of course, darling."

"Tell me."

"What?"

"Tell me what you need."

"I need you, sweetheart. Only you."

"Show me then. Show me what you need."

The particular shade of red of the Colonel's canopy is nearly identical to that of the Red Rectangle Nebula, located in the Monoceros constellation. Discovered in 1973, it is a highly compact, protoplanetary, bipolar nebula that is curiously symmetrical. Just two years ago, Vincent Icke demonstrated that gas ejections from a dying star could create bow shocks that might account for the shape of the nebula. Sometime over the next few thousand years— seconds, really, in astronomical time—the Nebula should make the transition from protoplanetary to planetary as its central star heats into a white dwarf. In this capacity, it will become a great galactic recycling bin, dispersing material from the star's core across the cosmos to aid in the creation of stars, planets; the birth of life; a system without waste, where every individual molecule is assembled into something beautiful, in which even annihilation is only a step in a process to miraculous, total, whole creation.

Contemplating this is all Ginny can do to keep her sanity as she dutifully sheds the remainder of her clothes, lies back, and spreads her legs for the man who butchered her Mary.

———

After dinner, Nicolette puts on a Clannad album and watches the window. It is an important night. She must be in the proper frame of mind. She must wait until the time is exact. She rises and goes to her garage. She removes the blanket from the cage. Inside, a dog lies on bed sheets, staring up at her. Its coat is relatively clean and its body unblemished. It had not been at the pound for long when Nicolette found it. The dog is small but packed full of compact muscle. It looks to have some pit bull in it. Even caged, its presence is intimidating.

Nicolette loads the dog into the back of her van. At this hour of the night, the streets leading to the landfill are almost deserted. At the entrance to the landfill, she shows the guard her identification and is permitted entry. The guard does not question her presence or attempt to examine the van. Without her identification she is sure that the proper sum of money would also gain her access.

Once she has driven deeply enough into the landfill, Nicolette turns out the headlights on her van. To shine artificial lights within these sacred halls would be high blasphemy. The silver luminescence of the moon is sufficient to guide her home.

At her destination, Nicolette parks her van and gets out. She stands for a long while beneath the moon, gazing up at it. Its image is reflected in the lenses of her glasses. The craters churn, mercury oceans full of alien life, chanting down the names of the ancients to her. She closes her eyes and hears their song.

When she is ready, Nicolette opens the rear of the van, unloads the dog. She waits. Slowly, from amongst the rubble and the ash heaps, the others begin to appear. They circle her at first, heads low, cautious. Some snarl. Those with tails tuck them between their legs. The new dog growls back, stays close to Nicolette. Their noses sniff the air. They smell her scent. The dogs stand down. They congregate before her, smelling the new dog. Nicolette is ceaselessly fascinated by them. Though she has conducted extensive research on feral dogs, she has no frame of reference for the behavior of her own particular pack.

To her knowledge, no one has ever attempted to artificially construct a pack made entirely of bitches.

Nicolette treads her secret paths until she has reached The Altar. It's here that the world of the Meadow and the world beyond her body converge; where she can stand between both realms and exist as her true self. She closes her eyes. She reaches up to stroke her horns. Two years ago she had been eating lunch in her office and enjoying a tome of Károly Kerényi when her eyes had fallen upon a curiosity in the text. The chapter she had been reading recalled how the god Poseidon, angry at King Minos of Crete for his failure to sacrifice a prize bull, had induced Minos' wife to copulate with the creature. Thereafter she had born a child. The child bore the head of a bull and the body of a man. Its ferocity knew no bounds. It demanded human flesh for sustenance. As the issue of a Queen, the creature could not be executed. Minos, in pity, had commissioned the construction of the great labyrinth, a palace-maze for the child to inhabit. To provided sustenance, Minos had demanded fourteen youths each year from the conquered kingdom of Athens, to be ushered into the labyrinth and hunted as tributes. The story had touched Nicolette. She had long conceived of herself as someone apart from the world. Then she had seen it. The thing which had opened her eyes. The thing which had made sense of her life. The thing that opened her ears to the voices of The City and filled her heart with such paralytic joy that she was certain she would die.

Looking up from her text, Nicolette had gazed out her window at the landfill beyond. Her eyes had fixed on a point beyond the horizon, beyond that which she could see. She had put her book down and left her office. She had entered the landfill on foot. She had walked until her feet ached and the heat of the day leeched sweat from her pores in such volumes that her hair lay plastered to her scalp. Then she had stopped. Where there had been refuse only moments ago there was grass, green and lush.

There were rose bushes, winding round and round, rows and rows converging into a giant maze. She had known then that she had reached the appropriate place. *This* place. She had dropped to her knees and wept, and thrown up her arms to the divinities above. Where there had once been purposelessness there was now hope. Where there had been despair there was peace. She understood, then, that afternoon, that the entire trajectory of her life, every moment of cowardice and every second of fear, every taunt levied at her, every punch thrown, every abuse inflicted on her body had been for a purpose.

Nicolette studies her Altar. The dogs swarm around her, sniffing, licking, crouching. It has been crafted over time, assembled with great reverence and care by Nicolette with the assistance of her attendants. Each piece was carefully selected not just for its aesthetic beauty but also for its durability and structural integrity. Nicolette runs her paws over its surface, her nerves calm. She stands there a moment and breathes deeply the smell of her home. Then she begins her patrol.

It's difficult to see her watch by the light of the moon so Nicolette does not know how long it takes for her to collect all of the poison. When she is done, she returns to her van. The next time a crew conducts an observation of the West mound, they will find several living dogs, no dead dogs, and no poison. They will be forced to conclude that the poison is somehow ineffective. There will be no choice but to isolate this region of the landfill. It will be sealed off from the workers and abandoned to the dogs.

Then, it will belong to Nicolette.

The drive back to her house is leisurely. Though the night air is hot, she rolls down her windows and lets it tousle her hair. Occasionally she hears stray words carried on the wind, gently caressing the lobes of her ears, speaking to her of greater glories to come. She turns down the radio to hear them more clearly.

At home, Nicolette crosses the day off of her calendars. She maintains a Gregorian calendar to keep abreast of important dates at work. She keeps an Athenian calendar beside it to track the progress of The Cycle. As the Gregorian calendar is solar and the Athenian calendar lunisolar, the two enjoy some minor overlap but are nominally separate entities. This year, Skirophorion, the final month of the Athenian calendar, falls between June 11th and July 10th. It's a time of celebration and preparation; crops are blessed in the hope of a bountiful harvest; the altar of Zeus at the Acropolis is consecrated, to keep the King of the gods appeased for the next year; The City offers up its tributes.

Nicolette consults her puzzle book. The City is running on schedule. It must offer her tribute roughly every other day to meet its quota. So far, she has collected two.

After tomorrow night, it will be three.

———

Kneeling on the floor in front of the television set, reaching forward for the fifth time to hit rewind on the VCR, watching Johnny Carson monologue in reverse, the candy-colored curtains swaying gently behind him, Ginny thinks how foolish she's been, how short-sighted, how the solutions to the day's problems have been at the forefront of her mind all along, how her exhaustion, Mary's situation, Tammy's indoctrination, all could have been made to flow smoothly.

All she needed was to get really, really drunk.

"*Avez-vous jamais pensé à papa?*"

"Huh?" The question travels to Ginny at the speed of sludge, mucking its way into her ears and echoing down her auditory canal so sluggishly that it takes her a moment to fully comprehend what she's just heard, let alone recognize that she has, in fact, heard anything at all.

"*Avez-vous jamais pensé à papa?*"

"You've been getting into my French tapes. You're supposed to be learning German," Ginny slurs, reaches forward, rewinds the tape.

"I'm sick to shit of fucking German. When I get to college, I want to sound hot, not like I'm ready to invade Poland. I want to be the girl who knows French. *Ooh la la. Mon Cherie amor. Tu as envie de coucher avec moi ce soir?*"

"…No."

A beat. Then, Tricia, her voice more modulated than usual, stripped of its usual acerbity, chilling to Ginny in how different it sounds this way, how adult: "You're trying to avoid answering my question."

"What question?"

"Is it wrong to think about dad?"

Ginny reaches forward and rewinds the tape. Tricia pushes her chair forward and jams Ginny in the back with her foot rest.

"Hey. Fuck you."

"I've got more where that came from."

Ginny sighs, hits pause. "I don't see why you'd want to."

"I don't know. I, like, do sometimes, though, you know? Don't you ever?"

"No."

"So is there, like, something wrong with me? Like, wondering how he's doing?"

"We know exactly how he's doing. It doesn't take a lot of imagination."

"I don't know. I mean, there's like, pecking orders, right? He's not totally at the bottom."

Ginny shrugs. "I guess not."

"But, I don't know... I mean, like, there were good times, right? And I mean, it's normal to miss those, right?"

"If you want to."

"Omigawsh, you said that *so* sad. You are *so* totally trying not to feel feelings right now."

"Your... face... is trying not to be sad right now."

Trish shrieks; Ginny jerks around. "What?"

"Omigawsh! You miss him, too. What do you think about?"

Ginny looks up at her sister; the expression on her face is so hopeful, so hungry, so shining like the light of a bright afternoon sun that she cannot stay focused on it, instead looks back to the floor, to the television, to the floor again. "He gave me this book of quotes for, like, my fifteenth birthday. And I went through and highlighted all of the ones that were from scientists. And I think about... that microscope he got me for my eighth birthday, and how you fucked it up."

"Omigawsh, you have so totally got to let that go." Tricia stops a moment, gnaws on her cuticle. "I just like to think about times before shit got all fucked up. It's, like, how a comedy starts out really funny but then the writer realizes he's got to wrap up the story and the jokes stop like thirty minutes before the end and then you're just watching some bullshit drama and you're like, 'why aren't you assholes making me laugh anymore?'"

"Our life is not a comedy, Trish."

Tricia sneers, leans forward. "The Elizabethans, who, like, came after the Tudors? They said that a comedy was any story with a happy ending. So I totally hope that we are living a comedy. Oh, and, by the way? Fuck you."

Ginny smiles weakly. "Elizabeth *was* a Tudor. And I'm still waiting for '99 Luftballoons.'"

Tricia frowns, runs her hands through her sister's hair. "You're, like, way more fucked up tonight than usual." A quiet, uncomfortable pause. "I'm sorry, Ginny."

Ginny leans back against Tricia's legs, lets her continue rubbing her hair. "You didn't do anything. It was a lousy day. A really fucking lousy day, and all I want to do now is watch Carson and get really fucking trashed."

"Hey, Ginny?"

"Yeah?"

"You can talk to me. I mean, like, about shit that bothers you and stuff. I mean, you don't really ever talk to anyone, right? You never spend time with any of the girls. And you don't really talk to Roger about heavy shit, do you?"

"We are, like, so totally not having this conversation."

"But, I'm, like your sister and stuff. You're supposed to

be telling me all this shit."

"You're seventeen and you've taken enough shit in your life. You don't need me piling all of my problems on you."

"But, I mean, like, you're going to go like totally fucking insane, you know? I mean, that shit happens, right? Like, I saw this thing on this talk show this afternoon about this guy, like, in the fifties, right? And he had all these bills and shit, and didn't tell his family that he got fired from his job, and he'd, like, go to the bus stop every day in a suit and just, like, sit there and totally bake in his own juices, and finally he goes totally fucking apeshit and he guns everyone down."

"Shit, Trish, I'm not going to kill you."

"I know you'd never hurt *me*. But, like, I'm worried about *you*." Tricia stops running her hands through Ginny's hair, looks down at her. "You know, I could work for you, right?"

"...What?"

"I mean, like, all I do is sit here all day and read books and shit and listen to tapes and watch TV and just fuck around, and, like, you're working for the both of us, and, I know the reason that we're still here and the reason you have to work the way you do is because I'm not doing anything. And like, I mean, I could do it, you know? It's not like I'd even feel anything, right? And there have got to be some real sick fucks out there that'd, like, totally get a hard-on and a half for a girl in a chair, right? And then, like, maybe we could save some money and we could maybe leave here one day."

Ginny's jaw slackens. She leans forward, stumbles, gets herself to her feet, turns around and kneels back in front of Tricia, her eyes glazed, glassy with tears. "You are not responsible for me. I am responsible for you. And you do not worry about a job or money or... Your job is to learn what I tell you to learn, and to do good at your school work, and… to be as normal fucking a kid as you can be right now, okay? And my job is to give that to you." Ginny grabs Tricia's thighs, shakes her in her chair. "Okay?"

"You still blame yourself."

"What?"

"You, like, want to do all of this for me because you still blame yourself."

Ginny smiles weakly, rubs the back of her hand over her eyes. "Hey, listen. You're going to be going to college in, like, a year. And then I'll be out of this. We'll both be out of it and then we don't think about it anymore. And once you've, like, conquered the world, then you can worry about taking care of me, okay?"

"Take over world, provide for sister. Got it."

"Hey. Hey. Do I tell you that I love you enough, Trish?"

Tricia shakes her head. "Oh, no. No, no, no. Do not do this."

"I love you so much, Tricia. And I'm so sorry for everything that's happened to you."

"Oh, grody, you're, getting snot all over me. It's a pain in the ass to shower, you know? Like, hello, paralyzed?"

"It's… it's important for… for girls your age to… feel loved? And… accepted? By, like, their parent? And… and since our parents were shit… I, like, I am your parent, right? I mean, I know it's biologically impossible to have given birth to you at four, but, I'm sort of your mom, aren't I? So, I mean, it's important that you know that I love you. Which… I…. do."

"Okay, okay, I get it, you're, like, all sloppy drunk emotional right now. So, like, I'm just going to accept that and ask you to go take a fuck at a flying donut. I mean, if you're done hogging the VCR, I *did* tape my stories this afternoon. I'm not *always* slacking off of my work."

Ginny pulls back, suddenly feels very ashamed, very surprised, though her mind cannot quite articulate why or at what. "You poor, sweet girl. I am... so sorry. You watch your soaps. You watch them and you enjoy them."

"And you, like, pass out in the position you want to wake up in, because it is a major pain in my ass to move you when you're out. And I can't even feel my ass, so, that should tell you a lot."

Ginny backs away from Tricia, arms extended in front of her. "I am so sorry..."

"Say you're sorry again and I'm going to, like, fucking go all like *Cuckoo's Nest* on you, all like native guy on Jack Nicholson and, like, kneel on your face with a pillow and then smash my wheelchair through our window and escape this shithole. Only, we're like, five stories high so I would die. So, if you say you're sorry again that means you want me to die. Why do you want to kill me, Ginny?"

Ginny smiles wanly, bends over to kiss Tricia on the forehead, nearly collapses into her. "Goodnight, Trish. I love you."

"And I love *All My Children*. So please don't stand between me and it. Like, literally. You are literally in between me and the television right now."

Ginny bows, staggers to the bedroom. Despite her inhibited physical state, she is feeling, essentially, happy. It seems that despite everything that came tumbling down around her, despite Mary, and the Colonel, and fucking Roger's stupid fucking paranoia, that everything will be okay. Mary will be okay; the morning light will bring her clarity and wisdom, a solution to the whole sorry affair that will make the desperation of this evening comical in hindsight. The Colonel is now, always has been and forever shall be the Colonel—nothing new there to contemplate or anticipate. Roger...

He had, at first, been just another body on 42nd Street, another man, another source of sensory input. She could tell, the way he looked at her that first day, that he was attracted to her; appreciated that he didn't stare, that his eyes moved over her in quick, fleeting glances; appreciated more that he didn't say anything about it, maintaining his quiet, almost disarming civility; appreciated most that he came to pay attention to Tricia. He joked with her, he argued with her about who would win against whom in a fight, what the best coalition of supervillains would be. He treated her like any other kid in a comic shop. He never saw the chair. It had been more than enough to endear him to Ginny, though she never gave any consideration to interaction with him outside of Hobbs's End. Then...

Late last Summer in the Colossus, *The Evil Dead* onscreen, Ginny utterly repulsed at what she was witnessing, the grotesque tableaux of a demon-infested tree molesting a helpless girl, wondering what in the world had possessed her to see this a second time, wondering even more what was keeping her glued to her seat. At the apex of her disgust, prepared to exit the theater, a familiar voice had called out from a seat in the aisle in front of her:

"I hope she doesn't get splinters!"

It had been all Ginny could do to stop herself from laughing, a little snicker turning into a spiteful cackle. It was absurd; it was as absurd as what she was seeing onscreen was absurd, and the stranger knew that and understood that, and he was sharing this with her, a running commentary developing as the film progressed, the barbarity and brutality diminishing by the moment along with her rage, fury replaced with something far more powerful: simple, derisive scorn. When she had calmed herself, she had leaned forward to identify the peanut gallery, and discovered it was Roger. She had offered him some of her popcorn, then hopped over the seat and sat beside him, joining him in ridiculing the remainder of the film.

Though she finds it difficult to articulate why, especially now, on her knees, rummaging beneath the bed for her suitcase, Roger's simple presence has transformed over time into something profound for her. Though she has no lack of faith in her own abilities to protect herself, something about her proximity to Roger makes her feel, if not physically, then emotionally, *safe.*

Ginny pries the suitcase free, opens it. Inside, the spoils of her pitiful empire: stacks of wrinkled bills secured crudely in brittle rubber bands, not jammed together as Ginny would hope but rather evenly spaced; the kick-up to the Colonel eating into her earnings and food for Tricia eating into her earnings; condoms and makeup eating into her earnings; new clothes for herself and new clothes for Tricia, school supplies, books for the girls; Tricia's disposable adult diapers because she will not force her sister to endure the added indignity of having to clean her own filth out of the cotton sort. Alcohol. Blessed, cursed alcohol bought with increasing regularity eating into her earnings. Three years on the job—the amount before her is soul-rendingly minuscule. Still—nestled in the space between the bills, hope. The hope that this, like all of the tragedies of her life, shall pass, not leading into different or stranger tragedy as the rest have, but dissipating, a final test of resolve before the world finally permits her to pass into a life resembling, if even only remotely, normalcy.

If—*when,* always *when*—that day comes, the one thing she will miss will be Roger.

Ginny shuts the suitcase and pushes it back beneath the bed. It's to her own surprise that she manages to lift her upper body onto the mattress, surprise the last registered thought or emotion before blackness abruptly overtakes her; surprise the first emotion when her eyes open to the morning sun, her body tucked securely beneath the covers, head sore from hanging off the foot of the bed, her feet cool but comfy, propped up on her pillow. Beside her, Tricia snores loudly, dead to the world, still seeming to grin lasciviously.

4

Friday, June 17th, 1983

T HE FIRST GERMS OF THE IDEA COME TO GINNY AS
she brushes her teeth, and by the time she has
finished her practice and completed Tricia's lesson
plan and is skipping down the stairs two at a time it is fully
formed, Ginny marveling to herself what intellectual feats
she is capable of with the assistance of a really good night's
sleep and a fine Irish coffee for a pick-me-up.

"Ladies, as you can see, we have a most unfortunate absence at our table," Ginny begins, taking her seat at the
head of the table, Shannon setting a plate before her. "As
dear, sweet Shannon told you all last night, poor Mary and
I were struck most unrighteously by a seriously awful case
of food poisoning yesterday." She places a hand over her
heart, pauses for emphasis, shaking her head, eyes downcast.
"Unfortunately, the repercussions were much more severe
for our little sister than for myself."

Quiet murmurs of concern drift around the table. Ginny raises her hands, shakes her head. "Ladies, ladies, please,
don't concern yourselves. Now, the truth is, Mary is going
to be out of commission for, like, at least the next week.
While she is expected to make a full recovery, it's going to

be a very long and difficult process."

"Damn, Miss Ginny, you lucky! Why Mary laid up like that while you down here?"

"Constance, darling, please, speak in turn? But to answer your question, it would appear that some tainted beef is the dastardly culprit in all of this. And while Mary was absolutely famished at lunch yesterday and helped herself to seconds, I only had, like, half off of my plate. I will, of course, mention here that I very strongly advise you to stay away from our little diner, lest you want to lose a few extra pounds the hard way."

"What's going to happen to her?" Sandra asks.

"Mary is under a strict quarantine for the duration of her illness. You see, her particular type of food poisoning is *viral* as opposed to *bacterial*; specifically Escherichia coli, commonly called E. coli. And all of her... we are ladies here, still, aren't we, so I'm going to say *bodily waste*—of which she is generating a most copious and gnarly amount even as we speak—is absolutely crawling with it."

"That's some seriously grody stuff, Miss Ginny."

"It is quite, Michelle. But please, rest assured, ladies, that Colonel Baniszewski takes care of his own. Mary has absolutely nothing to worry about while she rests, recuperates, and recovers; though, she will, of course, be paying it back with considerable interest."

Snickers abound around the table. Ginny nods, smiles, closes her eyes, raises a hand above her head. "Yes, yes, darlings, it's all completely terrible, but, as a great man once said, life, of course, *is* terrible. And with that bit of business out of the way, I see a little bit of extra time on my watch. So, ladies, have any of you begun Chapter Four? Let's hear some thoughts."

Ginny listens raptly to the responses she receives as she works her way around the table, sipping her coffee, pleased,

pleased very much this morning, at the work the girls are accomplishing, at the rebound she's made from yesterday, at the path she sees laid out before her. Mary will be well cared for; she will maintain her position of authority and trust with the girls; the Colonel will, absolutely, be kept out of the loop.

Ginny usually has two donuts for breakfast along with her eggs and coffee. This morning, as the girls share their recollections of Chapter Four, Michelle thinking Gatsby's fascination with Daisy romantic, Candice finding it pathetic, she reaches forward and grabs herself a third. Customarily, she dislikes rewards given or received before an accomplishment. She has never permitted Tricia to indulge in a comic or video tape or record intended as a prize for achieving a particular grade or completing a specific assignment before the completion of the task at hand. In certain circumstances, though, she feels it acceptable to make exceptions. The donuts *will* be all gone later.

As breakfast ends and the girls begin to drift out of the dining room, Ginny remains seated, catching Tammy with her eyes, gesturing for her to remain behind.

"I think Miss Ginny needs to see me," she says to Michelle, turning back, joining her at the table. Ginny waits for all of the girls to have vacated the room before she turns her head up to look at Tammy.

"Have a seat, sweetheart. Would you like anything else? Any more donuts? If you want anything else, sweetheart, anything more from the kitchen, let me know, and it's all yours."

"Um, thank you."

"You are so totally welcome. You know, sweetie, you did absolutely fabulous yesterday. Shannon told me. Do you know that you had the biggest take yesterday?"

"I... I did?"

"It looks like someone has got a natural talent. Or maybe just a natural appeal. I don't know. But the point is this, darling, you made an incredible amount of money for yourself yesterday. And that's why I'm so eager but so reluctant to come to you with this. And, believe me, I would totally not be having this conversation with you under most other circumstances." Ginny takes out a cigarette, lights up, the cross-sensation of tobacco smoke and coffee and residual vodka in her mouth an utter delight. "You want one?"

"No thank you."

"You're a Christian."

"I try to be. Tried, before this, I guess."

"Everyone's got to make her own way, sweetheart. I won't hold against you what you won't hold against me."

"You quoted from Psalms yesterday."

"Proverbs, darling, though I used to confuse them in catechism myself."

Tammy cocks her head. "You're Catholic?"

"Confirmed Virginia Maria Joan Kurva. The church and I have had a parting of the ways, though, and we are very steadily drifting off topic now. Right now, *your* devotion is of more concern to me. I absolutely love my girls to death, sweetheart. There isn't a solitary thing that I wouldn't do for any of them. I don't know if you're quite ready to believe that yet, but it's the honest truth. When something hurts one of them, it hurts me. I've always told them that they can come to me with any problem and that I would help them. That's what makes what happened to Mary so... devastating."

"You couldn't help no food poisoning."

"That's just the thing, sweetheart. Mary and I weren't dealing with food poisoning last night. You remember how I sent you off yesterday afternoon? Mary wanted to speak to me alone. She wanted to confess. She'd gotten herself pregnant, sweetheart. Now, now, I don't know who, I have no idea what the circumstances were. I wasn't going to shame the poor dear any more than she already was. What was more pressing was that she came to me because..."

At this, Ginny looks around the room, measured shame in her faux gravitas, wearing her expression of utmost distress. "She wanted to get rid of it, Tammy."

"Oh, no."

"I didn't tell her to do it, Tammy. I never told her to do it. That is the absolute, total, honest truth. We went to the diner and we discussed her situation. I counselled her on all of her alternatives. But come the end of the day, it was completely her decision, and..." Ginny sighs, stubs her cigarette out on the edge of her plate. "Here we are."

"What happened?"

Ginny puts a hand over her face. Although she has always found a certain self-loathing pride in her own capacity for improvised histrionics, she has never mastered the art of the fake cry.

"Oh," Tammy says. "Oh, no. She..."

"It's awful. I don't want to disgust you with the details. They are like, so, so totally grody to the max you would not believe it at all. Everything you have heard is completely true. And that asshole didn't even have the nerve to fix her up afterwards. She's ashamed, sweetheart, she is broken and ashamed and she is completely terrified right now."

Tammy begins to rise from the table. "Where is she? I want to pray..."

"*No!* No, sweetheart. She is in a very fragile place right now. Safe, but fragile. She's ashamed, darling, to face anyone. That's why I'm letting her rest away from the other girls. She needs her privacy right now, not just to heal physically but emotionally. Like, spiritually. In the meantime, though, there is another, more worldly but still very pressing matter, sweetie. Do you have any idea how much they charge to do something like that?"

Tammy shakes her head, Ginny thankful that she's accurately gauged the girl's knowledge of such things. "A thousand dollars. And poor, frightened Mary gave it to them. It was almost all she had to her name, sweetheart. She thought that she could make it back once it was over, she thought that she'd just put forth the extra effort, thought, I guess, like... I don't know. But with her being so hurt, sweetie, she can't make that money back now, at least not yet. She's going to need a lot of care. I want to give it to her, sweetheart, but... Like I told you, I have a sister. A biological sister, I mean. She lives here with me."

"Does she... does she work with..."

Ginny reels. "Fuck, no." One of Tammy's eyebrows cocks. Ginny touches her shoulder. "*No.* She couldn't if she wanted to. She was on her way to a friend's birthday party one night a few years ago when, like, some drunk hit the car she was in. The girl she was with and the girl's dad didn't make it; my sister was paralyzed."

"Oh, my goodness. That's awful."

"I'm just glad she's alive. I only hope the driver made it long enough to get himself right with the Lord before he met him." A complete lie; Ginny takes comfort in the image of the bastard burning. "She's how I first ended up doing this. So that I could take care of her. But it's a lot of money to feed and clothe a growing girl. Things are already tight. And that's where I need you, sweetie. Shannon is the only other girl who knows about this, and I can't ask her for help. She's a diabetic, darling, the money she doesn't use to eat goes straight to her insulin. She's not in any better of a position to help another person than me. But, you. You are a Christian, aren't you, sweetheart? You believe in doing the right thing. Caring for your parents, your neighbors, your brothers and sisters. That's why I knew I could come to you. I want to help Mary. I'm going to help Mary. But I can't do it alone. I need you, sweetheart. I need your help. I know that what we give to the Colonel's already a lot… But, at night, when you give your kick…"

"Of course." Tammy flings herself forward, arms wrapping around Ginny, squeezing her tight. Ginny returns the embrace warmly, nodding slowly to herself, thankful, that this has worked, that things will be all right as she anticipated them to be all right. "Of course, Miss Ginny. I couldn't not. I couldn't not help someone out like that."

"This remains between us, of course. You can't let anyone know, not even the Colonel. He's weird about some stuff."

"Sure, sure."

"Oh, Tammy, sweetheart. You have got no idea how thankful I am right now. You are, like, an absolute angel."

Tammy sniffs, crying now, nestling her head against Ginny's shoulder. "You are too. I see why all these girls love you so much now, Miss Ginny. It's strange, but, you got light around you, you know that? You're positively surrounded by light."

———

It's lunch time when Nicolette hears the ambulance sirens. Initially, she disregards them. There is no one at the office for whom she has any particular affinity, who she would be sad to see harmed or killed. She knows that she is in good health and that the sirens are not for her. There is no need to interrupt her lunch. She continues moving her pen over the pages of her puzzle book.

Someone runs past her door, followed by another Someone. There is a commotion in the hallway. People are panicking. She hears a woman scream. She closes her eyes. She attempts to travel to the Meadow. A multitude of voices all mix together. Realizing that she will not be able to enjoy the remainder of her lunch in peace, Nicolette decides she might as well at least amuse herself by seeing what's going on.

Outside, a crowd has converged. The ambulance is parked near a sanitation truck. In the bed of the truck, a sanitation worker is helping a pair of paramedics move what looks like a large animal carcass onto a stretcher. Nicolette's breath catches in her throat. They have killed one of her bitches. They have brought it back to investigate it. She begins moving close to the ambulance to try and identify which of the dogs it is. The carcass has been shredded in multiple places, as if by machinery. Hair and blood and bone intermingle in a viscous pink sludge that oozes up out of the body and drips onto the ground in sopping puddles as the men lay it onto the stretcher. One limb has been broken completely in two, and a piece of exposed white bone juts out to the sky, gently twitching. The dog's jeans have been torn apart in multiple places, scraps of frayed denim flapping with the movement of the body, spraying little drops of blood as they go.

Nicolette stops in her tracks.

It's not one of her dogs.

Cautiously, Nicolette approaches Someone.

"What happened?" she asks.

"Joey and Ed went out to check on the poison traps," Someone says. "Now I ain't gotten to talk to Joey personally yet, but what he called in on the radio, they got out there and the coast was clear. The traps were empty. Looked like the dogs took every last damn bit of it. Next thing they know the damn things are coming at them every which way. Joey made it back to the truck, Ed didn't quite. Joey drove the truck up on 'em, spooked 'em away, but by that time…"

The person that Nicolette supposes is Ed is loaded onto the stretcher and rushed towards the ambulance. A man turns and vomits onto the skirt of the woman standing beside him. Pitiful people; frightened and revolted by such ordinary things.

"Dammit. We gotta do something about those fuckin' dogs."

"This is very upsetting," Nicolette says. She removes her glasses; the world transforms into a psychedelic blur. It's a feeling of helplessness she is not comfortable with. She quickly turns her head, wipes an imaginary tear from her eyes, places her glasses back on and turns to Someone. "This is awful. I should have come up with a better idea. This is my fault."

"You can't fight nature, Aster," Someone says. "Shit. Go home. Consider it an extended weekend. I'm gonna ride down to the hospital, check on Ed. Come Monday, we're gonna figure this out. Even if we do gotta fence the fucking mutts in."

"Thank you, sir. That's very kind. Please call me later and let me know how… he… is doing."

Nicolette keeps her head down as she walks away from the scene. She contorts her face to generate the appearance of great anguish. She imagines she looks like any other hysterical bitch, losing her mind over a mouse in the kitchen. Once she's reached her van, her face slackens, returns to normal. Things have gone much better than she could have anticipated, and she's gotten some extra time, too. She checks her watch. Plenty of time until sundown. She turns the key in the ignition and heads towards the florist.

———

"If my Spidery Sense is correct, I do believe that someone is dreadfully thirsty. And, would you look here, I have just the cure for what ails you." Ginny's face is positively radiant as she says this, glowing in the darkness of Number Two at the Colossus, offering the little paper-wrapped package to Roger.

"What is it?"

"Well, someone is just going to have to open it up and see, now isn't he?"

Roger smiles at Ginny, his upper row of teeth hidden by his mustache. He tears open the package, continues smiling at the little bottle inside.

"Just a peace offering, sweetheart. My brand—Nikolai. The vodka that kisses and never tells. Just like me." She sits beside him, sighs; the afternoon has followed the pace set by the morning, perhaps her most profitable day of the past several weeks. While she has spent most of it in the minimal space between consciousness and mental absence, her body and brain numbed to the events unfolding around her, the time before and after each transaction has been jubilant, dates drifting in and out of her path with a regularity she hasn't experienced for some time, money accumulating in such an amount that the simple olive branch of a kind word and a smile she'd intended to offer Roger ceased to seem enough. "I was positively *curt* with you yesterday, and you were only looking out for little old me."

"It's your *Spidey* Sense."

"…Of course it is, sweetheart."

Roger unscrews the cap of the bottle, takes a mouthful. His face freezes, eyes widening; he swallows, coughs.

"I'll admit, it is an acquired taste."

"Son of a bitch. Where did you acquire it, a junkyard?"

Ginny frowns. "Darling, you're not being particularly gracious about this. It's considered polite to accept all gifts."

Roger raises an eyebrow. "Who, ah, who said I wasn't accepting it?" He takes another mouthful, turns back to the screen. "I think we're going to need it for this one."

"Whatever are we watching?"

"It's called *Hausu*."

"I saw the name on the ticket, darling, that wasn't my question. *What are we watching?*"

"That woman there, I think she's, ah, a vampire, or maybe it's just her cat who's the vampire. And that girl there? *Her* friend got eaten by some mattresses, and that one there, she's being haunted by her friend's severed head, and it wants to eat her."

"I see."

"I'm enjoying it, but, ah, I also think I might hate it."

"Why's that?"

"I, ah, can't figure out what's going on enough to make fun of it." Roger takes another drink, offers the bottle to Ginny. "I actually think, though... ah, I'm not sure... but I think it's making fun of itself. All I've been able to do is keep a running tally on how many boobs I've seen."

"How many?"

"None... I don't like it when you're mad at me. It makes me worry."

"Hmmm?"

"I know you don't like anyone coming to your room, so I can't come to apologize. And I know that... I, ah, I know that you're going to leave one day. And, ah, when we argue... I'm always afraid it's going to be the last time I'll see you."

Ginny turns towards Roger in her seat, smiles, reaches out to touch the side of his head. The little muscles in his bare temple twitch and tighten. Ginny drums her fingers against them.

"Sweetheart, you know what I do. You know what kind of life I live. I'm a saleswoman. I sell my time. And any man walking the Earth right now could buy it if he has enough cash and he pays up front. And then that time is his to do with whatever he wants. But I have a little bit of time, darling, just a very little bit, that's *mine*. That's Ginny time. And that's the time I don't sell. And most of it goes to my sister, and some of it goes to me. And a little bit of it—time, like this, right now—a little bit of that goes to you. And unlike every other man walking this earth, Roger, you don't have to pay for it. That's yours. That's what I give to you. Because you're, like, really fun to be around, and you listen to me and shit, and for that little bit of time that we're together, I'm not the girl who does what I do. But, Roger, you can't do with our time whatever you want. There are conditions. What you cannot do with my time is fuck it up for me. Because our time has got to end just like everyone else's, sweetheart. And when it does… Well, I've got to go on ahead and make another sale."

Roger, eyes unmoving from the screen, nods slowly, sniffs heavily, loosened mucous and phlegm rattling around inside of his sinuses, magnified eyes visibly moistened.

"No feelings, sweetheart. Just you and me and a shitty movie and whatever happens to be annoying us at the moment." Letting someone down gently is a foreign concept for Ginny. In high school, all of the propositions she received were of the profane variety, answered initially by running away to cry in the bathroom, later with blows to the genitals carefully timed to coincide with a lack of attention from any nearby authority figure. She has, up to this point in her life, only had the opportunity to gently break off one relationship; and while it is not the first time the similarity has occurred to her, it strikes Ginny again how much like Paul Saunders Roger is, if not in his appearance than in his general temperament, quiet and dry and withdrawn as he recorded data in his immaculately maintained notebook, entire stretches of lab time spent in silence before he would pipe up with some strange, random factoid of information, breaking Ginny's concentration on the experiment with the declaration that atomic weight of Cobalt is 59.3 or that blue light is vital to circadian rhythms or that her eyes had the same shimmer as pure beryllium. Paul, sandy-haired and cruelly handsome, his face swarthy and clean shaven but much more pockmarked than she imagines Roger's must be beneath the beard. Paul Saunders, not really like Roger at all though, really: Paul cultured and stately and infinitely fascinated with chemistry and Isaac Asimov and Greek cuisine and stargazing on blankets under clear skies on chilly Autumn nights and Ginny Kurva, whom he'd kissed one night after walking her back to her dorm , who had kissed him back that night and almost every other night of the next three weeks leading up to the Christmas break from which Ginny Kurva never returned. Paul Saunders, not the type of boy who would truck with trade, who would willingly idle his time away making conversation with that particular type of woman. Paul Saunders who probably waited stone-still beside a phone for the gentle letdown that never came and who has probably by now, for his own good, really moved on to some other quiet, shy girl who wasn't hiding all along the darkness that would finally consume her.

"No feelings, sweetheart. Understand?"

"Yeah."

"So no tears then."

"I'm not crying," Roger says, his voice choked. He rummages around inside of his shirt, comes out with a paper napkin, wipes his nose, his eyes. "It's allergies." Ginny is surprised that Roger's voice has cleared so quickly by the time he says this, no note of any strain or tremor in his voice, no sound of tears, so that she has to wonder herself if he's telling the truth; is surprised that some small part of her is disappointed at the prospect of this, even as the rest of her is relieved. "The fucking heat's been killing me. I thought the rain would've cleared it up, but, ah, maybe the next one."

Ginny smirks. "And when is that?"

"Saturday." Roger blows his nose. "You still going to watch the space launch?"

"Darling, I wouldn't miss it! I'm waking Trish up early, which probably means I'm going to have to drug her the night before just to get her out of bed before ten."

Roger chuckles. "It'll only get worse when she gets to college."

"I never knew you went to college."

"Sure. It sucked."

"Meteorology. You're, like, some sort of, I don't know, what, meteorology prodigy?"

"No." Roger shakes his head. "I can just tell when it's going to rain. Ever have since I was a kid."

"Aha! So you *were* a kid once."

"That's debatable."

"Surely you weren't spawned somewhere, darling? Only terrible things spawn."

"I had rheumatic fever." Roger grunts, clears his throat, does something that Ginny has never seen him do before—he takes off his glasses. Roger untucks the tail of his shirt, begins using it to clean them. "I, ah, spent a lot of time watching movies. I, ah, spent pretty much all my time watching movies. Sort of got to be a pro at it. Ah, some stuff doesn't change, does it?"

Ginny looks at Roger, his sad eyes, his defensive posture, the morose expression he wears as his neutral face, and a lifetime unravels before her: the sickly boy, bedridden, friendless, returning at last to school as the frail, blind, overprotected recluse, coming of age awkward and cautious, his intellect perhaps enough to make up for his lack of physicality but his social manners too crippled to cement the relationships he is always reaching out towards. Then, at last, left behind by the unknown joys of youth, he settles into this life, more secure in the chilly embrace of the lonely dark than the unwelcome gaze of the lit world; a subterranean dweller staring up at the sunlight from the gutter.

Ginny looks at Roger and, she thinks, for the first time, really sees him.

Roger puts his glasses back on, turns to look at her, blinks to reacquaint himself with his restored vision. "I stepped into your comfort zone. So I let you step into mine. Now, ah... now we're even." He turns back to the screen; Ginny sits in silence. Onscreen, a giant, snarling cat face materializes over the visage of a grinning vampire, bedecked in traditional Japanese wedding attire.

"You see what I mean?" Roger throws his hands up in exasperation. "What do I do with that? I, ah, I've got nothing." He sighs, settles back into his seat, takes another drink. Without looking at her, he offers the bottle to Ginny; she takes it, drinks. There's a sting behind her eyes but not in her throat. She hands the bottle back to Roger; he sets it between his legs, places his hands on the armrests. Without looking away from the screen, Ginny reaches over, places one gloved hand on top of Roger's, squeezes, pulls her hand back. Roger wipes his face with his palm, sniffs, smiles, shakes his head.

"And, ah, still no boobs."

In her adolescence, Nicolette Aster was never entirely certain of where her family obtained its money. She supposed, based on the scope and location of her childhood home on Long Island, that they had become wealthy long before even her father was born. It was not until her mother's passing, when her presence at the Aster estate became a hindrance to her newly single father and she had been sent to *get well* that some of the nurses at the institute informed her that her family's fortune came from the mass manufacture of fertilizer. Despite her general lack of humor, Nicolette recognized the irony in this. Yet, as a child, the origins of her family's wealth had no relevance to her. She lived in a large home, her father was always around, and this was all that mattered.

As a child.

Carefully, Nicolette arranges the orchids around her father's side of the grave. She is careful not to allow any of them to touch the segment of the plot beneath which she believes her mother lies buried. Though Nicolette does not enjoy consciously dwelling on the past, she has never permitted her father's grave to go without fresh flowers for a period longer than a week. She has never permitted weeds to overtake or obscure any part of the headstone.

Had her father died when she was a child, this would have been an act of benevolence.

Now, it is a show of force.

Nicolette completes the arrangement. She studies it. She ensures that every flower is in exactly the right place, to create the maximally pleasing aesthetic effect. When she is satisfied, she rises, and calmly addresses the grave.

"Where're your sluts now?"

The sun is descending below the horizon. Orange

beams penetrate Nicolette's back as she moves towards her van, tapping into the base of her spine and flooding her with electric vigor. It's time to go home and prepare.

———

"And that, *damen,* is how you use a bo staff." Ginny finishes swinging the broomstick, offers a polite bow to the girls, congregated around her in a semi-circle in the middle of the dining room. "Now, take that as your incentive. I expect you all to be ready for sparring next Friday and, if I'm impressed with what I see—and if I can track down enough broomsticks—I'll *consider*—that is a strong *consider, damen*—starting a few of you on weapons. Questions? No? Fabulous. This way!" Ginny leads the girls to a table in the corner of the dining room, haloed beneath a single operating light.

"You actually have to give a friend of mine credit for this," Ginny says, hovering over the table, meticulously moving bamboo around a little clay bowl, tired eyes studying each individual shoot to ensure that it's properly in place. "I hadn't really planned on this at all. Then we saw a movie this afternoon and, wham! Inspiration."

"Oooh, damn," Michelle says, "Miss Ginny has a *friend*." Numerous girls snicker; Shannon smirks, rolling her eyes. Ginny clears her throat, begins speaking above them, feeling her ears turning red.

"The Japanese have a legend, about Altair, Deneb, and Vega. Why are those names important? Candice?"

"Altair is the brightest star in Aquila and Vega is the brightest in… Orion?"

"Oh, sweetheart, you were very, very close. But that was good. Vega is the brightest star in Lyra. Now, Altair, Deneb, and Vega. The ancient Japanese had a legend that Altair and

Vega were lovers—the rancher and the weaver. The weaver was a princess, the daughter of the King of Heaven. She'd spend all of her time on the banks of the river, weaving and dying new clothes for her father, and he loved them and he loved her. But the weaver was sad because she was alone and wanted a husband, so her father arranged for her to meet the rancher, who lived across the river, by building a bridge—Deneb. They fell most passionately in love and married in secret but, they were so busy with one another, that the weaver stopped weaving and the rancher let his cows, like, shit all over Heaven. The King was super pissed so he separated them across the universe and made his daughter into Vega and the rancher into Altair, separated for all time by the Milky Way itself."

"This is so sad," Tammy says. "Why are you telling us this?"

"Patience is a virtue, *damen*. The story doesn't end there. The weaver continued to make garments for her father, but they were woven with her tears—tears of sadness that soaked into his skin and tore into his heart whenever he wore them. To please his daughter, he promised her that, on the seventh day of the seventh month of every year, she and the rancher would be together again. But only for that day." Ginny finishes her arrangement, steps back; she had sorry little practice with the art before arriving in New York, and now, in the absence of a book to use as reference, she isn't entirely certain that what she's accomplished is correct at all. "That's Tanabata—the Festival of Stars. We're about a month away, but I think in light of what's happening this Saturday, a celebration of the stars isn't out of place, is it, dear girls?"

"I guess not," Sandra says.

"Me neither. So let's allow Vega and Altair to come together a little earlier this year. Now, everyone come closer.

I want you to take a look at this. Ikebana is the Japanese art of flower arrangement. Regardless of the connotations our culture gives to men with an interest in flowers, ikebana was, in fact, a traditional a pastime of the Samurai: the warrior philosophers of feudal Japan."

"Like the Jedi," Candice says. Ginny cringes.

"No, no, *no,* darling, not at all like the Jedi; and pray tell where did you learn such an awful word?"

"Like, *Return of the Jedi,* man," Shannon says. "You mean you haven't seen it? You're always at the theater, I figured you were, like, eating that shit up. It's all outer space and rocket ships and…"

"*Return of the Shit-heap* is a much more accurate title, sweetheart. Fantasy is all well and good as long as you don't go gussying it up like science fiction. There is, like, a very definite line that should not be crossed. The… *Jedi…* belong riding white horses to rescue maidens from towers, not among the stars. Now let us never speak that name again, shall we? Besides, the Samurai were much more similar to the *Vulcans.* Anyway. On Tanabata, once an Ikebana arrangement has been made, you've got to make a wish and write it down and hang your wish on one of the bamboo shoots. When the weaver and the rancher are reunited, their joy will make all of the wishes come true." Ginny retrieves a little stationary pad, one of the Colonel's cursory gestures towards legitimacy. Tissue-thin, goldenrod paper bears at the top of the page the legend ST. JUDE'S in gothic lettering, surrounded on either side by a cluster of red, twisting vines. She distributes slips of paper along with the two-inch long pencils issued to every room.

"Here. Go ahead and write it, then fold it up. Don't let me see it, *damen*—that's between you and our celestial lovers."

The girls all begin writing on their respective slips,

some giggling, some taking on looks of somber earnestness. As each one finishes writing, she folds the paper into a little square and punches it over one of the bamboo shoots.

"And that brings our evening to a close, damen. Now, I hate to be the kind of woman to give out homework on the weekend, but I expect that most of you—*all of you?*—will be watching the space launch tomorrow morning anyway. If any of you weren't planning on it, I'm not making it a requirement, but extra credit goes to anyone who wants to discuss it on Monday. And no cheating by asking someone else to describe it. I'm looking at you, Sandra. Other than that: your quadratic equations worksheets are due next Wednesday, and remember, *show your work.* All right then. Class dis…"

"What about you?" Tammy asks.

"What, sweetheart?"

"You didn't write out a wish."

"I have all of you in my life, sweetheart. My wishes are fulfilled. But it is so sweet of you to think of me. Now. Class dismissed."

The girls file out, handing over their money to Ginny as they leave, Tammy giving a little, knowing nod as she hands over the thickest wad of bills of the evening. Once all of them have left, Ginny collates the night's kick up, retrieves the bamboo plant. As she's about to leave the dining room, she places everything down and tears off a sheet of stationary for herself. She begins to write something down, stops, laughs derisively at herself, at the whole exercise. She's about to wad the paper up when she hurriedly finishes writing, folds the paper into a little square, and shoves it over the top of one of the chutes. Then, she heads upstairs to collect her final wish of the evening.

———

Nicolette drives up 42nd for half an hour. She checks her father's watch. She has arrived too late to take another of The Girl's pack. Through careful observation, Nicolette has learned that they are diurnal. This does not disappoint her. She knows that The Girl is intelligent. She is observant. One or two of her bitches trailing away from the pack at a time will not draw her attention. To receive them in quick succession would be to awaken suspicion. She must receive tribute from elsewhere tonight. Her eyes dance across the billboards and marquees. She waits. Twinkling lightbulbs begin to flicker with greater urgency, drawing her near. Nicolette obeys.

Beneath the marquee, a small gaggle of pornai stand gathered together. No, they do not stand. They do not speak. They wallow. They squawk. They open their mouths and expose tongues glistening with filth. The City wants this. It begs Nicolette to take this wasted flesh.

Nicolette rolls down her window. She whistles. She is wearing a loose red polo shirt and a pair of jeans. Her pageboy is slicked flat against her head with pomade. With her flat breasts and square jaw and quiet warble, the image she presents is of a meek and needy little man desperate for what the refuge of the suburbs cannot provide.

One of the pornai approaches. She is slender and brown and shakes as she walks.

"What you need, baby?"

"Some company," Nicolette says.

"Oh, I bet you do, don't you, daddy?" The pornai says. "You need it real bad. I got your company, baby, I'll make you feel real good, you ain't gonna be alone anymore once Sheila get through with you. Come on, baby, what you need? French, Greek? Sheila does it all, baby."

"Around the world," Nicolette says. She extends a wad of soft, crumpled ten dollar bills. Nicolette learned early that fresh money arouses suspicion; has always made sure that her money isn't too new, like something a cop would offer. "This enough?"

"Baby, that enough for *two* trips."

Sheila moves around the passenger side of the van. Nicolette leans over, opens the door, lets her in. She shifts into drive and begins to move down 42nd and towards Hell's Kitchen.

"Call me Nic," Nicolette says.

"Call you anything you want, daddy."

"Don't call me daddy."

"Fine."

"Okay. Good."

"Don't go too far, sugar, I don't like going too far away from home. I'm gone too long, people wonder."

"We aren't going far," Nicolette says. "Somewhere private."

"Sugar, this thing here big enough, anywhere you take it is private."

Nicolette is silent. She looks for a poorly lit alleyway, one caked in sufficient shadow. Sometimes, the most vibrant colors of all are those found in the dark. They are the most powerful. Even Nicolette must sometimes cower in deference to them.

"Here," Nicolette says. She pulls the van into the alley and puts it into park. She does not switch off the engine. Sheila rises, begins to draw back the heavy cotton bedsheet which separates the front of the van from the rear.

"Wait," Nicolette says.

"I don't get paid to talk, sugar. I'm on the clock, see, I gotta make every second count."

Nicolette produces the wad of bills, offers some to the pornai. "Take them. We'll go when I'm ready. I'll make it worth it."

Sheila takes the bills. So easy.

"Do you like what you do?" Nicolette asks.

"I like eating, sugar."

"You could work."

"Honey, I don't know what you want to call it, but this here is work."

"It's spreading your legs," Nicolette says.

"You ain't got a problem with it."

"Do you like the way it tastes when they fill up your mouth?" Nicolette asks. Her voice does not waver. It does not raise an octave.

"You pay me enough, honey, I'll like whatever you ask me to like."

"Does it make you feel good? Eating filth? While other women work for their money?"

Sheila makes a face. Nicolette cannot register what emotion the pornai is attempting to convey. "Sugar, if this is your scene, you wanna talk to Delores. You can whip her till she bleed and she'll ask for more."

"I wasn't given Delores," Nicolette says. "I was given you. Now answer me. I'm paying you to answer me." Nicolette offers her another bill.

"Sugar, I don't love it, I don't hate it. I do what I gotta do."

"You don't *gotta* do anything," Nicolette says. The slurred word sounds unusual on her palette. "You had choices. Get in the back."

Throughout her life, displaying emotions has always been difficult for Nicolette. This is partially due to the concept of emotion itself being foreign to her. As a child, this was a matter of concern for her mother. Failing to have produced a child aesthetically worthy of her legacy, it had been the wish of Andrea Aster to at least raise up a girl with enough charm and social grace to make her place in society. She had attempted to train Nicolette in the art of conversation, proper etiquette, the correct manner in which to interact with boys. Nicolette had no concern for these social niceties. She had the Meadow and that was all that mattered. So it had been while the other girls of Long Island attended playdates, studied at prestigious schools, came out at debutante balls, Nicolette Aster, at last forsaken by her mother, spent her days motionless in the quiet sanctity of her father's office, her very presence a silent rebuke to his loathed wife. All the while, whatever capacity for expression the girl had harbored grew ever more stagnant, buried beneath layers of color, flashes of light; until the singular emotion the girl was left capable of expressing was an indistinct affection for the man whose office she occupied, conveyed in the simple little nod bestowed to him on entering and exiting the room.

Then that was gone, and all that was left was the emptiness within.

Until she had received tribute.

Nicolette reaches down beside her seat and retrieves the chemical rag. The pornai is moving through the bedsheet. She enters the back of the van, sees what is waiting there, makes a noise, a silly little noise of terror like its fear is anything more than animal surprise, and Nicolette is screaming with her, screaming with absolute and complete and all-consuming fury, her face as red as her shirt, the veins in her forehead and the sides of her neck bulging through her flesh.

"*Eat it, slut!*" Nicolette's voice descends into a guttural roar. She wraps the rag around the girl's head, her adrenal glands emptying themselves, her frail body suddenly possessing enough raw power to knock the pornai onto her knees. She wraps an arm around the pornai's throat and squeezes, holding the rag in place with the other hand, grinding her knee into the pornai's spine and the pornai is gagging and struggling and Nicolette's spit is running down her chin and onto her shirt and onto the pornai's back. She forces the pornai down onto her face, taking her hand away from the rag, punching the wretched thing in the back on the skull until it seems that any more force might prove detrimental to the hunt and Nicolette must stop herself. Nicolette screams again, punches the floor of the van, the side of the van, thrashes her feet out at the pornai. She grunts, low, raucous noises echoing up from the base of her throat and ascending into shrill ululations that rattle her body until the noise trails off and the inside of Nicolette Aster is as calm and still as a lake on a windless day. It's time to head out to the labyrinth.

———

"You have got to drink your water, Mary, sweetheart. Hydration is very important to you right now." Ginny looks up from tweaking her arrangement; has just finished recounting the Tanabata story, giving it a bit more of a flourish than she did for the rest of the girls. Mary looks somehow worse today than last night. Ginny had figured that an entire day of unconsciousness would do the girl some good, reinvigorate her, but instead she looks even more like a living corpse now than the ghouls in a Colossus matinee.

"I'm not really thirsty."

"And you won't be thirsty until you shrivel up dead from dehydration. You've got to keep drinking. And I expect you to try some eggs tomorrow morning."

"I don't think I can make it downstairs."

"I'll get someone to bring them to you." Ginny opens the bedside table, retrieves the stationary pad. She notices, with a small amount of resigned consternation, a little bookmark sticking out of the Gideon Bible, something homemade, a strip of fabric torn from some old garment and hot-glued to cardboard. From its placement, it appears that Mary has been perusing the Gospels.

"Here. Write your wish out. Good. I'll put it on for you; don't get up. Now, darling, I can't know what you wished for, but I do have something to act as a little encore to all of your fabulous, fabulous dreams coming true." Ginny goes to the bag she brought with her to Mary's room, brings it to the bed, dumps it out. The bills are all small denominations, but Ginny thinks that it's a better effect not to have rubber banded them together, their multitude masking the relatively small amount they represent. Mary's eyes go wide, the shock jerking her briefly into a sitting position before she slumps back down with a wince.

"What is this?"

"You've got a benefactor, sweetheart. Now, now, no names are going to be spoken, but I've made a little arrangement to make sure you leave our humble abode with nothing short of a pleasant nest egg."

"Leave?"

"You can't stay here much longer. I put in a word for you, but... Colonel's orders."

Though Mary is only inches away from Ginny on the bed, her stare seems to come from across galaxies, from across eons. "Ginny... I... I don't have anywhere to go."

"You're going to have the money to get anywhere you want to go. Why did you choose to come here, darling? Do you remember what you told me? The same reason anyone runs away to New York. Because you could *disappear* here. It's time to change that. You're going to leave here and you're going to stop being invisible. You're going to walk out of the shadows you've been sitting in. A little bit of makeup, a new haircut, and you can pass for eighteen, twenty-one wherever you go. We can get you an ID; I mean, it's the easiest thing in the world. A whole new you, Mary. Don't you get what this is? This is a gift, sweetheart. I know how terrible things are now, I know, but when you are on that bus, going to—I don't know, Seattle—do you have any idea what that's going to feel like? Every mile away from here is going to be a pound off your shoulders. And this is all going to be a bad dream, sweetie, everything from the past year, the girls, me, it's all going to be a nightmare. And you'll just be waking up to a beautiful sunrise."

"I wouldn't want to forget you, Ginny."

"You should and you will, sweetheart. Remember everything I taught you. Don't remember where you learned it. Here, get comfy." Ginny resituates herself, adjusts Mary so that her head is resting on her pillow. "A lesson, sweetheart, that is going to be one of the most important things I'll ever teach you. A lot of good things are going to come to you from, like, completely awful places. And the best thing you can ever do for yourself is figure out how to separate them."

Mary nuzzles her head against Ginny's hip, her eyes shutting, her body relaxing. "I don't think you're part of the bad, though, Ginny."

"You really haven't been paying attention, sweetheart."

———

On 42nd Street, Colonel Baniszewski does indeed own the day, his rivals the night. Yet, the treaty which ended the period of rape and bloodshed immediately preceding Ginny's arrival stipulated yet a third temporal division to be meted out to the interested parties: the weekends. As a concession to certain economic and logistic realities, it was agreed that the privileges of working The Deuce from Sunset Friday to Sunrise Monday would be shared on an alternating basis. While different pimps have seen fit over the years to break this aspect of the agreement, resulting in varying degrees of violence being dished out in the name of maintaining peace and civility, Ginny has ensured that the Colonel's girls never work in violation of the treaty. Part of this is a practical matter. She desires, above all else, the peaceful maintenance of The Deuce status quo, of business continuing to flow as it has for the past three years, without the threat of violence coming down on herself or the girls.

She also desires a break once in a while.

These weekend reprieves are not solely for Ginny's benefit, though. While she takes advantage of the break to let her body heal, to indulge herself in two days of sleeping in, drinking, reading, and conducting experiments in the kitchen (she is still waiting for the City of New York's reply to her study on the water composition at the Misanthrope), it is also the only time that she has any significant opportunity to take Tricia beyond the confines of the hotel. To indulge in something more than a midnight stroll or an impromptu field trip to the Met, to spend time with her in the open, in the daylight, not as a caretaker but as a girl enjoying the weekend with her sister.

"Let the fattening begin!" Ginny shouts as she enters the apartment, the pizza box held aloft, bottles of Labatt's balanced precariously atop it. Friday night pizza is a Kurva family tradition that Ginny has transported to New York, one of the few fragments of her childhood that she's bothered to carry with her. Growing up, Friday meant the end of a long, dedicated week of studies, a late Saturday morning her reward for scholastic success, preceded by long hours spent in the backyard with her telescope and her transistor radio and her animal crackers. Friday nights were, to Ginny, almost as spiritual as Sunday morning Mass, a time that made her think that the old Jews were right that it's the true Sabbath, possessing an innate holiness woven into the very fabric of the day. While the experience has diminished for her since her time in New York, she has attempted, to the best of her abilities, to keep the tradition alive, and, in doing so, recapture a dull glimmer of that lost brush with the divine.

"Preparations set!" Tricia responds, snaps the waistband of her sweatpants. "If these still fit in the morning, it means the night was, like, a total waste."

"Waste? Waste is *exactly* what we are going to do with the night. We are not going to sleep until the pizza is gone, the beers are gone, we are sick, bloated, and too drunk to move and we have absolutely no reason to live anymore. That is how we are spending the rest of our evening. And have you, dear sister, taken on the momentous task of developing our itinerary?"

"Prepare yourself for a trip down memory lane... A memory lane soaked in *blood*." Tricia rolls to the VHS player, piled high with video cassettes, some store bought, others bootlegged, commercially unavailable releases obtained from Roger in exchange for old comic books, unwanted records, Tricia's long neglected and strangely amalgamated GI Joe and Barbie collection. "We begin our evening with *The Umbrellas of Cherbourg,* starring a butt ton of sexy French people and a butt ton of French butts."

"Body count?"

"None! But that's, like, just the appetizer to get us all depressed and sad before we move on to, drumroll please, *Escape from New York,* starring, sigh, Mr. Kurt Russel and enough guns to overthrow a small island republic—always a dream of mine, you know."

Ginny puts the pizza on the table, opens it; the smell of anchovies and Canadian bacon explodes from the box, instantly permeating the room. She bends down over the pizza, inhales deeply, sighs contentedly. "Death toll?"

"*Innumerable.* Then, to stop us from growing hair on our tits, we move on to the–*boo hoo*– 1968 classic *Sweet November,* starring, sigh, Anthony Newley and the remarkable Ms. Sandy Dennis. Aaaand, drum roll please, so that we don't end the evening on a, like, completely dismal note, I present to you a personal favorite of mine, and I hope it's one of yours too…"

"Bestill my ever-loving heart."

"…*Bring me the Head of Alfredo Garcia.* Enough dead bodies to totally clog the Rio Grande, brought to your courtesy of, drumroll please, Mr. Warren Oates."

Ginny clicks her tongue, takes a drink of her beer. "There was a man who did not look good with a mustache." She looks around the kitchen, seeking something out, doesn't find it, returns to the living room. "Where's your potato clock?"

"Hmmm?"

"Your homework assignment. I always go easy on you on Fridays. Today you were supposed to do some reading and make your potato clock. Where is it?"

Tricia holds up a finger, guzzles beer, Ginny sighing, waiting, putting her hands on her hips as Tricia continues guzzling, stops when the bottle is empty. She plucks it out of her mouth and belches, loudly. "I ate it."

"What?"

"All of that, like, fiddling with a potato made me want a potato. So, I ate it. But, I totally took pictures of it, so I could, like, prove to you that I finished it, like a good widdle student. They're next to the toaster."

Ginny returns to the kitchen, looks beside the toaster,

finds there a pile of neatly stacked polaroid photos. The first: The potato clock, fully assembled on the kitchen table, half of Tricia's face in frame, giving a thumb's up to the camera. The second: The potatoes, cooked, in a pair of bowls, split down the middle and slathered with butter. The third: Tricia shoveling a forkful of potato into her mouth, again giving a thumb's up to the camera. The fourth...

"Why did you take a picture of your armpit?"

Maniacal laughter emanates from the living room, Tricia attempting to interject words, failing, the laughter rising in pitch and psychosis. Ginny, confused, looks to the living room, back to the photo, realizes what she's really staring at and tosses the stack down in disgust. When she returns to the living room, she thrusts the plate of pizza perhaps a bit too harshly into Tricia's lap. "Omigawsh, really?"

...and the pictures and the potato and the homework really stop mattering by the time Tricia gets *Sweet November* rolling and the pair are transported back through time into the Technicolor world of their girlhood, Ginny realizing by this point that there's no way they are ever going to make it to *Alfredo Garcia*. The pizza: completely gone, the box picked clean of cheese, the Labatt's depleted, and she's sitting in front of her sister on the floor, a salad bowl inverted on her head, Tricia trimming the fringe of her hair around the perimeter of the bowl.

"This is *not* making me sad," Tricia says, pushing herself forward to try and get a better view of Ginny's bangs. "I just need you to know that. I, like, totally do *not* cry at movies."

"Don't you dare fuck this up," Ginny sniffs. "Don't you... dare."

"Do you... do you really need a haircut? I mean, like, right now?"

"...Yes," Ginny says, sniffs again, wipes her nose with

the back of her forearm.

And onscreen November is winding down and Sandy Dennis is telling Anthony Newley that the night is over, the month is over, she has done all that she can for him but it's over now, and Anthony Newley is indignant and telling Sandy Dennis that it isn't fair he has to go, and Sandy Dennis is telling him that she is sorry but it is for the best, he has to go, that he has to leave now, that she's done all she can for him and she's sorry but he's on his own now, and Mary is saying where am I going to go, why are you making me leave, and Sandy Dennis is saying that your time is up, you've got to move on now and Anthony Newley is trying to be stoic, trying to pretend he can make it now, walking out into the snow, leaving Sandy behind, leaving her behind to die while he wanders into the night. Ginny sobs, curling forward towards the carpet, Tricia watching her sister go in mid snip, the bowl rolling off of her head and towards the television.

"Hey, like, are you okay?"

And Ginny is on her stomach now looking up at her sister and she isn't on the grass in the backyard anymore and, really, since she left home three years ago, there haven't been any Friday nights.

———

Though the pack has provided her with unforeseen benefits in her reception of tribute, Nicolette has had to alter the ceremony accordingly to compensate for some of their behavior. In the early days, when there had only been one or two dogs, Nicolette had simply dumped the tribute at the center of the labyrinth before retreating to don her vestments. By the time she was dressed, the tribute would be awakening, and the hunt could commence. Since the number of dogs has increased, so has their territorialism. During the Last Cycle, they had shredded pornai before they even regained consciousness. Though the resultant mess had provided Nicolette with no small amusement, the subsequent meal was highly unsatisfying, and she'd set about at once reconfiguring the ceremony. Trial and error have demonstrated that the most effective process is to don her vestments while the pornai is still in the van with her. By the time she is complete, they have just begun to stir, and then she can toss them out the back and wait for them to fully awaken, and begin the hunt before the dogs sense their presence. This has proven beneficial in more ways than one. The process of getting dressed is time consuming, and, in the early days, permitted the tributes too much lead time. Now, she can watch them as she prepares.

During the scant time she spent in schools, between therapy sessions, periods of isolation, and institutionalization, Nicolette's favorite subject had been shop, and she had applied whatever academic acumen she possessed almost solely within the confines of the wood and metal working studios. The display of one of her welding efforts at a campus art show resulted in what was perhaps her mother's sole moment of parental pride. Following the revelation in the landfill three years ago, Nicolette had set about constructing vestments for herself using these skills, both as a means of protection and as a way to properly convey the right amount of ceremony to the occasion.

She wants the pornai to be able to see her true self; she wants them to know to whom they are being offered.

Hurriedly, Nicolette strips, quick to begin pulling on her armor so as not to be nude in the presence of the pornai for too long. Her pants and shirt are constructed of thick leather shafts chosen by Nicolette for their flexibility and durability. She must be able to move swiftly but be protected from blows in the event that the tributes attempt to delay their fate. Next come the motorcycle boots. Nicolette had initially considered cowboy boots, but found them to be too lightweight for her purposes, too flamboyantly decorative in their aesthetics. Too, none of them had thick enough of a heel; and the metal loop found at the side of the motorcycle boots is congruent with the rest of her vestments.

Next, Nicolette dons her helmet. She must place the helmet on before her gauntlets because the helmet fastens to the back of her head by way of a series of leather straps which she cannot properly buckle with gloved hands. The helmet proved to be the most difficult part of the vestments to construct, and it is the item of which she is the most proud. After consulting myriad historical texts for inspiration, waiting for the proper sign, one photograph in particular had illuminated itself for her, rising from the page in three dimensions and arcing to life in her living room, hovering in the air above her couch and bursting into flames of the brightest magenta. It was the helmet of a samurai warrior, held on display in the museum at Osaka. It met nearly all of the criteria for displaying her true face, both in the Meadow and the world beyond. It covered the entire head; it was designed to accommodate a pair of ceremonial horns attached to the temporal portions of the helmet. The circular shape of the eye holes even provided Nicolette with a template for inserting a pair of corrective lenses, when her early prototypes had demonstrated that she would not be able to wear her glasses beneath the helmet. Only one aspect of the design was lacking; Nicolette rectified this after the pricey acquisition of a real bull's head from one of the state's most renowned taxidermists. Once she had cast the muzzle and attached it to the helmet's maw, she knew that she had at last constructed a tangible representation of her true self. For several weeks afterwards, she had returned home from work and immediately placed the helmet on, until the horns—removed from the bull's head and mounted to the helmet—had proven too difficult to maneuver through her doorways and she'd had to saw them down into stumps.

Once she has put her gauntlets on, Nicolette crouches and waits. She contemplates where the axe will strike first. Sometimes she likes to begin by taking out the knees, forcing the pornai to squirm along the ground like the worms they are. Other times she enjoys striking first at one of their arms, a shoulder or elbow, severing the limb, watching them clutch desperately at the stump with their remaining hand, attempting to stop the flow of blood while still fleeing. On rarer occasions, when the essence of the pornai is particularly infuriating, and their mere proximity is enough to stoke the flames within Nicolette, she will simply bury the axe in their heads and be done with it. She isn't sure yet what she will do to this one.

Nicolette opens the rear of the van and shoves the pornai out. Then she situates herself in the driver's seat and pulls the van away. Once she has reached an appropriate distance from the center of the labyrinth, she shuts off the van and exits. She retrieves her axe from the rear of the van. Like the helmet, Nicolette cast it herself from bronze. The design is called the *labrys*. It dates to the ancient days of the Cretan civilization. It has two heads. Standing here holding it, the visage of the moon reflected in her lenses, the first snarling sounds of the dogs beginning to echo through the rose bushes and over the verdant hills of the Labyrinth, Nicolette Aster feels at peace. She feels herself. She is reminded of what she read in her office that day, years ago. What had drawn her out into the landfill, to find this place; to find her destiny.

Though the ancients had saddled Minos' stepchild with the sobriquet *Minotaur,* meaning "Minos' Bull," the king had granted a proper name at birth, lost to all but those who faithfully studied the lore of antiquity.

The child had been named *Aster*ion.

She is the Mighty Minotaur.

Tonight, she shall receive her tribute.

Nicolette charges forward, horns brushing against rose bushes, hooves treading through soft grass. She charges through the halls of the great labyrinth, rising up towards the Heavens, following the sound of vicious barks and the terrified shrieks of the pornai. Nicolette's hearing is excellent; she knows which direction to turn at any given intersection, when to head left or right, when to double back. She knows the halls and contours of the labyrinth as well as her own hands; there are no hiding places here, no corners of refuge, no undiscovered corridors in which to cower and wait for the morning light. Every pathway here leads onto one place: to the end of the axe; to the shedding of blood and the splitting of flesh; to the death agonies befitting the wasted life of the pornai.

It has been many years since Nicolette Aster was sent away to the institution; since her father sat her down and explained to her that in her mother's absence he needed *company,* that he needed *companionship,* that her presence would prove difficult for him to achieve that, and as her father he felt it best she go someplace to get well, someplace where the nice doctors and nurses might be able to help her. The only help there had been to sleep; to sleep and half-dream while drugged senseless in a small, white room, the lack of colors deafening, blinding, that agony only slightly greater than that of the strange nurses who wandered in and out and stripped her writhing body to change and bathe her. Her only company were the puzzle books and felt tipped pens they handed out to occupy everyone's time. On her release at twenty-one—an event roughly concurrent with her father's death from overdose in the bed of a sixteen-year-old pornai—the maid's tales had been borne out by bank statements and credit bills, of how her father had enjoyed his *company,* the endless parade of *pornai* who had cavorted in every room of the home and sprawled across the desk of the once quiet office.

The pornai belong to her now.

Now they will find their purpose.

Nicolette rounds a corner, sees tails disappearing around another corner, hears the scream of the pornai. She reaches down to her belt, retrieves the dog whistle, inserts the end of it through the hole in her muzzle, blows. The dogs shriek; she blows again. They come barreling back towards her, past her, retreating in terror and pain at the sound only their ears can perceive. Once the last of the bitches have left, Nicolette charges forward. Her legs propel her with strength unknown to mortals. Sweat drips down her face and off the tip of her chin. The pornai is before her, stumbling, toppling forward and catching herself, and then righting herself and then running again. The blade of the axe grazes her back, tearing a strip of fabric from the back of her shirt, taking a sliver of flesh with it. The pornai screams and breaks into a sprint. Nicolette follows. Her senses are keener than the pornai's. Her body is stronger and more well-conditioned. She has run these halls for millennia; she will run for them millennia more; she will not be bested by some scrap of humanity, running for her useless life, wishing only to survive long enough to choke down one last cock.

The pornai stumbles. Nicolette sees her ankle twist, the foot jerk at a gruesome right angle, the pornai's weight collapse on top of it. The pornai screams; she drags herself forward, blood trickling out of the minor wound on her back. She turns around, looks up at Nicolette, shaking her dirty little head, all caked in garbage and stink. In the light of the quarter moon, Nicolette can see fat, little tears rolling down the pornai's face.

"Please, oh God, please, don't do this!" The pornai blubbers. "I'll do anything, please!"

Of course you will, Nicolette thinks.

Then she swings the axe down into the thing's belly.

The pornai screams, an ululating noise pathetic in its intensity, that something so feeble and worthless could be capable of projecting so powerful a sound. Nicolette steps back; leaves the axe buried in the pornai's midsection, blood gushing out around it, the soft, brown little body pumped full of filth, spilling out its life in gallons by the minute. She watches the pornai squirm, groping at the axe blade, trying to yank it out as she scoots backwards on the ground.

As though mere inches will protect her.

Nicolette steps forward, raises a hoof, and brings it down onto the pornai's face. There is a satisfying crunch when the pornai's nose flattens; an orgiastic chill bursts forth from the base of Nicolette's skull and floods her bloodstream, her thighs and her abdomen and her breasts, twitching and coursing with paralytic splendor. She moans, long and low, raising her hoof and bringing it down again. The pornai writhes as her jaw breaks and Nicolette is racked again with delight. Nicolette keeps stomping until she is stomping her hoof into the earth. Then she stops. She steps back. She watches.

From where the pornai has fallen, the new attendant rises. She has been purified by her sacrifice. She is dressed in beautiful white. Her body projects an aura of crippling cobalt and meridian. No man has ever known her new body; none ever will. Where her face would be in the world beyond The Meadow—the world of imperfection—there is hollowness. Nicolette removes one gauntlet and checks her father's watch. The hunt lasted a good while. She is satisfied.

Nicolette and the new attendant lift the body from the ground and carry it to The Altar. Before the great structure, Nicolette bows and gives thanks to The City for its tribute. She is well pleased. The attendant watches in reverent awe, her fellow ladies greeting her, welcoming her into service. Then they gather together around their master. They help her disassemble the body of the pornai. The meal will provide Nicolette with great vigor. She will be able to color in another box in her grid tomorrow. The City owes her ten more tributes in this month of Skirophorion.

Then, she will have The Girl.

5

Saturday, June 18th, 1983

THE CLOCK IS BUZZING IN THE BEDROOM, RICOCHETING again and again against Ginny's eardrums, and even through the nearly impenetrable slog of her hangover, she knows what the sounds mean, what they signify, and she is peeling her face off of the carpet with perhaps a little more ease than she normally would, enjoying a little more vigor than would be customary on any other weekend morning, the sun not yet having risen over the skyline of 42nd street.

"Trish," Ginny slurs, maneuvering herself to the couch. She shakes her sister's shoulders, neglecting to notice or care that the salad bowl has somehow transported itself onto Tricia's head. "Trish. Triiiiicia. Patricia Kurva. Wakeup. Wakeup. It's almost time. The space launch is happening ..." Ginny checks her watch. "Soon."

Tricia fails to respond. Ginny grabs one shoulder, shakes her. Tricia comes to with a start, grabs the salad bowl off of her head.

"I didn't do it!"

"...Didn't do what?"

"Where am I?" Tricia asks.

Ginny grabs the salad bowl from her hands, sticks it back on her head, staggers to the shower. Although she bathed last night, sleeping on the floor has left her feeling inappropriately prepared for such a momentous occasion. Once she's dried off, she hurries to the bedroom, dresses quickly; the electric blue suit she puts on was her Christmas present to herself last year, purchased secondhand and altered by Michelle to fit her figure, a near exact replica of the one worn by Princess Diana when she appeared on the cover of Time Magazine two Aprils ago. Ginny makes a mental note to herself to introduce the Princess into the pantheon of female role models she has been developing for her sister; play on Tricia's love of the fantastic, the common woman who became a princess, through personal charm and proper manner and, most importantly of all, Ginny thinks, not at all without a good foundation of dance experience and a passion for teaching...

"Hey! Hey, come on!" Ginny says as she enters the living room, Tricia slouched over on the couch now, the salad bowl still on her head. Ginny sits beside her on the couch, shakes her.

"Omigsawh, wake me up when something interesting is happening."

"Come on. You need to see this. You'll regret it later if you don't. This is, like, your moon landing." Ginny smiles, briefly lost in memory, for a split second seven years old again and kneeling on the floor inches away from the television, squeezing Mrs. Butter Bunny, Tricia crying from some other room and dad telling her to move so everyone else could see too, and Ginny not particularly caring to mind anyone that night, her front row seat well worth being sent to her room afterwards.

Tricia rights herself begrudgingly, takes the bowl off of her head, rubs her eyes. Ginny switching on the television, darting to the kitchen to fetch coffee.

"What's happening?"

"Omigawsh, I think, like, you have the wrong channel."

Ginny panics. "What? What's happening?"

"A bunch of ugly people are all getting into an RV together. Omigawsh, I think this is, like, porno. Dammit, bitch, you didn't tell me we could get porn here!"

Ginny rushes into the living room, looks at the television, slaps her sister on the back of the head.

"Those're the astronauts being transported to the launch site."

"Well, burst my little bubble."

Ginny returns to the kitchen, retrieves the coffee, settles down on the couch beside Tricia. She takes a long gulp, recording in her mind the way that the light looks in the room right now, the smell of sweat and beer and fish coming off of Tricia, the dull footsteps out in the hallway, "Mexican Radio" on the Misanthrope sound system. As much of her life as she willfully forgets, she wants to remember this morning until the day she dies.

"Tricia," Ginny puts an arm around her sister, slouch shouldered, loudly sipping her coffee, staring bug-eyed at the television, "I want you to know that I'm so happy to be here with you right now. This is... such a great moment in history, and... I'm glad I get to experience it with you."

"Geez, Dad, don't get all emotional."

"I don't know why you aren't more interested in this. You like *X-Men*. They're sort of sci-fi."

"Hey, sis? When we send a bunch of mutants into space, and they're going up there because a crazy Holocaust survivor who can bend metal wants to blow up the moon? Front row seats. My treat. Some guy with a porno mustache who is, like, most totally not going up there to ball? Bzzzzz. Wrong answer."

On the television, the countdown has begun, the Florida sky just beginning to light up with candy-colored hues of tangerine and cornflower. Ginny puts her coffee down, clasps her hands together. Her whole body tingles; any sensation of drunkenness is gone, any thoughts of her life outside this room eradicated. She feels completely the privilege of this moment, of being born into the tail end of a century in which women have bled and died to vote, to work, to learn, to expand their possibilities beyond the confines of the kitchen and the birthing bed, to be one of the first generations to enjoy the benefits of her foremothers' struggles. It pleases Ginny to cease feeling a sense of her own individuality; to think of herself on this morning not as a woman but as part of the collective of women, mothers in bedrooms rocking babies in suburban homes and the engineers parked before small computers glowing green in dark rooms, and business owners and managers with shoulder pads far wider than her own, bag ladies pushing shopping carts across deserted parking lots against ghost gray skies and old grandmothers in television rooms waiting for the family to visit, little girls picking up their first books or first microscopes or pushing the buttons on a toy cash register. At this moment, Ginny is all of these people and they are her, and all of them together are Sally Ride and so while it may be her body riding the Challenger this morning she will not be alone. It will be all of them travelling together, breaching the confines of the terrestrial world, venturing into the final frontier and becoming one with the cosmos. There are no whores this morning, on Earth or in the Heavens. Only possibility, only knowledge, only pure, white light.

The thrusters ignite; Ginny digs her nails in to the sofa cushion. The Challenger lifts up from the launch pad, travelling, travelling, soaring onward and upward and Ginny has got her hands in front of her face now, tears rolling down her cheeks, and while trying not to sob, she's saying, "Oh my God, oh my God," and though she hasn't prayed for ages, there is some acknowledgement of the holy in her words, some awe at the splendor of creation and the possibilities of the human spirit, and Tricia opens her mouth, means to say something crass to this—an orgasm joke is her initial reaction—but then she shuts her mouth and she smiles, and puts a hand on her sister's thigh.

"It's so beautiful," Ginny says.

"Yeah, sis. Yeah it is. I love you, too."

———

As Ginny has long planned, she takes her sister to the roof of the Misanthrope after the completion of the launch. She wants to look at the sky; to look out into the atmosphere and know that just beyond the reach of her sight and mind, the Challenger is drifting in orbit, imagine that she is looking at the same sky that little girls all over the world are looking at, and feel the same sense of wonder they are feeling, the same sense she once felt before possibility became impossibility.

The sky above 42nd street is overcast this morning, the clouds so thick and densely packed as to give the impression that it's evening rather than just past sunrise. Ginny breathes deep, sighs, content, glad for even a mild reprieve from the heat. She throws her arms wide, squeals with joy, runs across the roof of the building, head back, watching the subtle undulations and flow of the cloud coverage. She imagines herself falling up, gravity reversing, pushing her upward, flying as she would swim in water, kicking and twirling and spinning in the sky, pleasantly adrift away from the confines and troubles of the world beneath.

"She did it, she did it, she did it!" Ginny leaps in the air, lands on her toes, *entrechats* and *assembles* around the roof before performing a *grand jeté* that lands her back in front of her sister. Tricia claps politely.

"We need, like, a space launch every day. You are, like, so much happier on space launch than on booze. Do they sell space launch at the corner store?"

Ginny bends down, hugs her sister, points up at the sky. "That's your future up there, too. There isn't anything that is ever going to stop you, okay? Anything you want, Trish, you can make it happen."

"Anything I want?"

"Yes."

"I… I…. I want to make love with Al Pacino."

Ginny pats her sister's face. "Babe, you're bigger than US steel."

Something hits Ginny then, on the tip of her nose, a little prick like a needle, followed by another. She wonders if she's had enough to drink this morning; looks at her hands to see if they're shaking. Raindrops land in her palms, settling in the lines, rolling out towards her wrists and dripping onto the roof. She looks at her sister, sees them beginning to splatter against Tricia's cheeks and lips and soak into the fabric of her t-shirt.

"Oh, gnarly. You are, like not using this as an excuse not to shop."

Ginny frowns, stands. The fear that gripped her bowels a moment ago releases, dissipates, replaced by a vast and cavernous sadness swelling inside of her. The rain intensifies, a soft roar in the air as the smattering of droplets becomes a downpour. Tricia spins herself in her chair, wheels towards the roof access.

"Come on or, like, you're going to get pneumonia. And I, like, cannot take care of you. You think *I'm* difficult? You would be, like impossible."

"Just a second." Ginny's voice is so quiet when she says this, the exuberance of a moment ago so abruptly sapped, that Tricia stops herself in her tracks, spins back around to face her sister.

"Hey... Are you... like, okay?"

"Yeah." Ginny rises from her kneeling position, puts her head back for a moment. "I just want to stand here for a minute. I like the way this feels."

"Sure."

Ginny opens her mouth and lets the rain pour in. It was hope against hope that she decided to turn today into the festival of Tanabata; to spit into the face of Roger Neiderman and his silly fears and weird predictions. Although she thoroughly recalled the story and traditions of the festival to the girls yesterday, what she neglected to tell them was this: That in addition to using the day before Tanabata to arrange flowers and make wishes, it is also a day of prayer. The people of Japan spend the day before Tanabata praying that it will not rain. For it to rain on Tanabata is disastrous; if it does, the river will rise, and the Milky Way itself will flood. The rancher and the weaver must wait another year to be reunited; nobody's wishes will come true.

The rain continues on, as it will for the remainder of the morning. Ginny stands in it, arms at her sides, until all of the tension that has risen up inside of her has dissipated, until the urge to scream or cry or thrash at the ground has gone, and all that is left inside of her is an eerie stillness that flows from the base of her skull down into the tips of her toes and fingers.

Ginny strides to her sister, shakes her head beneath the awning, splattering Tricia with the water flying off of her hair. "All right. So, like, I promised, so, I guess it's time to go get you some new comics."

———

It's a misconception that the experience of living on 42nd invariably corrupts all innocence; despite the amount of drugs in which they indulge, the diseases they contract, and the acts they commit in order to survive, the children who flock here from around the country are, still, ultimately children and still possess a child's desire for amusement and escape: a taste for sweets, a love of sports, a predilection towards games and entertainment. So even here, amongst the pornography theaters and crack dens, there still exist—indeed, thrive—the same hangouts and retreats to be found in any part of the world: video arcades and hamburger stands, magic shops, toy stores. Tricia Kurva's weekend destination of choice is the Hobbs' End comic emporium. It is, perhaps, the last place on 42nd street where one can engage in an earnest conversation on the merits of DC versus Marvel, Batman versus Superman, Kane vs. Kirby and Lee without the looming threat of sexual violence. It's to Ginny's great appreciation that the proprietor, an elderly man with a fondness for unbuttoned Hawaiian shirts and sunglasses worn indoors, has imposed a zero tolerance policy for any untoward conduct on his premises, which he liberally enforces with an aluminum baseball bat kept behind the counter. Whatever their lives on the street, once they step through the door, the patrons of Hobbs' End are children again, if only for the duration of their visit.

The rain has begun to diminish by the time Ginny and Tricia approach Hobbs' End, albeit barely. Ginny holds a transparent plastic umbrella over her head and follows tightly behind her sister to keep the both of them dry. While Ginny has been lost in her own ruminations since leaving the Misanthrope, her enthusiasm seems to have been transferred to Tricia, whom Ginny doesn't believe has been silent for more than a minute since their departure.

"...So then, like, they have to send Kitty Pryde back in time, okay? Because, like, her power's intangibility, okay? And..."

"How can intangibility be a super power?" Ginny asks. "Intangibility is a concept. You can't have a concept as a super power."

"Omigawsh, she can, like, move through anything, , like, walls or time or..."

"So she can quantum tunnel," Ginny says.

"That is, like, so totally not the point, okay? You're always on about how there are no, like, girl heroes, and this one is all about a girl hero, because Kitty Pryde's the only one who can go back to the 80s from the future and, like, stop Mystique from killing this senator. So, the hero *and* the villain are women, which you should think is, like, totally awesome."

"It's still within the context of a male-dominated series. This is only special *because* the women are getting center stage. I'd still prefer it if you read series *about* female heroes, not series that decided to make a big deal out of it when they feature them once in a while."

"Omigawsh, you have got to, like, nerd all over everything I love, don't you?"

"Oh, totally. I am *so* objecting at your wedding."

"And I am, like, so totally poisoning your glass at the reception."

"I'll switch it with the groom's."

"Then we'll get old together and go all *Baby Jane*."

"Fine."

"Fuck yo— Omigawsh, is that, like, Roger?"

On the corner outside of Hobbs' End is Roger Neiderman, a windbreaker pulled over his head, staring into space, smoking, trying and failing to whistle the Old Spice jingle, his eyes obscured behind a pair of mammoth, wraparound sunglasses. Tricia springs into action, propelling herself away from Ginny too quickly for her sister to object. Ginny bolts after her, the umbrella flapping by the wayside in the process, the result being that both Kurva sisters have become thoroughly soaked by the time they reach Roger.

"Well, hello, sailor," Tricia purrs. "What're you doing standing out on street corners? Don't you know you'll give a girl the wrong impression?"

"What?" Roger, taken off guard, turns, slams his hip into the building. Tricia giggles wickedly. "Oh, ah, hey there kid. How you doing?" He looks up at Ginny, smiles. "Ah, hey. What, ah, what brings you ladies out on this cheery afternoon?"

"I'm desperately ill," Tricia says. "I'm in grave need of a shot of vitamin R."

Ginny's face reddens. It's the '79 church picnic all over again.

"What?" Roger asks. He lifts his sunglasses, exposing his hyper magnified eyes.

"My, what big eyes you have," Tricia says.

"I'm a plus-eight hyperope. My eyeballs are too small so they focus images behind the retina instead of…"

"*No, no, no, sweetheart,*" Tricia says. The voice coming out of her mouth is a dead imitation of Ginny's. "You're supposed to say, *the better to see you with, my dear.*"

"Is she serious?" Roger asks Ginny.

"She is *not.* Now, *love,* hasn't your *darling* sister been teaching you proper etiquette so that you don't make everyone think that you were raised by wolves? If you want to make an impression on someone, show them a special talent or skill. Now, Roger's been very interested in the progress of your German. Why don't you show that off? Tell Roger 'Hello, beautiful weather, isn't it?'"

"*Kommen sie hier, bitte, mit der hosen in der hand.*"

"*Dammit!*" Ginny flicks the back of Tricia's ear with her index finger. "*Where do you learn this?*"

"Ow! You bitch!" Tricia lifts herself up on the arms of her chair, turning awkwardly to flail at Ginny. Ginny swats at her sister's hand, ears growing redder by the moment, Roger watching in stunned bemusement.

"Is this a bad day?"

"Not at all, sweetheart," Ginny says, gripping Tricia's shoulders, forcing her down into her chair. "We had an absolutely *fabulous* morning—*didn't we?*— and now we're out for an afternoon of leisure and shopping. Aren't we, *dear sister?*"

"She's trying to kidnap me. Get me out of here and I'll do anything. *Anything.*"

"...And after darling, *darling* Tricia has found everything she's looking for here, we'll be headed for a luxurious lunch followed by an evening of drinks and fine conversation. A positively cultured Saturday in New York for a couple of young women of the 80s."

"Oh. Okay." Roger nods. "Cool." He shifts from foot to foot, about to say something when he stops abruptly and looks into the unnavigable sea of traffic congesting the street in front of Hobbs' End.

"What's the matter, sweetheart?"

"I, ah, I just feel like someone's watching us."

"Nonsense, sweetheart. I would know it. You have been watching too many horror movies, haven't you?"

"Sure." He looks back at traffic, winces. "You two, ah, wanna go inside? I think the rain's going to start picking back up." He moves to open the door; Tricia scoots her chair in front of him, grabs the handle, flings it open. "After you."

"Oh, shit. Getting strong over there. One of these days,

ah, you're gonna be able to bench press me." The inside of the store is cramped, the floor space dominated by narrow aisles and racks of comic books, records, cassette tapes. Roger waves to the man behind the counter, the man waving in return, going back to looking down at the newspaper spread out before him.

"Let me hit you," Tricia says.

"Tricia," Ginny mutters. "Stop asking people to let you hit them. It's embarrassing."

"Ah, okay." Roger kneels down next to the chair, angles his shoulder towards Tricia. "Here, go on." Tricia giggles, pulls her arm back, punches Roger. The sound is audible. Ginny sighs; Roger flinches. "Ah, damn." He looks up to Ginny. "You got the next Muhamad Ali over here."

"We're all very proud."

"Hey, hey," Tricia says. "You and Ginny like really gnarly horror movies, right? With, like, lots of blood and shit?"

"Ah, yeah?"

"You wanna see me stab myself? I mean, like, in the leg? I so totally won't feel it. Just get me a pen…"

"Tricia, sweetheart, why don't you go start stocking up? I've got some things I'd like to discuss with Roger."

"Okay." Tricia begins to wheel away. Ginny starts to relax, the embarrassment that has coiled itself up in her shoulders and neck beginning to subside. Just as Tricia begins to disappear around the corner of an aisle, she stops her chair, pivots around, and shouts out to Roger: "Her favorite color is red, her favorite song is "Skateaway," her favorite movie is *2001* and she's an Aquar-i-usssss."

Roger and Ginny look at one another a moment. Roger is the first to break the silence.

"I, ah, I think she might have ruptured my deltoid."

"She really does think the world of you, darling. You have positively been a lifeline to her, you know. She loves her soap operas, but without her records and her comics I really don't think she'd hold on as well as she does."

"She's a really great kid. You, ah, you've done a really great job with her."

It seems to Ginny that sufficient pleasantries have been exchanged. She smiles, tosses her hair. "You have an absolutely uncanny talent for weather forecasting, you know that? You've really got to tell me how that works."

"Just, ah, just hunches, I guess. I ah, I used to like to read Almanacs when I was a kid."

"And pray tell, sweetheart, is there anything else that you'd like to make a prediction about?"

"Well, I, ah... what?"

"Seen any more of your green van?" Ginny opens her purse, rummages around inside, comes out with her cigarettes. She's putting one into her mouth when the man behind the counter begins shouting:

"Hey! Hey! Don't ruin the goods!"

"I wouldn't dream of it, darling!" Ginny kicks the door open with her foot, stands across the threshold, holding her cigarette out the lit door. "Now, anything?"

"Nothing."

"So you think it was nothing after all."

Roger shrugs. "I don't know."

"'I don't know' is not an acceptable answer after you've laid life and death on the table, darling. We're dealing in absolutes now."

Roger looks out the window, then down at the ground, everywhere around the shop except at Ginny. Then he clears his throat, grunts, and looks at her slightly below the eyes. "Reggie Washington."

"Yes?" Ginny recognizes the name as one of the Colonel's nighttime counterparts.

"One of his girls, this girl named Sheila, so, like, she's

like also his girlfriend, right? And, ah, so, like apparently, last night, she doesn't come home either. And, ah, one of the other girls, she says she saw Sheila talking to some guy she says is a weirdo. Now, ah, Reggie's girls, they do some freaky shit, right…?"

Ginny's brow knits. "*Do they?*"

"I mean, ah…" Roger drums his fingers on the top of his head. "They, ah, they've offered before, right? But I mean, I never, ah, I've never…"

Ginny shakes her head. "It doesn't matter, sweetheart. Do go on."

"Uh, okay. So, like, if they think this guy is weird, he's gotta be weird, right? And then she doesn't come home. Now Reggie's got guys looking up and down the block for this guy, only they don't got anything to go on, ah, except for a weird guy, which, like you say…"

"…Is every guy on 42nd. No one noticed his car?"

"One says a van, one says a moving truck."

Ginny takes a long drag on her cigarette, drops it on the ground. Through the wire racks, she can see Tricia's head scooting back and forth, bobbing up and down as she peruses her wares. "So we say that you're right. We say that there's some lunatic picking off girls. What do you suggest I do, sweetheart? This is, after all, your apparent area of expertise." A sudden, terrible thought occurs to Ginny, her stomach rotating around itself to twist into tight, pretzel knots. "You're not a cop?"

"Heh, heh. No. But, ah, on that note, they're, ah, they're not taking this very seriously."

"And how do… You went to the police, didn't you?"

Roger shrugs. Ginny smiles, pats the side of his beard. "You poor, sweet darling. You are just a little angel, do you know that? But, I could have told you exactly what they would say. A kidnapping isn't a kidnapping until it happens to a person. And as far as they're concerned, sweetheart, we aren't people." Ginny cranes her head; Tricia has moved out of her line of sight. She drops her cigarette out the door.

"Walk with me."

Ginny strides into one of the aisles, dodging around boys huddled over the new *Spider-Man*, finds Tricia digging through a record pile. Ginny watches her from the end of the aisle, arms crossed over her chest.

"But, ah, really, I guess, all you can do is take your girls off the street for a while."

"Excuse me?"

"If no one's out there, then no one can get hurt, right? So I guess, ah, what I guess is best is you pull the girls off the street for a while, and, ah, you stop working for a while, so, ah, nothing happens to your girls, and, ah, nothing happens to you."

"Sweetheart, you really have no idea how this works, do you?"

"I have some ideas, ah, I guess... No, not really."

"If we work, we get paid. If we don't work, we don't get paid, we don't eat, and the Colonel throws us all out of the Misanthrope onto our lovely little asses. And then what sort of position are we going to be in, sweetheart? A bunch of homeless girls on 42nd street? I have a lot of leeway where I am now. That means I can keep my girls a lot safer than I could in another situation. I cannot risk that based on chances and guesses, sweetheart. That is an assumed risk versus a guaranteed risk. Not happening."

Roger looks around, rubs the back of his neck. "Ah, okay, so, ah, you're right then."

"Aren't I always?"

Tricia wheels up to the pair, her lap piled with enough records and comics that she has to keep switching off arms to push herself forward, alternatingly turning one wheel while keeping her treasure balanced against her stomach with the other. She holds up an album, squeals with delight.

"They've got *Physical!*"

"And you've got a spending limit. Decide what you want."

"Yes, Frau Joykill." Tricia rolls her eyes at Roger. "You got one of these?"

"I got a brother in Tulsa."

"Is he an asshole, too?"

Roger looks at Tricia, back to Ginny. "There's no right answer to that, is there?"

Tricia wheels back to the records, takes a pile from her lap, indiscriminately dumps them back into the bin.

Roger turns back to Ginny. "So maybe you don't take them off permanently. Maybe just, ah, temporarily."

"*Temporarily?*"

"Reggie's girls tell me this, too. Something like this happened once before. Last Summer. Some other girl of his that he, ah, that he trusted. I forget her name. Her and, ah, this girl she was close with. They never come back to their place one night, and Reggie gets pissed because, ah, because the girlfriend owes him money. And he figures maybe one or both of them's split. And he busts into their place and all of their shit's still there, ah, okay? So Reggie gets pissed and he thinks maybe they jumped ship. He hits up a couple of other, ah, other guys on The Deuce. No one's seen them. But, ah, but like one or two other guys, they're, ah, they're missing girls, too…"

Something turns over in Ginny's head. "When was this again, exactly?"

"I don't know. Last Summer."

A faint glimmer in Ginny's memory; a girl very much like a fusion between Tina and Tammy, an inveterate runaway. Pam, Ginny thinks her name was, maybe Kim. She'd thought she had a real project in the girl, this bony, spooky little thing with a taste for bad dime store romances; had been really keen to get her into Austen. She'd come with nothing and left with the same thing about a week later, Ginny chalking it up to a lack of resolve and the siren call of the road.

"Go on," Ginny says.

"So I decide to ask a few other girls I know, ah, girls who buy stuff off me, trade stuff with me. No one thinks anything, because, you know, girls disappear all the time, right? And no one really talks to one another. But, ah, I figure something's weird about it. Girls come and go all the time, but, how often do they all go at once? I got ten girls, Ginny, ten girls last Summer, all from like, the end of May to the end of June. For a whole month girls disappear, they don't take stuff with them, maybe some of them don't have stuff to take with them but the ones that do, leave it behind. They don't say anything to anyone, not their friends or their boyfriends or their girlfriends. They're just, ah... they're just gone. Like they were never there."

"If you're right, it started in May last year and ended in June. Say that Tina, or Reggie's girl, or this other girl are the first. They're all recently, aren't they, sweetheart?"

"The past week."

"Not in May."

Roger shrugs, grunts. "Something Lunar, maybe? I, ah, ruled out the Summer solstice. That's, ah, June 21st. It's not the Jewish or Muslim calendars, either."

Ginny thinks for a moment; it seems that the periods Roger is discussing have some sort of significance, something that she relegated to the corners of her memory where she tosses factoids she deems insignificant: zoological data; trigonometry; Transcendental literature. She scratches the back of her neck, grinds her tongue against the roof of her mouth; thinks how very nice a drink would be right now; how soft Roger's beard felt against her hand, how he must be using something other than the Misanthrope's complimentary conditioner, how pleasant it might feel now to shove her face into it. She continues digging through her mind. The information seems just at the tip of her tongue when Tricia wheels back to the pair, aiming a ray-gun at Roger's abdomen.

"Hands behind your head. The beard gave you away. We know you're the terrorist of love. You stand accused of car bombing my heart. Move and I'll incinerate you with my ray gun of passion."

"Dammit, Patricia, Roger and I are..." Ginny snatches the gun out of Tricia's hands, is ready to do something with it in anger, throw it or break it or smack her sister across the head with it, realizes that it's a nearly mint, gently used *Star Trek II: The Wrath of Khan* Federation phaser toy.

"...Talking. Go back and look at your records."

Tricia, noticing the arch hostility in her sister's voice, turns silently and returns to her browsing. Ginny smiles at Roger, runs her fingers over the phaser.

"A sister's work is never done, sweetheart. Nor is a den mother's. Now, I appreciate all of this so very much, and I'm going to take it into *great* consideration. You know, sweetheart, I always know the right thing to do."

"So, then, ah, what's the right thing to do now?"

Ginny cocks her head at Roger. "You let me figure that out, sweetheart."

Roger grunts, nods. He turns around, follows Ginny's eyes following Tricia as she continues through rows of comics. After a moment, Ginny realizes that Roger's gaze has moved away from Tricia and back onto her.

"Something you'd like to say, sweetie?"

"I enjoy spending time with you, Ginny."

"I know that, sweetheart, though it's kind of you to say so."

"And I'm sorry if I've ever done anything to upset you."

"Roger, darling, you're talking like you're going away somewhere."

"*I'm* not going anywhere."

Ginny, confused for a moment, looking at Roger with his implacable face and his big, wet eyes, what he's saying dawning on her slowly. "Roger ..."

"Hey." Tricia wheels up to them again, her bounty reduced to a far more manageable—and affordable—quantity. "I'm kind of bored and kind of hungry now. So, like, can we like, check out?"

Ginny looks to Roger; she intends the expression she gives him to be chiding, unsure if there isn't too much sympathy played out on her face. The three head for the checkout, Tricia eagerly wheeling herself forward, colliding with the counter. The old man there mumbles gently to himself, scratching exposed tufts of chest hair as he begins ringing them up on the cash register.

"So, like, mister guy," Tricia says, beginning to pass comics and records across the counter, "You've got a super awesome place here."

"Thanks, kid."

"What does it take to run it?"

"Huh?"

"Like, did you get a college degree, or what? Did you study, like, business or, social science, or math, or, like, what? I mean, say I wanted to run a place like this. What am I looking at?"

"I dropped outta the ninth grade." He continues ringing her up; the daggers that Ginny bores into his forehead create such a sensation of discomfort that he almost immediately clears his throat, adds: "But, uh, you know, I been runnin' this place, for uh, a long time now. If I wanted to get into the game today, I'd hafta to go to school for something. Business'd be a good place to start. Get yourself a background in management, maybe something with finance. Math's important."

"I'm good at math," Tricia says.

"She is," Ginny says.

"Okay, it comes out to eleven dollars."

Tricia frowns, looks up at Ginny. "Spot me an extra dollar?"

"Hey, uh, Freddy," Roger says, "Take it out of my end. They're, ah, they're with me."

Tricia turns in her chair, smiles at him. "Like, omigawsh! Thanks, *dad!* You were right! This really is the best day ever!"

Ginny looks to Roger, pushes the money back towards him, reaches into her purse, comes out with a five. "You are just too kind, do you know that, sweetheart? But I've never taken charity before and I never will." Ginny hands Freddy the five. He's broken the bill and is handing her the change when she places the phaser on the counter. "And that, too."

———

Nicolette awakens earlier than usual, before the sun has begun to rise, and spends an hour walking around her house, listening to Zamfir, strolling back to the record player when her favorite song ends to reset the needle. Then she goes back to walking around. When she grows hungry, she cooks an omelet. She uses three eggs and two slices of cheddar cheese. While the eggs cook, she unwraps one of the fresh packages from her refrigerator. It is breast.

She dices it into little cubes and sprinkles it into the frying pan. When her food is ready, Nicolette sits down at the kitchen table and turns on her little portable television. Nicolette does not typically enjoy television but she does occasionally watch the news during breakfast or dinner. This morning, all of the programs are talking about the dykey looking bitch going up into space. Nicolette holds a great deal of disdain for dykes. The image of one woman copulating is enough to fill her with furious disgust. The idea of two together is intolerable.

After breakfast, Nicolette dresses herself and heads for Times Square. The weather is nice. It will be a good day to shop. She would like some new albums and perhaps a new puzzle book. She might even take in a movie.

It's raining by the time Nicolette arrives on 42nd Street. She is thankful that she always keeps an umbrella in the back of her van. One of the few worthwhile pieces of advice Andrea Aster passed on to her daughter was to always be prepared in the event of a rainstorm. "It'll ruin your hair. And your makeup." Nicolette has no concern for the former and does not wear the latter; nonetheless, she dislikes being wet. She dislikes it even more when raindrops get on her glasses.

Nicolette has not been on 42nd Street for long when she sees The Girl. The Girl is across the street, pushing another girl in a chair. Nicolette believes that the girl in the chair might be The Girl's sister or daughter. Her face is not clear enough to determine age. She has seen them together before, when she has driven 42nd at night. Sometimes she has followed them for quiet hours, watching them go around the block again and again, watched their bodies glow and fade as they passed beneath neon signs and into little columns of darkness.

Nicolette falls into step with The Girl, mimicking her

rhythm, moving with her on her own side of the street. It's with no small level of disgust that Nicolette realizes The Girl is wearing almost the same outfit that Diana Spencer wore on the April 1981 issue of Time Magazine. She already knows that The Girl sees herself as superior to the other pornai; this is another level of *audacity*. This is blasphemy. Nicolette waits for traffic to thin out, to provide her with a straight shot at The Girl. It will be simple and elegant in its brutality. She will bolt across the street and gore the girl with her horns. Knock her through one of the plate glass windows of a store front. Nicolette can see the resultant evisceration, shards of glass sticking out of the girl like porcupine quills, her innards bulging out of holes, the little cripple screaming. Nicolette begins to cross the street, but then the faint whisper of The City echoes up through a manhole, uttering a gentle reproach. This is not the ceremony; this is not how it is done; The Girl is the final offering. Nicolette listens and obeys.

Nicolette returns to her side of the street and continues to follow The Girl. She briefly loses her in the throng, finds her again outside of a comics and novelties store. The Girl and the cripple are speaking to a tall, bald man. They seem to be enjoying themselves. Nicolette wonders if bald man is The Girl's lover. She has witnessed that several of the pornai on 42nd street have regular partners in addition to the men with whom they ply their trade. Nicolette finds such an arrangement particularly loathsome. She wonders if the bald man knows what The Girl does; if she only comes to him in the vestments of royalty and presents her false face to him. Perhaps he knows exactly what she does. Perhaps it excites him. Perhaps he thrusts into her while she chronicles the exploits of the day. Nicolette wonders if they incorporate the cripple into their sessions. It was with some disappointment that Nicolette acknowledged she would not be able to take both The Girl and the cripple at once. The logistics would prove too difficult. She would very much like to see how the pair would behave, facing tribute together. Would one offer her life in exchange for the other, or would they beg to be spared at one another's expense? Would they cling together and cry like mewling pups desperate for the tit? Too, she would like to see how they would react to one another's demise. If she could take them both, Nicolette thinks she would like to begin by removing The Girl's legs. Permit her to experience the little one's condition for a few moments before the end. Then she could set the pair to crawl alongside one another through the halls of the labyrinth.

The three enter the store and are gone from the street. Nicolette is disappointed. She checks her watch. She waits. When The Girl does not reappear after a few minutes, she continues on her day.

Soon, she and The Girl will be spending plenty of time together.

————

It is still drizzling as Ginny and Roger and Tricia exit Hobbs' End. Taxis kick a fine mist up from the wet pavement, the constant flow of traffic creating a gentle, drifting cloud that floats above the curb. Early mornings in St. Louis, Ginny thinks. She'd never bothered to study the city's precipitation data but it seems that in a large number of her memories it was raining on school days, just like this, seven in the morning and the sky a cool slate blue, caked over by gentle rainclouds.

"Still too fuckin' bright," Roger mutters, fits his wraparounds over his eyeglasses.

"Omigawsh," Tricia says. "Are you, like, Cyclops? Tell

me you're Cyclops. Please?"

"I'm Cyclops. Oh, hey, uh, before you go." Roger slips back inside the store, appears a moment later. He extends to Ginny a set of well-worn Sheena comics, the covers sunbleached and torn. "What you wanted. A dollar. They're useless to a collector."

Ginny reaches into her purse, comes out with a little coin bag. She counts change out into Roger's palm. It strikes her that while most tall men she's interacted with have mitty, meaty hands to match, Roger's are more spindly, more delicate; like the limbs of a friendly daddy long legs.

"Oh, and, ah, you'll find some Archies in there, too. Take these to Mary for me?"

"Mary?"

"Mary, ah, your Mary. I heard she's sick. I heard, ah, contagious. I recover from everything I catch, but, ah, I catch everything. I'm not interested in the trots today. Would you collect for me? I'd, ah, I'd wait until she was better but I figure she'll want something to read."

Ginny flips through the comics; had no idea that Mary read anything she didn't assign her. "I had no idea you knew Mary."

"Is that, ah, is that okay?"

"You're allowed to know anyone you want, sweetheart."

"I sell, ah, I sell tapes to Candice sometimes, too. So you, ah, so you know. "

"Perfectly acceptable."

"They're, ah, they're just friends."

"I'll get you your money the next time I see you," Ginny says.

"No, no rush. Tell her I said… Tell her I said 'get well.'"

"I will."

"Hey, like, what're you doing with the rest of the day?" Tricia asks.

"I got work to catch up on."

"Do you want, to, like, cut out and hang with us? We can have lunch, and try dresses on, haircuts, omigawsh, *facials*. Have you ever considered a mustache, Roger? You know, it'd make you look totally just like John Caz…"

Ginny places a hand on Tricia's shoulder. "It sounds like darling Roger has got a busy afternoon ahead of him, and what would a girl's day out be with this poor, sweet man dragged along for the ride?"

"Fucking hot."

Ginny flicks the back of Tricia's ear. "I'll catch up with you Monday, sweetheart. And remember, when the rain soaks through your underwear, and you wish you'd tucked your pants into your socks, and a gentle mist coats your glasses… That's me."

"Heh."

"See you on Monday."

"Hey, Ginny?"

"Yes?"

"You see the space launch?"

"Of course."

"That was, ah, that was something, wasn't it?"

Ginny smiles. "It was."

"Hey Ginny? You, ah, you look nice today."

Ginny lowers her head at Roger, looks up at him through her eyebrows, smiles severely. "Thank you, Roger."

"Ah, ladies." Roger nods to them both, seems momentarily confused as to whether he's properly dismissed himself, seems to come to the revelation that he has, and goes back inside.

When she's reasonably certain that Roger isn't turning back around, Tricia hauls back and punches her sister in the stomach. Ginny grabs herself, stumbles back against the wall of Hobbs' End.

"What the hell, bitch?"

"That's for being completely fucking stupid. I am *never* playing wingman for you again. I, like, totally *handed* you that."

"Okay, number one, totally not interested."

Tricia rolls her eyes. "Like I said, completely fucking stupid."

"And you hit on him for like, half an hour straight!"

"Hello? It makes you seem sexier in comparison!"

Ginny recovers herself, shoves her sister by the shoulders. "How the hell does that even make sense?"

"I hit on him, you get jealous, you grab his ass, bam, total alpha-bitch moment, boner city, hello, goodnight. Omigawsh, you are like, still *so* totally clueless about boys, aren't you?" Tricia spins herself around. "Come on. We are so not done with this day yet."

———

The rain continues for the rest of the day, through window shopping at boutiques, trying on second-hand clothes, breakfast-for-lunch at a diner, so that by the time the Kurva sisters reach the late matinee showing of *Flashdance* at the Colossus—the auditorium barren, audiences, Ginny supposes, having dumbly flocked to *Star Warped: Return of the Shit-heap* over in Number 1—she has begun considering the possibility that the Milky Way might really flood after all.

Yet it has dried up by the time the show ends, the girls exiting into a warm, damp night, the air heavy with fog and street signs dripping with the vestiges of the storm. Tricia avails herself of the puddles that have formed on the sidewalk, slowing herself at the sight of each one, assessing it, then either wheeling herself back a few feet or rushing headlong towards it, the result the same each time, water splashing up in little fans on either side of her chair, Ginny figuring out after that the pause before each puddle attack is due to her sister determining the correct speed and distance required for the maximum arc. It pleases Ginny, to see her sister applying her knowledge in such a way, to find such joy in the wonders of physics and mathematics and science the way that she always has, fills her with a pleasant warmth that lasts until they get to the Misanthrope lobby and it occurs to her that she'll be carting a soaking wet wheelchair up five flights of stairs.

The phone is ringing when they reach their room, a sound which strikes Ginny in the pit of her stomach, filling her with a sense of hopeless desperation. Barring a wrong number, there is only one person who could be on the other end of the line, a person with whom she has no desire to communicate today. She lets it continue ringing as she and Tricia change out of their clothes. Tricia prepares a bath for herself, Ginny goes to the kitchen to find the vodka and pour herself a glass with hands she doesn't realize are trembling until the vodka begins to spill over the rim. She takes down the entire glass in a gulp and pours herself another. She looks at her hands; the shaking has subsided. She gives them a moment, takes another sip. When they've completely stopped shaking, she goes to answer the phone.

"Hello?"

"You haven't answered your phone." The Colonel's voice sounds panicky, nervous, almost unaccented. Ginny is struck by the use of the contraction; wonders if she really heard it. "I been calling all day." Ginny wonders if the Colonel's assertion is literal. A sad, if not entirely sympathetic thought occurs to her, the Colonel alone in his suite in his sock garters and bathrobe, a cigarette in one hand and the phone receiver in the other, waiting for her to pick up as the sun moves across the horizon through his bedroom window, arcing and diminishing as the ring sounds again and again in his ear.

"I'm so sorry, sweetheart, but, you know, a girl's got to enjoy her free time. I'm actually glad you…"

"Not on phone. Come to my room."

The line goes dead. Ginny sits on her side of the bed, her hands no longer shaking, her heart no longer pounding, nothing going on inside of her at all, really. She looks out into the living room, at the dead television set, and wonders if this morning really happened at all. Couldn't have, now that she thinks about it; just a dream, a dream within a nightmare within a nightmare. Wherever Sally Ride flies tonight, she flies alone; and here, on Terra Infernis, all the little girls in the world snuggle into bed in their jammies and get their goodnight kisses and lie staring at the ceiling in the dark, and share in nothing but the putrid delusion that there exists something to strive for, that it will one day matter how great their aptitude at mathematics or language or science is, that there is anything the world will value of them other than how well they'll be able to take a cock.

Giny goes to the bathroom. Most of Tricia's body is hidden beneath the mammoth cloud of bubbles filling the tub, only her head and arms visible above the surface, a copy of Sheena in her hands. She looks away from the book, sees her sister re-dressed, knows.

"Hey," Ginny says.

"Hey."

"I've gotta go."

"I figured."

"I'll try and be back soon."

"Sure."

"Have a nice night." Ginny turns to leave.

"Hey, Ginny," Tricia calls out.

"Yeah?"

"I had a great day."

"Me, too."

Ginny returns to the living room. Before she leaves, she finds her purse beside the door, rummages around inside of it, and retrieves her phaser. She holds it for a moment, turning it over in her hands. She aims it at an imaginary Ceti Alpha Eel, pulls the trigger. The batteries are dead. She's not surprised. She puts the phaser on the coffee table, detours to the kitchen for a quick swig, and heads off to do what she does best.

———

Against Ginny's expectations the Colonel is almost fully clothed, padding around his suite in his robe and a t-shirt and red briefs. He carries a nearly empty bottle of merlot by the neck, rubbing the side of his head with his free hand. Ginny sits at the foot of the Colonel's bed, watches him as he moves around the room, mumbling to himself, occasionally taking little sips from the bottle.

"You not come see me today."

"Sweetheart, you know, that was like, completely unintentional." Ginny bats her eyes, leans back on her elbows. "I meant to, really, but, well, my sister is such the little dickens, and she hasn't been out of her room for so long now…"

"You take her out just other night." The Colonel stops in his tracks, wobbles as he turns to face Ginny. "I saw you. Saw you walking her up and down street. I have eyes, see everything in hotel. Everything on street. I know what you do on weekends, weeknights. *I know you have boyfriend.*"

Ginny flinches. "Excuse me, sweetheart?"

"Bald boy. Beard. Skinny, big shoulders. Bad eyes. Like mole."

"Sweetheart... Roger is just a friend."

"I not mind you have boyfriend, if you take care of responsibilities..."

She reaches down, wads her skirt up in her palms, slowly pulls it above her knees. The Colonel waves his free hand at Ginny, grabs the chair situated at the little desk beside the television, pulls it in front of the bed and sits down. "That all you think about? I care about other things, you know."

"What's worrying you, sweetheart?"

"We down girls," the Colonel says. "We lose Mary. That take us back to seven."

"Zarek, sweetheart, I was, like, so hoping you'd reconsider that. Mary's making, like, a spectacular recovery. She's going to be back in tip-top shape in just a few..."

"Mary done! What did I say?"

"Of course, darling. Please, forgive me. I was, like, totally out of line."

The Colonel snorts and sighs, a strange, defeated sound which Ginny isn't used to hearing out of him. "Two girls go in one week. Not good. Make me worried. Make me think fate against me."

"Setbacks, sweetheart, only setbacks. Everyone has them once in a while. Like, surely you didn't win every battle you were in."

"Hmmph." The Colonel crosses his arms; like most men, Ginny thinks, he's really just a spoiled little brat when he can't get his way. She smiles. The correct course of action at this point seems very clear. Simple, even. The Colonel is far too relaxed to see an attack coming; she could have the bottle neck in her hand before the Colonel realized what was happening. Break it over his head; he'd be on his knees, staggering for his gun by the time she had her switchblade out. She thinks she'd like to start between his legs…

"You've got a much sharper mind than I have, though," Ginny purrs. "I'm still so new at this. Still learning, still figuring things out. It's so much work to keep all of the balls in the air, sweetheart, to keep things running so smoothly."

The Colonel nods. "I know you work hard. I know you not incompetent. Everyone have bad week, once in a while. But you still need to make things right. I need eight girls on street."

"You know," Ginny says, leaning forward, placing a hand on the Colonel's thigh, her fingernails slowly, softly stroking his puckered flesh, "the girls have been working very hard this Summer… and it's been such a hot, *cruel* Summer, too. And I've been thinking, like, maybe our losing two little darlings in one week *is* fate trying to tell us something. Maybe we need to, like, slow down for a little while. Now, sweetheart, I don't know much about war, of course; that's, like, just a little too much for me to wrap my pretty little head around. But I do know that my dear, sweet father was a proud member of the Corps, and there was this little concept called 'R&R.'"

"R and R," The Colonel repeats.

"Time away from the front. I've been thinking, what about giving that to some of the girls? Not all at once, of course. I know you couldn't afford that. *I* couldn't afford that! But we need to give some of them a break, and, well, it has been a very profitable year, hasn't it? I'm thinking, like, four is a divisor of eight, so, maybe enjoy half the luck for a little while?"

"Four is Japanese number of death," the Colonel says. "*You taught me.*"

"…Maybe just some of the younger girls, then. Sandra, Candice… oh, and poor Shannon has been positively *kill-*

ing herself lately. Let the new girl and some of the others pick up the slack for, oh, I don't know, the rest of the month? Just two weeks, sweetheart; just to let them recharge. Didn't they have something like that in the Armia Krajowa?"

"I never in AK." He stares at her bemusedly, his eyes swimming in his head.

"Pardon, sweetie?"

"I never serve with AK."

"I'm confused, darling. You've talked about fighting the Germans. Were you… were you a Colonel in *our* Army?"

"No. Colonel in the Army of Baniszewski," the Colonel says. There's a strange, maniacal pride in his voice; loneliness and booze have loosened him up like she's never seen before. "War start, I working for man who sell papers, help Jews leave country. That man know men who sell guns. I take money I make selling papers, go to man with guns, buy guns. Then I sell guns to AK. Best guns, I tell them. Biggest guns. AK buy guns, I make lot of money. Then I go to SS. Tell them I know where AK hiding, what guns they have. Brrt, brrrt." The Colonel sweeps the room with an imaginary gun. Ginny unconsciously reaches for a cigarette, sorry now she forgot her purse.

"AK all dead. No one left to tell SS that I sell them gun. I take some gun off of dead AK, go to other AK, tell them I sell them gun. Start over again. And over again. War over, I have lot of money; but then AK figure things out. Some of them not die. Go to camps. Survive. They put out reward. I leave on boat. Leave everything behind. Wife, sister, daughter, just weight on me, coming to America. All I need shirt, shoes, pants, briefcases. Briefcases have gold."

"You… have a family?" Ginny feels a cold sensation traveling up her thighs, her spine.

"Maybe, maybe not. Maybe they alive, maybe they die.

I not need them. I not need family, not need country. I see some stupid people die fighting for country, for family. Country not give them clothes, country not give them house. Wife say love you, daughter say love you, this not feed me, this not feed them. Money get clothes. Money get house. That all I need. That all you need. That all anyone need. Girls want R&R, they pay for R&R."

"Of course, you're right, sweetheart," Ginny says. "It was, like, just a thought."

"You need to stop thinking about things that not matter. Start thinking new girl. I need eighth girl. I lay awake at night thinking about empty spot. Like empty chamber in cylinder. Time might come I need last bullet. Bullet not there, I not have last bullet. This worries me." He puts a hand over his face, a gesture of exhaustion, as though the very act of being himself is an endeavor.

"It takes a lot out of you, doesn't it?"

"Yes." His voice slurs. He lets his hand drop limply to his side. "I keep everything moving. Keep hotel going, keep business going. Keep the money flowing. No time for me. No time for me to just... be me."

"But that's what I'm here for, isn't it, sweetheart? For you to enjoy yourself? Don't you forget all your problems when you're with me?"

The Colonel smiles weakly, nods. "Yes."

"So forget about them now." She moves her hand to his face, strokes it, her other hand taking his forearm, pulling him towards the bed. "It's time for you to rest." She helps him onto the bed, towards the headboard. The Colonel collapses into a heap the second he's reached the vicinity of his pillows. Ginny reaches towards her bra, feels the heft of the knife situated there. Effortless now, simple. A few quick thrusts to the jugular; he might not even feel it.

"I need to sleep. To dream."

"Dream, darling." Ginny is staring at him, her hand on the knife in her bra and her hand still and her breathing perfectly regular, no hitches in her breath, no quickened pace, and as the Colonel's eyes close, she draws the knife out, pressing her thumb to the blade so that it makes no sound when she opens it, turning it over in her palm so that the point is downward. The Colonel shifts, moving onto his back, lying prone, eyes shut but still staring up at her, staring up at her through his lids, muttering under his breath.

Ginny pulls the knife back; her arm is steady. A simple command from the brain, impulses travelling through nerves, and her arm will descend and drive the knife into his jugular, bleeding him out within seconds. Nothing to it; nothing but a few moments of blood and agony and maybe some vomit if she can't keep it under control and then it's over, it's all over and one more piece of shit will have been wiped off the Earth. And then she'll be free, and the girls will be free, free if only for a moment before the thrill of that moment is gone, the seconds of victory negated by the cold reality of what happens in his absence, the men more cruel and barbaric than him waiting in the wings to take his place.

The Colonel mutters something Ginny can't understand; she doesn't care to. She folds the blade into the knife and slips it into her bra. She rises from the bed, prepares to leave.

"Darling?"

The Colonel snorts.

"It's, like, totally beside the point, but, can I ask you something?"

He snorts again. Ginny takes this as an affirmative.

"What was your daughter's name, sweetheart?"

"Aniela," he replies. Ginny's gut reaction is that the name

hasn't crossed his lips for a good long while; she wonders if she detects regret in his voice or if she's attempting to project human emotion onto him as a rationale for not having slit the miserable bastard's throat. "The angel."

———

Nicolette arrives home this evening with a bag of new puzzle books, a new outfit, and a ceramic cow. She does not tend to collect tchotchkes but when one calls out to her, she has learned that it is best to listen and purchase it. On those occasions she attempts to leave something behind, she will find herself awake at night, turning around and round in bed or on the couch, unable to get the image of it out of her mind. Sometimes, she will be able to make it to the store the next day and it will still be there. Then, everything is fine. Other times, when she returns to the store, whatever it was will be gone and Nicolette will return to her van and shake and sweat, and it will take several days for a vague sense of dread to leave her, as though she has missed out on an important turning point in her life and can never retrieve it.

She is glad she bought the cow. It will look nice on her kitchen counter.

She is ambivalent about the outfit.

She has been considering buying it now for several weeks. The idea first struck her on 42nd Street one evening, staring at the lights, tingling with growing anticipation at the approach of Skirophorion. It had come on her suddenly, like a bullet to the heart. The vision conveyed to her, her body clad in these vestments, was initially so profane that she trembled in disgust. Yet in the intervening days she found herself returning again and again to the vision, first with an obsessive revulsion, then a dark fascination. The tribute of the Omega bitch only fortified the compulsion. While out today, her body buffeted by the wind and the rain, pausing before a storefront to wipe stray droplets of mist from her glasses, she had looked up and seen it there in the window, exactly as it had manifested itself in her brain, presented to her on a majestically face-less mannequin, its spindly arm beckoning to her. There had been no choice but to enter the store and make the purchase. Carrying the bag around with her the remainder of the day, she had made sure to keep looking over her shoulder, to make sure no one followed her, to be certain that no one who had seen her buy it would float after her down dark alleys.

Nicolette moves to her bathroom on jelly legs, setting down the bags with her puzzle books and clothes and cow. She drapes a towel over the mirror. Then she removes the outfit from the bag. She places it on the edge of the tub and runs her fingers along its fabric. She strips slowly, fear-fully; once she is naked, she begins to redress herself in her new clothes. The process takes even longer than stripping. Once she is clothed again, she removes the towel from the mirror and steps back to study herself. A great, heaving sob rises up out of her gullet, and she grips her own face in clammy palms.

She does not look away.

The tank top hugs her slender torso; her pale thighs shine brightly against the black of the fishnet stockings. After a moment she extends a hand towards her own im-age in the mirror and grunts softly. She moves her free hand over her abdomen, her breasts, her thighs. There is no tactile stimulation; no sensations of desire. She is exploring an alien body reflected to her as her own. Nicolette won-ders if The Girl can feel it; feel her angry, gripping hands roving over her. Nicolette digs at her own flesh through the stockings, her nails raking red lines up her thighs. She hisses at the image before her in the mirror; of the beautiful girl that Andrea Aster would envy as her daughter; at the little slut versed as she is in the ways of conversing with men and boys and girls; at the putrid little body so loathsomely desired that desperate men fumble their wallets in the eager search for bills to pay for it.

In a singular movement, Nicolette reaches down, snatches up one of her puzzle books, and thrusts it at the mirror. The glass shatters, cascading down into the sink, the image of The Girl disintegrating into a silver waterfall.

When she is back in her own clothes, Nicolette takes her bags to the kitchen. She removes her ceramic cow and places it on the counter beside her microwave. It looks as good as she anticipated. Perhaps she will paint it. Red, green, and gold. This is her only concern now.

———

The shaking, Ginny tells herself as she exits the Colonel's suite, is just stress, just nerves. She is not that person; she is not at that point. She would very much like a drink; a drink would very much calm her down; she does not need it; she could do without it, if she wanted, which, at this moment, she does not.

She is reaching for her own doorknob, anticipating the burn of the vodka at the back of her throat, deciding whether or not to make it a screwdriver, when a hand lands on her shoulder. Her response is instinctual. She grips the wrist, spins around, is prepared to simultaneously knock her assailant to the ground and break their wrist when she sees that it's Tammy. She demurs but does briefly consider flinging her into the wall. For all of her adeptness at detecting the aura of the male gaze, Ginny's ability to identify female predation has always been regrettably lacking.

"What are you doing here?" Ginny asks. Her face is slack; she doesn't have the patience for any pleasant formality this evening.

"I… I needed to see you."

"You see me at breakfast, on Monday. Didn't we go over this?"

"Over… over what?"

"This is my room. This is where I live. This is where I do things when I'm not working. Work does not come here. Work does not come anywhere near here. Okay?"

"Okay. Can you let go of my arm, please? You're hurting me?"

"Oh." Ginny releases Tammy's wrist, steps back from the girl, blankly watches her inspect herself for a bruise.

"So, like, you're here, so… What do you need?"

"I… I wanted to give you this." Tammy reaches into her jeans, comes out with a neatly folded stack of bills. Ginny takes it, thumbs through it.

"What is this?"

"It's for Mary."

"I figured. Where did you get it?"

"Working."

"Tammy…" Ginny wobbles forward, puts a hand on the girl's shoulder. "I know you're new, and… And there's that temptation, at the beginning, to want to hold out… It's good for you to have brought this to me, and, I want you to know I appreciate that. And nothing is going to happen to you for it. But in the future, you have really got to kick up the whole amount, okay?"

"Oh, no," Tammy says. "I made that today."

"…what?"

"I went out and…"

Ginny's hand tightens its grip, goes from conciliatory

to confrontational. "I understand what you mean by 'work.' What were you doing out there today?"

"I… I wanted to make some extra money. For Mary. To help her…"

"You will not help her by getting yourself killed, and getting the Colonel killed, and getting the rest of us killed. Which is, like, so totally what will happen if you break the agreement. The rules are in place for a reason. We do not own the weekend. Men that are way worse than the Colonel own it. I will phrase this bluntly, Tammy, because maybe I haven't been quite blunt enough with you: Do not fuck with them, and do not fuck with me. I will be the absolute best fucking friend you've ever made in the whole fucking world, as long as you do your work and do what you're told. But never, *ever* put me in danger. *Got it?*"

Tammy looks at Ginny with wide, frightened eyes. It's the expression of someone who is seeing something familiar become suddenly frightening. "Okay."

Ginny hands her the money back. "Mary's room 203. Give it to her yourself. Wait."

Ginny unlocks her room, steps inside, retrieves Mary's comics, brings them back out.

"Give her these, too."

"I'm sorry, Ginny, I didn't mean to…"

"Go."

Tammy turns to leave, humbled. Ginny watches her slip off down the hall, vacillating between thinking to herself that she was too harsh, was not harsh enough. Unable to make up her mind, she opens the door and goes inside.

6

Sunday, June 19th, 1983

LTHOUGH THE RAIN DOES NOT RETURN OVERNIGHT, there are still puddles left on the sidewalk and in the gutters Sunday morning. Tricia, however, does not charge through them in her chair, nor does she pause to consider such a feat, opting instead to carefully wheel around them, even slowing her pace so as to avoid causing any unnecessary splash up.

She doesn't want to ruin her clothes.

The cream taffeta dress is Tricia's only nice outfit, the one article of clothing she insisted upon taking with her from home. She has worn it faithfully every Sunday since confirmation, the slight development of her body requiring only minor alterations over the ensuing four years. In contrast to the havoc she wreaks on the rest of her clothes, Ginny is amazed at the level of measured prissiness that Tricia puts into caring for the dress: her routine spot-checks for rips or tears, the special wooden hanger she keeps it on, the well-maintained plastic bag which is kept draped over it the other six days of the week. It might be endearing, Ginny thinks, were it not for the conversation they have every Sunday morning at the steps of the Holy

Cross, the sidewalk heavy with foot traffic, other congregants attempting to make their way around the Kurva sisters and up the steps.

"You're going to rip it."

"I'm not."

"The fabric is, like, totally bunching up in your pits and… did you shower last night?"

"What?"

"After you got back, did you shower? Your pits are clean, right?"

"I'm wearing a jacket," Ginny says.

"Omigawsh, I know, but you sweat like a pig. Are you sweating right now? Are your pits dry?"

"Okay, like, will you forget about my pits for a minute?" Ginny reaches the top of the steps, not sweating before but sweating now, the perspiration threatening to soak through the fabric of her suit at any moment. She takes Tricia to the doors, Tricia grabbing the handles, dangling there while Ginny sprints back down the steps to retrieve her wheelchair. Tricia refuses to be set on the ground; it would get her seat dirty.

Once she's situated in her chair, Tricia conducts the customary examination of her clothes, checking the hem of her dress for tears, her sleeves for any dirt strains. That operation completed, she retrieves a compact from her purse, checks her makeup, her hair. Although she witnesses the ritual on a weekly basis, it remains a surreal sight for Ginny, her sister out of a t-shirt and shredded jeans, her fingerless gloves removed; even the presence of the purse, the makeup, the compact cause a momentary disorientation, as though her sister is replaced for brief intervals every Sunday by someone with something approaching a sense of decorum.

"Okay, like, I'm ready," Tricia says. "Let's go in." She

wheels back towards the door, grabs the handle.

Ginny stays put.

"Like, hello? They're going to start."

"Trish, you know... I don't."

Tricia releases the door, wheels back towards her sister. "But, like, you're all dressed up today. I thought, like, you were going to come this time."

Ginny looks away. The Holy Cross is the oldest building on The Deuce. It has seen the rise and fall of presidencies, the passage of wars, the transformation of Times Square from a clump of unpopulated Earth to a mecca of enterprise to a melting fleshpot of debauchery, the stained glass windows filtering the light of the rising and setting sun onto a sanctuary which has housed and comforted those souls who've sought refuge in her walls from the transforming world. It seems perverse, though perhaps Biblically appropriate, that directly across the street, the façade visible from the front steps of the Holy Cross, sits the Port Authority Bus Terminal.

"I've got to work today," Ginny says.

"...Oh," Tricia says. "You kind of, like, got my hopes up and stuff. I thought that, like, after yesterday with, like, the rocket shit and everything you maybe had some kind of... I don't know. Shit." Tricia sighs, spins herself around in her chair. "You know, it'd be cool if you'd come with me sometimes."

"That's not really for me anymore."

"Oh, like, bullshit. I mean, hello, Mary Magdalene?"

"Mary Magdalene was not a prostitute. That's apocryphal."

"Okay then, like, woman at the well?"

"Adulteress."

Tricia glares at her sister, says defiantly, "*Rahab.*"

Ginny frowns. "That's not what I'm talking about, anyway."

"Omigawsh, then, like, what're…"

Ginny's eyebrows furrow, some of the natural fire fading from her eyes. Tricia knows. She sighs, looks away from her sister.

"Ginny… I'm sort of like super mega pissed right now, because you're making me feel feelings and shit, but… You know, there's no reason for me to say this, 'cause, like, I never blamed you for anything… but, if you need to hear me say it… I forgive you. Okay? It was never your fault anyway, but, I still forgive you. Okay? So you can, like, cut out the martyr shit and, like, come with me sometime, okay?"

"Sure," Ginny says. Going to breakfast afterwards?"

"Uh, like, hello? Free pancakes? Fuck-a-doodle-yes."

"About three hours then?"

"Unless they kick me out."

"Please don't get kicked out of a church breakfast."

"Omigawsh. I was joking. Give me some credit." Tricia shakes her head, exasperated, turns around in her chair.

"Hey Tricia?"

"Yeah?"

"Would you… light a candle? For me?"

"I do every week," Tricia says. "I light four."

She pulls the door open. An usher appears, holding it for her as she wheels herself over the threshold. Ginny peeks inside, watches her sister vanish into the rows of the blessedly assured.

Inside, the organ starts up, the voices of the congregation lifting their praises. Ginny smiles, pausing for a moment outside the door, listening to the familiar hymn, humming along. Then she finds a cigarette in her purse, lights up, and heads off to work.

———

Nicolette awakens Sunday morning with a dread chill in her gut, carried to her on the malevolent screams of the tortured dead echoing to her through the soundless vacuum of space, where they drift for all eternity in their nightmare cavalcade.

Her phone is ringing.

Nicolette is not unused to getting phone calls during the week. One of her superiors at the landfill. Someone trying to sell her something. Her dentist or optometrist reminding her that it is time for a checkup. This is the weekend, though. The phone should not be ringing. Sometimes, the phone will ring on the weekend and Nicolette will cease what she has been doing and go to the garage and retrieve her axe and wait there in the dark for something to come.

Nicolette considers her best course of action. She could go to her van and drive away, and come back later when the phone has stopped ringing. She could go down to the kitchen and make herself a hearty breakfast of cheek and tongue, and feast upon it while cradling her axe. She could wait here in bed. Nicolette fortifies herself. Fear is not becoming of her. She has crossed eons and civilizations to be here. She can face whatever threat awaits her.

Nicolette rises from bed. Calmly, she goes out to the garage. She returns to the bedroom with her axe. She holds it clumsily in one hand while she lifts the phone with the other. She holds the receiver to her ear and waits. After a while, a voice:

"Hello?"

"…"

"Miss Aster? You there?" It sounds like Someone from the landfill. Nicolette relaxes a little.

"Yes, sir. Hello. How is your weekend?"

"Ain't no weekend for me, girl, I tell you that."

"I'm sorry to hear, sir. Is... something the matter?"

"I don't know. That's why I'm calling you."

"How can I help, sir?"

"You busy? Church services or any such stuff?"

"No."

"All right, well now, I hate to ask this, but, I need you to meet me up at Plant 1, say, ten?"

Nicolette moves the phone away from her face. The hairs on her neck are still standing. She brings it back to her face. "Is something the matter?"

"I'm... not sure of it. Look, I was doing a little trouble-shooting of my own up here today, I want you to take a look at it."

"Yes, sir."

"You doing all right, Aster?"

"Fabulous, sir."

"See that there space launch?"

"Sir?"

"Sally Ride, gal goin' up to the moon or whatnot. Thought that'd be up your alley. I tell you, the cojones on that girl."

"Yes, sir."

"See you soon."

"Yes, sir."

Nicolette hangs up the phone. She begins to pace her room. Valleys of worms squirm beneath her toes. Something is wrong. Someone knows something. Maybe. If he knew something, would she be here? Would there be men in the corners of the room waiting for her? Men in the garage? There are none. Perhaps the trip to the landfill is a trap. No. If they knew, they would not wait. They would come for her now. Someone might know something but he does not know enough. He has suspicions. If he suspected her, would he let her know? Or is that a part of his plan? Nicolette sits down on her bed and tries to steady her breathing. Her eyes bulge. Her mouth slowly opens and closes like a suffocating fish. She is sweating.

Stop.

Nicolette stands up. She has handled the dog situation well. She has collected great tribute. Whatever challenge might arise, she will see to it, and swiftly.

She is powerful.

She is unstoppable.

———

"Omigawsh, that is, like, so fascinating," Ginny says, although she isn't quite certain what exactly she's just said it to, just smiling broadly at the little waif in front of her, holding a cigarette out at a jaunty angle, watching the world slowly swimming around her. While Tricia Kurva spends her Sundays in devotion to the Almighty, it's Ginny's custom to drift down to a diner, order a pot of coffee and scrambled eggs, and while away the morning doing the Times crossword. That ritual taken from her, she had to settle for guzzling half the contents of her flask in the Port Authority women's room, staring hatefully at her own reflection in the mirror, noticing for the first time the tiny little lines descending from the corners of her nose down to her chin, the heavy circles beneath her eyes. She reminds herself of the progress all of her girls have made: how Constance has gone from counting on her fingers to factoring polynomials; how Shannon, under her guidance, found a voice for her rage through the embracement of the punk philosophy; how Sandra has developed a love of botany and successfully cultivated a small atrium in her room; how Mary was passed around like a pack of cigarettes between her father and brothers and now she's got a twelfth-grade education and a butchered twat; how what she is doing now is good, how the world itself is really just one big brothel anyway, with its moral compromises and its emotional prostitution, and so what's the big deal about going ahead and literalizing it, if it means safety and security and actualization and the occasional botched abortion? "Really?" the waif says. "I never really thought that my life was interesting before."

"Everyone's life is, sweetie. We just want to pretend other people aren't interesting so we can keep on paying attention to ourselves."

"Oh, wow. That's, like, really heavy."

"Heavy like lead, darling."

The waif gives her a sad little ingénue smile; doe eyes to match her own, brown instead of gray, maybe a hundred pounds, soaking wet. Stacy, her name is, maybe Susan. Sally? Ginny can't really remember right now; had been thinking about what name she and Trish would play under if they formed an all-girl New Wave group, settling eventually on *Cuntagious Disease,* thinking this absolutely hilarious, the delight a thin veneer over a vague sense of unease over how simple this has become. Glancing at her watch she sees that she's been at the Port Authority for nearly forty five minutes. Across the street, the wine and host are being brought before the altar, the elements consecrated. Ginny reaches into her purse, pulls out her flask, drinks. The waif regards her concernedly.

"You want some of this?"

The waif shakes her head.

"You know, I wanted to be an altar server. Father Walther said that *only* boys could do it. I told Father Walther that Jesus never had a problem with women bringing him anything, and if the fat son of a bitch thought he was so much better than Jesus then he really ought to go fuck himself." Ginny nods purposefully. "Oh, yeah. You better believe my folks got a call about that one." Ginny giggles, takes another drink, pops her flask back in her purse, and recomposes herself. "Sorry, sweetheart. Sundays send me down memory lane. I guess I, like, really need to stay away from Sundays. Now, where were we?"

"You were telling me how interesting it was that I ran away from home."

"Of course, sweetheart, of course." Ginny nods; after a moment, she realizes that she's still nodding and stops. "And refresh my memory, why was that again?"

"Because my parents kicked me out of the house…"

"Because of the drugs. You poor, sweet, sweetheart." Ginny reaches forward, puts a hand on the girl's shoulder.

"…because I'm a lesbian," the waif says.

Ginny nods slowly. "Of course." She looks at her hand on the waif's shoulder, looks back to the girl, considers removing it, doesn't. "I want you to know that I am totally okay with that."

"You're only half listening to me, aren't you?"

"Darling, whenever I do anything, I go whole hog. Do you know what that means, sweetheart? Do you know about Flannery O'Connor? I think about *her* a lot on Sundays, too. Would you *like* to know more about Flannery O'Connor? Get your GED? You're…" Ginny thinks. "Sixteen…right? I can get you your GED. I can get you a lot of things. My agency…"

"I'm not stupid," the waif says. "I need a place to sleep and I need food. I knew this is where I was going to end up." Tears well up in the corners of her eyes. She offers Ginny a weak smile; the pretty little shield that all women learn to raise against the threats of life, to keep their pleasantness intact and so retain their value. "Where do we go?"

The landfill is closed today but the gates are open and Someone is waiting there when Nicolette arrives, sitting in his car, smoking. His car is small and feeble. It's a tiny vehicle for a tiny man with a tiny mind. When he exits the car Nicolette is confused to see that he is wearing a polo shirt and khaki pants and athletic shoes. It's outside of her schema for the landfill for anyone in a position of authority to come to work dressed so casually, even if it's the weekend.

Nicolette shuts off her van and gets out. Someone approaches her.

"Damn, girl, what're you so dressed up for?"

"I'm at work, sir."

"It's the weekend, Miss Aster, ain't no one gonna see us."

"Okay."

"That there an Econoline?"

"Yes, sir."

"Seen it around before, never knew it was yours. That there's a beast. You got kids?"

"No, sir. I enjoy metal working projects during my time off. Sculpture. It lets me carry supplies."

"Huh. Never figured you an arty type. People are surprises, though, ain't they?"

"Yes, sir."

"Hope this wasn't too much an inconvenience, coming up here."

"No, sir." Nicolette has learned that it's considered polite to lie when the truth would indicate that someone has been inconvenienced. "What did you want to show me?"

"Come around here."

The pair begins walking.

"Now let me tell you, after what happened, I was mighty pissed. Didn't sleep a wink, let me tell you. Not gonna lie to you, Miss Aster, I been spending some time with Mr. Daniels, first name Jack. Got up this morning, what do you know? Sometimes a hangover is exactly what the doctor ordered. Knew just what I had to do. Grabbed my daddy's .30-.30, grabbed me a truck, had myself a little huntin' trip."

Nicolette stops in her tracks. "Excuse me, sir?"

"Well, I figure if these super mutts are gonna eat our poison and not have the courtesy to drop dead, maybe what they needed was some lead poisonin'. Of the old fashioned variety. Now, I know what you said about them burrowin', so I hauled out some nice old tenderloins, tossed 'em out, waited to see what turned up. Damn if a few didn't take the bait."

The pair reach their destination. Nicolette must fight the urge to vomit. Laid out at the base of a heap, like discarded pieces of garbage, are three of her pack. Their bodies have been left cruelly exposed, flies hovering around them in thick little swarms. Pieces the size of tangerines have been taken out of each, ribs blown apart, chunks of head missing, legs blasted away from their bodies. Someone lifts the hem of his shirt over his face. His belly looks soft and vulnerable.

"Little bastards ain't so tough now, are you?" Someone says. "Or should I say little bitches?"

"...Excuse me?"

"Reason I wanted you to take a look at this. You're my resident mutt expert. Now, see there. I ain't got the smarts you have, but I did spend summers on my grandpappy's farm. I know how to tell one set of gonads apart from another. After I took 'em down, I remembered what you said, about there only being one does the breeding. Then I remembered the three that got taken down by the last round of poison. Now I didn't think anything of it until now, but I got me a gander at them, too. They was all females. Now, what're the odds that every one we took down was gonna be a bitch? I mean, that's weird, right?"

"I'm not sure I understand, sir."

"Hell, Miss Aster, neither do I. That's why I wanted to make sure I was seeing what I was seeing. Bounce it off of you. Try and figure this out."

"They are all bitches, sir."

"All right, so, what the hell does that mean?"

"I have some books back at my house that I've been consulting," Nicolette says. "We can go back there and check."

"Oh, now, that ain't necessary, I know this here's your weekend, I don't wanna invade that much. Just needed a second set of eyes on this. You take a look into it, see what you can figure out."

"It wouldn't be a problem at all, sir," Nicolette says. On the gentle breeze wafting over the dump, she begins to hear the apprehensive whispers of The City. The cacophonous murmur is unsettling. She has never heard such disquiet before. A dozen commands are given, each insistent and desperate, all contradictory. Nicolette attempts to process them all, choose a satisfactory option.

Awkwardly, Nicolette takes a step towards Someone. She realizes that there are still about three feet between them and takes two more steps forward. She hopes that she has come into close enough proximity to seem provocative. "It would be nice to… have some company… I was… spending the day alone, anyway. It's… awful to be alone… sometimes. Why don't you… come over… *sweetheart?*"

"Well, I… Sure, I can come over, if you want, shoot the shit, get to the bottom of this." Someone shrugs. He shifts his feet. Nicolette cannot be sure if he is enticed, or if he is feeling sorry for her. She isn't certain which would be worse.

"It'll be nice. I… have some ideas. Some books I've gotten from the library. Just… follow me. It'll be… *absolutely fabulous... darling.*"

Nicolette opens her mouth, smiles. With a great amount of difficulty, she winks. Then she turns and heads back to her van. She waits in the passenger seat for a moment, watching Someone get into his car in her rearview mirror. She starts the engine. Looking into her rearview mirror, she can see the festering corpses of her bitches slowly rising up from the refuse, their decaying and desiccated bodies moving with slow, determined rhythm, wandering back out into the mounds to rejoin the pack, their entrails dragging behind. Nicolette sobs. Then she puts her van into gear and heads towards home.

———

At the Misanthrope, Ginny steps out of the cab, moves around to open the passenger side door for the waif, finds herself opening the Colonel's office door, her heart rising into her throat as she realizes the missing time and space between the two actions. She stops in the doorway, looks at her watch. No real time lost; Tricia probably now just starting to dig into a plate of pancakes, chatting up some little old woman, hopefully minding her manners and her tongue. Ginny nods to herself, opens her purse, rummages through it.

"Are you okay, lady?" the waif asks from behind her.

"Just checking something," Ginny mutters. Good; nothing missing. She steps aside, leads the waif into the office, situates her on the couch.

"I'm going to find your new boss now," Ginny says. "Okay? You just wait here and... I told you about him, right? He's a Colonel. Only, not really. But don't tell him you know that. I just found out, too. I'm kind of surprised, you know? Because all this time, I'm like, he's a Colonel, my dad was a Sergeant… that makes sense, right?"

"Sure," the waif says.

"Just checking," Ginny says. "Hey. Hey. Are you all right?"

"Yeah."

"You… you're going to have to do some stuff, you know? I mean, normally I'd be, like, sugar coating this shit out the ass, right? But, I mean, you get it, right?"

The waif nods. "I get it, lady. Look, that coffee we just had is the only food I've had for two days, okay? I'll… I'll do what I have to do. I just really need to eat and get some sleep."

"Omigawsh! Sweetie… sweetie, you should have said so!" Ginny digs back into her purse, pulls out a box of animal crackers, tosses it to the waif, accidentally hitting her in the face. Ginny puts a hand over her mouth, initial shock turning into a soft giggle. "You… you eat that, okay? I'm sorry. But you… you enjoy that. And I'll… I'll be right back."

Ginny goes to the Colonel's door, knocks on it. "Zarek! Hey, Zarry! It's me…. It's… the Big G! Come on, I know you're… in there. C'mon! Put the gun down! It's just me."

The door cracks, opens, Ginny staggering in, flinging herself down into the Colonel's desk chair. She sighs, giggles, wipes her forehead of imaginary sweat.

"Sweetheart, I come to you from, like, most far off lands with most spectacular news. You see that precious little thing out there? There's your new number eight. Record time, darling. Record time. And let me tell you something else, sweetheart. Are you ready for this? Ready? Okay, here it goes: She likes *girls.*" Ginny claps her hands, fist pumps the air.

"You not usually this drunk until later in day," he says.

"It's the cure for what ails me, darling, and what ails me today is the task at hand. But—voila! Finito! Look upon your peephole and tremble, sweetheart."

The Colonel moves to the door, looks out the peep-hole. "Girl small. You sure she not break?"

"Positive, sweetheart. She and I had a good, long talk on the way over here, and, let me tell you… the heart of a lion, that one."

"If girl too small, girl break. *I know.*"

Ginny shudders. "I'm sure that she's… perfectly up to the task, darling. Come on. Right now, like, Candice and Shannon are our only bi girls. Three out of eight? That's… that's almost half. Over one third. Thirty-seven-and-a-half percent."

"You can't have half girl."

"Oh? I thought that's what Mary was," Ginny snaps, smiles immediately, giggles off the remark. The Colonel cocks his head at her, then smiles along.

"You in good spirits. You need drink in day more often. I was having bad day. You make me feel better. Give me a minute, to get ready."

Ginny smiles, rises, wobbles to the door. Back in the anteroom, the waif is munching on crackers, black rivulets of eyeliner having run down the sides of her face, smudged up on her cheeks from where the girls tried to dab at it with a tissue. Ginny sighs, shakes her head. She sits down beside the girl, takes a package of moistened towelettes out of her purse, opens one and begins wiping at the girl's face.

"Sweetheart, no, no, *no.* We cannot have this. This is completely unacceptable. You're going to be working an image once you get out there but that image most assur-edly cannot be a clown. That is far too narrow a clientele to attract."

The waif nods. "I'll be all right. I just need to… I'll be okay, okay? Like, you know, once I've done it a few times, you know? I just need to be ready for it."

"Of course, darling, it isn't easy for anyone in the beginning. But just because I brought you here doesn't mean you get the job, right? You've got to pass your audition." Ginny notices something on the girl's thigh, a little photo, the kind made to be kept in a wallet, deep white creases formed where it's been folded over and over to be slipped into a pocket. "What have you got there, sweetheart? Is that... that your family?"

"Yeah," the girl says. She passes the picture to Ginny. A photo of an American family in happy times: Christmas morning, dad in a robe on the edge of the couch, mom just out of frame, smiling as she hands a wrapped box down to a little girl at the foot of the tree, a slightly older girl beside her, already in the process of opening another gift.

"Is that... you and your sister?"

"Yeah." The waif sniffs, shoves a few crackers in her mouth. "She's back with the folks."

"Oh," Ginny says. The chill which first swept over her a moment ago begins to spread from her spine to her bowels, her thighs, her feet.

"I get why my folks kicked me out. But they didn't even let me say goodbye."

"That is...like... so awful," Ginny says. The hand holding the towelette begins to shake.

"She turns fourteen next month," the waif says. "I already got her a record for her birthday. It's still in the back of my closet. If my folks find it, they'll probably throw it away. Or say it's from them."

"That's *terrible,* sweetheart," Ginny says. "Now, let's talk about that image, shall we? What do you like to do? Do you play tennis? I could use a sporty girl. I bet you would look absolutely... precious... in a little pleated skirt."

"Fuck knows what they told her about me," the waif continues, blowing her nose.

Ginny takes a deep breath in, lets it out; feels like she's hyperventilating. "Once you've got some money, we can… we can make some arrangements, you know? Call a friend of hers, while she's at their house, let you… talk to her. Maybe send a package to a place in town where she could pick it up? You are going to have… a lot of opportunities."

The waif shakes her head. "There's no reason. She looked up to me, you know? I was, like, her fucking hero. Now as far as she knows, I'm just some fucking dyke."

Ginny isn't entirely certain what happens next; can't be sure what set of synapses and nerve impulses fire, what thought processes occur that lead to her open hand striking the girl in the side of the face, the waif shrieking, recoiling, Ginny rising from the couch and yanking the girl to her feet by the arm and then striking her again, sweeping her legs out from beneath her. The girl collapses onto the floor and then Ginny is on top of her, grabbing her by the throat, the girl's nose crushed and blood flowing down the front of her face.

"You think you're tough, bitch?" Ginny says. Her voice is trembling, desperate, her teeth clenched. "What? Huh? You think you're tough? You think you're ready for this? You aren't ready for shit. You listening to me? Huh? Are you listening to me?" Ginny reaches over, grabs her purse, finds her wallet. With shaking hands, she yanks it open, pulls out a wad of bills, tosses them at the girl. "You get your pretty little ass out of here, back on that bus, and get back to… to… to wherever the fuck you came from, and you do whatever it takes to make it right. You got me? Because whatever—*listen to me!* Whatever you have to do to make it right back there is *nothing* compared to what you're going to do here. Do you understand me? Are you listening to me? *This. Is. Hell.*"

The girl, eyes bulging, nods. Ginny scuttles back off of

her, breathless, sits on her haunches as she watches the girl gather up the money and dart out of the room, blood still pouring out of her face and onto her t-shirt. Ginny puts one hand over her own face, punches the floor with the other. Behind her, she hears tumblers turning over as the Colonel's door unlocks. She turns, sees him step into the room, looking more confused than concerned.

"You beat her up."

Ginny smiles, rises from the floor. She moves to the Colonel, smiling, giving him the doe eyes, puts her arms around his neck. Looking down, she sees that she's inadvertently transferred blood from her jacket and blouse onto the Colonel, the flecks looking like little red teardrops against the fabric of his polo shirt.

"Can you believe it, sweetheart, that right before you came out, the little dickens tried to plant one on me? Not that I minded, of course—it was flattering, really— but, believe it or not, when she came in for the clinch, do you know what I saw poking out of the corner of her mouth? *Herpes.*" Ginny, in trying to whisper the word, manages only to slur it. "Can you imagine what an absolute disaster that would be? I will not have you known as the man responsible for giving herpes to 42nd. Not at all, darling."

The Colonel snorts. "I would have seen it. No need for you to beat her up."

"I couldn't have risked it, sweetheart. I care too much."

The Colonel looks over her shoulder to his couch, the floor, the blood splattered there. "You pay to clean up office. Pay for new shirt. This crocodile shirt." He points at the little logo over his chest. "Expensive. Show world that I arrived. No one think I arrived if alligator shirt has blood on it."

"Of course, darling."

The Colonel steps back, extends his palm. Ginny sighs,

retrieves her wallet, begins counting out the remaining bills into the Colonel's hand, the Colonel continuing to gesture with his index finger until her wallet is empty. He unceremoniously stuffs the bills into his pocket, crosses his arms. "Go now."

She turns to leave; as she reaches for the door, he adds: "And clean yourself up."

———

"I'm sorry about the mess," Nicolette says. She has learned that it's polite to always apologize for the mess your home is in when having guests over. She has not been to many people's homes in her life—a few disastrous play-dates, a handful of coworker's birthday parties, just to maintain appearances—but it seemed to her that every host and hostess apologized for the mess the home was in. Someone slowly looks around Nicolette's living room, then at her. She cannot read his expression. Nicolette surveys her own living room. Nothing is out of place. She wonders if perhaps this seems unusual to Someone. Wordlessly, she reaches down and knocks over a vase on the living room table. Then she looks back to Someone. He clears his throat.

"You've got an eclectic taste, Ms. Aster, I, uh, I'll give you that."

"I'm sorry, sir?"

"Oh, don't get me wrong, I wish my old lady'd keep our place half as clean as this. You keep a real fine home, looks of this. I just never seen every wall in a house painted a different color is all. That, uh, that something the young people are doing today?"

"I'm thirty-seven."

"Still younger than me." Someone puts his hands in his pockets and looks around the room. He jiggles the change in his pockets. Nicolette wonders if he's waiting for her to take her clothes off. He seems eager and agitated. Perhaps he is contemplating raping her.

"Would you like a drink?" Nicolette asks. "I have wine. And coffee. And water."

"Ah, water's fine, thanks." Someone has a seat on the couch. Inside, Nicolette shudders. Though she thinks she will be comfortable with shampooing the carpets, the couch, for all intents and purposes, is now ruined.

Nicolette goes to the kitchen and fills a glass with water from the sink. She looks out the kitchen window. The gentle azure of the sky has given way to a sickly copper. Nicolette feels her heart begin to slowly accelerate. The shade is menacing. It means to warn her. The voices of The City continue to mutter in rising urgency. Nicolette looks down at her ceramic cow. Gingerly, she turns the cow to face away from her. Then she returns to the living room.

"Here." Nicolette thrusts her arm out towards Someone. Some of the water sloshes up on the sides of the glass and spills over the edge. Someone looks at her and takes the glass.

"So, down to brass tacks, then," Someone says.

"What do tacks have to do with anything?"

"The dogs, Ms. Aster. You, uh, seem to think you have an idea as to what's going on here."

"I do," Nicolette says. "But just… sit right there. I need to… fix my face."

"You, uh, don't have to do that on my account," Someone mutters.

"*No, no, no… sweetheart…* Just… wait right here." She lifts the legs of her pants a quarter of an inch, holds them up a moment, lets them fall back down. Someone tilts his head back and forth. Nicolette turns and hurriedly moves out of the room.

The voices are ricocheting around inside of her skull with such force by the time Nicolette makes it to her bedroom, that she must steady herself against the doorframe for a moment before switching on the lights. They are angry. They are terrified. In the Meadow, the attendants gather together before The Altar and bow their faceless heads, offering up their prayers and their strength. Nicolette takes their strength. She swallows it deep, deep, deep inside of her. It takes root in her belly and fills her. She begins to calm down. Slowly, determinedly, she turns on the light, takes ginger steps forward. She strips and redresses in her new outfit. Once she has gotten her tights straight, she wanders serenely to the garage. She removes her glasses. She fumbles for her helmet on the work bench. She places it on her head and tightens the straps.

From the living room, Someone calls out: "Ms. Aster? You doing all right back there? Ms. Aster?" He is in the middle of calling out again when Nicolette enters the room. His body jerks on the couch. He begins to rise and Nicolette screams, and the scream must startle him because he collapses back onto the couch.

"Son of a bitch, the hell is this?" Someone says. It is barely a whisper. For all of his loathsome might with a gun, he is helpless before her fury. His fear is pleasing to Nicolette. It frees her of apprehension; it makes sweet music of the rambling voices of The City, purifies and synthesizes them into a harmonious chorus. Nicolette screams along with it. She charges across the room and swings the axe. Someone raises his hand to guard against the blow but the force of Nicolette's swing is enough to take it off as the blade arcs down and lands directly between his legs, and Nicolette screams again when it makes its impact, her body vibrating as she watches Someone's face turn purple and the tendons in his neck bulge, his mouth opening but no sound coming out, blood gushing forth from the crotch of his pants. Nicolette grunts, giggles, plants her foot in the crimson waterfall soaking into the fabric of the couch and steadies herself. She rips the axe out. Someone rolls onto the floor, twitching. Tiny fountains of blood spurt out of the stump of his arm. Nicolette pauses a moment to watch, to catch her breath. A thin film of sweat covers her body. Someone isn't even trying to get away. His remaining hand fumbles meekly at his groin, trying to grip his severed member. Nicolette giggles. She raises the axe again. The blow is not quite enough to decapitate him. The second swing is sufficient. Someone's head wobbles beside his convulsing body, trailing severed tendons from the neck like the tentacles of some feeble and gelatinous deep sea creature waiting to be preyed upon by a beast more fierce than itself. Nicolette collapses backwards onto her haunches. The voices of The City have become quiet. This is only slightly reassuring. She knows that this sacrifice was made to her in retribution for the lives of her bitches, but she is unsure if this is a tribute or not. She has never hunted outside of the labyrinth; she's concerned that this perhaps invalidates it as an offering.

Nicolette rises and returns to the garage, removes her mask, puts her glasses back on. Looking down at herself, she sees that she's become splattered in Someone's blood. Once she is calm, she goes to the bathroom and strips. She showers quickly and dresses in her armor. She goes to the kitchen and turns on the oven. Then she heads to the living room and the busy afternoon in front of her.

———

Taking the Colonel's advice, Ginny does indeed clean herself up, showering quickly, drying herself with just enough time to get into clean clothes and make it back to the Holy Cross as breakfast is letting out. Tricia, her dress immaculate, her face smeared with dried syrup and powdered sugar, regards her sister's new outfit quizzically.

"Do I want to know?"

"Let's go home," Ginny says.

Ginny is quiet on the trip back to the Misanthrope. Tricia is mindful of her sister's desire for silence, even refraining from the customary grunts that usually accompany the process of getting her back upstairs. In their room, the frustrated silence takes on a consumptive life of its own, Tricia silently wheeling about, cleaning her face, removing her dress, inspecting it for damage, hanging it up, changing into pajamas, Ginny all the while sitting on the couch, staring at the blank television set, her fingers idly flipping through the pages of a copy of *Persuasion* plucked from the little shelf beneath their coffee table. After what seems to be sufficient time has passed, Tricia wheels herself into the room, situates herself beside Ginny. Though she is used to a certain amount of introversion on her sister's part, prolonged periods of silence such as this profoundly disturb her. Her memories are very sharp of the days, years ago, when she herself was still too young to understand, when her sister would spend entire weekends situated quietly in front of the dining room window, staring at nothing, slowly flipping through the pages of a book she would never read; and while those days abruptly stopped somewhere around the time that Ginny learned karate, the memories of them have never ceased to haunt Tricia Kurva.

"I know what it means when you're quiet. I, like, fucking hate it when you're quiet. I'd rather you be all, like, throwing some kind of Godzilla temper tantrum. Do you want to break the television? Let's break the television. I read in a magazine it's good for sisters to do, like, bonding activities together? So let's destroy the TV. *Together.*"

Ginny sighs, plops the book down. "I'm in no mood, Trish."

"Okay, okay. Like, I was saving this for dinner tonight, but, I've got a surprise for you."

Ginny looks at her sister. Deep beneath layers of rage and self-loathing, the prospect of a gift from her sister elicits a faint tingle of joy. "Yeah? What?"

"Close your eyes."

"Tricia…"

"If you don't close your eyes, like, Tinker Bell will die and it won't come true. So, you've got to like, close your eyes."

Ginny sighs, shuts her eyes, becomes acutely aware of Duran Duran on the Misanthrope's sound system. Tricia's wheels move over carpet; she rummages through something, finds what it is she's looking for, opens something. A second later, Duran Duran is overwhelmed by Michael Sembello blasting out of the record player, the recognizable *Flashdance* theme pounding out of the stereo at amped-up bass. Ginny opens her eyes slowly, delight and confusion mixed on her face.

"What is this?"

Tricia wheels to her, grabs her hands. "Omigawsh, come on! Alex in the loft, *hello?* Dance with me. Dance the dance of life!" She pushes herself backwards, pulling Ginny to her feet, spinning herself in a circle.

Ginny smiles in spite of herself. Tension that she didn't realize had been mounting in her shoulders begins to dissipate; awkwardly, in the cramped space afforded by their living room, mindful of the movement of Tricia's chair, Ginny begins to move, closing her eyes, vanishing into the darkness there, letting the music fill her up and guide her. Her smile widens; besides her brief rooftop performance yesterday, it has been a long while since she's danced for pleasure, losing her thoughts to the idleness of a pleasant song. There is freedom in the dance, in the music, in the fusion of her body with something creative, rather than the flesh of a needy, desperate man; freedom to move according to her own impulses, to the sensations that the song elicits from her. She continues to move for a few moments after the song has finished, unwilling to stop, finally slowing herself, out of breath, panting, a film of sweat built up over her. She collapses on the couch, giggles, smiles to Tricia.

"You did it. You made your mix tape. It sounds, like, really good, Trish."

"Omigawsh, I wish!"

"What?"

Tricia goes to the record player, lifts the needle. "Okay, so, like, I know you're going to be, like, mega ultra pissed, but, like, after you left last night, I knew you were like, uber down…"

"…Yes?" Ginny is acutely aware of her own heart rate, slowly gaining in momentum.

"So, like, I got ahold of Roger, and, like, omigawsh, you will not believe it, but he was able to find, yes, now the prized possession of my beloved sister, the original motion picture soundtrack to *Flashdance*. Sorry it doesn't have 'Gloria,' though. I know that's your favorite."

Ginny's eyes go wide. Her teeth clench. "Roger? How did you get to Roger?"

Tricia mimes holding a telephone to her ear. "Um, hello, front desk? Because, like, I live in a hotel and there's a front desk? Like, I'm looking for skinny, blind, bald guy with a beard who lives here? Wait, you mean there's only one? Can you put me through?"

"Roger… was… here? In… our room?"

"Omigawsh, like, he handed it off to me at the door. It

was, like, two seconds."

"*He saw where we live?*"

"Two seconds. He handed me the album, I handed him some of my comics. See? I even traded for them. So you don't have to feel bad about taking something on charity. I know that your, like, femismo pride won't let you. Hey... Ginny?"

Ginny's limbs tremble; Tricia looks on her concernedly, her own eyebrows slowly rising up on her face.

"...Ginny?" she repeats. Ginny grips the arms of her chair, spins her around so that she can look her directly in the face.

"You... know... that you are never... ever... supposed to have anyone... anyone here."

"Ginny, you're scaring me."

"You know where we live! You know what's out there!"

"Omigawsh, Mother Fear-esa, it was fucking Roger. You've known him for, like, a year!"

"I don't know him and he doesn't know me! He's some bum who spends all his time watching gore movies! He could be a fucking rapist, serial killer! Did he touch you, Tricia? Tricia? You tell me right now. Did he put his hands on you?"

Tricia pushes herself backwards with enough force that Ginny nearly loses her balance. "No, you fucking pervert. Not that I'd tell you, though. That'd by my secret."

"You are seventeen! He is twenty-seven! I should have put a stop to this whole little sick fantasy of yours the first time the two of you met. I should have known it, the way he looks at you..."

"The way he looks at me? Looks at me? He looks at me like I'm a kid, you twisted bitch. He looks at you like you're the most awesome fucking woman on the planet, which, you like, so totally are."

"Roger knows exactly what I do. Exactly what I am. What kind of issues do you think he's got, huh? What kind of sick, twisted, perverted son of a bitch would want that, huh? Where do you think that would go? Don't you get that, Tricia? Don't you get that any guy who'd want to be with me is exactly the kind of guy I don't want to be with?"

"Maybe," Tricia says. "Or maybe he doesn't care. Maybe he's just really fucking radcore. But you're too fucked up on booze to even try and find out."

Ginny moves towards her sister. "I am out on that street every single fucking day…"

"Yeah, I know what you're doing out there. I don't need to be reminded, and I don't need to talk about it. And, I'm like, super fucking grateful that you've kept us alive. But you know what else, Ginny? Fuck if it doesn't piss me off sometimes. Because at the end of the day I'm still the one in the chair, and I'm still the one who's never going to get to do what you're doing out there. Fuck yes, I wish Roger would look at me like that. I wish any guy would look at me like that. But they don't. Because I'm not Wonder Woman, Ginny. I'm not Sheena. I'm Professor X. I'm the fucking cripple. But you know what? I know that and I don't give a shit. I'm not in some kind of fucked up, self-loathing, I-hate-myself-and-I-wanna-die punishment trip. One day, I'm gonna get everything I want. Yeah, I am. I don't know how, but, yeah, I'm gonna do some really incredible shit with my life. But you? You're the baddest bitch in this whole fucking building. And all you do is work and then you lock yourself up here with me, and you drink your life away like you're fucking worthless. Like, you only used to drink at night, but lately… how fucking trashed are you right now, exactly? I know your life is shit, Ginny, I know both of our lives are fucking shit. But I've got my stories and my comics and, like, I've got stuff that matters to me, that makes it a little bit better. And you... you, you've got, like, you've got those girls that love you, that'd, like, totally fucking die for you, the way I'd fucking die for you, and a guy who is, like, so totally into you it's actually really pathetic. But you don't give a shit. Because you are made of suck, Ginny. You are made of nothing but fucking suck. And you're killing yourself. And that hurts because, like, I don't want you to die, or shit. *Especially* not for me. You've already killed for me, Virginia. I don't want you to die for me, too."

Ginny pulls her hand back. It freezes in the air, suspended in time, awful and terrible rage bubbling forth from the darkest, most infrequently explored depths of Ginny's soul. She turns around, grabs the record from the turntable, throws it to the floor with enough force that it explodes like glass.

Ginny feels her heart rate begin to slow, her breathing return to normal. The wanton destruction feels good, purifying; a release of the rage and agony that has festered within her for far too long. Without another word to her sister, Ginny storms from the apartment. She needs to get away, for just a little bit, to clear her mind, to remove herself from the situation. She needs a drink, and she needs to destroy some more things today.

———

Impulsive rage has faded from Ginny by the time she makes it down to the second floor; the desire to inflict real, permanent damage ebbing out of her mind as she reminds herself once more that she did not condition her brain and her body to inflict blind vengeance but rather justice. That what she is about to do is not only right but it is good; it is called for; it is necessary.

Truth be told, though, it's also something she's always wanted to do.

Ginny stops before the door to Roger's room, closes her eyes, inhales deeply, letting the stale air and odor of marijuana and cigarettes and sex and blood fill her up. She holds it in, exhales, negativity going with it, hatred, impulsivity. When she opens her eyes, she knocks, drops both hands to her sides. Watches the bottom of the door; sees a shadow drift across as someone checks the peephole. The door opens, catching on the pull chain, Roger's quizzical face appearing above it.

"Ginny?"

One kick is all it takes, the chain snapping out of the wall, the door flying open. Roger barely moves quickly enough to avoid being hit, the door continuing on its arc, slamming into the interior wall of his room, one of the narrow cracks snaking up from the base bursting apart, splitting the door open up to the doorknob. Ginny smiles, satisfied; kicking in a door really is as cool as it's always looked in the movies.

"Hello sweetheart," Ginny says, strolls in, gives the door a neat little kick behind her. Despite its clutter, the room is far neater than Ginny would have anticipated. From her vantage point she can see into the little bedroom space, torn posters tacked up to the walls, the bed unmade, the breech shotgun propped beside the nightstand.

"Ah, Ginny?" Roger asks. "Are you, ah, are you okay?"

"Fabulous, sweetheart. Now that I'm here with you." Ginny thrusts her body forward, knocking Roger onto the couch. She climbs on top of him, pinning his knees down with her own, one hand gripping his neck.

"Shit, Ginny, you smell like a fucking brewery exploded."

"I got your present!" Ginny slurs, stroking Roger's face with her free hand. "That was, like, so fucking thoughtful of you to do that. I mean, it takes so much consideration to, like, totally violate my privacy like that!"

"Look, Ginny, maybe we should, ah, talk about this in the morning when you're..." He tries to stand, pushing himself up on the arm of the couch. Ginny tightens her grip on his throat, thrusting her knees down into the tops of his thighs

"Oh, no, no, no, sweetheart! Where are you going? What are you doing? I'm here now, sweetheart. You've got what you wanted all along. All this time hanging out with me, making fun of movies together, talking about shit, this is what it all came down to, isn't it? You wait around, you sniff after me like some little dog waiting for the smell of blood, and then, then when I hit the absolute bottom, when my life is just shitty enough, you swoop in and make it all better? Because you're such a decent guy? And then what, sweetie, what then? I, like, come to your door, and I crawl into your lap, just like this? Because I'm, like, so turned on? And I just want to fucking throw myself at you? Is that what you want, sweetie?" She thrusts her free hand down between his legs. "Oh, just what I thought."

"C'mon, that's, ah, that's involuntary."

"Shut up. You wanted me, Roger? You always could have had me. You didn't have to pretend to be my friend. You always knew I was for sale."

"I was never pretending."

"A friend... would have listened... to my rules. And my rules were... no one... ever... comes to my door. Ever. No one. You knew that and you broke it..."

"Hey, you know what, Ginny? It was for Tricia. She wanted it for you. She's looking out for you. Because you sure as fuck aren't."

"That is, like, the sweetest fucking thing that I have ever heard. But you're both wrong. Records can't make me happy, Roger, and little jokes in theaters can't make me happy and telling me about some maniac running around killing girls who probably doesn't even... He's not real, is he, Roger? Your little van man? What was that, one more part of your sick little plan? What, you saw Tina run off and cooked that one up? To scare me, to get *widdle* Ginny all terrified so that she'd need her big strong man to take care of her? Here's news, darling. I have never needed anyone to take care of me before, and I sure as fuck don't now. What I need is for my sister to have enough food to eat, and clothes to wear, and a chance at getting the fuck out of this shithole and not ending up like me. And that takes money, sweetheart. That's what makes me happy. So go ahead. You want me? You can have me. Just pay for me. That's all you ever had to do. Because I'm not your girlfriend, and I'm not your buddy. I'm a fucking street walking whore and I'm totally up for sale."

"I, ah, I never looked at you and saw a whore. But, ah, you know, if that's all you really see when you look in the mirror, then get the fuck out of my room, Ginny. Because that line of thinking, ah, it's not gonna come to a good end. And I don't wanna be around to see it."

Ginny stumbles back off of Roger, nearly collapses over the coffee table. She moves backwards, her legs wobbling beneath her, one arm outstretched, pointing.

"You come near me again... it better be with a wad of cash. A lot... of cash. And if it isn't... or if you ever... come near my sister again... I'll do to you what I did to the door."

Roger nods. "Sure, Ginny. Sure."

She continues moving backwards towards the door, continues pointing at Roger, not entirely sure why but certain on some level that this is a good thing, that it conveys something very powerful and determined and so she keeps her hand stretched out until she has reached behind her and opened the door, moved out into the hallway and shut the door, and then she lets her arm drop to her side while she stands and stares at the closed door. She stares and stares at the closed door until she knows that something has just ended and that she isn't quite sure how she feels about that.

What she feels is like seeing a movie; and after another moment, she heads towards the stairs and makes the long trip down and out onto The Deuce.

———

The movie lasts the rest of the afternoon, beginning and ending, beginning and ending, the teenagers venturing out into the woods and getting slaughtered only to be resurrected for the next showing, an eternal loop, an endless night of blood and death, Ginny hunkered down in a seat in the rear of the auditorium, nursing her flask. She periodically checks her watch, the red numbers growing more blurred as the afternoon wears on, until at last the booze is gone and her ass is numb and if she's seeing things correctly it's probably late enough that Tricia has gone to bed and she won't have to talk to her.

The walk back home seems to take longer than it should. Ginny realizes eventually that she's passed the Misanthrope by at least three blocks; she arrives back at peak hour, the lobby jammed, the stairs lined with bodies, foaming beer bottles being passed above heads and joints being passed between fingertips, Ginny snagging one for herself on the way up, slipping through the crowd quickly so as not to have to give it back, toking leisurely as she makes her way up.

Tricia is in fact asleep, nestled into bed, the covers pulled up and over her face, the apartment in immaculate condition; it looks like she spent the duration of the afternoon and evening cleaning. This pleases Ginny; it indicates a falling in line, an acceptance of obedience. Perhaps things will be all right in the morning. Perhaps they can get back to normal after all.

She curls up onto the couch, turns on the television, lying there on her side and smoking in the dark, awash in the blue light of the screen. Her mind drifts far away from the Misanthrope, back through time, before the Christmas break that began but never ended, before she returned home to a nightmare she herself had permitted, back to a night very much like this one: Tricia asleep in her room and mom and dad asleep in their room, and Ginny wide awake on the couch, unable to sleep, thinking about the world that lay ahead of her, of the next day's trip to college and the experiences waiting for her, the hard-earned and long-awaited reward for four years of high school brutality. Hugging Mrs. Butter Bunny and watching Carson's monologue, all of the evil that had preceded that point in her life seemed acceptable, stubbed toes and banged elbows on the path to happiness. Though she's thought it before, tonight, lying here, perhaps because of the events of the day, perhaps because of the combination of the booze and weed, perhaps because of Sally Ride, perhaps because the hatred inside of her has built up so much that it doesn't have any place to go anymore, Ginny wishes now more than ever that instead of lying there and watching the monologue, she'd instead gotten up and grabbed Dad's gun and finished it all then.

Ginny rubs her eyes, but there aren't any tears there. This pleases her. Maybe she's cried them all out. Maybe she's moved past the need for them now, past the need for sorrow, past the ability to be hurt or feel pain. Past feeling any feelings. As recently as last week, the prospect might have frightened her; tonight, she thinks that might be very nice.

7

Monday, June 20th, 1983

"M S. ASTER?"

Nicolette looks up. There is Someone standing in her doorway. The Someone is a woman. Her outfit is remarkably similar to Nicolette's. Nicolette looks down at her own body to make sure her clothes have not been taken from her surreptitiously. They are still there. Good.

"Yes?"

"Ms. Aster… Police are here to see you," Someone says. She walks in, slowly, whispering. It occurs to Nicolette that this might be her secretary.

"What?" Nicolette asks.

"Ms. Aster… Mr. Ellis didn't come home last night," Someone says. "I heard… I heard they saw you talking to him on the security cameras."

Nicolette nods slowly. "Yes. I was here with him yesterday. We discussed the issue with the dogs. Please, send them in. I'm very sorry to hear that something might be wrong."

Someone leaves. Nicolette reaches up and smooths her hair. She removes her glasses and wipes them with the little cloth she keeps in her desk. She neatly arranges the stack of paperwork on her desk. She drums her fingers on her blotter. When the police enter, she rises with great formality. She wishes she had known they would be arriving today. She would have worn one of her good outfits.

"Nicolette Aster?" one of the detectives asks.

"Yes."

"My name's Detective Dafoe, this is Detective Spears. May we have a minute of your time?"

"Of course, gentlemen, please. Sit down." The men sit down. Nicolette is pleased. They waited for her permission to use her chairs. She feels more at ease now. She sits herself. Her throne has grown cool in the minutes since she rose. She shifts uncomfortably, trying to find a warm spot.

"Ms. Aster, you work with a Patrick Ellis?"

"I do."

"Ms. Aster, Mr. Ellis's wife reported him missing this morning. Says he drove up here yesterday morning and never came back home. Now we've reviewed security footage from the landfill, and it shows you and Mr. Ellis meeting here yesterday afternoon. Do you want to tell us about that?"

Nicolette has never understood the curious police tactic of asking people if they would like to speak. They are figures of authority; they should wield that authority with brutal confidence. The men who came to speak to her about the missing little ones were the same way. They asked her gentle, mincing questions, as though the children were her own. They sat in her living room and drank her tea while flesh cooled in the refrigerator.

"Is it lunch time?" Nicolette asks.

"Excuse me?" One of the detectives asks.

"I thought someone had to be missing for forty-eight hours before an investigation could begin," Nicolette says.

The detectives look at one another, then back to Nicolette.

"What?" one of them asks.

"Just something I thought I'd heard," Nicolette says. "We met up here yesterday, me and Mr…"

"Ellis."

"Yes. To discuss the dogs."

"The dogs?"

"Yes. Recently a pack of feral dogs has taken up residence in the landfill. Near the West Mound. They've been attacking workers for some time now. We've been attempting to rectify the situation but it's been going poorly. They mauled a worker last week. It was… bloody. He… Mister…"

"Ellis?"

"Yes. He took it poorly. He called me yesterday morning from the landfill. He'd been drinking. He said he had come up here with a gun and hunted some of the dogs. He'd shot them. He showed them to me. I can show you where he put the bodies."

"Wife confirmed a rifle was missing from the house," one of the detectives whispers to the other.

"He was angry," Nicolette says. "Ranting. Screaming. He'd been drinking. He blamed himself for what happened to that man. It was… it was awful, *darling*. The crying. The swearing." Nicolette leans across the desk. "He's always been such a gentleman. He's never… said such things in the presence of women. Awful things." Nicolette sits back. "After he showed me the dogs, I asked him what he was going to do now. He said he was going to drink some more, and that he might go visit the family of the man who was mauled. I can't… remember his name. " Nicolette puts her face in her hands and produces a sob. "I should have stopped him. If anything happened to…"

Nicolette cocks her ear. One of her attendants leans

down and whispers, "Ellis." Through her ravaged lips, it sounds like "Uh-is."

"...Mr. Ellis..." Nicolette continues, "I... I don't think I could forgive myself." She sobs again. "I should've helped him... I should've... And now I'm just thinking of his car at the bottom of some river, some ditch..."

"Actually, Ms. Aster," one of the detectives says, "His vehicle has been recovered."

Nicolette looks up. She has the urge to urinate. "Excuse me, sir?"

"Vacant lot, out near Willowbrook. Some college kids went out there to drink, thought it was weird. Got spooked and phoned it in."

Nicolette looks back and forth between the detectives. It makes sense now. She understands. *They know.* She must now ascertain whether they have been sent here on orders from The City, to convey to her through their secret language that she will remain protected, that they are true and loyal servants to the royal Asterion, or whether they are agents of a darker force.

"Was there... any sign of him?"

"None," one of the detectives says. "We were wondering if he might've mentioned anything to you yesterday, anything about Willowbrook? Any reason he might be going out there?"

Nicolette shakes her head. "I don't know. I don't remember if he did or not. We spoke only briefly, as you saw on the cameras. He was very agitated. He was more interested in the dogs than anything else."

"Ms. Aster, we realize that this may be a delicate subject matter, but... Do you know if there was anyone else? Another woman? Another man?"

One of the detectives sneezes. Nicolette goes rigid. He knows that she knows. She must tread carefully.

"I don't believe so, no," Nicolette says. "He was... fond... of women. But... what man isn't?" Nicolette smiles. She thinks the detectives smile back.

"*Was?*" One of the detectives asks. They look at one another, then back to Nicolette. *He knows she knows he knows.*

"Was he fond of you, Ms. Aster?"

The hairs on the back of Nicolette's neck go up. Why would agents of The City ask such a question? "Of course not. He knows I'm not like that."

"Like what?"

"Like... *that.*"

The detectives regard one another. "Are you a lesbian, Ms. Aster?"

Nicolette gags. "I am not. And I fail to see how that has any bearing on what's happened to Mr. Ellis. While you're here asking me what my... preferences... are or aren't... whether I... debase myself... Mr. Ellis is... still missing." Nicolette stands up. "Gentlemen, if you don't have any more relevant questions... Please go find Mr. Ellis."

The detectives rise. "I apologize," one of them says. "If you think of anything that might be of assistance, please, call us." He hands her his card. Nicolette accepts it. She walks them to her office door. She shuts it behind them. She waits until their footsteps fade. She locks it. She returns to her desk. She sits on top of it, facing the window. She tucks her knees beneath her chin. She begins to slowly rock back and forth. She wishes she had a record player here. She travels to the Meadow. She needs peace. She is stunned by what she finds. There is music there. It is discordant and descends from the sky, one note at a time on threads of burning tinsel that evaporate into a red mist as they reach the ground. The attendants flutter around, whispering amongst themselves, wringing their hands. Black warning smoke rises from The Altar. It writhes in a fleshy mass, oozing violet blood that rains down onto the rose bushes. Her ravaged dogs sniff around it, lapping at it with bleeding tongues. Nicolette opens her eyes and looks out over the gulfs of trash and refuse before her. She shuts them again. The same sight greets her. She approaches The Altar on trembling legs. Someone squats before it, naked, raindrops splattering his bloated and masticated body. He cradles his head against his chest with his single hand. He opens his mouth. A dog's bark comes out.

Nicolette stands up from her desk. She turns towards it and knocks it over. Her papers and blotter and stapler and pens soar around the room, rolling over the carpet, hitting the wall. A moment later, Someone begins banging on the door.

"Ms. Aster? Ms. Aster, are you all right?"

Nicolette opens the door. Though she and Someone are the same height, Nicolette looms tall over her. She considers tearing the little slut's head off right here. Someone steps back.

"Ms. Aster?"

"What are you bothering me for? I don't have a cock to shove up your hungry little cunt. Can't you go get that on your own, you filthy bitch?"

Someone steps back. She makes a surprised little noise. She is frightened. She is offended. She has no idea how close she came to an audience with the Mighty Minotaur. Nicolette hopes she knows how lucky she is to have been spared. Tonight, one of the pornai will not be so fortunate.

———

Ginny wakes up sticky and damp, the result of having slept not only in her clothes but her shoes as well. She pries herself up from the couch, rubs her face, feels the indentations there from the pattern in the sofa upholstery. Doesn't bother to go look at herself in the mirror; has a pretty good idea of what will look back at her.

She skips her exercises this morning, feeling particularly sluggish, the pot not completely out of her system; doesn't see any real point in showering, either, so just refills her flask for the day, taking a shot now as a little pick-me-up, sad that she can no longer feel the burn of the vodka, just the numb, raw sensation of something going down. Sits down at the kitchen table, draws up a lesson plan. She decides not to go too hard on Tricia. An emphasis on German today, a little bit of chemistry, the next chapter in Gatsby.

Moving through the dining room this morning feels to Ginny like moving through a heavy fog, the lights dimmer than usual, the acoustics seeming off somehow, as though someone has tampered with the carpeting or the wall upholstery in such a way as to make it into one giant echo chamber. Approaching the table, she stops, staring at the girls, their conversation having halted abruptly at her appearance, but not in the usual way, with greetings offered and happy smiles. Instead, she's met with stunned silence, the sort afforded to the sudden appearance of gunshot victims in ERs or naked homeless men wandering into corner gas stations.

Sandra is the first to break the silence. "Oh shit, Miss Ginny got mugged!"

The girls begin rising from the table. All the color drains from Shannon's face as she bolts around the rest of the girls, scurrying to the head of the table. Ginny smiles to herself, shaking her head, moving to take her seat. "Ladies, ladies, please. Today is a morning like any other. I'm allowed a rough Sunday night every once in a while, aren't I? And while I may be disheveled this morning, it's, like, no indication of any issue on my part. Now, please, everyone, take a seat, and, please, stop shouting."

A few of the girls look at one another, to Shannon. Shannon bends down as Ginny sits, whispering in her ear: "Nobody's shouting."

Ginny winces, pulls away from Shannon. Silence envelops the table as Shannon prepares Ginny's coffee, brings it to her. Ginny studies it, the little white spiral floating on the surface, leans over the cup and inhales deeply. The smell is weak, pitiful; the Colonel is skimping on the beans again.

"What is this weak fucking shit?" Ginny mutters. "How in the *fuck* are we supposed to operate on this fucking garbage shit here, Zarek?"

Everyone stares. Someone clears her throat; Ginny isn't sure who. She picks up her mug, knocks it back, the heat soothing on her masticated throat. She drums her fingers on the edge of the table. What were they supposed to talk about today?

"Do you... do you want to talk about the space launch, Frau Kurva?" Michelle asks. "I... watched it."

"Yeah, me too," Candice says. "That was some shit right there."

"I think we all watched it," Shannon says.

"Did we?" Ginny asks. Something in the tone of Shannon's voice seems unnecessarily shrill, petulant, accusatory. "And what did we think about it? What were our thoughts, our feelings about that? Sandra, let's start with you."

"Well, I..."

"I'll tell you what your feelings were. You all felt inspired. You felt like this was something special. And you felt that because it's what you thought I wanted you to feel. None of you gave a shit about space before you came here, I mean, am I right? I mean, like, let's be totally honest here, I'm still the only one at this table who knows what a pulsar is, right? None of you have ever seen a nebula. You couldn't tell the Horseshoe apart from the Horsehead apart from the Red Rectangle apart from the Orion apart from the Carina apart from my ass... But you wanted to make me happy and be all excited about this. Right? I mean, am I right?"

It occurs to Ginny that everyone is staring at her now, no one saying anything, expressions blank or puzzled or worried, and she doesn't understand why and it makes her angry for people to look at her this way, makes her angrier for her own girls to be looking at her this way, frustrated, at herself, at not being able to articulate herself in such a way that she is easily understood. "All right. Let's move on. Literature. We haven't... we haven't talked books in a while, have we? Well, here's an exercise I thought up, okay? I'm going to go around the table. I want you all to think about literary characters. Any one. In books we've read here or books you read in school or comic books or... or, anything. And I want you to think, if you were a literary character, which one would you be? Okay, are we thinking? I'll give you another minute." Ginny beats her hands on the table like she's performing drumroll. "Aaaand, okay, ba-da-tum, Tammy, go!"

Tammy looks at the other girls, at Shannon, looks back to Ginny. "I... I don't know... I guess I'd be... uh..."

"Bzzt!" Ginny imitates a buzzer going off, hits the table with her fist. "Wrong answer, sweetie. No. The correct answer was Esmerelda. Esmeralda, from *The Hunchback of Notre Dame*? Are you familiar?"

"I... I seen the movie," Tammy says.

"Good. Has anyone else seen the movie?"

A few hands go up around the table.

"Good! Because you're all Esmerelda. You're Esmerelda,

and you, and you, and I'm Esmerelda. We're all a bunch of fucking, luckless, loveless, whores, and our lives are shit, and our mothers are bitches, and our goats are completely fucked, and all we've got left to look forward to is the day we hang and we end up rotted in some God forsaken cemetery getting felt up by the twisted freak who loved us while we were alive. Have you all got that?"

Everyone stares. Shannon begins to rise, move towards Ginny.

"Hey... Ginny..."

"It is *Frau Kurva* and you sit the fuck down! What? You don't like the truth? Have I been sugar coating it for too long, sweetheart? I am, like, truly sorry for that. So, please let me enlighten all of you now. There... is... no... exit. We do not get out. This is what we're doing today, and it's what we did yesterday, and it's what we're going to do with all of our tomorrows, until we're old and crippled and we can't even give gum jobs anymore, and then we're all going to fucking die. You understand that? Any of you? Mary understands it. Oh, yeah, I know that Mary understands it. Sweet little, precious little, beautiful little Mary. Oh. Oh God. Oh, Mary." Ginny puts her face in her hand.

"Hey," Candice says. "Frau Kurva. She gonna be okay."

"No she isn't!" Ginny shrieks. "Don't any of you get that? Are you all that fucking stupid? Mary...had... an abortion. Oh, yeah. Yeah. A totally fucked up, totally awful, totally, like, slaughterhouse abortion, because I told her that was the right thing to do. *And it was! It was the right thing to do! She had nothing else to do! Nowhere else to go!* And I'd have done the same for any one of you. Every... thing... that I have ever done here, that I have ever done here, I have done for each and every one of you. I have sold my fucking soul for every one of you only God knows how many times! *Every night!* For three years! Every night... with...

with that man… upstairs… with him… Oh, God…" Her voice cracks and for the infinitesimally long, brief moment before she regains control of herself, her body rocks so violently that it appears as though she's ready to burst.

"And it was to keep all of *you* safe. Because this is as good as it gets here, really. For any of us. What? You think there's something better? You want to go do this job down the street, with Reggie Washington, who'll put out cigarettes on your tits when you don't make bank? With Claude Blanchard, working his girls over with box cutters, shoving… shoving *beer bottles* up their cunts because he's so high he thinks it's funny? This is as good as it gets. So if you have a problem with any of this, if you have a problem with the way things are, the way things really are… You can all go, right now. You can all go right to Hell."

There aren't many dry eyes around the table when Ginny stands up. Those who aren't crying have their heads down, eyes fixed on the table. Ginny wipes her face with the back of her arm, grabs a donut.

"OK. Yeah. That's what I thought. Class dismissed."

———

Nicolette's breath is heavy by the time she makes it to 42nd Street. Even without the pomade in her hair, the sweat would have it slicked flat against her scalp. The lights of The City are red. Pulsating shades of crimson, vermillion, scarlet envelop her in a suffocating veil. From beyond the veil, she hears laughter: hateful; spiteful; *female*. Shrouded figures standing in pitch black alleys point and gesture to her, and then vanish back into ether. The City has grown insolent; it must be reminded of its place. It must be reminded of the disgrace which brought it to its knees; which forced it into servitude to great Minos.

She pulls up to the hotel. She can barely see it through the haze of black gas hovering just above the ground, billowing up out of the cracks in the sidewalk and obscuring the air with its charcoal shroud. Nicolette adjusts her glasses and looks. There, just outside the door, the Beta lingers, talking with the new girl. Nicolette had hoped to save her for later in the Cycle. She has seen how The Girl relies on the Beta; how she spends much of her free time talking to her on the sidewalks, how they sometimes go into buildings together with their men. To have taken her at just the proper time would have been a great strike. Now Nicolette must advance the plan. She must reassert her thrall over this domain. Taking the Beta will restore order. She has already planned it. It will be a great and terrible tribute. She will remove the Beta's legs. Then she will remove the spikes from her collar and insert them in to every one of her holes. Eventually, she will insert the final two into her eyes.

Nicolette rolls down her window and beckons. She waves. She cocks her ear and listens.

"Past time," The Beta says. "Come on. Let's head in."

"Wait," the New Girl says. "I got to... just make a little more."

"Shit, kid, you see what kind of shape Ginny was in this morning? The fuck you think's gonna happen you work past curfew?"

The New Girl looks between the Beta and the van. Nicolette reaches down and holds up a wad of bills, nodding. Perhaps she can take the both of them.

"Let me... let me just go talk to him," the New Girl says. The Beta is about to say something when the New Girl sprints to the van.

"Hey mister," the New Girl says. The drawl in her voice is repugnant. Nicolette makes the mental note to carve out her voice box. "Whatcha lookin' for?"

"I need... some company. That's all."

"Look, I'm not supposed to be out here right now. My friend over there's gonna be real mad if I don't make this worthwhile."

"I've got... friends in the back. One of them's getting married tomorrow. This is his... party. Before he gets married. My friends... all think you're... cute. If you'll... be with them... I'll pay you for all of them. It doesn't have to be... all at once. Just... one at a time... I can pay you." Nicolette reaches down and retrieves the rest of the money she keeps beside the seat. It is several hundred dollars, all in tens and twenties. She learned during the last cycle that quantity of bills has a greater lure than quality.

"How... how many?" The New Girl asks. The disgust in her voice is matched only by the greed. Nicolette knows which will win out.

"Five," Nicolette says. "Plus me."

"All... all that money?"

"Half up front," Nicolette says.

"One minute."

The New Girl runs back to the Beta. They squawk like birds. The Beta protests; the New Girl insists. The New Girl turns back towards the van.

The New Girl gets in.

"All right," she says. "I'm ready. Let's do it."

"All right. Good."

Nicolette puts the van into drive. The New Girl is apprehensive. She shifts in her seat and wrings her hands. She does not even think to try looking behind the curtain until Nicolette is about to pull into the alley. Then, Nicolette is ready to show her exactly what is behind the curtain.

———

The shoulder of Ginny's tank top has torn and the hem of her skirt has ripped by the time she arrives to collect the kick-up, the girls drifting in for the night, Constance and Michelle and Sandra all waiting around the table, and Ginny pulls up a chair at the head of the table, turns it around, slumps against it with her elbows folded over the top, the girls glancing at her, looking but not looking, turning their eyes down to the floor. Ginny tries not to giggle, thinking for some reason that this is either hilariously pathetic or pathetically hilarious, she doesn't know which, these girls who've done things, such things, not able to look her in the eye after a simple bit of the truth.

Ginny becomes more agitated as the minutes wear on, the silence beginning to grate on her, her eyes on her watch, eyes on the door, Shannon wandering in, Candice wandering in, only Tammy left to show up and still no one is speaking. Ginny looks at her watch and she feels eyes on her, boring through her, looks up and catches Constance turning away and then rotating her eyes to look at her askance. Ginny begins staring back at her, not liking the defiance in her gaze, leaning further and further forward, almost toppling her chair, the near collision of her face with the table upsetting her even more . Then, she's rising up from her seat and Candice is rising up from her seat when the doors open and the Colonel enters, one half of his collar popped, the other folded over, his eyes visibly glazed even beneath the faulty lighting. All eyes are on him standing there in the doorway, looking at his watch, looking back at the girls, confused. Ginny checks her own watch, seeing that somehow twenty minutes have passed since she last checked it and it's now far past kick-up time. The girls begin looking at one another nervously; they have usually departed by the time of the Colonel's arrival. Ginny's schedule has, for the most part, diminished their interaction with him; past their initial auditions, some of the newer girls have never seen him again.

"Well, ladies, it has been a fascinating evening," Ginny says, rising up from the chair, getting her legs tangled around it, "but I think that it's time for all of us to, totally, make like trees, and, uh…"

She makes eye contact, for a moment, with Shannon, and though the initial glance between student and teacher is spiteful, resentful, the absolute helplessness that crosses Ginny's face as her words trail off prompts Shannon to rise, say, "Leave."

"…Right," Ginny mutters.

The girls file by Ginny, each briefly stopping, leaving their money for her before heading out of the dining room. The Colonel watches each one pass, some looking down to avoid eye contact, others opting to move several feet away from him. The last to pass is Shannon; she lays her money down, makes a step forward, about to leave, stops, reaching back to grab Ginny's arm, pulling herself backwards to look Ginny in the eye.

"The fuck happened, man? You could've said something to me, man, if it was getting this bad. You know? I don't have shit figured out. But I'd have listened. I mean… A year and a half ago I went to get a fix at the Port Authority and I ended up getting dragged into a bathroom by two guys. And the rest of the assholes in there just stuffed their dicks in their pants and walked out. But you followed me in. And, I guess I've always loved you for that. I'd have… been with you, if that was your deal. And I'm kind of afraid right now that you're the one going into the bathroom. And if you can go, man… what about the rest of us?"

"Sweetheart… *Please.* I have absolutely everything under control."

"Do you?"

"Where's Tammy?"

"Last trick," Shannon says. "Was going to pull a train."

Ginny nods. "Good for her. She's learned quick."

"Sure," Shannon says.

"I've got a date," Ginny says, looking to the Colonel, his arms crossed over his chest, tapping his boat shoe against the floor to the rhythm of the Misanthrope sound system. "I can't keep a gentleman waiting."

———

Though Ginny doesn't get back much later than usual, Tricia is already asleep in front of the television. Swaying to the refrigerator, she finds it bare except for condiments and cans of soda and a few remaining bottles of beer. She looks down at the sopping tinfoil in her hands, the hamburger patty and water-thin mashed potatoes packed inside, what should have been her sister's dinner tonight. It was a Monday after a hard weekend.

A bad day.

She is permitted bad days.

She will do better tomorrow.

Ginny pulls blankets from the bed, brings them out to Tricia, bundles her up. Then she turns and looks at the television. She's made it for Carson's closing monologue. The candy colors sing to her; they sing to her of the pleasant abyss into which she is falling, where the currency of memory has no value.

Ginny stares at the television until the monologue is over and the colors are gone, departing with the sweet promise of a return from tomorrow. Tricia snores behind her. Ginny's thighs ache; her breath is rancid with the stench of cheap wine and vodka and the vestigial odor of semen. She is drunker than she has perhaps ever been and she is completely, utterly wide awake.

MTV holds her attention for a good half hour, Ginny closing her eyes, trying to fall asleep to the music, feeling as though she's about to drift away and then opening her eyes abruptly, looking at her watch, expecting some significant time to have passed, finding that none has passed at all. After a while she rises, paces the room. Tricia's snoring grows progressively louder. When, at last, it occurs to Ginny that she isn't going to be sleeping after all, she shuts off the television, blows her sister a kiss, and staggers out the door. She's made it up to nineteen screenings of *Flashdance* this Summer; it's as good a night as any to break an even twenty.

———

When the film ends, Ginny is still as wide awake as she was when she sat down in the Colossus, her vision slightly more distorted but her hearing keenly sharpened, picking up on every sound coming in from the adjoining theater, and as the credits roll, Ginny rises and saunters out to the lobby to stand in the concession line. She figures that she might as well try and salvage the day, accomplish something good, and tie her *Khan* record.

Ginny is the last in a line of five at the concession stand, the sole woman in a queue of stoop shouldered, restless men, just as sleepless as she, desperate in a different way, here for the girls who work the balcony by night or in search of a quiet place to light up, or perhaps just to simply escape into the fantasy onscreen. Looking over them, fat and tall and muscular and short, handsome, homely, bearded, clean shaven, Ginny thinks how she could have them all, how if she wanted she could advance herself to the front of the line right now with just the right placement of her hands, just the right obscene promises, that she could take one of them into the auditorium with her and not only recoup the cost of popcorn but make a profit. Looking past them, past the concession stand, past the theater wall and the auditorium and through the dimension of time, Ginny sees into a future, a classroom somewhere, the PTA meeting in full swing and bake sales being hotly debated and she is there somewhere near the back, more than a little bit frustrated that she's the one having to attend when they are Tricia's children after all, and in this hypothetical classroom hypothetical Ginny roves her eyes over the fathers, looking very much like the men in the line around her, and she knows that she could have them, too. That any issue, any point of contention, any quarrel between their children and Tricia's could be easily and quickly solved in the back of their cars...

Oh, God, is that how it's always going to be?

Ginny reaches the counter, places her order, plunks change down on the filthy glass counter with trembling hands. The pimple-faced boy in the bow tie and the starched, butter stained shirt takes it, offers her a toothy smile, Ginny thinking that perhaps she took his virginity in a room back at the Misanthrope, if that wasn't some other boy who looked exactly like this one. She does not smile back.

The movie is nearly over, Ginny is wondering if she could pull off a tuxedo vest with no shirt underneath, shoveling popcorn into her mouth and letting kernels fall into her lap, when the picture shuts off and the end comes. There is at first the collective groan that drifts across the lips of any Deuce audience when a picture goes out, shouts at the projectionist, cups hurled at the screen. Ginny sighs; the very nature of The Deuce makes it unconducive for a theater to own or maintain the latest or even reasonable quality projection equipment. The occasional breakdown is to be expected, a hazard of filmgoing on 42nd street.

Then, the lights come up and she knows that this time it's different.

"May I have your attention please?" The voice is authoritative, sober; all eyes turn towards the rear of the auditorium, towards the quartet of young police officers making their way into the theater, dispersing, moving through the aisles. One of them stops at the last row of seats to address the crowd. "I need you all to listen up, all right? By the authority of the office of the mayor, this establishment is hereby closed. None of you are under arrest. Okay? None of you will be searched, none of you will be detained. But you all gotta get out of here." The other three officers have begun approaching patrons, crouching down to address them individually, reiterating the general address. The one at the back of the theater continues: "So just go on, get your stuff together, go on and go home. We're not looking for anyone, none of you are under arrest. I don't care why you're here, you just gotta leave now."

Ginny's chest aches; her mouth goes dry. She shifts towards the edge of her seat, then back, then forward again, spilling her popcorn. One of the officers approaches, reaches towards her.

"Hey, miss? Hey, I know you were watching the show, but you gotta go. We're closing this place down." His hand touches Ginny's wrist; she jerks it away with such ferocity that the officer is momentarily stunned.

"Don't you... Don't you... Oh, no, no, no, sweetheart, there must be some sort of mistake."

"Miss, we don't want a scene, nobody wants a scene. We just want everyone to go real quietly. Come on now."

Ginny stands, dazed, putting a hand over her eyes, the lights of the auditorium blinding. She has never seen it like this before, completely lit up and vacant looking and sad and dead, and in her confusion she finds herself being ushered out along with the handful of other souls who'd been watching the film, out into the lobby, joining the rest of the confused patrons being hustled out of the other three auditoriums, out onto the sidewalk, police cruisers parked up on the curb. A man with some air of authority about him talks to a man Ginny presumes to be the Colossus manager and an usher and another officer and Roger, the little bastard, is chatting it up with the cops and the manager and it becomes clear to Ginny what has happened. This is his doing, his perfect revenge; she doesn't know how or through what mechanism but the raid is his design.

Ginny turns to the nearest officer. "Sweetheart, I will, like, be totally pleased to go home when this is all settled, but as a taxpayer, I think I'm fully within my rights to know why my money is being used to close down a perfectly lovely establishment."

The officer looks her up and down, her outfit, her unwashed hair, the stains and streaks running over her skirt and fishnets. "Look lady, I'm sure you're a fine, upstanding citizen, but a lot of stuff goes down in that place that the mayor don't want going down here anymore. Understand?"

"I don't think you understand, sweetheart. This place is a... lifeline. My friends and I count on this place for... moral support. We rely on it."

"I'm sure you do, miss, but you girls can all go find someplace else. This theater's in violation of the health code."

"Don't you dare tell me that this place is being closed down for anyone's good. I know what's going on here. I am being *persecuted.*"

The officer rolls his eyes, turns away from Ginny, begins to address the next batch of patrons being brought out. Her eyes bulge; she grabs the officer's shoulder, turns him back to face her.

"Don't you turn your back on me!"

"Miss, what you need to do is go home, right now." The indifference is so infuriating to Ginny, the injustice of the situation so blatant, the loss of so vital a part of her operation so unbearable that there really seems to be only one response, only one rational way to react to the situation. Ginny's leg swings and sweeps the officer's legs out from beneath him as he's turning away from her, going down onto his knees, Ginny elbowing him in the back of the head. Then, another officer is on her from behind and she's elbowing him in the midsection, turning around to strike his jaw with her palm, the first officer getting back onto his feet now and Ginny spinning back to knee him in the groin, sending him to his knees. A third officer runs up on the fray as a circle begins to form around the scene, catcalls and hollers, cheers of the displaced Colossus crowd and of the denizens of 42nd, the children of the night in assembly around this battle between one of their own and the ancient enemy. Ginny swings at the third officer, a chop catching him across the chest, turns back to see who's coming up next. Two more officers are forcing their way through the crowd and Ginny is delivering kicks to the ribs of the man on the ground when their clubs come out, quick blows raining down on the back of her head, the back of her shoulders, and she screams and turns towards the blows and gets in another groin kick before a club catches her in the side of the face and she reels back around, onto her knees. She staggers forward, tries to rise up and is almost on her feet again when another blow comes down. The pain is electric; she is fairly certain by the sudden loss of mobility in her left arm that her shoulder has been dislocated. She screams; she tries to rise again, the rain of clubs continuing, forcing her onto the hot, filthy pavement, grit and dirt and ash and cigarette butts grinding against her flesh and her clothes and her hair, and she wraps her one functioning arm around her face to protect it. She is suddenly stone sober and completely terrified and against her will a great, pathetic, pitiful sob escapes her mouth and she knows that she's done it, she's finally done it, she's accomplished the great and fascinatingly difficult task of completely and utterly fucking everything up once and for all. Her shouts are wordless; she will not give anyone the satisfaction of calling out for help. Even if she were willing, there is no one left for her to shout for; and as she tenses herself against the next swing of the club, the next after that, waiting for the one to take her over the sweet oblivion of life's event horizon, she opens her mouth and whispers, inaudibly above the shouts of the crowd, what she is sure will be the final word to cross her lips: "*Patricia.*"

"Hey, hey, hey, hey! Ah, get off, ah, get off my sister!"

Ginny can't quite place the voice at first, familiar in its cadence if not its pitch.

"Back off, buddy, this don't concern you."

"...supposed to be peaceful. No publicity, ah, that's what I heard, right, yeah? You, ah, you think there isn't going to be any publicity for this?"

The blows have stopped; Ginny braces herself a moment, removes her arm from her face, turns to look up. Roger stands there, hands raised beside his head, trembling.

"Come on, man, get back. Your sister's going in."

"My sister, ah, my sister's a sick woman. Why, ah, why do you think she looks like that? She, ah, she starts to think she's getting better and so she, ah, she stops taking her pills, and then... well, then this happens."

The officer looks at his fellow officers, bruised, breathless, some bloody. "You fucking with me, man? What, she goes off of pills, she turns into fucking Lou Ferrigno?"

"I'm very, very sorry."

"So am I, man, but we gotta take her in."

"Give her to me. I'll take care of her. She'll listen. No troubles. Look, ah, I, ah, I heard about this, ah, from, ah, Lenny Caruso?"

"You know Lenny?" Another officer asks.

"Sure, ah, he buys comics from me for his kid sister, for ah, Angie? Mayor doesn't want any publicity. You think there'll be no publicity if it gets out you shut this place down and, ah, five guys got the shit kicked out of them by a teenage girl?"

"Teenage?"

"Seventeen, sure, ah, she's had a hard life, and she's a minor, anyway, so what do you think's gonna happen? They'll just release her back to me anyway, and then that's it for her. But you guys... Ah, you guys want someone from the Post putting your names in the paper, that you, ah, that you all got manhandled by a sick seventeen-year-old girl? You wanna get sued for beating up a mental patient? You wanna get called on the carpet for that? Look, ah, I'm, ah, I'm really sorry, but, arresting her doesn't do anyone good, does it? We, ah, we've all been in bar fights here, am I right?"

The officers eye Roger skeptically. "*All* of us?"

"...Sure. So let's, ah, let's chalk it up to that, all right? Chalk it up and go home."

"...Get your sister and get the fuck out of here."

And the officers are collecting themselves and the hooting and hollering and cheering crowd is dispersing, wandering away to find other delights with which to fill the night. Roger approaches Ginny, whimpering and still immobile on the concrete, trying to push herself up with her one functioning arm.

"Get the fuck away from me. I don't need your fucking charity." Her arm gives out and she collapses, screaming.

Roger hovers over her, hunched down, moving around her. At last he stops, reaches forward, grips her wrist.

"Get off of me, you son of a bitch!"

"I'm sorry, but ah, this is really gonna hurt."

One of Roger's shoes come down onto her shoulder. Ginny squirms beneath it, a final scream before the sudden, fierce jerk, Roger exerting more force than Ginny thought he was capable of, his wiry chimp arms stronger than they look, and then her arm and her shoulder are back in place; soothing warmth flows through her as sensation returns, the pain ebbing. Slowly, she rises into a sitting position, examining her hands, her arms. Roger kneels in front of her.

"How does it feel?"

"...Better."

"I know, ah, I know I'm the last face you wanna see, but, ah, but I'd really like you to come with me. The, ah, the light's not too swift here and, ah, and I'd really like to see if you got a concussion."

———

"I really thought they were going to start with the Anco," Roger says, standing over Ginny, shining a Maglite into her eye. "The night shift was, ah, pushing crack at the concession stand. Or the Oracle; the manager there, he ah, he's been filming porno in his office. And so I figured you'd get the message when one of those went down, or when they both went down, and you'd, ah, you wouldn't have been caught off guard. So, if I'd have known, I'd have told Shannon or someone. So, ah, sorry."

Ginny squints against the brightness; hadn't noticed the last time how dim Roger's room is, thinks to offer to have the bulbs changed before it hits her that he's already changed them all himself, put 40 watts in place of the customary 60s and turned the place into his own private theater.

"So what exactly is going on, sweetheart?"

"The city's getting tired of dealing with a particular, ah, element. They've, ah, they've always been all right with 42nd as long as what happens here stays here. But what was bad in the 60s was worse in the 70s, and it's, ah, it's, I guess, much worse now. So the mayor's office, ah, they decided to take a look at certain, ah, epicenters of dissolution. The Anco for the drugs, the Oracle for the porn, and, ah, well, the Colossus for, ah…"

"For me."

Roger grunts, continues his examination. He has her look around the room without moving her head, has her follow the movement of the flashlight around in a circle, stands away from her and holds up a magazine, this month's issue of *People*, asks her to read the headlines as he flips through pages. When he's commenced the visual examination he begins moving his hands over her head, his fingertips prodding different bone structures of the head, what Ginny remembers from Tricia's lesson plan are the mastoid processes, the occipital bone, the foramen. The gentility with which his spidery fingers move over her skull is surprising, in light of the brute force exerted on her shoulder in front of the Colossus. Were it not for the circumstances, Ginny thinks, not for the throbbing in her shoulder and her abdomen and in the sides of her head, it might even feel nice. When he's completed his examination of her skull and he turns his attention towards her ribs, she shudders.

At last Roger stands back, pulls up a chair from the little writing desk, positions himself in front of Ginny.

"You've, ah, you've had the shit beaten out of you."

Ginny claps her hands over her mouth. "Omigawsh.

Really?"

"You don't have any skull depressions, no bruising, no blood in your ears, so, ah, I don't think there's any cranial damage. And, ah, there's no signs of any visual impairment or, ah, other abnormalities. So, I, ah, I think you're going to be okay."

Roger folds his hands in front of him. He sits there looking at Ginny, Ginny looking at him, across the Milky Way between them. When the silence becomes too un-comfortable, she is the one to break it:

"You work in a comic shop, sweetheart."

"Uh-huh."

"And you just gave me a half-assed triage exam. That's not an insult; I wouldn't have even expected quarter-assed."

Ginny smiles; Roger, awkwardly, smiles back. They fall quiet again. This time, Roger speaks first.

"I was always sick as a kid. I, ah, I told you that. The rheumatic fever. My eyesight. This thing where I stop breathing when I sleep. I, ah, I didn't have much, except for my books, and my movies, and the hospital. A lot of time in the hospital. Lots of time to wonder what was wrong with me, why there was something wrong with me. Lots of time to get to know kids a lot worse off than me. This one guy, his name was Peter. You know I couldn't even tell you half the stuff we talked about; just that he was always there and I was always there, and we both liked Buck Rogers and blue, and then one day he wasn't there and then he never was again. I don't even know what was wrong with him, really, or if my folks knew, either. Don't even know when he went or why. Just that he did and I was sad when I found out. And that's when I knew what I wanted to do when I grew up."

Roger sighs, looks past Ginny to some long forgotten place. "There's no jump start on premed like growing up in a hospital. I heard once that the best psychiatrists are the ones trying to figure out what's wrong with themselves. I think maybe the best doctors are the ones that got something wrong with them, too. Who want to fix in other people what they can't fix in themselves. I was good. Ah, not great. But pretty good. Made it to my residency. So, you know, I had that going for me."

"What happened?"

Roger's already nasal voice grows higher in pitch. "You ever kill someone?"

Ginny does not respond. Roger nods.

"Well, it feels like shit."

Ginny still does not respond.

Roger goes on: "I thought I'd be ready for it. I mean, losing the first one. Everyone does. The bleeding you can't stop, the heart you can't restart, ah, the brain you can't get firing again. They said it wasn't on me; that no one could've saved him. But it didn't make me feel any less that it was my fault. That he hadn't died; that I'd killed him. And that was when I realized that for all the diplomas and studying and wanting to change things, I was still really just a sick kid in bed who wanted to play doctor to make the world feel better. And so… that was it. If I was going to do any good for anybody… It, ah, it wasn't going to be there. I left Oklahoma. And then, ah, then I came here. The way I've always seen it, ah, if I'm gonna make a difference, it's gonna be in a way no one gets hurt. Even if that difference was just treating kids who had to grow up too quick like they were still kids. And, you know what? Maybe that's all I gotta do. I feel good about that. And I get to watch a lot of movies. That's pretty cool, too. And so that's that. And I guess, really… that's me." Roger nods quietly, looks around the room, back at his own folded hands, and then to Ginny, offering her the floor; the opportunity to make her own confession.

"I was going to be a teacher," she says. "I saw the moon landing when I was seven and I was like, oh, shit, this is like, the best thing ever, right? And I was, like, the only girl excited about it the next day at school. No one else wanted to talk about it. They wanted to talk about Barbie and shit. And Mrs. Simmons was okay with that, and I wasn't. And I pretty much always knew from then on that one day I wanted to make as many little girls as excited about the stars and the universe and chemistry and physics and all the really awesome stuff as I was. Because I knew that there are so many other little girls out there who could do some really awesome things, if someone would just show them how great it was. So that's what I worked towards. I got, like, accepted into the teaching program at Avila on a scholarship. And it was like, oh shit, it's going to happen. But, then it was, 'oh, some shit happened.' And then me and Trish came here. And that's, like, more than I've ever told anyone. You're very privileged now, sweetheart. I hope you realize… I hope we're cool."

Roger smiles. "We, ah, we gotta be. Us sad sacks have got to stick together."

Ginny smiles back. Though the music continues to drone on the Misanthrope's sound system, the room seems almost quiet; peaceful. She reaches forward and puts her hand on Roger's, squeezes it.

"You're, ah, you're welcome here anytime, you know," he says. "Now that, ah, now that the Colossus is gone. I've got, ah, I've got a Beta. Or we… could just watch television. I'll, ah, I'll even sit in the chair."

"Sweetheart, that sounds absolutely fabulous." Ginny stretches, rises, puts either leg out in front of her, rotates it. No pain there; good. "I really have got to be going now, though. It's getting early and a girl needs her sleep. Especially after tonight."

"I'll let you out."

Ginny lingers in the doorway, looking up at Roger, Roger leaning there, shifting his weight from foot to foot, looking down at her.

"Well, sweetheart, thank you for a fantastic night at the movies," Ginny says. "We, have totally got to do it again sometime."

"Thank you for, ah, thanks for walking me home," Roger says.

"A girl's got to look out for her best fella."

Roger visibly begins to sweat. "Ah, well, thanks. Ah, really?"

"The best, sweetheart. Goodnight."

"Goodnight."

Ginny reaches up, runs her fingers through his beard, steps back from the door. Roger smiles, steps back, closes the door. Ginny watches the bottom of the door for his shadow to drift away, leans against the doorframe, sighs. She looks at her watch; late for the world, early for The Deuce. Some of the girls might still be awake. She needs to make the rounds; smooth things out with them as she has with Roger. Perhaps she can arrange for a group of street thugs to engage in a faux attack on her in the Misanthrope dining room tomorrow morning, let the girls save her, be the heroines riding in on white stallions. It seems to have done the trick nicely with Roger.

Ginny heads down the hall to Tammy's room; best to start her mea culpa tour here. The new girls always bruise the easiest, are the quickest to run. She can arrive on the pretense of collecting the night's kick-up, segue into something best resembling an apology. She scans her mind for those Biblical verses pertaining to forgiveness, brotherly love, atonement, settles on the two or three she thinks will most effectively resonate with the girl.

She knocks on Tammy's door. "Tammy? Tammy, sweetheart? Are you still awake?" She waits a moment. No answer. Knocks again; waits.

"Tammy?"

The girl could, of course, be downstairs, availing herself of the nightly revelry; could be on the toilet; could be working The Deuce again in violation of her orders. Something nags at Ginny, though, something she cannot quite articulate, something conveyed to her in the depths of her drunkenness that the sudden, brutal onset of sobriety has eradicated from her mind, and with this nameless dread bobbing beneath the surface of her mind, she thoughtlessly puts her key into the lock and lets herself into Tammy's room.

The quarters are as Ginny expected; no mess, no clutter, barely any signs that the room has received any use at all over the past week except for the placement of the Gideon Bible on the little table before the couch.

"Tammy? Sweetheart? Are you decent?"

She walks around the room, as though the girl might be crouching somewhere impossible, hidden beneath the sofa, in the closet. The bed is still made; Ginny runs her hand over the fabric. It's cool to the touch. She sits there, bobbing her foot to Culture Club, wishing she had a drink, thinking how awfully that's worked out for her over the past few days, opens up the bedside table, finds a pack of cigarettes there and takes one. Something of Tammy's base nature, she feels, has rubbed off in this room; become a part of its essence. Something homey and gentle, a quietly dignified perseverance. She wonders if Tammy's ever had a beer before; will try to tacitly pry it out of her, maybe get her a bottle. Ginny checks her watch. Maybe she can even bolt out somewhere, get back before Tammy returns, have

something nice and cold waiting for her. Ginny's pulled her share of trains in the past, knows the toll it takes, the gross anonymity of it. At once, Ginny feels a sudden respect for the girl; she's held out this long, met her fate here admirably. A bit of petulance and disobedience are to be expected, especially from someone coming to her from so stable a background. A world better than little Tina, polluting the world around her with her negativity, sucking the life out of rooms rather than putting any in, Tina who never even came back…

Ginny stands up. She moves to the door, shuts out the lights, heads into the hallway. Rushes to Shannon's, smoothing her skirt on the way, tidying her hair. She stops before knocking, to gain composure, to make sure that the acceleration of her heart and the tremble of her stomach are not audible in her voice.

"Shannon? Sweetheart? Are you awake in there?"

Ginny hears movement inside the room, soft voices before the door cracks; women's voices. She relaxes a bit. The thought of Tammy having found a confidant in Shannon is comforting to her. She'd have thought that the girl would have opened up sooner to Mary; isn't really in any position to question the peculiarities of human relationships, though.

"Ginny?" Shannon opens the door, but keeps the chain lock in place. Looking past her, into the room, Ginny can see a nude blonde girl splayed across the bed, looking up from a magazine. Her heart starts to race again.

"Sweetheart… I know it's late and I, like, totally hate to ruin your private time. But, you have no idea how badly I feel about before."

"Everything cool?" The girl calls from the bed.

"It's the boss," Shannon yells back, undoes the chain lock, steps into the hallway.

"Shit, man, are you like, okay? What the fuck happened to you?" Shannon's eyes move over Ginny's body, the developing bruises on her shoulders, the deteriorated condition of her outfit.

"Nothing but a very much needed and very much appreciated dark night of the soul, darling. The point is that I'm here with my hat in my little hands asking for your forgiveness. You have been so super awesome to me and I have been, like, so not awesome at all the past few days. You didn't deserve today. None of the girls did. And I am *so* going to make that up to all of you."

Shannon nods. "You and me are always going to be cool, man. It may take some work with some of the other girls, though."

"You are so totally right, sweetheart. As a matter of fact, I was just by to see Tammy; she's still so fresh, you know, I figured she probably took it the worst. But, do you know, the little dickens still isn't back yet?"

Vague concern crosses Shannon's face. "Pulling a train's a hell of a thing. She seemed cool with it, though. The guy was offering her a load of cash."

"Guy, sweetheart? As in, the singular?"

"Well, sure, the guy with the money. I didn't see the rest."

"Where were the rest?"

"In the back of the van, I guess. That's where he said they were."

"Van, sweetheart?"

"Well, sure. It was a bachelor party."

"What... sort of van, sweetheart?"

"'73 Ford Econoline." Shannon pauses, thinks. "Sea pine green."

Ginny grabs the doorframe with one hand, grips her stomach with the other. The vomit burns on its way up.

"Oh, shit man. Are you sure you're all right?"

Ginny nods violently, evacuating the remainder of her stomach, trying to do Shannon the courtesy of not hitting her. Shannon tries to help her rise, Ginny waving her off with the hand she's not using to brace herself. Shannon opens the door, calls back into the room: "Hey, Lana, get me a washcloth! Boss is sick!"

"…Fine, sweetheart, perfectly fine. Just a little… Oh. Just a little upset stomach. I have really got to eat better food, you know that? I know my metabolism is absolutely marvelous but I can't live on donuts forever, now, can I?"

Lana appears at the door, offers Ginny a damp washcloth. The girl has a chain connecting her nose to her ear. Ginny looks between the two as she wipes her forehead, her face. "I'm, like, so sorry that you've got to meet me this way, sweetheart. I do hope that darling Shannon here has told you enough stories to make up for this most unfortunate first impression."

Lana looks her over, shrugs. "I've had hard nights too, man."

"You're an absolute doll, do you know that? Shannon is a very lucky woman. Now if you ladies will excuse me, I have got to take care of some business before turning in for the morning. Shannon, sweetheart, you two have a lovely evening. Lana, it's been a pleasure. I, like, do hope that we get to meet again soon, under much more fortunate circumstances."

Ginny smiles, offers a polite little curtsy. Lana smiles wryly, she and Shannon disappearing back into the confines of their room. Ginny waits for them to resume talking before she turns, bolts upstairs.

————

"You bring new girl?" The Colonel says this as he rubs his eyes, squinting at Ginny from the darkness of his room.

He reeks of sweat and piss and his bathrobe is splattered with cheap merlot. "I not ready yet. Let me make phone call, get cocaine, then I ready."

"We need to talk." Ginny moves past the Colonel into the room, switches on the light. The Colonel shouts, puts his arm over his eyes.

"Too bright! My eyes sensitive at night." He moves to the light switch, turns them back off. Ginny sighs, shuts the door behind her. In the faint light coming through the curtains, Ginny can barely make out the Colonel's figure shuffling around the room, picking up empty bottles, shaking them beside his ear, finally finding one with a few last drops of wine in it before settling down on the foot of his bed.

"What so important you wake me up? I asleep."

"Tammy's dead," Ginny says. She's spent enough time in the Colonel's room in the dark to make her way to his desk, find his cigarettes, light one up. She smokes it quickly, lighting another, taking this one a bit slower. "Tina, too. And maybe this girl named Sheila. And maybe a whole shitload of other girls, too."

The Colonel is still on the foot of his bed. He takes another drink. Ginny registers his silence as tacit instruction to keep talking.

"I've been hearing stories over the past week about a guy in a green van picking up girls who never come back. I wasn't sure what to believe at first. Then, like, more information started coming in to me…"

"Information from boyfriend?" The Colonel snorts. "I know bald boy knows things. People bring him things, he buy them, sell things for other things. Bald boy a lot like me. Best thing man can be in war zone is source of information. Information most valuable thing in war."

"If you must know, sweetheart, yes, Roger has been absolutely wonderful about keeping me abreast of the situation at hand. And the situation at hand is this: We are completely fucked."

The Colonel snorts, takes another drink.

"Someone is out there killing girls, sweetheart. *Our* girls. Other girls. He may have killed a lot. I... I think that he's going to stop soon. He may have done this last year and if he did, then he's going to be slowing down pretty soon. But, until then... We've got to take the girls off the street, sweetheart. I could tell the girls not to service guys in vans, but I don't know if he's going to get wise, change cars... Just for the next two weeks. I'll work them like an absolute taskmaster through July, sweetheart. We won't have a second's rest. It'll be the last days of Rome out there. But, until then... We've got to stop."

Neither of them speaks for a long while; the Go-Gos fade in and out on the sound system. Finally, the Colonel speaks: "Why?"

"Excuse me, sweetheart?"

"Girls stupid enough to die, they not need work for me. I not need stupid girls. Stupid girls make mistakes, get robbed, beaten up, lose money. Mary stupid. Tina stupid. Ginny see what happen to them. Stupid girls cost money. I not here to spend money. Girls die, that not my problem. Let them die. Then we get better girls."

"Sweetheart... He could get me, too."

"...No. You too smart for that."

"And if I'm not, sweetheart? If he gets a sedan, a truck? If he walks up to me on the street and offers to bring me back here?"

The Colonel contemplates his bottle, turning it around in the dark. "I seen the world come and go. Watch men younger than me die screaming for mothers, watch men older than me die begging for life. I watch sun set over camps, sky red, filled with black smoke of burning bodies. I watch boys run screaming into dark with guns… Boys still running today. And I still here. That all I need. You walk with me, that good. You not able to walk with me… I still here. I always here."

At once the Colonel is on his feet and his hand has got the back of Ginny's neck, pulling her towards him, onto him, down onto the bed, yanking her face towards his own.

"You so worried about going…I make sure to enjoy you while you still here."

The only thing that gets her through the next half hour is knowing that it's the last time.

———

Tricia Kurva screams as she wakes up. No nightmares molest her mind, no nascent terrors dancing on the periphery of her subconscious. The source of her fright is quite real, sitting before her, slouched over in her wheelchair, red-eyed, shoulders bruised, her bathrobe draped loosely around her. Tricia clasps a hand over her mouth, reaching out to her sister with the other.

"Omigawsh! Ginny! What happened? What happened?"

Ginny brings a cigarette to her lips, smiles faintly. Her other hand slowly works the length of Tricia's rosary, passing each bead determinedly between her fingers.

"Pack the VCR," she says. "We're leaving."

8

Tuesday, June 21st, 1983

THE ALARM CLOCK LULLS NICOLETTE OUT OF A dreamless sleep. Her first revelation upon opening her eyes is that she is still wearing her glasses. Her second, on rising, and finding the sheets stuck to her body, is that she is still in her armor. Her breath catches in her throat.

She doesn't remember how she got home.

She tugs at the sheets; they peel away from her with a long, soft, scratching sound. Some of the places where the blood is particularly caked tear away from the rest of the sheet. Nicolette tosses them in a heap at her feet. The room is dark. Though she can see the light of the sun beyond the blinds, it's not penetrating the house.

Nicolette moves out and into the hall. As her eyes adjust, she can see small, dark patches in the carpet, two by two, that were not there before. They are accompanied by dark streaks on the walls. She continues moving down the hallway. It's brighter in the living room. She can see now that the spots and streaks are blood. She can tell because there is blood everywhere in the living room; not just where Someone was sacrificed yesterday but elsewhere, too. On the walls. On her coffee table. On her record player. Nicolette begins panting. She walks in a circle for several minutes, until she grows dizzy. Then she stops and begins walking in a circle again. She can see into the kitchen from here. The table has been tipped over. One of the chairs is broken. Her ceramic cow is on the floor, shattered into small pieces. She continues walking in a circle.

Somewhere in the house, something drips.

Nicolette stops in her tracks. She stands still. Listens.

It's coming from the garage.

Nicolette bolts to the garage door, flings it open. She switches on the light. The doors of her van are open. Dried blood trails out the back, onto the garage floor. It trails across the floor to a point beside an overturned stool. Beside the stool there is a small puddle of blood. From above, a droplet strikes it. The blood ripples. Nicolette looks up. Dangling from the ceiling by a length of rope is a crimson husk of soggy meat that Nicolette supposes was the New Girl. The head and some of the limbs have been clumsily removed; odd lengths of bone poke out at strange angles.

Vague flashes dance through her mind. The trek to the dump. The hunt. The dogs converging on the tribute. She must have grown tired after the sacrifice. She must have decided to butcher her here. She must have spent the night taking her apart. Yes. This makes sense. It makes perfect sense.

It must.

Nicolette goes to sit in the back of her van. Some of the blood has not yet completely dried and the upholstery is still damp. She rests on the edge a moment, staring at the pornai's body, blood and ooze trailing out onto the garage floor. Then she lifts her legs up into the van and shuts the doors. This is a result of her own foolishness. The City intended her to take the Beta. She should not have

attempted to deny its offering. This pornai was weak, pitiful; perhaps the most vile and low of all the pornai she has
taken; perhaps lower even than the little ones. Her vitality
was in such weak supply that it actually drained Nicolette's.
That is why she is here now; that is why her home is in
shambles. It's still fine. It's still good. Tribute has still been
made, but she must rectify the situation. She must make it
right. She will phone in sick to work today. She will clean
up her house. She will be on 42nd Street early tonight. She
will collect what belongs to her.

—————

Little planning went into Virgina Kurva's flight from
St. Louis; it had been borne of equal parts necessity and
impulsivity, and beyond her sister and a few cursory odds
and ends, she had taken little with her in the way of use
or value. Such a decision had naturally resulted in multiple
unforeseen circumstances; the trek north in their father's
Impala had required the sale of multiple articles for gas
and food money—both girls' jewelry, the cassettes in the
car, Paul Saunders' class ring; the sale of the Impala for bus
fare; and, ultimately, in the name of sheer survival, the sale
of the last thing Ginny had *to* sell. All things considered, she
feels that she and Tricia's lives have turned out far better
than they could have. As such, she's sure that, with half a
day's planning, she and her sister will be running San Francisco by this time next year.

"Okay, but, like, I think we totally need to review some
of the cons, too," Tricia says as she slurps her coffee. Ginny cannot recall the last time she and her sister sat at the
breakfast table together on a weekday; she'd very much
like to change that when they get to California. "Like,
beach, check, weather, check, that's all fan-fucking-tastic.

But, hello? Everyone is gay there? That's, like, totally cool for all of them, but I want to get laid before I die."

"Not every man in San Francisco is gay."

"All the hot ones are. And, like, why San Francisco?"

"Same reason we came to New York. We can disappear there." Ginny takes a drink of her own coffee. She's proud of herself; there's only one shot in it.

"But we don't need to disappear anymore. I mean, like, we never really did, did we?"

Ginny winces. "Maybe not. But we might after today. I mean, as far as I know, the Colonel's small fry, really. He's got the Misanthrope and he knows some half-assed coke pushers. But I mean, I don't know what he's really into, what he's really got. I'm not taking any chances in pissing him off. And he's going to be totally pissed when no one comes back tonight." Ginny considers what she says next carefully, not entirely sure she's comfortable with it yet. "That's why I'm leaving you with Roger today."

Tricia stares. Ginny is not sure she's ever seen her sister at quite such a loss for words.

"You *will* be on your best behavior."

"...So *I am* getting laid before I die."

Ginny wads up a napkin, throws it at her sister. "Women are dead. I'm glad you're taking this so well."

"Omigawsh, like, I'm not a monster. But give me some credit, okay? I've lived with you for the past three years. I could, like, survive nuclear winter now."

"I'll take you down before I go to breakfast. You'll have on two pairs of your clothes and one of my suits on over that..."

"What about my confirmation dress?"

"...I will, like, so totally buy you a way better dress in California."

Tricia's face melts. "*Ginny!*"

"It would look weird. I'm sorry. I will buy you the nicest, prettiest, most expensive dress I can afford. California style. Haute couture. And you can wear it when you're introduced to the new congregation. But we can't leave with much. And the VCR. Roger's got Beta. If anyone's watching, if anyone asks, you're going down to watch tapes with him. People have seen him and me together before. So now I want my sister to spend some time with him, to get to know him, right?"

Tricia stares again. "Oh, shit."

"What?"

"You guys did it, didn't you? Last night, after he put you back together?"

"He did not put me back together. He… helped me out of a rough situation."

"Was he like, all weird and awkward? Or did he, like, totally just go all rabid chimp and throw you down on the floor?"

"Tricia…"

Tricia squeals.

"*Listen to me.* You're going to spend the day with Roger. I'll meet the girls in Mary's room. We'll say our goodbyes. I'll come back for you. We'll already be on the second floor so it'll be a quick shot out. If I schedule everything right we'll be out of the Misanthrope before the Colonel comes down for dinner and at the Port Authority just before boarding time. We'll be leaving the city before the Colonel knows anything."

Tricia doesn't say anything for a minute. Then:

"What about the girls?" Her tone has turned serious.

"If they're smart, they'll be leaving, too."

"No, I mean…like… the other girls? I mean, the other girls working on the street. What'll… what'll happen to them?"

"I don't know. Roger's already tried to talk to the cops once. And if they don't believe… Whoever it is will slip up one day. He'll be spotted. Someone will remember his plates, some kind of detail. And then the next time he tries something, there'll be some pissed off pimp waiting."

"Until then, though?"

Ginny shakes her head. "We can't worry about that. As much as you'd like, we're not the X-Men. We're a bunch of people who're in way over their heads."

"That is such bullshit," Tricia says.

"What?"

"*Nothing* is over your head, asshole."

————

"Rise and shine, sweetheart. The breakfast patrol is here!"

Roger Niederman, still in his bathrobe, has no choice but to step back and out of the way as Ginny pushes Tricia's chair into his room. The chair contains a tableaux which Roger isn't quite certain he is actually seeing, Tricia dressed like Ginny, a black and violet plaid suit and lavender bow-neck blouse, holding in her lap the Kurva girls' VCR, their portable record player aloft that. Tricia balances them beneath the balls of her thumbs, holding in either hand a cup of coffee and a burned English muffin.

"Hot and fresh, just like us!" Tricia chirps, thrusts the mug and the muffin forward. Ginny pokes her head out into the hallway, checking either direction, quickly ducking back in and shutting the door.

"I think we're clear," she says.

"I, ah… what?" Roger asks.

"Tricia, go on to the bathroom and get changed. I don't need you sweating through my good suit."

"Aw, but I was having fun pretending to be a massive

fucking dork."

"So get into your own clothes and you can stop pretending."

"Ahhh, what's happening?" Roger asks.

"Omigawsh, like, ow. My self-esteem is, like, critically injured," Tricia says. "I think I've got, like, trauma now. Thanks for the emotional scars, sis. I really wanted to spend my savings on college but now I guess I'll have to put it towards therapy."

"*Go change.*"

Tricia sighs, rolls her eyes. She drops the VCR and record player off on the couch, disappears into the bathroom. Once she's gone, Ginny smiles at Roger, nodding, grinding her heel into the carpet.

"So…"

"Thank you again for last night," Ginny says. "You were wonderful…"

"I knew it!" Tricia calls from the bathroom. Ginny picks up a magazine from the coffee table, hurls it at the door, turns back to Roger.

"…And I would have absolutely loved to have spent more time with you. But…" She sighs. "The new girl's dead, sweetheart. Ninety-nine percent sure. The man in the van. I'm very certain he got Tina, and Tammy, and, like, probably this girl last year whose name I can't remember. I think it was Pam. And I'm pretty sure they're all dead. I've let… I've let a lot of bad things happen in my life, sweetheart." Ginny runs a hand through her own hair, sits down on the couch. "I can handle a lot of things. I've accomplished a lot of things. But sometimes… Sometimes, when there are things I don't know how to handle… Sometimes I try and pretend they aren't happening. Because I'm *not* used to not being able to handle them. And then they get out of control and I have to take care of them anyway, but they've had time to get worse. And this is one of those times. And I've got to stop things now before they get worse. I'm sending the girls away. Tonight. Then Tricia and I are getting on a bus. I'm having them all meet me at Mary's upstairs, then I'll come down here and get Tricia, so we can get out of here before the Colonel comes down. And I'm sorry to bring you into this, and I don't know if you'll be in any kind of danger after we're gone, and I'm sorry for that too, but…"

"Ginny." Roger puts the coffee and muffin down, places his hands on her shoulders. "I'll call in sick. You know I'll help. You know I will. You, ah, you knew I would. You, ah, you wouldn't have come here if you didn't know."

Ginny smiles, tries to keep smiling, can't. "I always meet the best guys at the worst possible times." She reaches out a hand to touch his face, hesitates, puts her arms around him. Roger embraces her back.

"I really would have loved to have spent time with you here, sweetheart. I really… You helped make something awful bearable for me. I mean, with working, and taking care of Trish… Being with you was the only time I felt like a normal girl."

They both squeeze one another tighter. Ginny runs her fingers over the back of Roger's head, over the side of his beard, committing the sensations to tactile memory, to retrieve at some future date, when the world grows too cold.

From the bathroom, Ginny can hear the faint sound of crying.

"Write to me?" Roger asks.

"Of course, sweetheart. Of course I will."

"Where are you going?"

"California. I figure it's like here but with a nicer beach. I think… I think I'll fit in just fine."

Roger sits back. His eyes are damp. He wipes them

with the back of his hand. "You're still, ah… still?"

"There aren't… I don't have many options that will take care of two people, sweetheart."

"What if, ah… Well, what if this wasn't goodbye, then?"

"Excuse me?"

"I've ah, I've got nothing here for me. I've got a shitty job that pays me enough to live at the Misanthrope, and I can, ah, I can watch movies anywhere I live. And if you were working, ah, a straight job, and you had someone else working a straight job, ah, well… then you would have enough, wouldn't you? It could be even somewhere nice. Somewhere Tricia could go to a real school. I mean… We wouldn't be much better than here, I don't think, ah, not really. But a little better than here is still better, right? What, ah, what I guess I'm trying to say is that, ah, I think we'd make a hell of a team."

Ginny smiles, runs her hand over Roger's head. She opens her mouth to speak. Before she can, Tricia's voice resonates from the bathroom:

"Say yes, bitch!"

Looking into Roger's eyes, the gentility there, the expectant, twitchy smile on his face, a life unfolds before Ginny. A Midwestern town perhaps not unlike St. Louis, more trees, a moderate pace, not quite New York, not quite Mayberry; a generously sized school with equally well-funded arts and science programs; a nice little laboratory with plenty of flasks and beakers and burners to accommodate all of the bright wondrous minds sitting at the lab tables, a decent telescope for astronomy club, a well-ventilated gymnasium, mats for karate on Monday, Wednesday, and Friday afternoons, a study barre for ballet Tuesday and Thursday and maybe Saturday mornings. A well-trafficked movie theater in want of a reliable, caring manager, someone with a good mind for an entertaining double bill, a cozy little office in the back, dimly lit. A novelties store for the town's youth, comics and records and games and toys and like the theater needing someone of a particular temperament to watch over it, and to watch over all the little patrons; a town where night means night and the lights go out in houses down verdantly lawned streets one by one as up above, in the yawning void of the sky the stars come on. In the cool of the spring and the heat of the Summer two lawn chairs would appear in a high-fenced yard and two bodies would sit in them and they would watch the nightly show, stories of the day traded across the flickering light of a mosquito candle until the night is through with them and they would slip off into a cool, dark house, to watch television, to make love, to lie beside one another in a wide open bed, to wake up to warm, white light bathing the room, and it is a beautiful life that Ginny sees, stretching out before her, through birthdays and anniversaries, down through vacations and research trips, graduations, weddings, births, retirement parties, travels, until they are ancient and feeble and they trek off together on their final voyage into the undiscovered country.

It's a beautiful life and Ginny so wishes that it could be her own.

"Oh, sweetheart." Ginny searches her mind for the right words to say, the proper way to put things. How does she articulate reality for someone who's lived so close to the cusp of it yet still exists so deep in another corner of the universe? "You are so totally the coolest guy I've ever met. You have always been there for me when I needed someone. And I'm never going to forget you. And I'm going to write to you. But, like, us? There isn't really an us, sweetheart. There can't be. Because you *are* the coolest guy I've ever met. And I couldn't do that to you. And no matter how much you think you're helping me out now, and how

little other stuff might matter… It's going to matter later on, sweetheart. I know. Because I know people. And I
know you'd start to wonder. How many men, how many
boys, who was better looking and who was worse and
what I did and how many times…"

"Ginny…"

"…I know that, even though I'm going to try, really try
to be different, it's going to be a very long time before I
can go to bed without a drink or three. And I know that
even if I like myself when we're together… I've played a
part for so long, sweetheart, and I've done it so well, I'm
not really sure who I am anymore. And I don't know if
you'd like the answer when it finally comes. I don't know
if I will, either. Because you don't know the things I've
done. What I'm going to have to finally face when the
last bottle's empty. And you'd have to find those things out
about me, one day. And when you did… well, that'd be it,
sweetheart."

"Ginny…"

"You're going to get this one day. And when you do,
sweetheart, you are going to be so totally grateful. Until
then, I know it's going to hurt like shit. But it's totally the
right decision. And it's *my* decision."

Ginny checks her watch. She doesn't need to wipe her
eyes in order to see the time clearly. She's proud of this.

"It's time for me to go, sweetheart."

"Sure," Roger says. He's nodding slowly, trying to smile.

"I'll see you tonight. Take… take care of my sister, okay?"

"Ah, sure. Of course."

Ginny stands up, puts a hand on Roger's shoulder.
Without thinking about it, without playing out the possibilities in her head, without arranging the chess pieces on
the board and playing them out, simply because she feels
like doing it, she kneels forward and kisses him on the

forehead. It feels nice.

"I'll be back tonight. For Tricia."

Roger takes off his glasses, wipes his eyes. He doesn't put them back on; it occurs to Ginny that he's keeping them off so that he can't see her.

"See you later, sweetheart."

Ginny doesn't look back on her way out the door. Even above the music on the Misanthrope sound system, she can hear the sobbing coming from Roger's bathroom.

———

"*Guten tag, damen.*"

"*Guten tag, Frau Kurva.*"

Ginny looks out across the table—*her* table—at the sadly diminished number of faces looking back at her, and with a perverse wistfulness realizes she is going to miss *this* part of her life.

"I hope you all had a most excellent rest last night. I know that I did, and I feel a world better for it. And I have got to apologize to each and every one of you for the way I behaved yesterday. I know that it isn't an excuse, but well, I did get rather excited about the space launch this last weekend, and we girls do know how to celebrate, don't we?"

Ginny mimes knocking back a bottle; the taciturn faces of some of the girls begin to dissolve.

"But again, that's no excuse. I don't always speak frankly with you girls, but let me do it right now. Each and every one of you is as important to me as my own sister. And what happens to every one of you matters to me, as much as what happens to myself. More than what happens to me. And, if I have ever done anything to hurt any of you…"

Ginny feels eyes on her, someone staring laser beams

through the back of her skull. She turns; there, silhouetted in the doorway, leans the Colonel, one arm folded behind his back, the other supporting himself against the wall. She smiles, waves, waits for a response that does not come, turns back to the girls, annunciates clearly, loud enough to ensure all of the girls are paying attention but not so much that it seems out of place.

"In any event, as you can see, we are, like, so very sadly short another body this morning. Our darling little ingénue Tammy, bless her heart, has come down with a case of something positively awful." Ginny raises her eyebrows as she speaks, makes careful, concentrated eye contact with each of the girls as she does, not moving her gaze until she registers on their faces their understanding that something is happening, that they are not receiving the truth and are meant to be aware of that. "So I want each and every one of you to be at your best today. That means positively no breaks, *damen.* I want a grade-A day out there. Now! For a change of pace. Today we're going to discuss the latest chapter of *Gatsby* in *Deutsch. Jetzt sind Sie bereit, zuhören, richtig?"*

The girls look at one another, some confused by the abrupt shift.

"Ja, Frau Kurva."

"Gut. You see the Colonel back there? Now he isn't the sort to go around telling anyone, but today is his birthday. The big six-five! And let me tell you, ladies, it has gotten him seriously down. Now, we all may have our opinions of the man, but he does keep the trains running on time, doesn't he? So I've gotten something planned this evening. Don't come here for kick-up; I want you all at Mary's, half an hour ahead of schedule. Understand?"

Some of the girls look at one another, then back to Ginny. *"Ja, Frau Kurva."*

"Gut. Now I'm going to say a bunch of random things

and I want you all to respond with more random things. We've got to make this look like a book discussion, haven't we? Candice, why don't you go first?"

Ginny travels around the table, asking girls to name their favorite colors, childhood pets, best convey what they did last weekend. When she's completed the circuit, she checks her watch, finds that they are right on schedule. She turns around, sees that the Colonel has left. For the first time this morning, she comes close to relaxing. Everything is fine. Everything is going according to plan. She picks up a donut, takes a bite.

"Alright then, *damen*. It's time to get out there and earn our keep, now isn't it? And, like, I cannot stress this enough... *earn*."

The girls rise and file out. Ginny keeps her seat, watching them go one by one, until she is alone at the head of the table with a fleet of empty chairs before her. When she's sure that everyone is gone, she pops the remainder of her donut in her mouth, stands, walks around the table, eyes moving from chair to chair, remembering the girls who have occupied them, those now out on the street, those who have left 42nd, those gone forever from this world. When she's made it back to the head of the table, she quietly pushes in her own chair and heads out of the dining room. There's no use for her in turning around for a last look. There's a final day on the job to complete; too much ahead of her to busy herself with what's behind.

––––––––

As she instructed her girls, Ginny takes no breaks today, no detours into the auditoriums of the Anco or the Roxxy to catch a few minutes of a film between dates or to give herself reprieve from the too-eager attentions of any of her johns; what she does today, what she earns today, has got to matter. There will be plenty of time for rest on the bus. She works with a vigor slightly above her norm, an aggression beyond that which she normally employs, though she supposes that, similarly, the level of detachment which she engages once the coupling has begun is likewise heightened, the seconds bleeding into hours, time vanishing for her more quickly than usual. Only once does she permit herself to slip out of the confines of her own mind, while she's lying on her back, transfixed on the ceiling, a little tear in the corner of the wallpaper, the windows dirt caked, and the thought comes to her, crystalline, exploding in her mind like a bullet: *Is this the last thing Tammy ever saw?* Her date does not appear to notice when she begins to scream and brings one hand up to her mouth to stifle the sound; if he does, he does not care.

Forty-five minutes before the end of the day, Ginny Kurva slips out of a bed on the third floor of the Misanthrope, puts on her clothes, takes the money from the nightstand, and brings to an end the life she has lived for the past three years in New York. There is no sense of finality to the encounter, nothing momentous about the occasion. She has simply quit working for one agency with the aim of pursuing employment at another across the country.

Tricia and Roger are in front of the television when Ginny gets back, playing one of those electronic games that Tricia has been onto her about, Roger frantically trying to position a cursor around the screen and tiny projectiles descending down onto quiet little cities in the desert, Tricia hunched forward in her chair, gripping the armrests, shouting, "Faster, dammit! They're gonna die! They're all gonna die, man," and Ginny can smell the dwindling aroma of something cooked and eaten, some kind of prepackaged meal. Empty cans of Coke stand on the coffee table and Roger turns to look at her and he smiles, and she smiles back. Tiny little electronic explosions sound from the television; and Tricia is saying, "Oh, wow, thanks a lot, Dr. Strangelove, I'm glad my sister's tits are more important than the fate of the free world," and Roger smiles wider and Ginny smiles wider and then she remembers herself.

"I've got to get ready." She stops to hug her sister on the way to the shower. She bathes quickly, just enough to get the scent of funk off of her, figuring she'll be picking up plenty of grime the second her ass hits the bus seat. Once she's dressed, she takes a moment to stop and study herself in the mirror. Though the outfit is not conducive to a clandestine flight from the city, Ginny cannot help but feel that some amount of ceremony is appropriate, if only out of respect for her girls.

It is, after all, graduation day.

"I'll be back soon," Ginny says, coming out of the shower, retrieving the record player. Tricia has taken control of the video game, her eyes fixed on the screen.

"Uh-huh."

"You need to be ready. As soon as I get back, we have to go."

"Right."

"Hey, Tricia?"

Ginny moves in front of the television set, blocking the view of the screen. Tricia's eyes grow wide and then she throws the controller down on the ground. "Dammit, bitch…"

"Tricia. Really." She smiles weakly, puts a hand on her sister's, looks back and forth between her and Roger. "When I get back… we're going. This is going to be, like… it. Okay?"

Tricia is looking down at the controller on the ground now, her hands folder in her lap, and Ginny can see that she is digging her fingers into her knuckles, wringing them, can hear her grinding her teeth. "Yeah. Yeah, okay."

Ginny turns to Roger, Roger standing up and putting a hand on her shoulder, Ginny putting her own over it. "Roger, I... I'll see you in a minute, sweetheart. All right?"

"Ah, sure."

"You two enjoy your game."

Ginny heads out the door. If everything goes according to plan, within minutes, her girls will be safe, far away from the reach of whatever demented heart is preying on The Deuce; she and her sister will be safe; if everything goes according to plan, she will, hopefully, be able to slip away from the Motel Misanthrope without having to say good-bye to the Colonel.

————

"What's going on?" Mary has gotten some of her color back since Ginny last saw her. She's sitting up and watching television and doesn't look at all like someone who was almost taken apart from the inside out less than a week ago. Ginny is happy about this, knows too well from experience that a girl bearing a certain abused, defeated look about her is choice picking for precisely the wrong sort of person.

"How are you doing, sweetheart?" Ginny asks, sets the record player down. She moves to Mary, hugs her, kisses her forehead, kisses it again, lets her arms linger around her a little while longer than usual. "You feel cool. That's good. You're looking incredible, darling, absolutely fabulous."

"I feel... I don't feel that bad. I'm better, I guess. I mean, I guess I'm doing okay."

"That's great. That's wonderful."

"Why'd you bring the record player?"

"Mary, sweetheart... Mary, the rest of the girls are going to be coming here, soon, and we're all going to have a very serious talk."

"Um...okay. Should I... should I be worried, Ginny?"

"No, no, no, sweetheart. Not at all. Everything is going to be just fine. But there are some very big things happening. I'm... I'm going to be going away, Mary. You'll understand why in a little bit, once everyone gets here. But before they show up, I wanted to talk to you privately. Girl to girl. Woman to woman. I know you haven't had the best life, Mary. None of us have. None of us would be here otherwise. And I... when I found you, and I found out about you, and your life... It was very personal to me. It hurt me more than some of the other stories, from some of the other girls. And I'd promised myself that you were going to be special to me. That I was going to make things better for you. And I don't know if I've succeeded in doing that or not; and if I haven't, I'm, so sorry, sweetheart. I'm so very sorry. You know I've never tried to play favorites with any of you. But ... You know, I've never really thought of having my own kids, and I don't really think I ever want any. But if I did... I'd want to have a daughter like you, Mary. And wherever you go from here... I'm proud of you, sweetheart."

Mary has begun to cry by the time Ginny reaches the midpoint of her speech, and when she is finished she throws her arms around her, squeezing tight, too tight, and Ginny squeezes back too tight and the women are still embracing when a knock comes at the door. Ginny rises to check the peephole and seeing that it is Candice, lets her in. Candice grins wide and bellows greeting to Mary. Shannon shows up next, physically lifting Mary out of bed and spinning her around and Mary is crying and squealing as Ginny goes to greet Sandra at the door and it's like a reunion, all of the girls meeting not in some communal space to conduct business but returning home. As she looks around the room, women lounging on the bed and hunkered smoking on the floor, playing with the remote for the television, turning on MTV, it occurs to her that while for the past three years she has always thought she was protecting herself by not allowing any of these women into her life, she has been harming herself by keeping them out.

"Ladies," Ginny says once everyone has arrived, quieting the room, raising her arms. "Your attention, please."

"Damn, Miss Ginny," Constance says. "You come back here early to change, you didn't tell any of us we should change! We gonna look like damn fools, throwing the Colonel a party and you the only one dressed up!"

"Maybe she has something special planned," Michelle snickers.

"It's a special occasion, darling, but not the kind you think. The fact of the matter is that it isn't the Colonel's birthday, and I'm sorry I had to lie about that to get you here."

"Dammit," Sandra mutters, pulls a small Hallmark envelope out of her jeans and begins tearing it up.

"Girls, I'm… I'm sorry I've got to make this quick. The Colonel is going to figure out that we aren't downstairs, and I don't know what that's going to look like. But you all need to know… Girls… Tammy is dead. Tina, too."

Gasps, murmurs, tears begin to fill the room. "Who did it, Miss Ginny?" Candice stands up, pulls out a butterfly knife. "You tell me. We kill him together."

"That's a… that's a very sweet offer, darling… But, I don't know. Roger Niederman, from the comic store— some of you know him—he's my friend, too, and he's been telling me some stories that have turned out to be true.

That there's a man who's been killing girls on The Deuce; he did it last Summer, too. We think he only kills in the Summer. And we just know he drives a van and no one's ever gotten a good look at him. I guess because there's nothing special looking about him. He's just, like, some guy. And that's why he's dangerous and that's why it's a risk for any of us to be out on the street anymore. I tried to tell that to the Colonel and he refused to let us do anything about it. So *I'm* doing something about it. If you listened to me, you worked hard today. The money you've got now is yours. No kick-up. You take it, you take whatever you've got in your rooms and you get off The Deuce tonight. I know not all of you are in a position to walk away yet, and, like… I'm sorry. I wish this was happening under better circumstances. And I can't tell you where to go. But if you want to stick around… If you want to go see the Colonel after this, give him your kick-up, tell him what happened… You can do that. I don't think he'll be angry with you. One of you might even be the next bottom girl. *Shannon.*" Ginny wags her finger accusatorily at Shannon. She laughs; so do a few other girls.

"But I don't advise it. I advise getting out of here. And… and it may not help much, but…"

Ginny retrieves the record player, pulls out her switchblade, uses it to pry open the casing. From inside, she retrieves the stacks of money which constitute her pitiful savings and begins to distribute them amongst the girls.

"This is from my savings. I'm keeping enough for me and my sister to get out of here. The rest… The rest belongs to all of you."

"Ginny…" Sandra says. "We can't…"

"Shut up," Michelle mutters.

"You're my girls," Ginny says. "All of you. And I love you all. I love every one of you, and I know… I know you're all going to do great things. This is officially the commencement of the Misanthrope High School graduation, class of 1983. It won't mean shit in any state, but you are all hereby recipients of the Ginny Kurva GED and entitled to all rights and privileges thereof. And your final assignment is to finish the Great Gatsby, and perfect your German, memorize the periodic table, and to go forth and be totally awesome. And, that's all I have to say, I guess. I love you guys. Class dismissed."

Ginny has her hands over her face. Girls are getting up and hugging her, hugging one another, and they begin to leave the room, Ginny proud of them, no one panicking, though it's clear from the pinched, pained expressions on Constance and Sandra's faces they want to lose their cool right there, girls telling Ginny that they love her, that they'll miss her, and Ginny accepts their gratitude in turn, sure to shake everyone's hand before they leave, until there's just her and Shannon and Mary left in the room that only moments ago was so full of life, which now is stifled with an air of residual dread.

"So this is it, man," Shannon says.

"It would seem so, sweetheart."

"Lana's got an older sister in Philly she keeps bugging me to visit. I guess this is the best time to do it. Her last name's Voyou. V-O-Y-O-U. You look us up, you get where you're going. Drop me a line. You're one badass chick, man. I wish you swung my way."

"You'd be the first girl I'd call on, sweetheart."

"You ever come back this way, you can roll with me anytime."

"Where *are* you going?" Mary asks.

"California, I figure," Ginny says. "I think I'll do okay there. What about you, sweetheart? You've got enough money now to go almost anyplace, start over anywhere."

Mary shakes her head. "I don't… I don't know, Ginny. I… I came here to get away from stuff because this is, like, where you're supposed to run away to, right? So, I don't know, how can you run away from the place you're supposed to run away to?"

"Ever been to Philly, kid?" Shannon asks.

"I, uh… no."

"C'mon. Pack your shit. Lana's got three other kid sisters. The fuck's one more? You don't like it there, then you're on your own. "

Mary looks to Ginny.

"You'll be in good hands, sweetheart."

"Let's get your stuff together," Shannon says. "I wanna be out of here before the Colonel comes knocking. You'll like Lana. She's a reader. The two of us have been going through Gatsby. Three of us will finish it together. You know the guy wrote other shit, we figure we're gonna start on something else of his next. We'll take turns." Shannon turns to Ginny, puts her hand on her cheek. "The hell you waiting for, sister? Get the fuck out of here. I got this shit under control. I learned from the best."

———

"One more game?" Tricia is asking, clutching the joystick, Ginny standing over the couch and Roger standing alongside her and Tricia is asking "Please?" Not really asking, Ginny knows, there's no bite in the question, no pleading, only the words of a girl who's old enough and smart enough to know that something is coming to an end, and there's more virtue for her in pretending to fight it than giving in straightaway.

"I should have been with the Colonel ten minutes ago," Ginny says. "That's, like, dangerously past schedule. Come on. Get the VCR, get our stuff. We've got to move."

Tricia sighs, puts the joystick down on the floor. She turns to Roger. "Hey, c'mere. I got something to say to you before you go."

Roger kneels down. Tricia puts her hands on his shoulders. "Goodbye, man. Out of all the weird, loner, blind, bald guys in the city... I'm glad I got to know you."

"You're, ah, you're a strange kid. And don't let anyone ever tell you different."

The two embrace; after a moment, Tricia shoves Roger off, wipes her face, and wordlessly moves off to grab the VCR. Roger turns back to Ginny.

"So, ah... uh..."

"I'll write to you at Hobbs' End," Ginny says. "When we get where we're going. It might be a while. I don't know. But I will. I promise."

"I'm sorry, ah... I'm sorry we didn't get to watch a last movie together. I'd have liked that."

"This... This isn't goodbye, Roger. It isn't. Whether you end up out west, or whether I end back here... We'll see one another again. We'll find the absolute most batshit insane movie they've got showing and we'll tear it a new one. And... Until then... When your cable goes on the fritz, and all you can get is local crap, and there's nothing on... That's me."

"You take care of yourself, Ginny. The both of you."

"I always have, darling."

"Hey, Ginny?"

"Yes, sweetheart?"

Tricia breezes past the pair to the door, the VCR in her lap, and she is drumming her fingers on the casing, sighing heavily, impatiently, occasionally wiping at her eyes with the back of her hands. "Omigawsh. Bang me backwards on a bulldozer, you've had a year to get all touchy feely and shit. Let's just go, okay? Don't make me feel..."

The force of the door breaking inward is enough to knock Tricia sideways, her legs becoming entangled in her chair as she spills out of it, the chain lock catching and ricocheting the door back into place, and though Ginny rushes forward, tries to brace it with her body, the Colonel's second kick is violent enough to snap the chain and permit him entry to the room. The arm holding his pistol wavers between Ginny and Roger, and he is about to move towards them when he stumbles over Tricia, looks down at her, and, a more opportune target presenting itself, aims the barrel at her face.

"Your sister not as smart as I give her credit for," he says, stomps on her hand. Tricia shrieks, writhing, curling in on herself. Ginny moves forward, making a run towards him, the Colonel swinging the gun around to aim it at her face.

"No one move. No one leave. You move, I make it worse. Don't worry. I not want to hurt girl. I need girl. Ginny send all my girls away. I look in dining room. You not there. I look in your room. You not there. I look in Ginny's boyfriend's room." The Colonel smiles, nods.

"I'm, ah, not her boyfriend," Roger says.

"*Quiet!*"

Ginny glances to her sister, hopes that the look she conveys will adequately reassure her, help her not to panic, help her not to be afraid, moves her eyes back to the Colonel's gun, drifting softly to and fro. He is, she can tell, in the most volatile stage of drunkenness, hostile enough to use a weapon, not sober enough to aim straight with it. He turns the gun back to Ginny.

"You think you can ruin me? Better people tried. They dead now."

"No one was trying to ruin anyone, sweetheart," Ginny says. "That wasn't my intention at all. Tell me now, darling, what sort of business can you conduct if all of your employees are dead? This was a strategy, sweetheart. If our girls aren't on the street, then who's going to get killed? Everyone else's girls. If we remove them from the equation, why, there's no way that they can die, is there? And when, when the killing's over, who's going to have the only complete stable on The Deuce? You, sweetheart. All you."

"Girls gone," the Colonel says. "You send them away. That fine. I know better now. I start over. No more bottom girl. I pick girls myself. Make sure they work. I start with this one." He gestures to Tricia, nudging her with his shoe. "Perfect girl. She not need to get out of bed anyway. Leave her there, bring men to her. Let men do anything. She not even feel it." On the floor, Tricia begins to sob.

"You son of a *bitch*..." Ginny makes another move towards the Colonel. He pulls back the hammer on his gun. Roger puts his hands up over his head, speaks:

"Hey, look, ah, you're mad at me, you're mad at Ginny, I get that. Let's go upstairs, the three of us. Okay? The kid's, ah, the kid's got nothing to do with this."

"This not involve you. Get out, I let you live."

"Ah, sure, sure, ah, no." Roger says, and he nudges Ginny, steps on her foot. He is shifting slowly and strangely, and in the intensity of the moment it seems almost surreal until she realizes that he is attempting to position himself between her and the Colonel's gun. "See, ah, here's the thing. This was, ah, this was all my idea."

"Roger," Ginny hisses.

"You, ah, you think she'd stab you in the back after, ah, after all this time? Sure, she, ah she wanted to take the girls off the street, but when you said no go, ah, she was ready to listen. I, ah, I told her though, 'The fuck does he know?' So, ah, so you see, this was all my idea, and, ah, I realize what a bad idea that was now. So why don't, ah, why don't you and me talk this over, man to man?"

"Man?" The Colonel snickers. "You blind. You weak. Can barely even talk with gun in face. You know how many times I have gun in face? You afraid. I not afraid of anything. You no man. No idea why Ginny like you. You make Ginny scream? You make her come? Colonel make her come, every night, she want it or not. You pet for Ginny. Little dog for when she bored. Just like Ginny pet for me. Sad when pets turn on owners. Have to put them down."

Ginny has forgotten how loud a gun is in real life, has been desensitized by three years of hearing them go off in the distance or on television screens or movie screens, has forgotten that they do not sound like bangs or booms but violent, spitting cracks, a bowling ball dropped from the school roof during physics class, the sound of the lion tamer's whip at the circus for Tricia's birthday. There is a big blur beside her as Roger topples backwards and over the couch. Ginny does not flinch; does not cry out. The rage inside of her does not break through to the surface. It concentrates; it waits. It's patient, standing ready to burst forth when she wills it to, when she is best prepared to unleash it of her own volition, to focus it on a target.

The Colonel has begun to sweat, droplets pouring down into his eyes. He is blinking rapidly; it's been a long time since he's fired a gun and the experience has startled him. Perhaps he hadn't really thought through the implications of this, is realizing now that he's begun something he maybe wasn't ready for, and has to see it through. His arm is wavering even more violently, cresting back and forth, up and down, Ginny watching for an opening, her body tensing every time the barrel crosses back in front of her face. One second, God, one second is all she needs, one instant to strike, get him on his back, stomp him to death beneath her heels… and if she can't have that second… If she can't have that second, and she ends up with a bullet in her...

Then she'll just need to be quick about it.

"I hope you not disappoint me. I figure it take two to put you down. You tough. I know that. That why this sadden me. I had big plans for us. Think you with me for long time."

"You better make it good, sweetheart," Ginny says. "Because you're only gonna get one shot. And if that doesn't do it... I'm going to make it slow."

The Colonel smiles broadly, chuckles. When he speaks, it's in perfectly unaccented English, layers of obfuscation melted away to reveal the all-knowing heart of filth beneath: "All right, then. Go ahead, you stupid cunt. What've you got?"

The shot that reverberates through the room is much louder than the first, and in the utter silence that follows Ginny is sure that she's been rendered deaf. She cannot hear Tricia's screaming, cannot hear the sound of the Colonel's gun thumping to the floor. Her vision, though, it seems, has been rendered momentarily superhuman in compensation for this loss; she is seeing in more detail, seeing things unfold before her more deliberately, like the slo-mo feature on her VCR. She sees the Colonel's head expand like a water balloon made of flesh, torrents of blood erupting from his ears as the right side of his face separates and disintegrates, the bone of his cheek and jaw and forehead liquefying and splattering across the wall behind him, painting it with tiny flecks of gore, bits of skull and hair and wads of brain and fragments of teeth matting into the wallpaper. His eyeball, miraculously intact, sticks for a moment before it oozes down to the floor, trailing strands of optic nerve behind it. The left side of the Colonel's head remains briefly erect before it collapses down onto his shoulder like a discarded condom, blood rushing down the front of his polo shirt as his body sways and collapses on top of Tricia. Though Ginny cannot hear it, she can tell from the stretching of her sister's mouth that she is screaming even louder now. Ginny turns, her body moving as slowly as everything around her seems to be. She looks at Roger, barely supporting himself on his elbows over the back of the couch, shaking hands holding the shotgun, the side of his own face torn open by the Colonel's wayward bullet, a set of bloody lips smiling contentedly from his cheek, dousing his beard red.

Tricia shoves the Colonel's body off, drags herself away, braces herself against the wall, looking down at herself, covered in blood and little strands of hair and chunks of brain, and she wipes her body with her hands and then wipes them on the floor, on the wall. Ginny moves to her, kneels down, careful not to touch her, to remain the one person in the room not doused in human offal.

"It's okay," Ginny says, glad she can hear her own voice, her hearing beginning to return to her. "Shhh. Shhh. Tricia, Tricia? You've got to stop screaming. *Tricia!*"

Tricia stops, her eyes still wide, her mouth agape, nods slowly. "Oh...wow. Oh...shit."

"Are you okay?"

Tricia nods.

"Your hand?"

She nods again. Then: "Is...Roger...?"

Ginny stands, goes back to the couch. Roger has sunk back onto the floor, the gun between his legs. He's staring at it, the blood running down the front of his shirt and into his lap, pooling on his thigh. A trail leads back towards the bed, little broken streaks on the floor from where he dragged himself to retrieve the shotgun.

"Roger?"

Roger shakes. Looks up at Ginny, looks through her.

"Roger. Roger, sweetheart. Are you okay?"

"*Get out!*" He shouts. "Go…. Go on! Get out!"

"Ginny!" Tricia cries. "Come on. We've gotta leave."

Ginny puts both hands up, listens. Around her, the nightly sounds of the Misanthrope go on uninterrupted; she hears no frantic footfalls coming towards the room, no screams of surprise, no congregation of gawkers forming in the hallway. As far as the revelers are concerned, life is continuing on as normal at the Motel Misanthrope.

"If everyone will be quiet," Ginny says, "I am, like, totally capable of handling this. Now, Roger, sweetheart, do you own any cologne?"

―――――

For once, Ginny is glad of the throngs moving through the hallways of the Motel Misanthrope; amongst pierced faces and painted faces, shaved heads and purple hair, the sight of a man wearing a niqab made from a pillowcase, carrying a girl in a burqa made out of bedsheets, trailed by a woman in a violet suit carting a wheelchair and a VCR, attracts virtually no attention. Ginny is grateful when they're able to flag down a taxi relatively quickly. The driver regards them quizzically, his eyes moving between the three. The overpowering smell of Old Spice fills the cab, masking the odor of blood.

"Good evening, sweetheart!" Ginny chirps to the driver. "How are you doing tonight?"

"Where do you want to go?" The driver asks.

The ride goes smoothly, if not quickly enough for Ginny's liking. She makes small talk with the driver, distracting his attention away from the other two passengers, speaking loudly enough to cover the sounds of Roger's occasional groans. When they reach their destination, Ginny is sure to give a generous tip; big enough to seem like a token of gratitude, not so large as to arouse his suspicions.

Ginny is familiar with the dive as a hub of activity for some of the other girls who've come to the Deuce, some flophouse in Hell's Kitchen where the locals don't ask questions and don't talk to uniforms. Thankfully, a first floor room is available; based on the tremor of Roger's legs, she isn't sure he can make it much further.

In the room, Roger strips off the pillowcases swaddling his head. The gym sock wadded up against his wound has become coagulated to his face. Ginny sets Tricia on the bed as Roger heads to the bathroom. By now the blood on her has dried, and as Ginny strips the sheets off of her sister, she grabs her, holds her tight against her own body, stroking her hair, kissing her face.

"Oh, Tricia… Oh, Tricia, I'm so sorry."

"That was… That was fucking insane, right?"

"Are you okay?"

"Omigawsh… It like… It fucking *exploded.*"

"Are you hurt? Let me see your hand."

"It's fine. It's sore. The little prick couldn't kick a soccer ball."

"I thought you were going to die."

"Omigawsh, like, you? Even if fucking James Bond over there didn't step up, I know… I know you'd have taken him. That's why I don't need any comics with strong women, man. You … You're like fucking Jean Grey."

"I… have no idea who that is."

"It's a compliment. But you still suck for not knowing."

"I'm going to go check on Roger now."

"Omigawsh. Like, finally. Just get me the remote. I've… I've gotta do something, like, normal now, okay? What time is it? Is it time for Carson?"

Ginny finds the remote, gives it to Tricia. She returns to the wheelchair, propped against the wall beside the door, unfolds it. She removes the pillowcase; inside, the disassembled shotgun, the first aid kit retrieved from Roger's bathroom. She leaves the shotgun, takes the first aid kit to Roger in the bathroom.

In the bathroom, Roger has stripped down to his boxers, tossed his gore-soaked clothes into the tub, is now wiping his body with a damp washcloth. Ginny sits on the toilet opposite him, hands him the kit.

"I, ah, need one last thing. Ah, your flask."

Ginny obliges, retrieves it from her hip. Roger opens the kit, removes gauze, a pair of scissors, a spool of thread, a pair of manicure scissors, a little plastic container of needles. He retrieves one of the needles, sterilizes it with a splash of vodka and then takes a shot.

"Ah, old west anesthetic," he says.

"I could get you heroin, you know. I mean, after three years here, I know people."

"I, ah, I need to be clear-headed for this."

"Why have you got needles in a first aid kit?"

"Ah, because this way I never have to pay anyone to lance boils." Roger painfully pulls the washcloth away from his face. His hands begin to steady; Ginny watches as he carefully threads the needle, grits his teeth as he pours vodka over the wound. Assessing himself in the mirror, he sighs, mutters, "This is, ah, this is going to fucking suck," and sets about stitching himself.

Ginny watches the spectacle; she has seen enough ugliness—and participated in enough biology labs— that it arouses neither disgust nor revulsion. There is a certain amazement to it, this boy barely older than her, putting himself back together like this, sewing his own flesh like torn cloth and only wincing as tears flow down his cheeks.

When he's finished, he studies his handiwork, pokes at it with his index finger, opens and closes his mouth, ensures that the stitches are secure. Then, standing there, staring at himself in the mirror, a great, heaving sob racks his body and he collapses back onto the tub and begins to cry.

"Sweetheart. Shhhh." Ginny moves to sit beside him, wraps an arm around his shoulder, rests his head on her breast. His torso is as hairy as the density of his beard would have indicated; Ginny runs her hand over his back. It feels pleasant.

"I... I killed him."

"Shhh, shhh, sweetheart. Not so loud. Not so loud."

"I killed a guy."

"Roger... Sweetheart..." Ginny takes his head in her hands, lifts it so that he's looking at her face. She reaches to the toilet paper roll, tears off a section, dabs at his eyes beneath his glasses. "It was self-defense, sweetheart. Pure and simple. And there is nothing wrong with that. There is... there is nothing wrong with killing someone to protect the people you care about." Ginny inhales sharply, lets it out. She looks to the door, listens, can hear the faint sound of Carson coming from the television. She looks back to Roger, runs a hand over his head.

"I was... twelve when my mother started coming into my room at night. And... And I'd had such a great childhood before that, that I didn't even know there was anything wrong with it. I was... I was afraid at first, and I didn't know what was happening, why she was doing this, what I was feeling... But I figured, I didn't like the dentist, either, and... And I'd just started my period... And so maybe this was just another part of growing up that you had to deal with. No one talked about this stuff, you know. So it just seemed like, hey... Rites of passage. Baptism, first communion, your mom sticks her face between your legs before she tucks you in." Ginny shakes her head, instinctively reaches for her flask, bristles.

"I didn't think anything about that for a while, until the night I heard my father crying in the hall. Dad... He'd been at Iwo Jima, he ran his department at work... He taught me how to use a telescope and how to tie a fishing line... And he was just, like, this bigger than life guy to me... And hearing him crying... I knew something was up. And I started to think that something wasn't right about this. And then a girl in one of my classes, uh, I can't remember her name... Jamie? *Her* father... Well, after that, Sister Barbara took all of us girls aside one at a time and talked to us, about how we might have heard things, what happened to Jamie, and about how it was very bad, and about how if anyone ever tried anything like that with us, we should tell her or Father Walther right away, and the police would come and stop it. And... And I didn't want the police to come. I... I loved my mother. I didn't want them to take her away. I wanted her to stop but I didn't want them to take her away. And I was thirteen and, I don't know... I was afraid they would take Dad, too. I... I hated him so much then... That he didn't, wouldn't... But... I loved him... And I didn't want them to take him away. So I stopped going to dance class after school and I started taking karate. And I didn't tell anyone, and mom didn't find out until the night she put her hand under the covers and I broke her wrist. And I'll never forget she... She looked so hurt... Like... Like the way that some of the girls at school would look when their boyfriends dumped them... And she went to the hospital, and after that night things were great again. Things were fine, and... And it was like none of it had ever happened. We went to the movies. We had family dinners, church picnics, and... And everything was great. But I was worried when Tricia hit puberty, I was worried it was going to start with her, but, nothing ever did... Things were fine. And I went to college, and... And then there was the accident. And I didn't think anything. I was worried about Tricia but, like, not in that way. Or maybe I was. Maybe I knew and I... And I didn't want to think about it. I didn't want to think about her lying there helpless and what a temptation that would be... I wanted to be at school and learning and having fun and just be.... *normal*... And then I came home for Christmas... And I should have known when I came in and Dad was in the living room and... And the entire bottle was empty and just sitting there next to him, and he looked so... Gone... And I went into Tricia's room and she was asleep and I sat down on her bed.... And she woke up screaming..."

Ginny puts her hands over her face; she feels herself at the brink of tears, chokes them back down.

"Just...screaming... And I knew. I knew. And I... I didn't even hesitate. I knew that I had to make it right. That I had to do what I should've done in the first place. I knew where Dad kept his gun. And he... and he just sat there... He just sat there and watched me load it. And I re- member thinking, 'Good. Good, you son of a bitch. If you weren't gonna stop that, I'm glad you're not gonna stop this either.' She was asleep... And I turned on the lights... I wanted to see her. I wanted her to wake up and see me. I wanted her to know why it was happening. And she woke up, and she saw me... And there was that hurt look again... And she started to sit up and I shot her. I'd never fired a gun before. I think... I think I might've screamed. I don't know. It hit her in the stomach. And then she started to try and get up again... So I... I just kept pulling the trigger. I kept pulling it for, like, a long time. And then I dropped it. And I could hear Tricia screaming for me. I went into her room and I told her that it was going to be okay. And then… and then we left."

"Ginny…." Roger whispers. She can't tell whether the expression on his face is sympathy or awe or terror or some mixture of the three.

"I figured we'd disappear to New York. I'd get a job, take care of Tricia… I'd seen how far gone Dad was. I was afraid if I left her with him, she'd end up going into the system, go through the same shit all over again… And it wasn't until we were already here that I decided to look at the St. Louis papers, see what they'd written, if I could figure out if they had any idea where to look for me and… And that's when I saw… Saw that he'd turned himself in."

Ginny dabs a wayward tear with the ball of her thumb. "He'd told the cops almost everything. About what she'd done to me, to Tricia … And he said that I'd come home from college and taken Tricia, and he knew that's why I'd done it, and it had just become too much for him and so he'd gotten his gun and put the bitch down. Of course, neither of us were there to testify on his behalf, but… But I guess us not being there said enough. They went easy on him. Twenty-five years. He might get out in another two. I kind of hope he does. But I'm also kind of glad he's where he is. Because… because I think he kind of owes me that. And I'm telling you all of this because… Because you did what you had to do. Because you were there for me, Roger. And everyone needs someone there for them once in a while. And the people I've needed have never been there for me. And I'm telling you this because I'm sorry I told you I didn't want you to come with Tricia and me… I thought you'd be better off, but… Roger… Seeing that happen to you, I… I want you with us. I love you." Ginny smiles. "You make me feel feelings."

Roger wipes at his eyes, smiles pitifully. "I… I love you too, Ginny." He puts his head in one hand and begins to quietly cry.

"Roger... love... shhh...." Ginny takes his chin in her hand, raises his face, brings it close to hers, kisses him. It feels liberating to do something so intimate with her body of her own volition; like swimming through ocean waves rolling onto the shore, lying nude in a sunbeam in some deserted and exotic place. It's freedom to *decide* to kiss this man and then to kiss him, not because he promises her anything, money, protection, power, safety, but because she cares for him and he is hurt and she wants to show him her love, give him her physical affection, and in doing so heal that pain if even in some small manner. She kisses him because she thinks it will feel good to kiss him, and it does feel good. Roger's jaw goes lax against hers, letting her tongue enter his mouth, one of his hands gliding up her back to stroke her hair, and Ginny sighs and nestles her cheek into the unwounded side of his beard. This is happening because she wants it, and she is making it happen and she is, in the smallest, most infinitesimal of ways, happy.

"They're, ah... they're going to figure it out," Roger says, after they've broken away from one another, after Ginny's lipstick has become smeared around his beard and her hair has gone into complete disarray. "My room, my gun..."

"The Colonel didn't have the front desk keep a register. Too many of the other guests were pushing dope for him. So your name isn't anywhere on paper; and everyone the Colonel had working the front desk is going to be too terrified of who'll come after them if they start naming names. Think, love, was there anything you left behind in that room that could be tracked back to you? I mean, like, specifically you? Fingerprints don't count. There are, like, a thousand fingerprints in every room."

"I ah... I don't think so, no. My clothes?"

"Anything unique about them? Alterations?"

"No."

"Good, good. Listen now, sweetheart. They're going to find the Colonel dead. That's, like, completely true. And the first thing they're going to do is crack into his safe. And they're going to find two sets of ledgers in there. And it's going to become pretty clear exactly what kind of business the Colonel was *really* running out of his precious little hotel. The girls. The drugs. Who knows what else. Men like him don't die well, as a matter of course. I have a feeling that the police are going to be less than eager about tracking down whoever killed the fantastic Colonel Baniszewski."

"All right, fine. But the gun is registered to me, Ginny."

"And that's why we brought it with us, sweetheart. Now, listen to me. In a little while I'm going to go. I'm going to pawn the VCR. I'm going to get you and Tricia changes of clothes, some food. And I'm going to buy a file. And once the numbers on that shotgun are gone, it's going right in the dumpster. Even if they find it, they'll be nothing to link it back to you. No prints. Nothing. And then it'll be over."

Roger shakes his head. "No. Don't. Stay here, with us. I... I don't want you to go out. They... they might be looking in the area. For someone, for, ah, for something suspicious. If they stop you, ah, if they stop you and you've got the gun..."

"Neither you nor Trish have clothes to go out on the street in, and I wouldn't let Tricia do it anyway. And I... I don't like having it here. I'm going to get rid of it. I'm going to take care of things."

"Ginny, I... I've got a bad feeling about it. I'm afraid, ah, that if you leave tonight... I'll never see you again." A bitter chill fills the air of the bathroom. Roger and his warnings and predictions. How has ignoring them worked out for her over the past week? Ginny dismisses it. It's paranoia;

adrenaline from the shooting; a pin dropping would cause him to worry now.

"Roger, everything will be fine. Haven't you realized that now, sweetheart? That it's what I do? Take care of things? I'm going to get rid of that gun, and I'm going to come back here and the three of us are going to go someplace nice. Someplace absolutely fantastic. And… And I'm going to make you *so* happy to be alive, sweetheart. Do you know… Do you know you're going to be the first guy who's ever been with me who hasn't paid for it? Isn't that wonderful? You're going to be my first."

Roger smiles wanly. "Heh. So, ah, so are you."

"Excuse me?"

"I, ah, I hope I'm not a disappointment."

"You've, uh…"

"Ginny…. Even if I hadn't have spent all my time studying and holed up… I'm blind, I can barely breathe. And let's face it… I'm pretty weird. I've been, ah been too busy getting fucked by life."

"You've lived here a year. And, I mean, you were friends with so many of the girls… They'd have done it for you, you know. I mean, as a courtesy."

Roger shrugs. "I, ah, I met you pretty soon after I got here. And, ah, well… After the first time we watched a movie together… You're all I've wanted."

Ginny is torn between smiling and crying. She opts for the former; she takes Roger's hand, places it on her thigh, locking her eyes on his so she can watch his expression as she guides it up her abdomen, delight in the sensation of his palm through her blouse, at the little gasp he makes as she guides it over her breast, up her neck, to her face, to kiss the ball of his thumb. Her eyes never leave his, her smile turning teasing, coy, and then she pushes her hand away from him and grins evilly. Roger shifts on the edge of the tub, bites the inside of his mouth. Good; let his thoughts linger there a while; away from more unpleasant realities.

"And you're going to have me, sweetheart. After I do what I have to. All right?"

"Yeah. Ah, yeah, okay."

"Good. Now I'm going to take care of things. And I want you to take a nice, hot shower. Get clean. And think of me."

Ginny kisses him again before she leaves the bathroom. On the bed, Tricia is watching Carson, her eyes glazed over. Ginny sits down beside her.

"Is Roger okay?"

"He just got done stitching himself up."

"Omigawsh. I, like, told you he was totally fucking rad-core."

"You're an excellent judge of character. I'm glad you approve."

Tricia turns to her sister, sees the little smirk there, the smudged lipstick, turns away incredulously, punches the bed and claps her hands and giggles furiously.

"Really?"

Ginny nods. Tricia squeals, hugs her sister, then rapidly pulls away and slaps her.

"Omigawsh, what the fuck was that for?"

"For, like, taking this long to figure it out. So, he's coming with us?"

"Yeah. Yeah, he is. I don't know where we're going now. It doesn't have to be California. It can be anywhere. After tonight... After tonight, it's over. No more of what we've been doing, how we've been living. After tonight it's all different."

"Holy wooden shit Geppetto, you mean I'm gonna be a real girl?"

"Splinters and all."

"Hey, Ginny?"

"Yeah?"

"Stuff's, like, not *all* going to change, is it?"

"What do you mean?"

"I mean, this is gonna be really weird, but... Aside from the hooking, and the booze, and the solitary confinement... Like, some of the past three years have been really great, you know? I mean, you teaching me shit, and us just hanging out... I mean, I always *loved* you growing up, but you always seemed so much older, and you were such a big dork, that, like, I could never really *stand* you, you know? But over the past three years... I've really gotten to, like, *like* you. You're the badass queen mother bitch of all sisters. And, you know, I've always hoped you and Roger would get together, but like, now that you are... I don't want stuff to change between us."

Ginny hugs her sister; maybe too tightly. "Hey. You listen to me. You remember asking me, if I ever think about dad? You want to know what I think about when I think of dad? I think of him and me in the waiting room in the hospital when you were being born. And he was, like, so worried that I was going to be jealous. And he said he didn't want me to think that it made me any less special. And, like, I remember, I told him, I wasn't upset, I was happy. Because I was getting the best present I could. I was getting a sister."

"Omigawsh."

"What?"

"You're, like, making me feel feelings now. Stop it."

"You're my gift, Tricia. You're my best friend. Nothing changes that. Not ever. It's Tricia and Ginny for a hundred years. From here to Pluto and back again. You and me until the end, okay? But first I have to take care of some stuff here. Last bits of business, you know?"

"What do you mean?"

"I've got to sell the VCR for some cash. And I've got to get rid of the gun."

"Can't you wait until morning? I… I don't want you to leave me."

"Tricia… Look at me. It's going to be fine. You've got to trust me, all right? I'll be back, like, super quick. Until then… Consider this the first day of Summer vacation. You don't have anything to worry about for a while except how late you can stay up and how many comics you can read."

"Bullshit," Tricia says.

"What?"

"I'm finishing *Gatsby*," she says, looks back to the television. "I want to know how that shit ends."

"You *are* my sister."

"I know, like, how did *that* happen, right?"

"I love you, Tricia."

"And I love corn chips. Now go hock the damn VCR and buy me some."

Tricia is channel surfing as Ginny rises and collects the pillowcase and the VCR. Ginny prepares herself for her final night on 42nd Street. As her hand reaches for the door, she finds herself compelled to turn around, look to the bathroom door, listen to the sound of the shower running, to look to Tricia splayed there on the bed, and a look must cross her face because Tricia becomes acutely aware of something. She turns to look at Ginny, her own face seeming concerned, and she smiles nervously at her.

"You okay, Ginny?"

"Of course. Just looking at you."

"You know what I look like."

"Of course."

"Hey... I love you too, Ginny."

"I know. Enjoy yourself. I'll be back soon."

And then she's gone.

———

Traffic is comparatively light today on 42nd street and Nicolette navigates it smoothly, other vehicles shuddering out of her way in awesome reverence for the chariot that comes before them. Nicolette feels satisfied. She feels hopeful. It took most of her day but she is confident that the thorough bleach and peroxide baths which she gave to the back of her van have purged it of both the sight and smell of blood. Now the van is clean, clean, cleaner than it has ever been. It sparkles in the fading sunlight. It radiates an aura of pure and unadulterated cleanliness that chokes any filth which should wander into its path.

Nicolette drives up and down, up and down 42nd, her eyes scanning the bobbing heads and writhing bodies for the Beta. There are other girls like the Beta, and Nicolette sometimes mistakenly calls out to them, beckoning with the bills. The other girls are not pornai. They look to her with scornful faces and make sounds of disgust. They pretend that they would not spread their legs for her if it was enough to their advantage. They shout profanities. Once, Nicolette believes that she has successfully lured the Beta, gotten a girl to approach the van with an offer of money, the girl smiling and leaning against the window when she pulls a knife out from her brassiere and flashes it in Nicolette's face. Nicolette hurriedly rolls her window up and pulls away from the curb. She can see the girl raising her middle finger in the rear view window.

It's Nicolette's decision to allow her to live.

As the night wears on, Nicolette grows nervous. It begins to occur to her that she has not seen any of The Girl's other pornai out, either. She has not seen The Girl. She has not seen The Girl's lover or the little cripple. Approaching an intersection, an awful balloon begins to swell in the depths of Nicolette's mind, expanding with such fearsome rapidity that when it bursts, splattering the inside of her head with flaming shrapnel that burns the back of her eyes and incinerates the hairs of her nose, she nearly runs the light, slamming her brakes at the last moment. The front edge of the van leaps over the line at the intersection before rocking back into place, the vehicle behind her nearly colliding with her rear end. Horns honk. A man shouts. Nicolette grips the steering wheel and attempts to regulate her breathing.

The Girl has gone.

Nicolette executes a donut in the intersection. Considering the girth of her vehicle, it's a feat that she doesn't damage any other cars or strike any pedestrians.

She would not care if she did.

Each second towards the hotel is agony. She struggles to breathe. Her body vibrates with the ferocity of her wrath. Her face reddens. When she can see the hotel, she pulls to the curb, stops the van. Her hands knead the steering wheel. She shifts restlessly. She watches. When cars begin to honk at her she pulls away from the curb, travels to the next light, loops back around. She watches for any of the pornai she recognizes. She watches every window and every doorway and every car in every alley and every opened coffin propped against the street lights, their lids flapping in the breeze to expose the writhing masses of copulating flesh within.

The Girl has gone.

Nicolette is making her third round of the block, ready to haul the van up onto the curb, charge out with her labrys, when she sees the Beta leaving the hotel. The Beta is with another of the pornai, the one with pigtails. There is a third girl with them that Nicolette has never seen before. They are walking quickly. They are talking amongst themselves.

They are walking in the direction of the bus station.

The little pornai with the pigtails is carrying a suitcase.

Something is wrong.

They are leaving.

Nicolette looks behind her. She looks up to the tops of buildings and in the passenger seat and beneath her own. She looks anywhere for a sign. She strains her ears against the sounds of traffic and the sounds of voices, and listens for some directive from The City, some decree which will make sense of this. She was meant to take the Beta tonight; but she is too well accompanied, the bus station too crowded. Such an endeavor would be impossible. She cannot fathom why she would have been sent on this false mission. The City would not betray her. The City reveres her. It bows in fearful recognition of her eternal dominion.

They are leaving because The Girl is sending them away.

The Girl knows.

The Girl is moving against her.

Nicolette punches the steering wheel. The impact is so fierce that it cracks her thumbnail. She does not feel it. She watches with eyes that burn with all of the terrible majesty of her proud lineage, the fire blood of kings surging through her, her teeth grinding together in a slow, meticulous rhythm. It takes several minutes before she sees what she has been waiting for: The Girl, coming out of the front of the hotel, carting the little cripple's wheelchair and a video tape player. There is a figure shrouded in white beside her, carrying another figure also shrouded in white. Nicolette's heart nearly bursts. It's a message. She is conveying her knowledge of the situation. The Girl dares to blasphemy her faithful attendants by adorning her filthy entourage in their sacred vestments.

The Girl and the two figures enter into a cab. The cab pulls into traffic. Nicolette lags behind. She lets the cab stay as far ahead of her as possible without disappearing. The Girl has sent her pornai away and now she's attempting to flee. She thinks that she can escape into an electric night, smiling and laughing and filling her holes with the cocks of her clients and lovers, floating away to safety on a tidal wave of filth. She thinks that she will live to see another day, another city in which to flaunt her beauty, to use it to entice the trembling legs of hungry, desperate men to defile themselves in her.

Nicolette whimpers. She wipes her face with the back of her arm.

Tonight, The Girl will fall in tribute to the great Asterion.

———

The money Ginny is offered for the VCR is laughable. Under different circumstances, she would refuse, seek out another pawn shop, perhaps break something on the way out the door—nothing big, just something to prove a point. Given the events of the evening, she smiles sweetly, flips her hair, giggles, takes the cash, returns some of it seconds later for a file, and a hacksaw. Without letting the clerk see the contents, she drops the tools into the pillowcase, flings it over her shoulder, and heads out the door.

Ginny walks down the street with the pillowcase dangling at her side. She takes a detour down to the Misanthrope, lingers in a doorway, watches. No sign of any police or paramedics; the night goes on uninterrupted. If anyone had put in a call, there'd be a presence by now, squad cars on the sidewalk, ambulances, freaks with cheap cameras clamoring over one another to snap a photo before the coroner's wagon arrived. She checks her watch, waits, and checks it again. When five minutes have lapsed with no change in atmosphere, she heads back. Ginny is rarely glad of the city's general apathy; tonight, she'll embrace it as a virtue. The Colonel won't be found until late morning, when housekeeping makes the rounds. Even then, considering what the Colonel was paying them, Ginny has to wonder if the call won't go into the police until after lunch.

Back in The Kitchen, Ginny lets instinct guide her to an appropriate alley; once she's sure that no one is watching, that she is sufficiently hidden in shadow, she removes the barrel of the shotgun from the pillowcase and sets to work. The intensity with which she files the numbers, saws the barrel apart, is such that the task is completed much sooner than she had anticipated. If her shoulders weren't aching from the beating she took, she thinks she might have even accomplished it sooner.

Ginny lifts the lid of the garbage can; holding the barrel of the shotgun with the pillowcase, she rummages around the junk, spreads aside old newspapers and rotten food and aluminum foil, and once she's cleared a space, she stuffs the gun inside, as well as the hacksaw, the chisel, the pillowcase. When she places the lid back on, it feels like putting the lid on a lifetime; a lifetime lived in three years, and if in another three years she can't remember them, she'll count herself a lucky woman. Maybe she'll pick up a six pack on the way back to the motel to celebrate. Doesn't know what brand Roger likes; with the last name Niederman, he's got to have a bit of German in him. Probably a lager type.

This time tomorrow, maybe she'll have a bit of German in *her,* too.

Ginny giggles. The thought of a consensual sexual encounter is dizzying with novelty. Without thinking about it, she starts to giggle even more furiously. She's still giggling when the lights wash over her and she hears the belabored rumble of the engine sputter down and die.

When she turns around, Ginny's first instinct is to reach for her switchblade. There it is, hulking in the alley, barely able to fit between the two buildings: a squatting, mechanical monster, shrouded in darkness, leering down on her, the headlights blinding her to the visage of the driver. Ginny flicks the blade open. The lights cut out; Ginny shuts her eyes, blinks, tries to reorient them to the darkness of the alley. When she can see inside the cab again, it is empty.

She looks behind her; the wall is too high to scale. Doesn't want to take the risk, anyway, of turning her back. She squints, tries to make out the color; can't.

"You know, you're blocking my way, sweetheart," Ginny shouts. Wonders if anyone can hear her. The ambient sounds of the street have suddenly become too faint, too distant. "I don't know if you saw me back here, but I've really got to be on my way now."

From the van, silence.

"I don't know what you've got to do here, but I've really got to ask you to back up now," Ginny calls.

Ginny searches the cab for the outline of a shadow; some sign of movement. She sees nothing. Slowly, she approaches. She keeps the knife extended in front of her. The weapon is a front, really; she isn't sure that she's got enough energy or mobility in her upper body to effectively fight with it. If it comes down to it, she'll distract with the blade, attack with her legs. She moves slowly, carefully; hoping against reality that this is a mistake; that, somewhere in the back of the van, some slovenly painter lies in a drunken stupor, that some clueless electrician is fuddling over plans, that a girl much like the one she used to be is providing her professional services.

"I've got a knife here, darling, and let me tell you, those tires aren't going to survive the night if I've got to maneuver around you. I really don't want to go around committing any felonies tonight. I've got a very big day ahead of me tomorrow and I'd rather not have something like fucking up your car get in the way of my plans."

Ginny watches the van. Though she cannot tell if it's reality, an optical illusion borne of the poor light in the alley, or a product of her own panicked mind, the vehicle appears, almost imperceptibly, to softly rock. Perhaps someone on the street striking it from behind for amusement; perhaps some quiet breeze, indiscernible to the flesh or ears; perhaps the movements of a deranged and cunning killer.

"I know who you are. I know what you did to my friends. So, like, let's just stop fucking around, okay? Get out here so I can kill you."

Silence.

Ginny stares.

The headlights come on.

Ginny raises a hand in front of her face, holds the knife out, stares between her fingers, trying to make out the figure behind the wheel. She hears the engine grind, turn over, the van growling to life, and it backs up perhaps a foot before the driver switches it into drive, comes towards her. Ginny turns, bolts for the back of the alley, tosses her knife as she runs, the van tearing through the alley behind her, Ginny hearing garbage flying up against the windshield, trashcans crunching beneath the wheels. She throws herself at the rear wall, clamoring up it, pain erupting in her bruised and aching shoulders. She screams and tries to climb, gritting her teeth, her arms trembling and fingers slipping, tears of agony rolling down her face as her muscles give out. Sliding down the brick, Ginny screams again, screams in rage and fury and desperate hopelessness and she turns to face the van, doesn't want to die with her back to her killer, wants to die with her eyes open, wants at the very least to fuck up the son of a bitch's grille if she can, maybe crack the windshield with her body, and as she turns the vehicle jerks to a stop, and idles inches away from her.

Ginny pants; tries to catch her breath. The glow of the headlights surround her in filthy yellow light; she looks up into the windshield and sees only her own reflection, eyes bulging, hair wet with sweat, her jacket dusted in grime. She looks down; the spaces in the grille are just large enough to accommodate the toes of her pumps. Ginny jumps onto the front of the van, pushes herself up with her legs, keeping the weight off of her arms, her shoulders, scrambles up the front, steadies herself on a wiper blade, snapping it off in the process. She smacks the windshield with it as she mounts the top of the van, charging across the roof, little dents forming beneath her heels. Ginny leaps when she reaches the end, drops down at the rear of the van, proud that her legs are strong enough to absorb the impact of her descent, and as she turns around to face the rear of the van, the last thing she sees are the open doors and the blackness yawning within before the chemical rag wraps around her face and she's yanked inside.

9

Wednesday, June 22nd, 1983

A HELL OF A HANGOVER, GINNY THINKS, SLOWLY SITTING, eyes only half opened, the world dark and hazy, a hell of a hangover, and however much it was she had last night, she thinks that maybe she's finally found too much. The smell is awful; a great wave of shame washes over her, grave humiliation that she's finally reached the point of soiling herself, of vomiting in her stupor. She tries to inhale, gags, stuffs her face into the arm of her jacket. Something wrong; knows that she can't produce that strong an odor. It can't possibly be Tricia, either, but, then again, the girl can pack it away fierce when she gets her hands on it, an entire six pack and a large pizza extra anchovies extra cheese in a single sitting and *oh, sorry sis were you gonna have some of that?* It must be her, the little shit, making her think that she's done this to herself, going to have a talking to once she gets this cleaned up, and then Ginny rises and her foot slips in the muck beneath her feet and she sees the alley and the shotgun and the van and…

Oh.

Ginny rubs the sleeve of her jacket across her face. Her eyes begin to adjust; she can make out the hills of garbage around her, the wide, twisting pathways of waste and refuse rolling off into eternal blackness. Ginny checks herself, running her hands over her face, her neck, her abdomen, checking for some wound or mutilation that shock or the effect of the drugs have numbed. She feels between her legs; her underwear are intact. So are her stockings. She doesn't feel especially raw. Nothing's been done to her; not an unpleasant surprise but a surprise nonetheless...

Unless that's what's coming.

Ginny closes her eyes. She assumes the *musubi-dachi*; inhales deeply; exhales; opens her eyes again. She slips a hand into the pocket of her jacket, fumbles for something there, snatched quickly in her departure from the Misanthrope; glad when her fingers fall across the beads and fine silver chain of Tricia's rosary. She slips her hand back out of her pocket.

She's ready.

Ginny looks around; reassesses the garbage surrounding her. A landfill, obviously; looks up; smiles ruefully. The sky that greets her is black and wide, only picking up peripheral light pollution from some weak, nearby sources. There are easily forty, fifty stars visible to her here. A pittance, really, in the grand scope of the cosmos, but a veritable treasure trove compared to the paltry few that flicker dimly each night above 42nd Street. She checks her watch; hopes that it's still in working order, that it hasn't been banged around too badly, and thank you, Texas Instruments, the happy red numbers illuminate for her when she punches the button. It's just after midnight. Not enough time to travel far; too much of the sky visible to still be anywhere in the vicinity of Manhattan. And it hits her, suddenly, where she is, has read about it, in *Newsweek,* perhaps, or *The Times,* or *Astronomy Today.*

She's at the Staten Island landfill.

The one you can see from outer space.

Off in the distance she hears movement, something approaching. No, several somethings, tiny, rapid little pattering noises gaining in speed and intensity. Ginny turns to face it, just in time to see the dogs rounding a corner, shoulders hunched, teeth bared, snarling, growling, their slobber glistening in the moonlight. Ginny hesitates long enough to size them up; four of them, in varying degrees of physical decline, the weakest scrawny and mangy, ribs jutting out, one-eyed; the strongest looking fresh from a kennel, squat and powerful, a pit bull, maybe, its cubic face a vicious tribal death mask in the moonlight.

Ginny runs.

She races down serpentine passageways branching out before her, blackened highways into the realm of nightmares, her heels sloshing in the soft, putrefying soil beneath them, the pallid light revealing her path to her only feet at a time. Ginny runs, legs pumping fiercely beneath her, looking back over her shoulder every few seconds, seeing the dogs gaining on her, their blind fury audible in each snap, each violent bark offered up to her like a personal threat. Ginny runs, wonders if this is exactly what it was like for the others, if this is what the end was to them, fed to wild dogs in a pagan graveyard, a heretical temple to waste, mauled screaming in the pitiless dark. She wonders how far they were able to make it, neither Tammy nor Tina as athletically gifted as she, if they made it feet or meters or miles before they fell. Wonders if fear crippled them, if they were able to run at all or if they bowed in defeated, terrified acceptance of the cruel inevitable, sobbing prayers or begging for mercy from whatever perverted soul looms in the wings, watching the spectacle unfold for his pleasure.

If he wants a show, she'll give him a fucking show.

She eyes the debris as she passes, taking in as much as

she can without sacrificing velocity. She sees what she needs, a length of rebar, jutting out of one of the mounds of garbage forming an intersection. She grips it, keeps moving, yanks it as she turns the corner, has it at the ready as she spins around to face the mutts. She brings it down into the face of the big one at the same time she sweeps its legs out from beneath it, knocks it into the other three, turns and takes off running again. She looks back, sees the dogs righting themselves, scrambling over one another, snapping at one another in frustrated indignation as they resume their pursuit. She thinks she can see a line of blood coming down the big one's forehead. She keeps moving, pushes herself as she approaches another mound, gains momentum, propels herself up onto the side of the garbage heap, spinning as she leaps, turning back towards the approaching dogs, kicking the big one in the face with her outstretched foot and swinging the rebar down at the rest. Both blows meet their mark; the big one's head snaps back, crumpling to the ground, catching the small one in its remaining good eye. The mutt shrieks. Gore, black in the moonlight, gurgles up out of the ruined socket, and it falls back, tail between its legs. One of the smaller dogs snaps at Ginny, catches the hem of her skirt. She yanks away, lets the mutt tear out a swath of fabric, keeps running. She looks back; the big one is again in pursuit, its face matted in blood, its pace reduced by what looks like an injured or God willing broken leg, followed closely by one of the smaller dogs, the third remaining behind, reducing its piece of Ginny's poor forsaken skirt to purple ribbons. Ginny begins to slow; keeps her head cast back over her shoulder; waits for the big dog to gain on her. She twists around, waits for it to leap, its muscular, compact body soaring towards her like a vicious, hungry missile. Her foot catches it in the front of the ribcage; the animal shrieks, rolls sideways, its companion taking the opportunity to bite into Ginny's calf. She screams; her body tenses; rage and instinct combine and she brings the rebar down onto the dog while it still has its teeth in her, unaware of its victims' strength, her fury, her training. The pain in her shoulder prevents her from completely driving the rebar through the animal. Instead, it lodges in its side, so Ginny twists it, working it round and round, turns it before she yanks it out. The animal squeals, whimpers, staggers back.

Ginny looks down at her injured calf; can't be sure if the diminishing pain is due to a superficial bite or the onset of shock. Can't worry about that now; she looks to the big dog, righting itself on its hobbled legs, one eye caked over with blood now, blood dripping down the sides of its face, intermingling with its saliva. It snarls and crouches, Ginny preparing the rebar, preparing her foot, and the animal's legs bunch up and it releases a low, vile growl...

―――――

Nicolette freezes when she hears the first yelp of pain echo back to her, her own body racked with agony at the sound. Not possible. The Girl is strong but she is not invincible. She is a wild rabbit before her bitches, to be hounded back to the warren for culling. Nicolette disregards it. She relaxes. She waits—waits for the moment to come upon her; holds her wrist to her ear and listens for the muffled ticking of her father's watch, counting down the seconds of The Girl's life, each tick another moment shaved away from the cunt's miserable existence, another instant closer to at last fulfilling the great purpose for which she was put upon this earth.

When the time comes to dine, Nicolette thinks she'll start with her round little tits.

Then a shriek comes again, high and panicked, a howl of agony and desperation. Her dogs are in trouble. They are in pain. They are hurt. She cannot deny the sounds. She cannot deny the helpless pleas for salvation. Nicolette fumbles for the whistle. She must call them back. She must see what The Girl has done to them. Then she must make her pay.

———

Ginny is in mid-swing when the animal begins to shriek, recoils from her, hind end striking the ground as it spins around and begins to retreat. She holds the rebar in midair, watching it barrel away from her, back around a corner, into the great maze of the landfill. Ginny pants breathlessly, a mad giggle of panic and relief escaping between heaving breaths, then another and another. She keeps giggling until she hears the whine and then she is dead quiet. Can't quite identify it at first, something high-pitched and reedy, barely more than an echoing whisper…

A dog whistle.

Ginny begins turning around and around, making quick spins to identify all of the possible inlets to this corridor of the dump, every possible point of attack. She thinks she hears something behind her and jerks around—nothing—but footsteps are approaching from somewhere, determined yet quick, not running but moving fast, followed by a low, murky scrape. Ginny's heart races, sweat and blood intermingling on her legs as she turns, and turns, and turns, stopping at last as the shadow appears, a monstrous silhouette looming like a profane icon against the side of one of the mounds. Ginny feels as though she's about to soil herself at the sight. It doesn't appear to be entirely human in its formation or its carriage, something horned and lanky and slightly hunched like an injured animal, pulling something behind it in the filth. She begins to back away, eyes locked on the shadow, following it to its source as it appears around a corner. It stands there, silent, motionless, gazing at her. She sees the body, swathed in armor, thin limbs encased in what looks like leather, like a primitive version of the attack suits worn by self-defense trainers; she sees the axe gripped in one gauntleted hand, being dragged behind, the blade caked in dirt and stray bits of trash; follows the body up to the head, the mask, the horns, the giant, leering muzzle, and it makes sense to Ginny, for as much as this is all completely insane it makes sense. The dump, the corridors, this great labyrinth of debris and the maniac that has turned it into his playground.

The son of a bitch thinks he's the Minotaur.

"This is, like, all very fascinating, sweetheart," Ginny says. Her eyes never leave the thing in front of her; she shifts all of her weight onto her injured leg, tests it out. It stings but doesn't give out. Good. The bites are shallow. She can still run, still do damage. "But I think we're nearing the end of the story. Just tell me, which version would you prefer? The one where you're beaten to death, or the one where you're strangled? I was always more interested in Medusa, myself, so, I really don't have a preferred canonicity, you know? I guess what I'm really asking is, how do you want to die?"

The Minotaur stands stationary, leering at her across the clearing. He is completely motionless; Ginny can scarcely detect his shoulders rising and falling with breath. She considers making a charge, attacking while the axe is down; hesitates. Might be what he's waiting for; has no idea how strong he is, how quick. He's a little guy, but has got a definite height advantage, probably five five, five six in the boots; too, his arms look a good deal longer than her own. She waits, silent, holding the rebar before her. Interminable seconds pass before he wordlessly takes the axe up in both hands and charges towards her.

Ginny staggers back, swings the rebar, misses, hits the handle of the axe. The Minotaur raises it, makes his own swing. Ginny dodges sideways. The blade arcs down beside her, stops in midair, the Minotaur yanking it back to the ready position. Ginny keeps strafing, making little sideways jumps, not staying still long enough for him to get an accurate swing in, moving, moving, raising the rebar, holding it at the ready, preparing to swing it, tossing it down at the last moment and diving forward, gripping the axe handle in both hands. She yanks as hard as her shoulders will permit; the Minotaur makes a sound of enraged surprise, a higher pitch than Ginny would've thought, yanks back. If her shoulders were at a hundred percent, she's sure she could pull it away, at least put up more of a fight. As it is, their strength is evenly matched. The Minotaur thrusts the handle forward, strikes Ginny in the chest, knocks her back. She lands on her ass, the soft earth breaking the fall. She scrambles backwards on her palms. The axe swings down, striking between her open legs, tearing a yawning divide in the fabric of her skirt. The Minotaur yanks the blade up, readies it for another swing. Ginny takes the opportunity to kick at his ankles, sweep them out from under him. The Minotaur drops to his knees; Ginny shouts, jumps to her feet, advances on him, delivering kicks to the shoulders, the chest, the upper arms. The leather of his armor absorbs all of them; he kneels there stoically, no sounds of pain or injury escaping the mask. In the faint sapphire light, Ginny can make out a pair of furious eyes leering up at her from out of the mask, frighteningly gigantic, engorged veins pulsating in dense spider webs around the massively dilated pupils. Ginny screams in enraged frustration, delivers a final, panicked, desperate blow to his head, regretting it before her arm even makes contact. The metal of the helmet is invulnerable; pain ricochets down to the ball of her thumb and back up to her shoulder. She pulls back. The Minotaur rises, lifts his axe, stares at her a moment, charges.

Ginny runs.

The Minotaur is in tremendous shape, his legs longer than her own, giving him greater strides. Still, the armor weighs him down; the axe reduces his mobility. Ginny activates every toned muscle, every strengthened fiber; parts which she has not called on since her lost, lamented days of ballet come to life, resurrecting themselves from their long dormancy to return to the service of the woman who once so lovingly called upon them in the display of art and beauty. She rockets forward; she stays scant feet ahead of her pursuer but ahead nonetheless, so that the sharp swoops and soars of the axe blade swinging behind her remain just sounds. Still, she knows that she cannot run for the entire night; even if the dump is due to open come morning, there are hours before her, hours to spend evading someone more well rested and more well prepared than herself. Fleeing is a temporary solution.

Ginny veers to the side, stops abruptly, nearly losing her balance in the process. She catches herself against a mound of trash, her arm sinking in up to the elbow. The Minotaur bolts past her, comes to his own unsteady halt, turns back towards her. Ginny charges forward, swings her leg, knocks his legs out from beneath him again; before his knees have even hit the ground she's turned around and begun running again. She doesn't bother to look back over her shoulder; doesn't want to slow herself. She turns at every intersection she reaches, right, left, right, right, corner after corner, hiding herself so deeply within this labyrinth that it ceases to be her pursuer's domain but becomes her fortress. Give herself time to regroup.

Ginny is moving so quickly that she almost runs into it before she sees it; stops herself at the last moment, glad she did. Sure that if she'd hit it she would completely lose whatever remnants of food are left in her stomach.

It looks, Ginny supposes, to be some sort of altar, though beyond the general shape and basic structure, it bears little resemblance to those of her youth. The materials, certainly, are all wrong. There is no wood or marble to be found; the surface of the thing is comprised almost entirely of pelvic bones, crudely lashed together with what look like strips of leather and set upon a multitude of pedestals made from arms and legs, themselves supported by foot and hand bones laid flat against the earth. Atop the structure, a half dozen pillars made of spinal columns reach up towards the starry sky; and mounted on each pillar, through holes punched in the skullcaps, are totem poles of heads, some mummified, some putrefying, some long ago reduced to skulls. Ginny trembles, her eyes moving all over the hellscape before her. She sees that some of the bones comprising the structure are too small to be those of adults; then, she really does vomit, gripping her belly and keeling forward, splattering one of the legs of the monstrosity with burning bile. When she's empty, she rises, inspects the thing, her body and her eyes drawn towards one particular alignment of heads, vacant eye sockets and masticated faces staring back at her in pity and mournful regret. How many dreams died here? How many women have fallen prone to the piece of shit's blade, their lives and ambitions and loves and fears and desires and joys subsumed to fulfill whatever perverted fantasy dominates his mind? What possibilities have been snuffed out here, calling out to the starry sky, and then calling out no more?

Tears have begun to roll down Ginny's cheeks as her

shaking hand reaches forward to stroke Tammy's cheek. The flesh has already begun to decay in the Summer heat. Her face is frozen in a death grimace, her eyes squeezed shut, her mouth twisted open. Ginny grips the chin and shuts it. The expression, now, is at least something vaguely resembling peace. A final, pathetic gift to the lost soul who will never be going home to West Virginia.

"I'm so sorry, sweetheart," Ginny says. "I'm so, so sorry. I know that doesn't make it better now, but... Please. When you get where you're going, you... you let Him know that, all right? You let Him know I'm sorry. For everything I've done and... and for everything that I didn't do and... I know I don't deserve that but... If you could just... let Him know that, okay?"

Ginny steps back, removes the rosary from her pocket, and lays it before Tammy on the altar.

Somewhere in the twisting passageways beyond, Ginny can hear him approaching; hear the faint scrape of the axe dragging in the muck. She folds her hands before her face. She will fight. She will *not* go down *without* fighting. She will kick and claw and beat, even if it means breaking her own limbs against the fucker's little helmet. Still, she has never considered herself someone given to self-delusion; she is a scholar, a woman of science, and science demands practicality, a recognition of possibilities versus limitations.

She is going to die here.

She isn't going to die because of her sins; she isn't going to die because she has earned this fate through years of degradation. She's going to die because the universe cast the die and her number came up; because she was in the wrong place at the wrong time; because hateful forces stalk the dark corridors of the world and prey on women in the deluded hopes that broken bodies and consumed souls will fill the emptiness inside of them. She's going to die here;

she is going to die without ever holding her sister again, without seeing her grow and flourish. She's going to die without ever getting the opportunity to make love to her dear, sweet Roger, waiting for her back at the motel, poor Roger with his handsome beard and his funny laugh and his aura of gentility and comfort and his big, big, *big* eyes, *my, what big eyes you have…*

Ginny crouches down and tears a loose strand of fabric from her shredded skirt, wrapping it tightly around her bleeding calf. Then she removes her shoes, and, walking on bare, cold feet, trots through the muck and back towards the sound of the Minotaur's scraping axe; back towards Tricia and Roger. Roger, her darling Ariadne, who without knowing it has given her the thread she needs to make it out of the labyrinth.

She knows how to spot a plus-eight hyperope.

The Mighty Minotaur wears glasses.

———

Nicolette hurtles through the rose bushes, quaking, juddering, her fury barely contained inside of her own body, threatening to burst it apart at the seams, explode in a geyser of blood and muscle. The Girl dares to continue running from her; dares to prolong what has become too long a hunt. A certain amount of resistance is expected, welcomed even, but the time must come when all tributes realize their fate, their infinitesimal significance before her, and, in doing so, bow in supplication to the blade. She had intended to make The Girl's demise brutal yet swift. Now, she will prolong it. She will take her apart piece by scintillating piece. She will disassemble her like a building block puzzle, each finger a knuckle at a time, then the hands, the forearms, up to the shoulders. She will draw the process out for as long as The Girl's putrid biology will allow it.

Nicolette stops in her tracks when she sees The Girl. The Girl is lying on her side in the grass, dragging herself along with one arm. She has dressed her leg in a crude bandage. The dogs did more harm than she realized. The girl is whimpering; she is weeping. She looks to Nicolette and casts her head down to the ground and sobs. She is ready. She has realized her place.

The taste of victory is sweet in Nicolette's mouth; it tastes like rosebuds and caramel and melted strawberries. It flows over her tongue and down the back of her throat in delicious waves. She approaches for the kill. She sees glory before her. She sees The Girl's body, stripped to the bone, mounted as a great centerpiece to the sacred Altar. She sees the labyrinth quarantined and contained, her kingdom at last given over to her.

She does not see that The Girl's sobbing face produces no tears; she does not see that the girl has removed her shoes and is holding them in one hand. Nicolette lifts the axe above her head; it takes her off guard when The Girl leaps to her bare feet. Her arms freeze in the air; then, a pair of high heels strike her lenses and she sees no more.

———

Ginny screams. The agony that surges through her arms and shoulders as she swings her shoes is nearly crippling. The only thing that palliates it is the satisfying crunch the heels make on impact and the sound of shattering glass. She falls back, scoots across the ground, replaces her shoes on gunked up feet. She watches; she waits.

The great Minotaur shrieks and snarls. If Ginny were more supernaturally inclined, she would believe that the sounds coming out of the muzzle were not entirely human. He drops the axe to the ground, gripping the handle with one hand. The other swings impotently at the ground, casting off the gauntlet. A bare hand—delicate, Ginny is surprised how delicate—reaches behind his head, fumbles, pulls, fumbles, pulls, undoing straps, yanking them free. At last, his hand grips one of the sawn off horns, and, yanking at it, pulls the mask off.

The face beneath is barely female, Ginny thinks; not in its formation but in its lack of even base humanity. The eyes—small, now, in the absence of the magnifying lenses—are vacant, the wide jaw slack and gaping, the expression completely blank except for primal rage. If anything remotely human ever lived inside this body, it's gone now. What stands before her, staring into a blurred abyss, is entirely animal.

Nicolette takes up the axe, making blind, shallow swings. Ginny waits for her moment, charges, barrels headlong into Nicolette's abdomen as she lifts the blade, knocking her backwards. The axe falls wayside; Nicolette pushes her off, rises, grips the axe handle. Ginny staggers to her feet, steps back. The force of the axe's descent has lodged it in the ground. Nicolette struggles to pull it free. Ginny charges her, kicks her leg out from beneath her, delivers a weak elbow to her face, knocking her away from the axe handle. Now it's Ginny's turn to try and pull it free, wincing in pain as she tugs at it, the blade beginning to lift up out of the muck when Nicolette's arms wrap around her neck. The other woman bites at her, Nicolette's teeth sinking into one of the shoulder pads of her jacket. Ginny screams, bends over, flips Nicolette forward. Nicolette summersaults, is attempting to right herself when Ginny sweeps her legs out from beneath her, and in the same motion grips her by the roots of her hair. She brings her knee up into Nicolette's face. Then, she brings it up again, and again, and again.

She can feel it when Nicolette's nose breaks, feel it flatten, feel the warm spray of blood against her flesh. Ginny releases her, steps back, looks at her a moment kneeling there dazed, runs towards her and delivers a kick to one temple and then the other, the second blow knocking her onto her side. Nicolette begins to squirm down one of the passageways, trailing blood behind her.

Ginny turns back. She isn't sure how she pulls the axe out of the ground. The pain in her shoulders is excruciating, the weight of the axe pulling her body forward as she charges after Nicolette. Nicolette hears the sound coming behind her, turns, rolls onto her back. She opens her mouth and hisses.

Ginny intends for the axe to land between her eyes: bury it in her brain and end this. It takes the last of her strength to lift the axe above her head, but then her brutalized shoulders at last finally seize into place and the descent of the axe is clumsier than she'd have hoped. It misses the mark, bisecting the woman's lower jaw and lodging in her throat.

Nicolette writhes. One half of her jaw is wedged against the blade, the other flops up and down like a dying fish, her mutilated tongue twitching in the swelling pool of blood that is quickly filling her mouth, bubbles rising to the surface as she begins to drown. She grips the axe handle, and struggles to yank it out.

Calmly, Ginny steps forward, places her foot on the handle, and presses down. She keeps pressing until Nicolette's arms go slack and drop beside her; until her frightened, bulging eyes grow dim and roll up into her head and her convulsions cease, and she moves no more.

Ginny stares at the thing lying before her for a long time. A soft, fine mist begins to come down, not enough to cleanse her of the blood and filth caking her, but enough to cool her cheeks and soothe her eyes. She casts her head back, takes it in. When she's ready, she opens her eyes and studies the sky. If she recalls correctly, the Western border of the landfill is formed by Staten Island Sound; East seems as good a direction as any.

She checks her watch again; looks back to the stars, her long departed friends returned to her in her hour of need, to comfort and guide her. She scans over them, their names rolling through her mind as her eyes fall over each one, seeking out what she needs to find her way back. The Austrian astronomer Joseph Johann Littrow called it the Conspicuous Triangle; her own textbooks had referred to it as the Summer Triangle; the Air Force, she has read, calls it the Navigator's Triangle, and this is the purpose for which she seeks it out tonight, the unmistakable formation above her in the night sky, the brightly burning stars of Deneb, Vega, and Altair.

The rancher, the weaver, and their bridge, pointing her East; pointing her home.

Ginny looks back to Nicolette. Something catches her eye, a little token incongruous to the rest of the costume. Ginny kneels down and inspects her wrist. Though she can't tell for sure, the watch looks very nice. Carefully, Ginny unbuckles the strap, removes it, and slips it in her jacket pocket. Then, following her triangle, the weaver heads back to her rancher.

––––––––

The cabbie Ginny flags down seems hesitant at first to pick her up, barely rolling to a stop as she approaches. She smiles broadly, flings herself into the back seat, lets out an exasperated sigh.

"Omigawsh, sweetie, you have no idea what a life saver you are. Like, I really mean it this time, okay? No... more... tequila. I, like, so totally do not think I can handle another one of those nights."

The cabbie shrugs, relaxes; he doesn't speak much on the trip back to Manhattan. His tension rises again when Ginny directs him towards the pawn shop, tells him to keep the meter running. She waits while the man behind the counter inspects the watch. She can tell by the sudden lift in his eyebrows and the subsequent, forced nonchalance what exactly she has on her hands. She doesn't accept the first offer; prepares to walk out following the second; turns back towards the counter at the third. She demands an additional fifty dollars to the offered price; accepts thirty. She suspects that the wad of cash the broker retrieves from his safe has just about cleaned him out; knows that he'll probably get triple the price for the diamond alone. She doesn't care. Neither does the cabbie, once she tips him a twenty on top of the fare. It's been a long night; she's feeling generous.

The slog towards her room at the motel feels eternal, her thighs and calves burning, her knees threatening to buckle at any moment. She knocks on the door to her room, leans against the frame. When Roger answers it, she slumps forward against him.

"Ginny. Shit. What happened? Ginny, are you, ah, you all right?"

Ginny looks up into giant, loving eyes. She puts her arms around Roger and kisses him.

"You are so totally not going to believe any of this."

————

It takes the last of Ginny's energy to tell the story, sitting slumped beside Tricia on her bed, Tricia running her hands through Ginny's filthy hair, stroking her arm as she tells it all. The dump, the dogs, the thing in the Minotaur armor. Roger's eyes grow impossibly large, Tricia accompanying her story with a chorus of profanity. Ginny can barely keep her eyes open as she comes to the end of the story. The last thing she hears is her sister's assertion: "See, bitch? I told you that you're fucking Jean Grey."

"Glad... I'm back... too."

Then Ginny leans against her sister, and quietly goes to sleep.

———

While she's out, someone raises the window shade, and it's the hot, white glow of the late morning sun that lulls her back to the waking world. Ginny sits up slowly, achingly, looks at her sister curled beside her, one arm draped across her chest. She lifts it gently and lays it back across the bed. Roger is lying on his side on the opposite bed, his back to them, facing the door. Ginny creeps across the floor and carefully slips into bed beside him. She lies there for several minutes, her arm around his shoulder, softly stroking his beard, looking back every so often to see her sister safe in the bed beside them. The room looks quite different to her than it did last night, under the shade of darkness, when it was a weigh station on a journey out of Hell.

This morning, it looks like home.

———

"So, like, are we still going to California?" Tricia asks this as the bus prepares for departure, the engine humming, the door gliding shut. "Because, like, if we are, I so totally have to buy new clothes first. I, like, refuse to go to the beach looking like this." All Ginny was able to find for her at the thrift shop this morning was a denim skirt and matching blouse. Roger is more fortunate, being the beneficiary of a bowling shirt and Bermuda shorts. Ginny is the only real victor; can't understand why there were so many bow neck blouses and matching skirts to choose from.

"Our tickets get us as far as Chicago," Ginny says. "I figure that'll give us enough time to decide our next move."

"I haven't seen my brother in a year and a half," Roger says. "It might be nice to drop in on him. Tulsa's hotter than Hell this time of year, but he'd let us crash with him. Maybe, ah, give us a chance to sort through stuff. Figure things out. Where we want to go. What we want to do. Who we want to be."

"Is he single?" Tricia asks.

"Yeah. Why?"

"Tulsa it is," Tricia says.

"Just so you know, it's a job in itself watching after her," Ginny says.

"Ah, what?"

"Well, she's your responsibility now, too, you know. I mean, if you want her to be. If we're still doing this."

Roger smiles. "Yeah. Yeah, ah, yeah we are."

"Fantastic, sweetheart. Now, tell me, what do you know about quantum mechanics?"

"Ah, what?"

"Fabulous, sweetheart. Fabulous."

The bus pulls away from the Port Authority, merges into traffic. Ginny gazes out the window at the Western skyline, glowing crimson with the setting sun; to Tricia on her right, opening a new comic, quietly muttering the words to "99 Luftballoons;" to Roger, on her left, wringing his hands. Ginny takes one of them in her own. He looks at her and smiles; she smiles back.

From somewhere across the aisle, Ginny hears faint strains of music rise up, barely audible beneath the din of chatter on the bus. She leans across Roger, addresses the boy with the transistor radio in his lap.

"Excuse me, sweetheart? I hate to be a bother, but would you mind turning that up, please? I absolutely love this song."

The boy obliges; "Skateaway" swells throughout the bus. Ginny leans back in her seat, rests her head against Roger's shoulder. Sitting here, between the only people she needs, she feels something she hasn't felt since the long drive back home those three years ago: she feels optimistic.

Old sailors, Ginny knows, took a red sunset as a good omen. It meant clear skies above them, storm systems behind, and smooth waters ahead. To Virginia Kurva, travelling once and forever away from 42nd Street, it means all of this and much more. The images that materialize to her out of the kaleidoscopic medley of crimsons and scarlets, rubies and carmines, are more beautiful and majestic than any tongue could ever hope to convey. They are the wonders of the cosmos; they are the intricate mysteries of mathematics and the grand splendor of scientific discovery; they are the soul-soothing artistry of literature and the subtle intricacies of linguistics; they are the face of God. They speak to her of the future. They speak of great achievements to be made, of fantastic discoveries, of the interminable possibilities that lay before her, before Roger, before her sister. They speak to her of a fading darkness at her back, and a great yawning sunrise before her. She closes her eyes and lets herself sink into the sunset, into the gentle light washing over her; into Orion; Carina; Horseshoe; Rosette; Red Rectangle.

ACKNOWLEDGEMENTS

I would like to thank the following individuals for their contributions not only to this book, but to my life. Without their invaluable knowledge, friendship, and support, this work would not have been possible.

In order of appearance...

- My parents, Jim and Linda (who bear no resemblance to the Kurvas), for their love and encouragement.

- Uncle Bob and Aunt Janet, for being the best

- Kyle Ebert and Ian Thompson—the good parts of my childhood

- Judy Diepenbrock, a saint

- P.C. Cast, one of the earliest patrons of my writing

- Virginia, who was wise beyond her years

- Sgt. Michael Henderson, who taught me the discipline and professionalism that has seen me through

- Herman Raucher, who told me I had what it takes when I still wasn't sure

- Kat, who listened

- Prof. Cliff Hudder, who first printed my stories and brought my earliest incarnations of The Deuce to life

- Prof. Habib Far, because of whom I can now do math

- My wife, Kayleigh, who generously allowed herself to serve as a partial model for Ginny

- Eric Ogriseck, a dedicated reader and friend

- Mark Mattison-Shupnick, who gave me my first professional writing job and continues to support my endeavors

- James Spina, my mentor, friend, and editor at 20/20, who printed my first nationally-published fiction piece

- Mindi Lewis, a wonderful editor and friend

- Cory Brown, who brought me both cheer and my UPS packages

- Dave Alexander, who brought me into the world of horror journalism

- Ron McKenzie, who has always been there to lend an ear

- Jennifer and Sylvia Soska, who without knowing it put me back on the horse when I thought I could no longer write

- Andrea Subissati, who let me make the *Rue Morgue* blog my home for a while

- Richard Halfhide and Ron Seniscal, the best research partners a guy could ask for

- Darryl Mayeski of *Screem Magazine*, for having faith in one Hell of a crap shoot

- The Hobby Crew—Abra, Barry, Edgar, Jon, and Steve—the best

- Jessie Hobson, who in addition to being an excellent friend let me expand my journalistic horizons and kept some of my writing alive after it'd gone out of print

- Jason Howard, who's there with a laugh when I need one

- Fear Front, for first having faith in a project so many others thought was insane

- Jerry Winnett, for so vividly bringing the world of *OLOTI* to life

- Majanka Verstraete, who wisely discouraged that page-long paragraph

- Izzy Lee, who became one of *Our Lady*'s first evangelists

- Bradley Steele Harding and Dan Gremminger, a great pair of friends

- Dallas Sonnier and the fine folks at Cinestate, who finally gave me a place I can call home

- ...and to all of the friends and acquaintances who, in my haste and hubris, I might've forgotten. You're still awesome.

- A special nod must also be given to my most valuable resources for telling the story of *Our Lady*:

  » *Sleazoid Express*, by Bill Landis and Michelle Clifford, which constituted my grindhouse Bible

  » *Ghosts of 42nd* by Anthony Bianco, which provided me with valuable historical and geographic information on The Deuce, which I could then flagrantly ignore

  » Elizabeth McLeod, who patiently answered all of my questions on the architecture and operation of old movie theaters

  » The users of *CityData.com*, for giving me just enough information to intentionally get it wrong

ABOUT THE AUTHOR

Preston Fassel is a three-time Rondo Award nominated journalist and author. He was born in Houston, Texas and grew up between St. Charles, Missouri and Broken Arrow, Oklahoma. In 2004, he was a recipient of the President's Volunteer Service Award, Gold Level, for work conducted with the Broken Arrow Police Department evidence room. He graduated Summa Cum Laude from Lone Star College-Montgomery with an AA in 2009 and Cum Laude from Sam Houston State University with a BS in 2011. He is the author of *Remembering Vanessa*, the first published biography of British horror star Vanessa Howard, printed in the Spring 2014 issue of *Screem Magazine*. From 2015 to 2017, he served as the assistant editor of *Cinedump.com*; in 2017, he joined Cinestate as story editor and staff writer for *FANGORIA Magazine*. This is his first novel.

CPSIA information can be obtained
at www.ICGtesting.com
Printed in the USA
LVHW04s2034120818
586642LV00002B/2/P